TRANSITION

By Iain Banks

The Wasp Factory
Walking On Glass
The Bridge
Espedair Street
Canal Dreams
The Crow Road
Complicity
Whit
A Song Of Stone
The Business
Dead Air
The Steep Approach To Garbadale

Also by Iain M. Banks

Consider Phlebas
The Player Of Games
Use Of Weapons
The State Of The Art
Against A Dark Background
Feersum Endjinn
Excession
Inversions
Look To Windward
The Algebraist
Matter
Transition

TRANSITION

IAIN M. BANKS

www.orbitbooks.net

New York   London

Orbit
Hachette Book Group
237 Park Avenue, New York, NY 10017
www.HachetteBookGroup.com

First U.S. Edition: September 2009

Orbit is an imprint of Hachette Book Group. The Orbit name and logo are
trademarks of Little, Brown Book Group Limited.

Library of Congress Control Number: 2009930242
ISBN: 978-0-316-07198-7

10 9 8 7 6 5 4 3 2 1

Printed in the United States of America

For Alastair and Emily, and in memory of Bec

With thanks to Adèle, Mic, Richard, Les, Gary and Zoe

TRANSITION

— based on a false story

Prologue

pparently I am what is known as an Unreliable Narrator, though of course if you believe everything you're told you deserve whatever you get. It is, believe me, more than a little amazing – and entirely unprecedented – that you are reading these words at all. Have you ever seen a seismograph? You know: one of those terribly delicate and sensitive things with a long spidery-fingered pen that inscribes a line on a roll of paper being moved beneath it, to record earth tremors.

Imagine that one of those is sailing serenely along, recording nothing of note, drawing a straight and steady black line, registering just calmness and quiet both beneath your feet and all around the world, and then it suddenly starts to write in flowing copperplate, the paper zipping back and forth beneath it to accommodate its smoothly swirling calligraphy. (It might write: "Apparently I am what is known as an Unreliable Narrator . . .")

That is how unlikely it is that I am writing this and anybody is reading it, trust me.

Time, place. Necessary, I suppose, though in the circumstances insufficient. However, we must begin somewhere and somewhen, so let me start with Mrs Mulverhill and record that, by your reckoning,

I first encountered her near the beginning of that golden age which nobody noticed was happening at the time; I mean the long decade between the fall of the Wall and the fall of the Towers.

If you wish to be pedantically exact about it, those retrospectively blessed dozen years lasted from the chilly, fevered Central European night of November 9th, 1989 to that bright morning on the Eastern Seaboard of America of September 11th, 2001. One event symbolised the lifted threat of a worldwide nuclear holocaust, something which had been hanging over humanity for nearly forty years, and so ended an age of idiocy. The other ushered in a new one.

The wall's fall was not spectacular. It was night and all you saw on television was a bunch of leather-jacketed Berliners attacking re-inforced concrete – mostly with hammers, rather ineffectually. Nobody died. A lot of people got drunk and stoned – and laid, no doubt. The wall itself was not a striking structure, and not even very tall or especially forbidding; the real obstacle had always been the barren, sandy killing ground of mines, dog runs and razor wire behind it.

The vertical barrier was always more symbolic than anything else; a delineation, so the fact that none of the crowds of cheerful vandals scrabbling for a perch on it could do much to destroy it without access to heavy equipment was irrelevant; what mattered was that they were clambering all over this famously divisive, allegedly defensive symbol without getting machine-gunned. However, as the expression of a sudden outburst of hope and optimism and an embracing of change, one could ask for no more, I suppose. The al-Qaida attack on the USA – well, given that a nation was invaded and occupied using this as an excuse, and that this was done in the name of democracy, let's be both nationalistic and democratic about it: the Saudi Arabian attack on the USA – could hardly have offered a greater contrast.

Slung between these two wide-reaching levellings, the intervening years held civilisation happily if ignorantly scooped, as in a hammock.

Sometime about the centre of that sweet trough, Mrs M and I became lost to each other. We met again, then parted again for the final time just before the third Fall, the fall of Wall Street and the City, the fall of the banks, the fall of the Markets, beginning on September 15th, 2008.

Perhaps we all find such coincident place marks in the books of our lives reassuring.

Still, it seems to me that such congruencies, while useful in fixing what one might call one's personal eras within our shared history, are effectively meaningless. Lying here, during all this time after my own small fall, it has become my conviction that things mean pretty much what we want them to mean. We'll pluck significance from the least consequential happenstance if it suits us and happily ignore the most flagrantly obvious symmetry between separate aspects of our lives if it threatens some cherished prejudice or cosily comforting belief; we are blindest to precisely whatever might be most illuminating. Mrs Mulverhill herself said that, I think. Or it might have been Madame d'Ortolan – I get the two confused sometimes.

I am getting a little ahead of myself, so, in the light of the above, let us embrace rather than resist this effect.

You may, even as we begin, wish to know how my part in this ends.

So let me tell you.

This is how it ends: he comes into my room. He is dressed in black and wearing gloves. It is dark in here, just a night light on, but he can identify me, lying on the hospital bed, propped up at a slight angle, one or two remaining tubes and wires attaching me to various pieces of medical equipment. He ignores these; the nurse who would hear any alarm is lying trussed and taped down the hall, the monitor in front of him switched off. The man shuts the door, darkening the room still further. He walks quietly to my bedside, though I ought to be unlikely to wake as I am sedated, lightly drugged to aid a good night's sleep. He looks at my bed. Even in the dim light he can see that it is tightly made; I am constricted within this envelope of sheets and blanket. Reassured by this confinement, he takes the spare pillow from the side of my head and places it – gently at first – over my face, then quickly bears down on me, forcing his hands down on either side of my head, pinning my arms under the covers with his elbows, placing most of his weight on his arms and his chest, his feet rising from the floor until only the tips of his shoes are still in contact with it.

I don't even struggle at first. When I do he simply smiles. My feeble attempts to bring my hands up and to use my legs to kick myself free come to nothing. Wound amongst these sheets, even a fit man would have stood little chance of fighting his way from beneath such suffocating weight. Finally, in one last hopeless convulsion, I try to arch my back. He rides this throe easily and in a moment or two I fall back, and all movement ceases.

He is no fool; he has anticipated that I might merely be playing dead.

So he lies quite calmly on me for a while, as unmoving as I, checking his watch now and again as the minutes tick by, to make sure I am gone.

I hope you're happy. An ending, and we have barely even begun yet! So we shall begin, first with something that in a sense has yet to happen.

It begins on a train, the highest train in the world, between China and Tibet. It begins with a man in a cheap brown business suit walking from one swaying carriage to another, his gait a little unsteady as he holds a small oxygen cylinder in one hand and an automatic handgun in the other. He steps onto the sliding metal plates that separate the carriages, the corrugated collar linking the passenger cars flexing and wheezing around him like a gigantic version of the ribbed tube connecting the oxygen cylinder and the transparent mask round his nose and mouth. Inside the mask, he finds himself smiling nervously.

The train rattles and jiggles around him, moving ponderously up and down and side to side, throwing him briefly against the ribs of the connector. Perhaps a place where the permafrost has proved less than permanent; he has heard that there have been problems. He steadies himself, rebalancing as the train straightens and resumes its smooth progress. He sticks the oxygen cylinder under one arm and uses his free hand to straighten his tie.

The gun is a People's Army issue K-54, decades old and feeling worn smooth with age. He has never fired it but it is meant to be reliable. The silencer looks crude, almost home-made. Still, it will have to do. He wipes his hand on his trousers, cocks the gun and extends his fingers towards the code panel above the handle of the door leading to the private carriage. A tiny red light pulses slowly on the lock's display.

They are approaching the highest part of the line, the Tanggula Pass, still most of a day away from Lhasa. The air feels cool and thin here, five kilometres up. Most people will be keeping to their seats, plugged into the train's oxygen supply. Outside, the Tibetan plateau – a symphony of dun, beige and brown with a bitty overlay of early-summer green – has ridged and buckled over the last hour to create foothills that harbinge the crumpled parapets of low encroaching mountains in the distance.

The chief train guard had demanded a lot of money for the override code. It had better work. He taps it in quickly.

The tiny pulsing red light turns steady green. He feels himself swallowing.

The train rocks; the handle feels cold beneath his fingers.

And it begins with our young-sounding, young-looking, young-acting but in the end middle-aged friend Mr Adrian Cubbish waking up in his Mayfair home one London morning in – oh, let's say late summer 2007; the routine is the same for the majority of days. He is in his bedroom suite, which takes up most of what used to be the attic of the town house. A light rain is falling onto the slabs of double-glazed glass which point at forty-five degrees to the light grey sky.

If Adrian were to have a symbol, it would be a mirror. This is what he says to the mirror each morning before he goes to work, and sometimes at the weekends when he doesn't have to go to work, just for the sheer hell of it:

"The Market is God. There is no God but the Market." He takes a breath here, smiling at his still-waking face. He looks young and fit, slim but muscled. He has tanned Caucasian skin, black hair, grey-green eyes and a wide mouth which is usually fixed in a knowing grin. Adrian has only ever slept with one woman who was significantly older than him; she chose to describe his mouth as "sensuous," which he'd decided, after a little thought, was cool. Girls his own age and younger would call his mouth cute if they thought to describe it at all. He has a shadow-beard a night old. He lets his beard grow for a week or so sometimes before shaving it off; he looks good either way. He looks, if he is being honest with himself, like a male model. He looks just like he wants to look. Maybe he could be a little taller.

He clears his throat, spits into the glass bowl of one of the bathroom's two sinks. Naked, he runs his hand through the dark curls of his pubic hair. "In the name of Capital, the compassionate, the wise," he tells himself.

He grins, winks at his own reflection, amused.

And here, in a low-rise office suite in Glendale, Los Angeles, blinds slicing the slanting late afternoon sunlight into dark and shining strips draped across carpet tiles, chairs, suits and conference table, the noise of the freeway a grumbling susurrus in the background while Mike Esteros makes his pitch:

"Gentlemen, lady . . . this is more than just a pitch. Don't get me wrong – this is a pitch but it's also an important part of the movie I'm going to convince you that you want to help me make.

"What I'm going to tell you here is how to find aliens. Seriously.

When I'm done, you'll believe it might be possible. You'll think we can capture an alien. What we'll certainly be able do is create a movie that will capture the imagination of a generation; a *Close Encounters*, a *Titanic*. So, thank you for letting me have these few minutes of your time; I promise you they won't be wasted.

"Now, anybody seen a full eclipse? Anyone been in the path of totality, when the sun is just wisps and tendrils of light peeking out from behind the moon? You, sir? Pretty impressive, sight, yeah? Yeah, mind-blowing indeed. Changes some people's lives. They become shadow chasers – people who track down as many eclipses as they can, journeying to every corner of the world just to experience more examples of this uncanny and unique phenomenon.

"So let's think about eclipses for a moment. Even if we haven't seen an eclipse personally, we've seen the photographs in magazines and the footage on television or YouTube. We're almost blasé about them; they're just part of the stuff that happens to our planet, like weather or earthquakes, only not destructive, not life-threatening.

"But think about it. What an incredible coincidence it is that our moon fits exactly over our sun. Talk to astronomers and they'll tell you that Earth's moon is relatively much bigger than any other moon round any other planet. Most planets, like Jupiter and Saturn and so on, have moons that are tiny in comparison to themselves. Earth's moon is enormous, and very close to us. If it was smaller or further away you'd only ever get partial eclipses; bigger or closer and it would hide the sun completely and there'd be no halo of light round the moon at totality. This is an astounding coincidence, an incredible piece of luck. And for all we know, eclipses like this are unique. This could be a phenomenon that happens on Earth and nowhere else. So, hold that thought, okay?

"Now, supposing there are aliens. Not *E.T.* aliens – not that cute or alone. Not *Independence Day* aliens – not that crazily aggressive – but, well, regular aliens. Yeah? Regular aliens. It's perfectly possible, when you think of it. We're here, after all, and Earth is just one small planet circling one regular-size sun in one galaxy. There are a

7

quarter of a billion suns in this one galaxy and quarter of a billion galaxies in the universe; maybe more. We already know of hundreds of other planets around other suns, and we've only just started looking for them. Scientists tell us that almost every star might have planets. How many of those might harbour life? The Earth is ancient, but the universe is even more ancient. Who knows how many civilisations were around before Earth came into existence, or existed while we were growing up, or exist right now?

"So, if there are civilised aliens, you'd guess they can travel between stars. You'd guess their power sources and technology would be as far beyond ours as supersonic jets, nuclear submarines and space shuttles are beyond some tribe in the Amazon still making dugout canoes. And if they're curious enough to do the science and invent the technology, they'll be curious enough to use it to go exploring.

"Now, most jet travel on Earth is for tourism. Not business; tourism. Would our smart, curious aliens really be that different from us? I don't think so. Most of them would be tourists. Like us, they'd go on cruise ships. And would they want to actually come to a place like Earth, set foot – or tentacle, or whatever – here? Rather than visit via some sort of virtual reality set-up? Well, some would settle for second-best, yes. Maybe the majority of people would. But the high rollers, the super-wealthy, the elite, they'd want the real thing. They'd want the bragging rights, they'd want to be able to say they'd really been to whatever exotic destinations would be on a Galactic Grand Tour. And who knows what splendours they'd want to fit in; their equivalent of the Grand Canyon, or Venice, Italy, or the Great Wall of China or Yosemite or the Pyramids?

"But what I want to propose to you is that, as well as all those other wonders, they would definitely want to see that one precious thing that we have and probably nobody else does. They'd want to see our eclipse. They'd want to look through the Earth's atmosphere with their own eyes and see the moon fit over the sun, watch the light fade down to almost nothing, listen to the animals nearby fall silent and feel with their own skins the sudden chill in the air that comes with totality. Even if they can't survive in our atmosphere, even if they need a spacesuit to keep them alive, they'd still want to get as close as they possibly could to seeing it in the raw, in as close to natural conditions as it's possible to arrange. They'd want to be here, amongst us, when the shadow passes.

"So that's where you look for aliens. In the course of an eclipse totality track. When everybody else is looking awestruck at the sky, you need to be looking round for anybody who looks weird or over-dressed, or who isn't coming out of their RV or their moored yacht with the heavily smoked glass.

"If they're anywhere, they're there, and as distracted – and so as vulnerable – as anybody else staring up in wonder at this aston-ishing, breathtaking sight.

"The film I want to make is based on that idea. It's thrilling, it's funny, it's sad and profound and finally it's uplifting, it's got a couple of great lead roles, one for a dad, one for a kid, a boy, and another exceptional supporting female role, plus opportunities for some strong character roles and lesser parts too.

"That's the set-up. Now let me tell you the story."

And, too, it begins somewhere else entirely . . .

"Between the plane trees and belvederes of Aspherje, on this clear midsummer early morning, the dawn-glittering Dome of the Mists rises splendidly over the University of Practical Talents like a vast gold thinking cap. Below, amongst the statues and the rills of the Philosophy Faculty rooftop park, walks the Lady Bisquitine, escorted."

. . . like that, it begins like that, too.

And with a slight, stooped, unremarkable man walking into a small room in a big building. He is holding only a single sheet of paper and a small piece of fruit, but he is met with screams. He looks, unconcerned, at the only other man in the room, and closes the door behind him. The screams continue.

*   *   *

And it begins here, now, at this table outside this café on this street in the Marais, Paris, with a man dropping a tiny white pill into his espresso from a small but ornate sweetener box. He looks around, taking in the passing traffic and pedestrians – some hurrying, some flaneuring – and glances at the briskly handsome young Algerian waiter who is trying to flirt with a couple of warily smiling American girls, before his gaze settles briefly on an elegantly made-up and coiffured Parisienne of late middle age holding her tiny dog up to the table to let it lap some croissant flakes. Then he adds a gnarly lump of brown sugar from the bowl to his cup and stirs the coffee with a studied thoughtfulness as he slips the slim ormolu sweetener box back into a pocket inside his jacket.

He slides a five-euro note under the sugar bowl, replaces his wallet in his jacket, then drains the espresso cup in a couple of deep, appreciative sips. He settles back, one hand still holding the miniature handle of the cup, the other hanging by his side. He has now taken on the air of a man waiting for something.

It is an afternoon at the start of autumn in the year 2008 CE, the air is clear and warm beneath a milky, pastel sky, and everything is about to change.

1

Patient 8262

I think I have been very clever in doing what I have done, in landing myself where I am. However, a lot of us are prone, as I am now, to think we've been quite clever, are we not? And too often in my past that feeling of having been quite clever has preceded the uncomfortable revelation that I have not been quite clever enough. This time, though . . .

My bed is comfortable, the medical and care staff treat me well enough, with a professional indifference which is, in my particular circumstances, more reassuring than excessive devotion would be. The food is acceptable.

I have a lot of time to think, lying here. Thinking is what I do best, perhaps. Thinking is what we do best, too. As a species, I mean. It is our forte, our speciality, our superpower; that which has raised us above the common herd. Well, we like to think so.

How relaxing to lie here and be looked after without having to do anything in return. How wonderful to have the luxury of undisturbed thought.

I am alone in a small square room with whitewashed walls, a high ceiling and tall windows. The bed is an old steel thing with a manually adjustable backrest and slatted sides that can be raised, clanging, to prevent the patient falling out of bed. The sheets are crisp and white, glowing with cleanliness, and the pillows, while a little lumpy, are plump. The linoleum floor gleams, pale green. A battered-looking wooden bedside table and a cheap chair of black-painted metal and faded red plastic comprise the room's remaining furniture. There is a fanlight set into the wall above the single door to the corridor outside. Beyond the floor-to-ceiling windows is a small decorative balcony with iron railings.

Held behind these bars, the view is of a strip of grass and then a line of deciduous trees, with a shallow river behind them which sparkles in the sunlight when the angles are right. The trees are losing their leaves now and more of the river is becoming visible. On the far bank I can see more trees. My room is on the second, the top floor of the clinic. I saw a rowing boat glide down the river once with two or three people in it and sometimes I see birds. On one occasion, a high-flying aircraft left a long white cloud across the sky, like a ship's wake. I watched it for some time as it spread slowly and kinked and turned red with the sunset.

I should be safe here. They will not think to look for me here. I think. Other places did occur to me: a yurt on some endless rolling steppe with only an extended family and the wind for company; some packed and noisome *favela* spattered across a steep hillside, the smell of shared sweat and the noise of bawling children, bellowing men and beaty music jangling; camping out in some lofty ruin of a monastery in the Cyclades, garnering a reputation as a hermit and an eccentric; underground with the other damaged tunnel dwellers, ragged beneath Manhattan.

In plain sight or secreted away, there are always many, many places to hide where they'll never think to look, but then they know me and how I think, so perhaps they can guess where I'd head for even before I'd know myself. Then there is the problem of fitting in naturally or assuming a disguise, adopting a role: ethnicity, physiognomy, skin colour, language, skills – all must be taken into account.

We sort ourselves out, do we not? You lot there, this lot here; even in the great melting-pot cities we generally order ourselves into little enclaves and districts where we gain a comfort from a shared background or culture. Our nature, our sexuality, our genetic desire to wander and experiment, our lust for the exotic or the just different can lead to interesting pairings and mixed inheritances, but our need to group, grade and categorise continually pulls us back into set arrangements. This makes hiding difficult; I am – or at least I certainly look like – a pale Caucasian male, and the places I'm least likely to hide are such because I'd stand out there.

A trucker. That would be a good way to hide. A long-distance truck driver, beating across the US Midwest or the plains of Canada or Argentina or Brazil, or at the helm of a multi-trailer road train barrelling across the Australian desert. Hide through constant move-ment, seldom meeting people. Or a deckhand or cook on a ship; a container vessel plying the high seas with a tiny crew, turning around in twenty-four hours at vast, automated, nearly uninhabited container terminals far distant from the centres of the cities that they serve. Who would ever find me, living so distributed a life?

But, instead, I am here. I made my choice and I have no choice now; I must stick with it. I worked out my route, set up the means and the funding and the personnel with the required skills to aid me on my way into obscurity and unfindability, tested the ways those who might want to find me might set about doing so and worked out methods of frustrating their quest, then – with every-thing in place – went through with it.

So, thinking, here I lie.

The Transitionary

Others have told me that for them it happens during a blink, or just at random between heartbeats or even during a heartbeat. There is always some external sign: a shiver or tremble, often a noticeable twitch, occasionally a jerk, as though an electric shock has passed

13

through the subject's body. One person said that the way it happens for them is that they always think they've just caught a glimpse of something surprising or threatening from the corner of their eye and – as they turn their head quickly round – experience a distressing burning sensation like a sort of internal electric shock buzzing through the neck. For me it is usually fractionally more embarrassing; I sneeze.

I just sneezed.

I have only the vaguest idea how long I sat outside that little café in the 3rd, waiting for the drug to take effect, sinking into the waking dream that is the necessary precursor to navigating accurately to our desired destination. A few seconds? Five minutes? I trust I paid my bill. I should not care – I am not him, and anyway he will still be there – but I do care. I sit forward, look at the table in front of me. There is a small pile of change sitting on the little plastic tray with the bill clipped to it. Francs, centimes; not euros. So; so far, so good.

I feel a pressing need to rearrange the items on the table. The sugar bowl must be in the exact centre while the drained espresso cup needs to be halfway between the bowl and me, aligned. The bill tray I am happy to leave to the right of the bowl, balancing the condiments carrier. It is only as I rearrange these items into this pleasing configuration that I notice that the wrist and hand protruding from my sleeve are both deep brown. Also, I realise that I have just formed a sort of cross on the little table. I glance up, taking in the design of the cars and trams in the street and the dress of the pedestrians. I am where I thought, in a Judeo-Islamic reality; hopefully, in one particular one. I immediately rearrange the pieces on the table to form what would be called a peace symbol back where I just came from. I sit back, relieved. Not that I look like some Christian terrorist, I'm sure, but you can't be too careful.

Do I look like a Christian terrorist? I reach into my chest bag – I wear the salwar kameez, like most other men and women here, effectively pocketless – and bring out what would have been my iPod a few seconds/five minutes ago. Here it is a cigarette case of stainless steel. I try to look as though I am contemplating having a cigarette; in fact I am studying my reflection on the polished back of the case. More relief; I do not look like a Christian terrorist. I look like I usually do when I'm this colour and broadly like I always do no matter what colour, race or type I may be, which is to say unobjectionable, unremarkable, not bad-looking (not good-looking either, but that's acceptable). I look bland. But bland is good, bland is safe, bland blends: perfect cover.

Check the watch. Always check the watch. I check the watch. The watch is fine; no problem with the watch. I do not take a cigarette. I feel no need. Obviously I have not incorporated the craving into this new personification. I put the cigarette case back in the bag slung over my chest from shoulder to hip, checking that the little ormolu pill case is in its own internal pocket, zipped. Still more relief! (The pill case has never not travelled, but you always worry. Well, I always worry. I think I always worry.)

My identity card tells me that I am Aiman Q'ands, which sounds about right. Aiman, hey man; hi, pleased to meet me. Language check. I have French, Arabic, English, Hindic, Portuguese and Latin. A smattering of German and also Latter Mongolian. No Mandarin at all; that's unusual.

I sit back again, adjusting my legs in the voluminous salwars so that they are precisely in line with the X of legs supporting the little table. It would appear that while I have no tobacco habit I obviously do have – once again – some sort of mild Obsessive Compulsive Disorder, which is arguably just as annoying and distracting, if less health-threatening (though I should care!).

I hope it's mild OCD. Do I think it's mild? Maybe it's not mild after all. (My hands do feel a little clammy, like they might need to be washed.) Maybe it's severe. (There's a lot about this café that could do with being tidied, aligned, straightened.) That's something to worry about. So, I'm a worrier, too, obviously. That's annoying, that's worrying in itself.

Well, can't sit here all day. I'm here for a reason; I've been summoned. By Herself, no less. I feel quite recovered from any passing dizziness associated with the transition; no excuse for hesitating. I need to get up and go, so I do.

Adrian

I've told people I'm an ex-East End barrow boy, haven't I? Dad ran an eel stall and mum was a barmaid. But that's bollocks, a total lie. I only tell them that because that's what they like to hear, what they want to hear. That's one of the lessons I've learned, isn't it? You can go a long way just telling people what they want to hear. Of course, you got to be careful, and you got to choose the right people, but still, know what I mean?

Course, any fuckwit can just tell somebody else what they already know they want to hear. The creative bit, the real added-value bit is knowing what they want to hear before they know it themselves. They really appreciate that. That pays dividends. It's kind of a service industry thing. Anyway I'm really good at the accent. Highly convincing. You should hear me. The East End thing, I mean. Doing the barrow-boy routine. I'm fucking good at the geezah accent, that's all I'm saying, isn't it? Keep up.

Truth is I'm from Up North. One of those grim northern cities with all the grime and all. You don't need to know which grim northern city on account of the fact I'm sure you'll agree they're all the same, so it won't make any difference me telling you exactly which one, will it? So if you do want to know exactly which one, tough. Do what I do. Use your imagination.

Nah, my dad was a miner before they joined the list of endangered species thanks to Saint Margaret (with a little or a lot of help from King Arthur, depending on your outlook). Mum worked in a hairdressing salon. I'm serious about La Thatch being a saint, too, though you still have to be careful who you say that to back where I grew up, which is one of the many reasons I don't go back there hardly at all, isn't it? I mean, who the fuck wants to work all their life down a fucking hole in the ground anyway? Nobody in their right mind. La Thatch did them all a favour. They should have statues to her where the pit wheels were.

Anyway, by the time I came along that stuff was all ancient history. Well, it was as far as I was concerned. It might as well have happened yesterday from the way everybody around me kept banging on about it constantly. We lived in a semi so there was a family right next door, obviously, right? Well, we weren't allowed to acknowledge they even existed because the guy, who'd been one of dad's best mates apparently, had joined the Democratic Union of Miners of Britain or whatever and so he was a blackleg as far as my old dad was concerned and seemingly that was worse than being a paedo or a murderer. Only time my dad looked like he might hit me was when he caught me talking to the twins next door.

Anyway, it wasn't anywhere that I wanted to be. I was off down the motorway soon as I could escape from school, heading for the big bad city, and the bigger and badder the better. I sort of hesitated around Manchester for a month when it was just getting interesting but I didn't bother staying. I went on south. M6 to London. Always liked the bright lights, I have. London was the only place for me. Only place this side of the Pond at any rate. Suppose New York would have been all right, but then thanks to people like yours truly London eventually became better and cooler than NYC anyway.

Thing is, I sort of understand people wanting to stay where they were brought up, if they were raised in a big city anyway, I mean why would you want to stay in the country? You might want to stay where you grew up for sentimental reasons and your mates being around and so on but unless it's a really, really great place that's really, seriously going to add something to your life, you're kind of being a mug, know what I mean? If you stay in a place like that when you know you could have a go somewhere bigger and brighter with more opportunities you're giving more to it than it's giving to you, aren't you? You're in a net loss situation, know what I mean? I mean, if you like feeling like an asset to your local community or something then fucking yahoo for you but don't pretend you aren't being exploited. People talk a lot about loyalty and being true to your roots and suchlike but that's just bollocks, isn't it? That's one of the ways they make you do things that aren't in your own best interest. Loyalty's a mug's game.

So I moved to sunny London. Was sunny, too, compared to Manchester or where I come from. Bought my first pair of Oakleys day I arrived. I say bought. Anyway, London was sunny and warm and balmy even and full of totty and opportunities. Moved in with a mate from back home, got a job behind a bar in Soho, got a girl-friend or two, met some characters, started making myself useful to the sort of people who appreciate someone with a bit of sharpness about them and the gift of the gab. Thinking on your feet, like they say. Landing on your feet. That's useful, too. Better still, landing on somebody else's feet.

Long and short, started providing the high-flyers with the means to get them high, didn't I? Full of creative types, Soho, and a lot of people in the creative industries like to powder their nose, indulge in a bit of nasal turbocharging, don't they? Very big thing with the Creatives, certainly back then. And amongst said Creatives I would most certainly include the financial wizards and their highly exotic Instruments and Products. Plus, of course, they have the funds to really get stuck into it.

So I worked my way up, in a sense. And along, sort of. Along in the sense of east, where the dosh is. East of Soho, to the City, to be precise, and Canary Wharf, where a lot of them highest of high-flyers perched. Follow the money, they say – well, I did.

See, I had a plan, right from the start. A way to make up for my lack of what you might term a formal education and letters after my name. (Numbers after my name, that might have been a different story, but I managed to avoid that.) Anyway, what do people do when they've had a toot or two? Talk, that's what they do. Talk like fuck. And boast, of course, if they're especially impressed with them-selves. Which would cover just about everybody I provided for.

And of course if you spend all your time working, concentrating, making money, taking risks, being financially daring and so on, you'll talk about that, won't you? Stands to reason. Fizzing with testosterone and their own genius, these guys, so of course they talk about what they've been up to, the deals they've done, the money they've made, the angles they've got coming up, the stuff they know.

So a person who happened to be around them when they were talking about this sort of stuff, especially somebody who they knew wasn't one of their own and so not a threat, not a competitor, but somebody they thought of as a mate as well as an always available deliverer of their chosen leisure-enhancing substance, well, that person could hear a lot of interesting things, know what I mean? If that person acted a bit thicker and even less educated than they actually were and kept their eyes and ears open and their mind sharp they could hear some potentially very useful things. Potentially very lucrative things, if you know the right people and can get the right bit of information to them at the right time.

Just being useful, really. Like I say, I'm part of the service industry. And once you know a few secrets it's amazing how you get to know others too. People trade in secrets, and don't realise they're giving themselves away, especially if they trust you, or underestimate you, or both. So I found myself in a position where I could call in a few favours, use what our financial friends would call leverage to pick up some training, some recommendations, some patronage you might say, not to mention some working capital.

Long and short again, I went from being a dealer to being a trader. Swapped the powder for the folding, replaced the stuff that goes up the middle of the rolled note for the note itself. This was a deeply smart move, if I say so myself.

Don't get me wrong. Drugs are great, obviously they are. Great business to be in in a lot of ways, and definitely enduringly popular in good times and bad otherwise why would people spend so much of their disposable and risk prison taking them? But it's all a bit of a mug's game dealing them, when you really think about it, certainly for any length of time. You have to watch your back constantly and even the profits get eaten into keeping the boys in blue happy. I mean, serious fucking profits, there's still a lot left, but still, that's exactly what attracts some very heavy and uncivilised people to the business and you can't spend fuck all when you're dead, can you? Get in, make some of the filthy and get out while you still got a set of balls and an unslit throat to call your own, that's how you fucking do it if you've any sense. Use it as a leg-up to get into some-thing just as lucrative but a lot less risky. That's the smart way. That's what I did.

Amazing what you can accomplish by applying yourself and making yourself useful.

Madame d'Ortolan

Madame d'Ortolan sat in her orangery, discomfited. She had been accused of being a racist! And by someone she couldn't take any immediate retributive action against, too. Of course she was not a racist. She not infrequently had black and Jewish people here in her town house, though naturally she was always careful to keep an accurate note of where they sat and what they touched and might have used, subsequently having everything so contacted thoroughly cleaned and disinfected. One could not be too careful.

But of course she was not a racist. To the contrary, as she could point out, in appropriate company (that would be to say, highly limited and avowedly discreet company), had she not tasted of what she thought of as the Dark Pleasures, with blacks, on more than one occasion? The epitome of such enjoyment was, for her, to be taken anally by such a Nubian brute. Privately, she thought of this act as "going to Sèvres-Babylone," as this was the deepest, darkest and most excitingly, enticingly dangerous Métro station that she knew of.

Racist! The cheek of it. She had taken the call here in the orangery. The conversation had gone like this:

"Oui?"

"Madame, I'm glad I managed to catch you."

"Ah. Mrs M. I trust we can return the compliment."

Mrs Mulverhill had chosen to open by speaking English, always a sure sign that she wished to talk business and this was not a social call. It had been some long time since either had called the other for purely social reasons. "May I ask where you are?"

"I suppose you might, though not to any instructive consequence."

Madame d'Ortolan felt herself bristling. "A simple No would have sufficed."

"Yes, but would have been inaccurate. Are you well?"

"I am, as if you care one way or the other. And you?"

"Tolerably. And I do care, one way. Let me tell you why I'm calling."

"Do. It's been so long. I can't wait."

"Rumour has it you intend to divide the Council."

"Beyond my powers, dear. And, anyway, I think you'll find it already is."

"If it is divided—"

"Oh, it is."

"If it is, then it is largely due to you."

"As I say, you both flatter and overestimate."

"That is not what the people I've talked to say."

"People on the Council? Who?"

Mrs Mulverhill remained silent. There was a pause while Madame d'Ortolan – who had taken the call on the house phone, on an extension with a long lead – twirled the extension cord round her longest finger. After a few moments, a sigh sounded down the phone line and Mrs Mulverhill said, "So, what is the thinking on this matter?"

"The thinking?" Madame d'Ortolan asked innocently.

"What do you intend to do?" Mrs Mulverhill said, voice suddenly sharp.

"I think that matters need to be resolved."

There was a silence, then: "I hope that is not settled. It would be the incorrect decision."

21

"Is that what you think?"

"It is."

"What a pity we did not have the benefit of your opinion earlier, before the decision was made."

"Theodora," Mrs Mulverhill said crisply, "don't pretend that you'd have taken any notice of anything I'd have said."

"And yet you have chosen to call me now, my darling, and I presume you are only doing so in an attempt to influence that very decision, after it has been made. Are you not?"

A shorter silence, then: "I would appeal to your sense of prag-matism."

"Not morality? Decency? Justice?"

Mrs Mulverhill laughed delicately. "You are a card, Theodora."

"Yes, I like to think of myself as the queen of spades."

"I have heard something to that effect."

"And what do you think you might be? The joker, perhaps?"

"I could not care less."

"I'd imagine something like . . . the two of clubs, yes?"

"Theodora, enough of this. I am asking you to reconsider."

"Very well; the three."

A silence Madame d'Ortolan would have termed "tight" reigned for a moment. It sounded subsequently as though Mrs Mulverhill might be speaking through clenched teeth. "I am attempting to be serious, Theodora."

"They do say the struggle against adversity is highly character-forming."

"Theodora!" Mrs Mulverhill first raised her voice, then dropped it. "Theodora. I am asking you: please do not do this."

"Do *what*?"

"Whatever decisive, divisive step it is you intend to take. It would be a mistake."

"Oh, for goodness' sake!" Madame d'Ortolan was losing patience. She sat forward in her cane chair, flicking free the twisted phone cord from her left hand. "Alors, my sweet, my pretty! What do you really care about the fate of people you've already turned your back on? People you oppose by opposing the Council. What are they to you? A couple of mealy-mouthed, grinning half-castes and a lesbian Negress?" A thought struck her and she beamed. "Unless she excites you, of course, our crepuscular friend; so well camouflaged, in the dark. One would hardly know she was in one's bed of a night, would one? Well, until she smiled, at any rate. Don't tell me; you're a secret admirer. Has one put one's finger on something?"

Another telling silence, then: "You old, racist bitch."

And then she put the phone down! Just like that! The nerve of the woman!

Madame d'Ortolan was unsure who had come out best from the exchange. For most if not all the way through she had felt that she was having the best of it, but then the Mulverhill woman had been the one to hang up on her, which counted for something. Most vexing. And to be called a racist! Not for the first time, she wondered what Mrs Mulverhill herself might have to hide in that regard. She habitually wore a veil; Madame d'Ortolan had always assumed this was mere affectation, but perhaps the lady wished to conceal some angle from which she looked less than racially pure, when the race concerned was human. Who knew?

But still, to call her a racist. When it was meant as an insult. And, worse, "old!"

And now she had to meet that objectionable and seemingly unkillable little man Oh, or whatever he was called for now (at least they were meeting elsewhere and she didn't have to suffer his presence in the house; he never looked clean). And meet him not a moment too soon, if the Mulverhill woman had heard rumours already. Madame d'Ortolan smiled to herself. "Divide" the Council? Was that the best, or the worst, that she'd heard?

"I'll show you *divide*," she muttered to no one present.

She shooed the white cat called M. Pamplemousse from her lap and rose, smoothing her cream skirt. Madame d'Ortolan favoured her various cats according to the colour of the clothes she was wearing at any particular time. Had she been wearing dark grey or black, the black-haired cat called Mme Frenolle would have been the one allowed to warm itself on her lap. Though perhaps not for much longer; recently Mme Frenolle, who was eight years old now, had started to produce white hairs amongst the black, which was most annoying. Depending on how well she behaved over the next week or two, Mme Frenolle would either have to suffer regular visits to the *Maison Chat* to have her white hairs plucked or dyed, or be put down.

Madame d'Ortolan was, she liked to think, of elegant middle age, though to the casual observer this might imply that she expected to live to be about one hundred and twenty. Of course, being who and what she was, this was would have been a perfectly reasonable expectation on her part, had the truth not been much more complicated.

She used the house intercom. "Mr Kleist, if you would."

The gentleman himself arrived a minute or so later, a pale, slightly hunched, somehow dowdy figure despite being, to all appearances, quite smartly dressed in a conservatively cut grey three-piece suit. He looked to be about the same age as his employer, though the same dispassionate observer called upon to judge the lady's looks might have taken a second glance at him and decided he was really a decade or more her junior, just worn-looking. He came to her side, blinking in the orangery's hazy sunlight.

"Madame."

"Mrs Mulverhill," she told him, "is rapidly approaching the stage where she will know what I intend to do shortly before I do myself."

Mr Kleist sighed. "We continue to search for her, ma'am, and to look for her informants."

"I'm sure we do. However, we must start to act." She looked up at him. Mr Kleist could contrive to look only half-glimpsed in the brightest sunlight. He carried his own shadows about with him, she was sure. "I am seeing Mr Oh today," she told him, "for what I have now decided ought to be the last time. I think we set him on his way as fully wound as possible. You catch my drift?"

"Yes, I do, ma'am."

"And we take all further steps to make sure his work is carried on after whatever point he is no longer able to do it."

"I'll have the draft orders finalised."

"I shall leave in ten minutes."

"That'll be sufficient, ma'am."

"Thank you, Mr Kleist." She smiled at him. "That will be all."

For some moments after Mr Kleist had turned and gone, Madame d'Ortolan sat where she was, staring at nothing and tapping her long pink nails against each other with a hollow, clacking sound. The cat M. Pamplemousse jumped back onto her lap, startling her. She threw him off immediately, hissing.

She called for her car, left the orangery, freshened up in her downstairs boudoir, collected the orders for the objectionable Mr Oh from the efficient Mr Kleist as she walked down the hallway and then allowed the second most attractive of her Egyptian footmen to place her jacket over her shoulders before she walked out to the car and instructed Christophe to take her to the Café Atlantique.

The car swivelled on the ribbon of gravel looped in front of the tall town house and exited to the Boulevard Haussmann as the ornate black gates swung silently closed.

2

Patient 8262

I t is amazing what you can tell even with your eyes quite tightly closed. I can tell, for example, what season it is, what sort of day it is, which nurses and orderlies are on duty, which other patients have visited my room, which day of the week it is, and whether someone has died.

None of this is difficult and certainly none of it is in any way supernatural. It simply requires that one keeps one's ears open and one's senses attuned to everyday reality. A good memory for previous experiences helps too, as does a decent imagination. The imagination is necessary not to make things up – that would be wrong – but to come up with plausible scenarios for what one's senses are detecting; theories that might explain what is going on.

Sometimes I spend entire days with my eyes closed. I pretend to sleep – I do sleep, longer than I would otherwise – and I allow my other senses to paint the scene around me. I can hear wind and rain against the window and birdsong outside, I can tell from the faint draught and the definition and detail of the sounds outside that the window is ajar, even if I missed the creaking, scraping noise of it being opened, and from the scents that reach me from it and the feel of the air I know immediately whether it's a summer's day or an unusually warm interlude in either spring or autumn. I can smell the identifying body odours and perfumes of the nurses and doctors who attend me and so can tell who is there even without hearing their voices, though I know those too, of course.

Occasionally other patients wander in and I know they are there from their institutional, medicinal smell. I don't mix with them sufficiently to have built up a reliable database of them all as individuals, though one or two do stand out through body odour or what they do; one man smells of a particular cologne, one old lady carries with her the scent of violets, another always runs her fingers through my hair (I can peek through not-quite-closed eyelids and so see who is responsible when something like this happens). One small, gaunt man whistles aimlessly more or less all the time and another chubbier fellow never visits without tapping absently on the metal frame at the foot of the bed with his fingernails.

The rhythms of the hospital day, week, month and year are also obvious without recourse to sight and the place, of course, feels and sounds quite different at night; most noticeably, far quieter. During the day, meals are regular, drug rounds too (there are two drug trollies – one has a squeaky wheel), doctors perform their various rounds according to a certain timetable and the cleaners have an entirely predictable set of rotas that cover every temporal scale from daily dusting and wiping to the annual spring clean.

So, very little escapes me as I lie here, even with the most informational of my senses deliberately denied.

I can see perfectly well, though. This is really just a game, something to help occupy my time while I wait out my self-imposed exile and bide my time before returning to the fray.

I will, most assuredly, be back.

The Transitionary

Once, I watched her hand move above a lit candle, through the yellow flame, fingers spread fluttering amidst the incandescing gas, her unharmed flesh ruffling the very burning of it. The flame bent this way and that, guttered, sent curls of sooty smoke towards the dim ceiling of the room where we sat as she moved her hand slowly back and forth through the gauzy teardrop of fire.

She said, "No, I see consciousness as a matter of focus. It's like a magnifying glass concentrating light rays on a point on a surface until it bursts into flame – the flame being consciousness. It is the focusing of reality that creates that self-awareness." She looked up at me. "Do you see?"

I nodded, though I was not sure that I did see. We had taken certain drugs, and they were still affecting us. I knew enough to realise that one could talk utter nonsense in such circumstances and that it could seem unutterably profound at the time. I knew it but at the same time felt that this was quite different.

"There is no intelligence without context," she continued, watching her hand go through the flame and back. "Just as a magnifying glass effectively casts a partial shadow around the point of its focus – the debt required to produce the concentration elsewhere – so meaning is sucked out of our surroundings, concentrated in ourselves, in our minds."

One summer when I was a teenager some friends and I were walking into town, saving our bus fares to have more money to spend on sweets, burgers and slot machines. Our route took us down a quiet suburban street of houses with small front gardens. We came to one garden – mostly paved, with a few mismatched pots holding dry, bedraggled-looking plants – where a fat grey-haired man was lying asleep in a deckchair. We all stopped to look, sweating. A couple of the guys had taken their T-shirts off and were bare-chested, like the old man. He had lots of curly grey hair on his chest. Somebody whispered that he looked like a beached whale.

The garden was tiny; he'd had to angle the deckchair across it to fit in. He was so close that you could smell the coconut oil on his skin, so close that we could almost touch him.

We stood there watching him sleep and somebody else said they wished we had a water pistol. The sun was behind us, light beating on our backs. I was the tallest and the shadow of my head was putting the man's feet into shade. I remembered I had a magnifying glass with me. I'd been using it to burn holes in the leaves of my stepmother's prize flowers.

"Watch this," I said, and took the magnifying glass out. I held it so that it focused the sunlight on the skin of his chest, then moved it along and up through the forest of glinting grey hairs to concentrate the light on his little puckered left nipple. Some of the guys were starting to laugh already. I began to laugh too, which made the small, bright point of light waver, but I held it steady enough and long enough for him to shift a little, and for a frown to appear on his face. I still think I saw a faint wisp of smoke. Then his eyes flicked open and he bellowed, sitting up suddenly, his eyes wide, one hand flying up to his singed nipple. The other guys were already running, howling with laughter, down the street. I sprinted after them. We heard him shouting after us. We avoided that street for a few weeks.

I don't mention this story to her, either at the time or ever.

"I'd have said," (I said, instead,) "that we give, even . . . Even that we radiate, emanate meaning. We ascribe context to external things. Without us they exist, I suppose—"

"Do they?" she murmured.

"—but we give them names and we see the systems and processes that link them. We contextualise them within their setting. We make them more real by knowing what they mean and represent."

"Hnn," she said, shrugging fractionally, distracted by the sight of her hand moving through the flame. "Maybe." It sounded like she was losing interest. "But everything requires a leavening. Everything." She let her head fall slowly to one side, watching her hand moving through the flame with a perfectly absorbed intensity that left me free to look at her.

She sat bundled in a crumpled white sheet. Her hair, a brown-red spill of curls across her shoulders and along her slender neck, formed a quiet nimbus around her tipped head. Her deep brown eyes looked almost black, reflecting the flickering candlelight like some image of the consciousness that she had been speculating about. They looked perfectly still and steady. I could see the minuscule spark of the flame reflected in them, see it occluded by her hand passing over it. She blinked slowly, almost languorously.

I recalled that the eyes only see by moving; we can fasten our gaze on something and stare intently at it only because our eyes are consumed with dozens of tiny involuntary movements each second. Hold something perfectly and genuinely still in our field of vision and that very fixity makes it disappear.

"I love you," I heard myself whisper.

She glanced up. *"What?"*

Her hand stopped, poised over the flame. She jerked it away. "Ow!"

Madame d'Ortolan

In the main salon of the Café Atlantique – vast and echoing, with a ceiling lost in a layer of ancient-looking smoke stirred by giant wobbling ceiling fans – there is a Jupla band playing to the mostly indifferent crowd packing the spaces between the tables, which are variously set for eating, drinking and gaming. Stained-glass circular windows set high in the two gable walls struggle along with globular yellow lamps the size of bathyspheres to illuminate the chaotic scenes below, where small, sweating men wearing sandwich boards run up and down the aisles.

The pretty little Eurasian singer wears a vibrato collar and the snare drums are doubled, one set conventionally while the other is poised upside down directly above, separated by about half a metre.

As Madame d'Ortolan enters – her way cleared as best he can by Christophe the chauffeur – the singer on the low stage midway along one long wall hits an especially high and plangent note and uses the cable remote in her pocket to turn her collar to high speed. Batteries in the remote power up a tiny motor attached to unbalanced weights within the device itself, making the collar burr against the girl's throat just over her voice box so that she produces a sort of staccato ululation impossible to achieve without such mechanical artifice. The drummer has both sticks blurring in between the lower and upper snares, creating a crazed percussive accompaniment to match.

"Your table, ma'am," Christophe says, quickly dusting and polishing a seat with its back against the wall of a semicircular booth set almost directly opposite the band. He called ahead from the car to book this small, neatly placed table and the previous occupants are still arguing with elements of the management even as their half-finished drinks are being tidied away by white-jacketed waiters.

Madame d'Ortolan eyes the seat sceptically, then sighs, smooths her skirt and sits, prim and upright while Christophe pushes the chair in. She can see the one who is probably the Oh person making his way through the crowds towards her. He is dressed like a peasant and has either a peasant's skin tone or just that neither-one-thing-nor-the-other colour that Madame d'Ortolan finds irritating. He arrives, stands in front of her, glancing at the towering presence of Christophe. He smiles at her, rubbing his hands. He bows sinuously. "Madame."

"Yes?"

"Aiman Q'ands. At your service."

"Sit," she tells him. She has already forgotten the name he has just spoken. To her he is still Oh. There is shouting beyond the mouth of the alcove, where the table's earlier occupants have noticed that their drinks have been tidied away. A waiter flaps a pristine white tablecloth across the table, lets it settle and turns to take her order as the greasy-looking little man sits. Christophe, standing greyly

32

behind her, divides his time between looking suspiciously at the man who has just arrived and looking suspiciously at the arguing punters, now in the first stages of being shooed away by the management and a couple of bouncers who have just drifted up and who are even larger than Christophe.

Aiman Q'ands bows from a seated position. "Always a pleasure to see you—"

"I do not require your pleasantries," Madame d'Ortolan tells him, "and you should not expect mine." This one, she recalls, surveying his smiling, shining, annoyingly anonymous coffee-coloured face, has always responded well to being kept thoroughly in his place. She turns briefly to Christophe and glances at her shoulder; he lifts the cream jacket from her shoulders and places it carefully over the back of her seat. She suspects that he lets his fingers linger just a fraction longer than fully necessary as they touch her flesh through her silk blouse, and that he surreptitiously sniffs at her hair as he bends to her. This is agreeable but distracting. "Still water," she informs the waiter. "Bring it sealed. No ice."

"Double espresso," Aiman Q'ands says. He flaps the collar of his kameez. "And water; lots of ice." He drums his fingers on the table.

It is hot in Paris and hotter still in the Café Atlantique; the leisurely spinning ceiling fans are largely decorative. The small sweating men wearing the sandwich boards – which advertise today's specials and the services of various bookmakers, lawyers, pawnbrokers, bail-bond companies and brothels as well as conveying the latest headlines and sports results – are there principally to create cooling draughts as they pelt up and down the aisles. They are surprisingly effective. Aiman Q'ands squirms in his seat, looking up and all around. His hands knead each other. He seems incapable of sitting still and is making Madame d'Ortolan feel even warmer. "Fan, Christophe," she says over her shoulder. With a snap, a large lacy black fan is deployed and starts to move air gently past her face.

Aiman Q'ands sits forward, eyes glistening. "Madame, may I say—"

33

"No, you may not," Madame d'Ortolan tells him. She glances about her with a look of some distaste. "We shall keep this to the minimum."

Q'ands looks hurt. He sits back, looking down. "Madame, do you find me so repellent?"

As though she spared the wretch a thought at all! "Don't be absurd," she tells him. "I simply have no great desire to be here," she says, a glance taking in the smokily cavernous space. "Aside from all else, these crowds are, perversely, highly attractive to bombers."

"Christians?" Q'ands says, looking mildly surprised and also looking round.

"Of course Christians, you idiot!"

Q'ands shakes his head ruefully and tuts. "The religion of brotherly love. So sad."

Just for a moment Madame d'Ortolan thinks he might be trying to make fun of her. You can never be sure in how much detail these *passerines* remember previous encounters with things, events or people. Could he be baiting her? She quickly dismisses the thought. "The religion of zealotry," she informs him testily. "The religion that loves its martyrs, the religion of the doctrine of Original Sin, so that blowing even babies to smithereens is justifiable because they too are sinners." She jerks her head and makes a sort of dry spitting sound. "A religion made for terrorism."

She can see what might be a small smile on Q'ands's unpleasantly glowing face and can feel perspiration starting to gather on her brow. She leans forward and lowers her voice. "Are you properly ambiented? Have you fully embedded here yet?" she asks. "Any idiot ought to know this. Do you?"

"I know what I know, ma'am," he says quietly, for all the world as though trying to be mysterious. Meanwhile one leg is bouncing up and down as though he is trying to follow the beat of the Jupla band. The fellow is preposterous!

"Well, know that I wish to waste no further time here." She glances up at Christophe, then has, annoyingly, to clear her throat loudly because he seems distracted by the Eurasian waif warbling on stage. Her chauffeur collects himself, follows her gaze as it flicks to the man seated opposite and, sticking his free hand into his grey tunic, produces what looks like a cigar tube and hands it to Q'ands.

He looks at it sadly and then places it in his chest satchel. "Also," Q'ands says, "I am almost out of—"

"There are supplies for a dozen journeys in there," Madame d'Ortolan tells him. "We're not stupid. We can count."

He shrugs. "My apologies for so obviously inconveniencing you." He sounds hurt. He stands up and runs a hand through his wiry brown hair. As he turns to look out into the body of the salon, a sandwich-board man races past, clacking. The resultant breeze makes Q'ands's salwar kameez flutter. ". . . See if I can intercept my coffee . . ."

"Sit down!" she snaps.

He turns back. "But you said—"

"Sit!"

He sits, looking still more wounded.

"There are certain instructions specific to this matter which have not been written down," she says. Q'ands looks appropriately surprised. She is already finding the way his expression seems to reflect his internal state so immediately and accurately extremely vexing. Worryingly unprofessional, too, if he's like this with everybody. Has he finally gone off the rails? How vexing if her long campaign to destabilise the fellow has finally succeeded just when she needs him at his most implacably efficient.

"Indeed?" he says. He looks mystified. Madame d'Ortolan half expects a cartoon thought-bubble bearing a big question mark to appear above his head.

"Indeed," she tells him. "The written orders mention some names and actions that you may find surprising. Nevertheless, these instructions have been subject to particularly careful scrutiny at the highest level, by not one or two but several sufficiently security-cleared individuals and you may be assured that there is no mistake. Regarding the final action you are instructed to pursue in each case, ignore that course of action as written in your orders. Each of the subjects concerned is *not* to be forcibly transitioned; they are all to be elided. Killed. Expeditiously. Do you understand?"

Q'ands's eyes widen. "I am to ignore my written orders?"

"In that one detail, yes."

"Detail?" The fellow looks aghast, though probably more at the choice of word than the terminal severity of the action proposed.

"In writing," Madame d'Ortolan explains patiently, "you are instructed to find the individuals named, close with them and take them away. The spoken amendment I am giving you now is to do all the above, except you are to kill them rather than kidnap them."

"So that's an order?"

"Yes. That is an order."

"But—"

"The written orders issue from my office," Madame d'Ortolan tells him, her voice acidic. "This verbal order is also from me, has also been appropriately vetted and approved, and post-dates the written orders. What about this sequence of events is difficult for you to comprehend?"

There is a hurt silence while the waiter delivers their order. When he goes, Q'ands says, "Well, I take it the verbal orders will be confirmed by written—"

"Certainly not! Don't be an idiot! There are reasons why this is being handled in this manner." Madame d'Ortolan sits forward, lowers her voice and softens it a little. "The Council," she tells him, head tipped towards him, drawing him in, "even the Concern itself, is under threat, don't you see? This must be done. These actions must be carried out. They may seem extreme, but then so is the threat."

He looks unconvinced.

She sits back. "Just obey your orders, Q'ands. All of them." She watches as Christophe unseals her bottle of water, wipes her glass with a fresh handkerchief and pours. She drinks a little. Q'ands looks most unhappy, but drinks his espresso, finishing it with indecent haste in a couple of tossed-back gulps. She has a sudden unbidden, unwelcome and unpleasant vision of his lovemaking being similarly abrupt and curtailed now. Where once, of course, he had been quite pleasantly proficient. She pushes the memory away as something best forgotten and nods beyond the booth. "*Now* you may go."

He rises, gives a cursory bow and turns away.

Madame d'Ortolan says, "A moment."

He sighs as he looks back at her. "Yes?"

"What did you say your name was?"

"Q'ands, ma'am."

"Well, Q'ands, *do* you understand?"

His jaw works as though he is trying to control himself. "Of course," he says, voice clipped. "I understand."

She favours him with an icy smile. "As you might guess, this is altogether of particular importance to us, Q'ands. It is what one might term a high-tariff matter. The highest. The rewards for success will be as lavish as the sanctions for failure will—"

"Oh, madame," he says loudly, holding out one hand to her, his voice pitched somewhere between exasperation and what certainly sounds like genuine insult. "Spare me." He turns and leaves with a shake of his head, disappearing into the tumult.

Madame d'Ortolan is quite shocked.

The Philosopher

My father was a brute, my mother was a saint. Dad was a big, powerful man. He was what they used to call free with his fists. In school he was kept back a year and hence was always the biggest boy in his class. Big enough to intimidate the teachers sometimes. Eventually he was thrown out for breaking another pupil's jaw. According to him, it was a boy, a bully, from a couple of years above him. It was twenty years later and he was dead before we found out it had actually been a girl in his own class.

He always wanted to be a policeman but he kept failing the entry exams. He worked in the prison service until he was thrown out for being too violent. Feel free to make your own jokes.

My mother had a very strict religious upbringing. Her parents were members of a small sect called The First Church of Christ The Redeemer Our Lord's Chosen People. Once I suggested that they had more words in their title than they did members. It was the only time she hit me. She was proud that she didn't sleep with my father until after they were married, on the day she turned eighteen. I think she just wanted to be free of her parents and all their restrictions and rules. They always had a lot of rules. Before they could be wed dad had to promise the elders of the church and our local minister that he would have all his children raised strictly in the ways of the Church, though he only did this so that he could wash his hands of his parental responsibilities. He had as little to do with me as he could while I was growing up. He'd usually be reading his paper, lips moving silently, or listening to music on his headphones, humming loudly and out of tune. If I tried to attract his attention he'd put his paper down, scowling, and tell me to talk to my mother, or just glare at me without turning his music down and stab a finger first at me and then at the door. He liked country and western music, the more sentimental the better.

He made no secret of the fact that he had no faith himself, except that "There must be something up there," as he would say sometimes when he was very drunk. He said it quite a lot.

My mum must have seen something in him. Perhaps, as I said, she also thought that she was escaping from the petty rules and regulations and restrictions she'd had to accept living in her parents' house, but of course dad had plenty of those of his own, as we both discovered. My usual way of discovering a new rule was being slapped around the ear, or, if I'd been really bad, dad taking his belt off, throwing me across his knee and leathering me. Out of the frying pan and into the fire, that's what it was for my mum. I started out in the fire.

Mum made me her treasured boy and gave me all the love that she wanted to give dad but which just bounced back off him. Don't think that she turned me into a gay or anything. I'm not. I'm quite normal. I just had this unbalanced upbringing in this strange family where one parent worshipped me and thought I could do no wrong and the other one treated me like some pet that my mum had bought without asking him first. If I'd thought about it I'd have assumed my family was typical. It wasn't something I did think about, though, and I'd never have thought of asking other children what their families were like. I didn't mix much with other children at school. They seemed very noisy and dangerously boisterous and they thought I was quiet, apparently. Or cold. I was teased and picked on for being Christian.

I suppose people would say it was a troubled upbringing but it didn't feel like that to me, not at the time and not really since, not properly. Just one of those things. I worked hard in class and went for long walks in the country after school and at the weekends. I always did my homework to the highest standard. I spent a lot of time in the school library and the library in the nearest town, not always reading. On the bus to and from the town I used to sit looking at nothing.

We'd probably have rubbed along not too bad together, just the three of us, but then my sister came along. I don't blame her, not really, not any more, but it was hard not to at the time. I didn't know any better. It wasn't her fault, even though she caused it.

We lived in the country in a line of prison-officer homes, within sight of the prison. I'd grown up listening to mum and dad arguing over the years because the walls were thin in the house. Though you couldn't hear mum, just dad. She always kept her voice right down, whispering even, while he either shouted or just talked in his loud voice. I don't think he ever whispered in his whole life. When you listened to them it was like he was arguing with himself, or with somebody who wasn't there. I used to wrap my pillow round my head, covering both ears, or if it got really loud I'd stick my fingers in my ears and hum to myself to shut out the sound.

One time I must have been humming really loudly because the light went on and I opened my eyes and dad was there over me wearing just his underpants standing at the side of the bed and demanding what I thought I was doing making all this noise? He scowled at me as I lay there blinking in the bright overhead light, wiping my eyes and cheeks. I was sure he was going to hit me but he just made a grumbling sort of noise and left, slamming the door. He left the light on so I had to put it out myself.

I had already, over the course of the preceding few years, heard things I would not have chosen to hear, things about sex and so on, but the night mum came back from the hospital a week or thereabouts after giving birth to my sister was the thing that really made the difference, for me. Mum had had a bad time giving birth to me and she wasn't really meant to have any more children, but then she got pregnant and that was that. Dad would just have soon have got rid of what turned into my sister but mum wasn't having that because of her religion so she went through with it. But it was an unpleasant procedure and she needed a lot of stitches down there. I suppose dad must have been drunk – especially drunk, as he always liked a drink.

I tried humming but I knew they were talking about sex that evening when she came back from the hospital and because of the age I was a part of me was getting interested in sexual matters and so I partly wanted to listen, so I did. Thus I got to hear my mother begging my father to let her take him in her mouth, or even sodomise her, rather than have normal sex, due to the stitches and the fact that she was still very sore. I had heard dad in the past demanding these favours, or thought I had, but from the little I knew neither had actually occurred. That night, though, he wasn't to be fobbed off with such distractions, especially not after months of being denied.

So, not to put too fine a point on it, he had his way with her, and I had to listen to the gasps and gulps and then the screams. A lot of screams, even though despite it all you could somehow tell that she was trying to be quiet about it. I shoved my fingers into my ears so hard that I thought I was going to puncture my eardrums, and I hummed as hard as I could, but I could still hear her.

It took much longer than you might imagine. Perhaps it was the drink, or the screams. But eventually the screams stopped, to be replaced by sobs and, shortly, snores.

I had, of course, imagined myself bursting in on them and hauling him off her and beating him up and so on, but I was only eleven, and slight, like her, not big and burly like him. Therefore there was nothing I could have done.

Meanwhile my sister had been set off by all the screaming and she was crying the way that very small babies do, and had probably been crying like that all the time but I hadn't heard her over the screams from my mother and my own humming. I heard mum getting up from her and dad's bed and going over to the cot and trying to comfort her, though you could hear her own voice breaking and her sobbing as she did this. Dad snored very loudly, and mum was sobbing and breaking down and my sister was screaming in a high, unpleasant whine. It was only at this point that our next-door neighbours started hammering on the wall, shouting, their voices like a sort of tired, distant commentary on events.

I am not ashamed to say that I cried quite a lot throughout the rest of that night, though I still dropped off to sleep eventually and got up for school the next day, because it is amazing what you can put up with and get over. Almost anything, in fact.

Nevertheless, I think it was then that I decided I would never get married or have children.

3

Patient 8262

There is a certain purity to my existence. A simplicity. In a sense nothing much happens; I lie here, gazing into space or at the view presented by the window, blinking, swallowing, turning over now and again, getting up occasionally – always while they make the bed each morning – and staring open-mouthed at the nurses and orderlies. Now and again they'll try to engage me in conversation. I make a point of smiling at them when they do this. It helps that we do not speak the same language. I can understand most of the one that they speak – sufficient to have an idea what my perceived medical status is and what treatments the doctors might have in store for me – but I have to make an effort to do so and I would not be able to speak much sense in it at all.

Sometimes I nod, or laugh, or make a sound that is halfway between a sort of throat-clearing noise and the moans that deaf people make sometimes, and often I frown as though I'm trying to understand what they're saying, or as though I feel frustrated at not being able to make myself intelligible to them.

Doctors come and give me tests sometimes. There were quite a lot of doctors and quite a lot of tests, early on. There are fewer now.

They give me books to look at with photographs or drawings in them of everyday objects, or large letters, one to a page. One doctor brought me a tray holding letters on wooden cubes, from some child's game. I smiled at them and her and mixed them up, sliding them around on the tray, making pretty patterns out of them and building little towers with them, trying to make it look as though I was attempting to understand these letters and do whatever it was she wanted me to do, whatever might make her happy. She was a pleasant-looking young woman with short brown hair and large brown eyes and she had a habit of tapping the end of a pencil on her teeth. She was very patient with me and not brusque the way doctors can be sometimes. I liked her a lot and would have liked to have done something to have made her happy. But I could – would – not.

Instead I made that motion babies and toddlers make sometimes, clapping with fingers fanned, knocking down the little towers of letters I'd made. She smiled regretfully, tapped the pencil on her teeth, sighed and then made some notes on her clipboard.

I was relieved. I thought I might have overdone the kiddy-clappy thing.

I am allowed to go to the bathroom by myself, though I pretend to fall asleep in there sometimes. I always make mumbly apologetic noises and come out when they knock on the door and call my name. They call me "Kel," not knowing my real name. There was a reason, something between a conceit and a joke, why I was christened so, but the doctor who named me thus left earlier this year and the thinking behind this name is not mentioned in my notes and nobody can remember the reason. I am not allowed to bathe alone, but being bathed is not so terrible; once you get over any residual shame it is very relaxing. One even feels luxurious. I take care to masturbate in the toilet on the morning of a bath day, so as not to embarrass myself in front of the nurses or orderlies.

One of the nurses is a big kindly woman with drawn-on eyebrows, another is quite small and pretty with bleached blonde hair, and there are two orderlies or care workers, one a bearded man with a ponytail and the other a frail-looking but surprisingly strong lady who looks older than me. I suppose if one of them – well, just the pretty blonde, if I am being frank with myself – ever showed any sign of sexual interest in me I might reconsider my pre-emptive pre-bath self-pleasuring. So far this looks unlikely and I am bathed with a sort of professional detachment by all of them.

There is a day room at the end of the corridor where other patients gather and watch television. I go there rarely and affect not really to understand the programmes even when I do. Most of the other patients just sit there slack-jawed, and I emulate them. Now and again one of them will try to engage me in conversation, but I just stare at them and smile and mumble and they usually go away. One large fat bald chap with bad skin doesn't go away, and regularly sits beside me, watching the television while talking to me in a low, hypnotic voice, probably telling me about his ungrateful and dismissive family and his sexual exploits as a younger and more attractive man, but for all I know regaling me with lurid local folk tales, or his detailed design for a perpetual-motion machine, or professing his undying love for me and setting out the various things he would like to do to me in private. Or perhaps his undying hatred for me and setting out the various things he would like to do to me in private – I don't know. I can hardly understand a word he says; I think he talks in the same language as the doctors and nurses – most of whom I can understand well enough – but in a different dialect.

Anyway, I rarely bother with the television room or the other patients. I lie here or sit here and I think about all that I've done and all that I intend to do once the immediate danger has passed and it is safe for me to re-emerge. I smile and even chuckle to myself sometimes, thinking of these poor fools mouldering away until they die here while I'm back out in the many worlds, living and loving; an operator, getting up to whatever mischief takes my fancy. How shocked they would be, patients and staff both, if they only knew!

45

Adrian

Funny thing is, I always loved cocaine. I mean, obviously I loved it in the sense that I loved how rich it made me, how it helped me to drag myself up from the pretty much nothing I started with, but what I mean is I loved it when I took it.

It's a proper brilliant drug, coke. I loved everything about it, I loved the way it all seemed of a piece. The cleanness of it, for a start. I mean, look at it: this beautiful snow-white powder. Little yellow some-times, but only the way really brightly lit clouds are yellow though they start out looking white, from the sun. Bit of a joke it looks like cleaning powder, but even that seems right somehow. It feels like it's cleaning out your skull, know what I mean? Even how you take it goes along with all this, doesn't it? Clean, sharp, definite things like razor blades and mirrors and tightly rolled banknotes, preferably new, as big denomination as you like. I love the smell of new notes, with or without powderage.

And it energises you, gives you what feels like ambition and ability in one easily snorted package. Suddenly nothing's impossible. You can talk and think your way round any problem, batter down anybody's resistance, see the clear, clever way to make any challenge work for you. It's a doing drug, an enabling drug.

Back where I came from they were all into dope, or H, or speed, which is the poor man's coke, and they were starting to get into E. Speed's like laminate instead of real wood, or faux fur not pukka, or a hand job instead of proper sex. It'll do if you can't afford the real thing. Ecstasy's pretty good, but it's not immediate. You have to commit to it. Not as much as kosher old-fashioned acid, though, cos I've heard people old enough to be my dad talk of these trips that lasted eighteen hours or more and just turned your whole world inside out, not always in a good way, and you needed to organise everything, too, like where you were going to spend the time you were tripping, and even who with. Support staff, practically. Like, carers! How the fuck did hippies ever get that fucking organised, eh?

Anyway, compared to that time-consuming nonsense E isn't that bad, like drinking spritzers instead of whisky sodas or something, but you still need to organise everything to come up at the right time and it really is mostly about dancing, being loved-up in amongst lots of fellow travellers and boppers. Fine for that long drawn-out moment of collective euphoria, but it's more like part of a sort of rite, a ritual. What was that song that went, "This is my church"? Something like that. Like a service. Bit too collective, too chummy for my taste.

Cannabis was sort of similar in some ways in that it made you mellow, didn't it? Though how that squares with the fucking Hashisheen I've never quite understood. But it's all that lying around like old hippies, wreathed in smoke and talking bollocks, that I could never take. All that claggy brown tar gumming up the cigarette papers and your brains and making you choke and splutter and wrecking you to the point where it seemed like a great idea to drink the old bong water for the final hit that'll really take you over the edge into some other realm of understanding. What a load of bollocks. I can see it was a great Sixties drug when everybody wanted to smash the system by having love-ins and painting flowers on their bum, but it's all too hazy and vague and sort of aimless, know what I mean?

H is proper hard-core, got to respect that. It's a serious lifestyle commitment for most people, and it's like discovering the mother-lode of pure pleasure that all the other drugs including the legal ones like drink have all come from, like finding something utterly pure beyond which there can't possibly be anything better, but it's a selfish drug. It takes you over, it becomes the boss, everything else becomes about the next hit and it takes you away from the real world, seems to say that the one where the H is is the real world and the one you've lived in all this time and where everybody else still lives, the poor fools, and where the money is, sadly, annoyingly, is just a sort of game, a kind of grey, grainy shadow-place where you have to go back to far too often to make these sort of robotic responses that'll let you get back to the tits-out Technicolor of the wonderful and enchanting world of the H. Proper commitment, H is, and the way it's served up is potentially lethal too. Bit like joining the army or something.

Plus, all that melting the mucky-looking stuff in ancient-looking spoons and searching for a vein and pulling ligatures tight with your teeth and having to draw your own blood out to mix it up in the syringe. Messy. You don't need that. Not clean like coke. Exact opposite. And you need a bucket by you cos the first thing that happens when it hits is you chuck your guts up! Call me old-fashioned but I thought drugs were supposed to be about fun! What sort of fucking fun is that?

Like I say, respect to people prepared to suffer that sort of degradation for the sake of the river of warm bliss you end up submerged in, but fuck me, it's not a drug you take to make your life better, which is what I'm looking for, it's a drug that empties you out of one life and pours you wholesale into another one completely where it's all very fucking wonderful but the drug is the only way into it and the only way of staying there. It's like becoming a deep-sea diver in one of those old brass-helmet jobs with the porthole grilles and the air hose leading back to the surface. The H is the air hose, the H is the air. Total dependency.

No, give me coke every time. Not crack, though. Not cos it's instantly addictive, that's another load of bollocks. It's just overrated, that's all, and because you smoke it it's got that messiness factor again, know what I mean? Something a bit sordid about crack, frankly. It's like coke for junkies.

Proper, pukka coke is clean, sharp, accelerating, and like a smart drug, a precision munition you take exactly when you want it and need it and delivering for as long as you keep taking it. Of fucking course it's the drug of choice of your masters of the universe, your financial wizards, your high-financiers. It's like just-in-time exhilaration, isn't it? A toot in both barrels and suddenly you're a fucking genius and totally invincible. Just what you need when you're juggling telephone numbers of money about and making bets with everybody else's dosh. Not without its downsides, obviously, though for most people these days loss of appetite is brilliant. I mean, who wants to be fat? Collateral benefit, kind of. But the runny nose and paranoia and risking losing your septum and, so they say, having a heart attack, that's all a bit toss. Still, no gain without pain and all that.

So it's funny that I hardly ever took the stuff myself, given that I loved it, and still do, and I had access to the purest supplies at the best prices. Still do, too, through my contacts, of course. Just being cautious, basically. Also proving to myself who's the boss, know what I mean? It's called keeping things in proportion, keeping things balanced. I treat drink the same. I could guzzle vintage champagne and ancient cognac every day but that'd be giving in to that particular monkey, so that has to be rationed too. Same with the girlies.

I do love the ladies, but I wouldn't want to be totally beholden to one of them, would I? True love and wanting kids and settling down and all that, it's fine for most people and it makes the world go round and all like my old man said, but apart from the fact no it doesn't, it's gravity that does that, well, all right maybe it does make the world go round in the sense of creating the next generation, but it works just fine and dandy thanks as long as most people do it. Not all. Doesn't need to be compulsory, doesn't require every single person to take part, just most, just enough. What was that song, "Love Is The Drug"? Never a truer word, know what I mean? Just another temptation, another way of losing yourself. Making yourself vulnerable, that's what it's doing, giving in to all that romantic guff. Just putting your head on the chopping block, isn't it?

Don't get me wrong. I'm not stupid and I know it can happen to anybody and maybe one day it'll happen to me and I'll be giving it all that It Just Feels Right and She's The One and This Time It's Different, and if it does then I just hope I don't make a complete cunt of myself, excuse my language but you know what I mean. Even the mighty fall, they say. Nobody's invulnerable, but you can

49

at least show yourself the respect of holding out as long as possible, know what I mean?

The Transitionary

Temudjin Oh, Mr Marquand Ys, Snr Marquan Dise, Dr Marquand Emesere, M. Marquan Demesere, Mark Cavan; Aiman Q'ands. I have been called many things and I have had many names and though they sometimes sound very various they tend to gyrate round a certain set of sounds, clustering about a limited repertoire of phonemes. My name changes each time I flit, never predictably. I don't always know who I am myself. Not until I check.

I tap a tiny white pill into my espresso, rearrange the table condiments a little, drink my coffee in two gulps and sit back, waiting (another part of my mind isn't waiting at all, it's concentrating furiously, darting down a single filament of purpose within an infinitude of possibilities, a lightning strike zigzagging its way through a cloud, searching). I'm outside another pavement café, in the 4th, looking out across a branch of the Seine to the Ile St Louis, just entering the trance that will guide me to exactly the right place and person. Meanwhile, space to think, to review and evaluate.

My meeting with Madame d'Ortolan was most unsatisfactory. She was sitting asquint in the booth, and the tablecloth was off-centre, hanging down twice as far on one side as on the other. The only way I felt able to compensate was by jiggling one leg up and down, which was really no help at all. And then she treats me like an idiot! Self-satisfied salope.

"Plyte, Jésusdottir, Krijk, Heurtzloft-Beiderkern, Obliq, Mulverhill," I find myself muttering, for these things must be fixed in the mind. A waiter, scooping change from the next table, turns and looks at me oddly. "Plyte, Jésusdottir, Krijk, Heurtzloft-Beiderkern, Obliq, Mulverhill," I mutter at him, smiling. In theory a security failing, but so what? In this world, essentially, these are nonsense words.

Meaningless to anybody who knows only this reality, or any single world for that matter.

The little aluminium tube lies inside my chest bag. Amongst other things it holds a tiny mechanical one-time reader; a metal device like two miniaturised measuring tapes joined by a short collar, a sort of slide with a glass window in it. One of the spools has a little pull-out handle on it. You deploy this, wind it up and let it go; it starts to pull the paper strip from the other spool past the little window. You need to watch this very carefully. You can read about a dozen letters at a time before they're gone, into the other spool, where the specially treated paper comes into contact with the air and turns to dust, its message for ever unreadable. The clockwork mechanism, once started, cannot be stopped, so you need to pay continuous attention. If you miss any part of the message, well, you're stuck. You will need to go and ask for another set of instructions. This does not go down well.

I read my orders in the toilet. It was a little dim so I used a torch. Taken with the highly irregular verbal changes to the instructions, it would seem that certain elisions, as we call them in the trade, are called for. I am to elide. Rather a lot of eliding required, in fact. Interesting.

A sneeze, and when I open my eyes again I am a dapper gent in a frock coat with a hat, cane and grey gloves. My skin is a little darker. A language check reveals Mandarin is back and Farsi is my third language after French and English. Then German, then a smattering of at least twenty others. A much-divided world. Paris has changed once more. There is a canal through the breadth of the Ile St Louis, the street is full of gaily dressed hussars on clopping, head-tossing horses being politely applauded by a few passers-by who have stopped to watch and everything smells of steam. I look up, hoping for airships. I always like it when there are airships, but I can't see any.

I let the troop of horsemen pass, then hail a sleek-looking steam cab to take me to the Gare Waterloo and the TGV for England.

"Plyte, Jésusdottir, Krijk, Heurtzloft-Beiderkern, Obliq, Mulverhill," I mutter once more, and wink at the uncomprehending look of the cabbie. There is a mirror in the buttoned lining of the cab's passenger compartment. I look at myself. I am well turned out, with a very neat haircut and an exquisitely trimmed little goatee, but I am otherwise undistinguished, as usual. The cab is number 9034. These numbers add up to 16, whose own numbers then add up to 7, which – as any fool knows – is by convention the luckiest of lucky numbers. I adjust the sleeves of my chemise where they protrude from my coat until they are exactly equal in length.

I allow myself a deep sigh as I settle into the plush of the cab's seat, positioning myself as centrally as possible. Still with the OCD, then.

The Perineum Club sits on Vermyn Street, off Piccadilly. It is late afternoon by the time I arrive and Lord Harmyle is taking tea.

"Mister Demesere," he says, holding my card as though it might be infected. "Oh well. How unexpected. I suppose you'd better join me."

"Why, thank you."

Lord Harmyle is a gaunt, spare figure with long white hair and a face that appears halfway to being bleached from his skull. His thin lips are pale purple and his small eyes rheumy. He looks ninety years old or more but is apparently only in his early fifties. The two schools of thought regarding this anomaly cite either predisposing familial genes or an especially outré addiction. He eyes me beadily from the far side of the table. The Perineum is as calm, reserved and sparsely occupied as the Café Atlantique was frenetic, rowdy and crowded. It smells of pipe smoke and leather.

"Madame d'Ortolan?" the good lord enquires. A servant wafts to our side and dispenses weak-looking tea into an almost transparent porcelain cup. I resist the urge to swivel the cup so that the handle points directly towards me.

"She sends her regards," I tell him, even though she did no such thing.

Lord Harmyle sucks in his already hollow cheeks and looks as though somebody has laced his tea with arsenic. "And how is that . . . lady?"

"She is well."

"Hmm." Lord Harmyle's fingers hover thinly, like the claw of a predatory skeleton, over some crustless cucumber sandwiches. "And you. Do you bring a message?" The claw retreats and lifts a small biscuit instead. There are seven of the small, anaemic-looking sandwiches on one plate and eleven biscuits on the other. Both primes. Added together, eighteen. Which is not a prime, obviously. And making nine, the throwaway number. Really, this sort of thing could be both distressing and distracting, over time.

"Yes." I take out the little ormolu sweetener case and shake free a tiny white pill. It disappears into the tea, which I stir. I lift the cup to my lips. Lord Harmyle appears undisturbed.

"One is supposed to lift the saucer and cup together to one's mouth," Lord Harmyle observes distastefully as I drink my tea.

"Is one?" I ask. I replace the teacup on the saucer. "I do beg your pardon." I lift both saucer and cup this time. The tea tastes diffident, whatever flavours it might possess holding back as though ashamed of expressing themselves.

"Well?" Harmyle asks, frowning.

"Well?" I repeat, permitting myself a look of polite puzzlement.

"What's the message you bear, sir?"

I hope I shall never lose my sincere admiration for those able to invest the word "sir" – on the face of it a genuine honorific – with the level of brusque contempt that the good lord has just achieved.

"Ah." I put cup and saucer down. "I understand you may have expressed some doubts regarding the direction the Central Council might be taking." I smile. "Concerns, even."

Harmyle's already pallid complexion appears to lose whatever blood it previously contained. Which is rather impressive, really, given that all this is basically an act. He sits back, glances around. He puts his own cup and saucer down, rattled. "What on earth are you talking about?"

53

I smile, raise one hand. "Firstly, sir, have no fear. I am here to ensure your safety, not threaten it."

"Are you indeed?" The good lord looks dubious.

"Absolutely. I am, as I have always been, attached, *inter alia*, to the Protection Department." (This is actually true.)

"Never heard of it."

"One is not supposed to, unless one has need to call upon its services." I smile. "Nevertheless, it exists. You may have been right to feel threatened. That is why I am here."

Harmyle looks troubled, and possibly confused. "I understood that the lady in Paris was unflinchingly loyal to the current regime," he observes. (At which I look mildly surprised.) "Indeed, I was under the impression she herself formed a significant part of that regime, at its highest level."

"Really?" I say. I ought to explain: in terms of Central Council politics, Lord H is a one-time waverer who is now a d'Ortolan loyalist but who has been instructed by Madame d'Ortolan to seem to grow remote from her and her cabal, to speak out against her and, by so gaining their confidence, try to draw out the others on the Central Council who would oppose the good lady. She would have a spy in their midst. However, Lord H has been conspicuously unsuccessful in this endeavour and so fears he is caught between two very slippery stepping stones and is in some danger of skidding and falling no matter which way he tries to go a-leaping.

"Yes, really. I'd have thought," he continues cautiously, still glancing around the quiet, high-ceilinged, wood-panelled room, "that if she heard I was – that I had any doubts regarding our . . . prevailing strategies . . . that she would have been my implacable opponent, not my concerned protector."

I spread my hands. (For a moment, my brain chooses to interpret this movement as one hand diverging into two different realities. I have to perform the internal equivalent of a mind-clearing shake of the head to dispel this sensation. My mind is in at least two different places at the moment, which – even with the rare gift I have and the highly specialised training I've benefited from – requires a deal of concentration.) "Oh, she is quite placable," I hear myself say. "The good lady's loyalties are not entirely as you might have assumed."

Lord Harmyle looks at me curiously, perhaps not sure how good my English is and whether he is somehow being made fun of.

I pat my pockets, appear distracted (I *am* distracted, but I'm holding it together). "I say, d'you think I might borrow a handkerchief? I think I feel a sneeze coming on."

Harmyle frowns. His gaze shifts fractionally towards his breast pocket, where a white triangle of handkerchief protrudes. "I'll ask a waiter," he says, half turning in his seat.

The half-turn is all that I need. I rise quickly, take one step forward and while he is still swivelling back to look at me – his eyes just beginning to widen in fear – slash his throat pretty much from ear to ear with the glass stilleto I have been concealing up my right sleeve. (A pretty Venetian thing, Murano, I believe, bought on Bund Street not ten minutes ago.)

The good lord's earlier alabaster appearance deceived; in fact, he held quite a lot of blood. I ram the stillete into him directly underneath his sternum, just for good measure.

I have not lied, I feel I must point out. As I have already stated, I am indeed attached to the Protection Department (though I may have just constructively dismissed myself, I admit) – it is simply that said Department is concerned with the protection of the Concern's security, not the protection of individuals. These distinctions matter. Though possibly not here.

Stepping delicately away as Lord Harmyle tries with absolute and indeed near-comical ineffectiveness to staunch the bright blushes of blood pulsing and squirting from his severed arteries, while at the same time seemingly attempting to wheeze a last few bubbling breaths or – who knows? – words through his ruptured windpipe (he doesn't seem to have noticed there's a pencil-thin knife protruding from his chest, though perhaps he is just prioritising), I sneeze suddenly and loudly, as though allergic to the scent of blood.

Now that really would be a handicap, in my line of work.

4

Patient 8262

A small bird came and sat on my window ledge this morning. I heard it first, then opened my eyes and saw it. It is a fine, clear day in late spring and the air smells of last night's rain on new leaves. The bird was smaller than my hand, beak to tail; mostly a speckle of two-tone brown with a yellow beak, black legs and white flashes along the leading edges of its wings. It landed facing me, then jumped and turned so that it was facing outwards again, ready to fly off. It rotated and dipped its tiny head to observe me with one black sparkling eye.

Somebody passed the open door of my room, shuffling down the corridor, and the bird flew away. It fell initially, disappearing, then reappeared, performing a series of shallow bounces through the air, fluttering energetically for a few seconds to buoy itself up, then bringing its wings tight into its body so that it resembled a tiny feathery bullet, dipping down like some falling shell on an earthbound trajectory before deploying its wings again and fluttering busily to gain height once more. I lost sight of it against the bright green shimmer of the trees.

We live in an infinity of infinities, and we reshape our lives with every passing thought and each unconscious action, threading an ever-changing course through the myriad possibilities of existence. I lie here and ponder the events and decisions that led me to this point, the precise sequence of thoughts and actions that ended – for now – with me having nothing more constructive or urgent to do than think about those very eventualities. I've never had so much time to think. The bed, the room, the clinic, its setting: all are highly conducive to thinking. They impose a sense of calmness, of things remaining unchanged and yet being reliably maintained, without decay or obvious entropy. I am free to think, not abandoned to rot.

In Detroit I played pinball, in Yokohama pachinko, in Tashkent bagatelle. I found all three games enthralling, fascinated by the randomness that emerged from such highly structured, precisely set-up machinery knocking shining spheres of steel from place to place within a setting where, in the end, gravity always won. The comparison with our own lives is almost too obvious, yet still it gives us an inkling into our fates and what drives us to them. It is only an inkling, because we are submerged within a vastly more complicated environment than the clicking, bouncing steel balls and the pins and bands and buffers and walls they collide with – our course is more like that of a particle within a smoke chamber, subject to Brownian motion, and we are at least nominally possessed of free will – but by reducing, simplifying, it allows us a grasp of something otherwise too great for us to comprehend in the raw.

I was a traveller, a fixer for the Concern. That is what I was, what I made myself into, what I was groomed for and made into by others, what life made me. Across the many worlds I roamed, surfing that blast-front of ever-changing, ever-branching existence, dancing through the spectra of plausible/implausible, hermetic/connected, banal/bizarre, kind/cruel and so on; all the ways that we'd worked out a world or deck of worlds could be judged, evaluated and ranked. (This world, here, is plausible, hermetic, banal, kind. Yours is the same except closer to the cruel end of the relevant spectrum. Quite a lot closer. You had the misfortune to have a singular ancestral Eve and I guess she just wasn't a very nice person. Blame volcanoes or something.)

Of course, I cannot tell anybody here this, though I have thought to. I could talk to them in my own first language, or even English or French, which were my adopted tongues and operational languages and the chances are high that nobody here would understand a solitary word I said, but that would be foolish. It would be an indulgence, and I am not sure that I can afford even so modest a one. I have even been reluctant to think about my past life until this point, which is now starting to seem almost a superstition.

At some point I suppose I will have to.

I wish the little bird would come back.

Adrian

I suppose Mr Noyce was a sort of father figure to me. He was a decent bloke, what can I say? Old money, which made him unusual among the City people I knew at the time. Come to think of it, so did the being-decent bit, too.

I'd supplied his son Barney with enough dust to sink a cruiser, though I'm not sure Mr N ever knew this. I mean, he certainly knew Barney did toot by the sackful, or he must have guessed, because he was sharp, nobody's fool, that's for sure, but I don't think Barney ever told him he'd got so much of it through me. Getting introduced properly to Barney's dad was one of the favours I called in when I decided to make the transition to relative respectability. Barney owed me money and instead of taking it in folding I suggested that he might like to invite me to the Noyce family pile for a weekend in the country. I'd thought Barney might resist this idea but he jumped at it. Made me think I'd priced the deal far too low, but there you are.

"Sure, sure, there's a bunch of people coming down next weekend. Come down then. Yeah, why not."

We were glugging Bolly in a newly opened champagne bar in

Limehouse, all glitzy chrome and distressed leather, both of us coked to the eyeballs, jittery and voluble. Much drumming of fingers and over-quick nodding and all that sort of shit. I'd taken a lot less than he had but I've always had this thing where I start behaving like the people I'm with even though I'm technically not in the same state they are. I've been a designated driver once or twice and drunk nothing stronger than fizzy mineral water all night – with no drugs at all – and people have taken one look at me and tried to take the car keys off me because I'm slurring my words and have gone all giggly and smiley.

Same with the white stuff. I would take a little with clients just to be chummy while they got stuck in up to their eyebrows but I'd end up just as high and wired and frenetic as them. Thing is, I can always snap out of it pronto, know what I mean? I'd be sober the instant after somebody accused me of slipping vodkas into my Perrier, which, once they'd realised I was straight, meant they were happy to let me drive, but that came with its own problems cos you look like an actor, like you're taking the piss, just pretending to be drunk, know what I mean? People resent that. Especially drunks, of course. Caused a few arguments. I never was taking the piss, though. It wasn't something I did deliberately, it was just something that happened. Anyway, I learned to tone down this getting drunk/whatever on the atmosphere effect, but it still came into play.

"What sort of people?" I asked, suspicious.

"I don't know," Barney said, looking round. He smiled at a table with three girls. There was a fair amount of talent in the place. Barney was tall and blond to my average and dark. He worked out, but there was a sort of pudginess to his face that made you think he'd be a bloater if he ever stopped gyming every day. Or gave up toot. I've been called wiry. "Just people." He frowned at me, trying to smile at the same time. He waved one arm. "People. You know; people."

"Sorry, mate," I said, "I don't fink I can cope with this level of detail. Can you be a bit more vague?" I was doing the barrow-boy bit then, which was why I said "fink."

Barney struggled. "Just, I don't know . . ."

"Tramps? Kings?" I suggested, annoyed that we still weren't getting anywhere.

"Oh for fuck's sake," Barney said. "People. I can't say. People like me, people like you. Well, maybe not like you, but people." He sounded frustrated and glanced at the door to the Gents. It was only about fifteen minutes since his last toot but I sensed he was getting ready for more.

"People," I said.

"People," Barney agreed. He patted the pocket where his wrap of gear was and nodded emphatically.

Barney never was very good on specifics. It was one of the things that made him not very good as a trader. That and the over-fondness for the coke.

"This weekend?" I asked.

"This weekend."

"Sure there'll be room?"

He snorted. "Course there'll be fucking room."

There was lots of room cos it was a fucking mansion, wasn't it? Spetley Hall's in Suffolk, near Bury St Edmunds. One of those places where you pass a nice but deserted-looking gatehouse like something out of a fairy story and start off down the drive and begin to wonder if it's all a giant wind-up cos the gentle rolling parkland and distant vistas of follies and herds of deer just seem to go on for ever with no actual dwelling in sight.

Then this cliff of stonework dotted with statues and urns and tall windows with ornate surrounds and looking like a barely miniaturised version of Buckingham Palace heaves into view over the horizon and you suspect you're finally nearing the gaff. Still didn't get greeted by no butler or footmen or anything, though. Had to park me own car, didn't I? Though actually there was a servant of some description who did help me with my bags once I'd tramped up the steps to the front doors. He even apologised for not being there to greet me, just taken some other guests to their room.

It was all the wife's, Mrs Noyce's, really. She was something double-barrelled and a proper Lady with a capital L and had married Mr N and they'd inherited the place. There were at least twenty guests that weekend. I'm still not sure I saw all of them all together in the one place at any one time. Mrs N was a lovely old grey-haired girl, not stuck-up but seriously posh and she tried to get everybody to dinner and breakfast at the same time but what with one couple needing to stay the Friday night in London, somebody having a cold, a couple of children to be got ready for bed early and all that sort of stuff, I don't think we were ever totally quorate, know what I mean?

Plus I wasn't even that far off with the meant-to-be-facetious question to Barney about there being kings there, as one minor royal and his lady friend were present.

I'd left my own current main girl back at the flat. She was lovely, a dancer called Lysanne and all legs and gorgeous long real blonde hair but she had a Scouse accent you could have etched steel with. Plus she'd have been a distraction, frankly. And also Lysanne was one of those girls who never really managed to hide the fact she was always on the lookout to trade up. I was definitely a catch compared to her earlier boyfriend, another dealer a level or two down the chain of demand, but I never fooled myself that she thought I was the best she could do. Bringing her somewhere like Spetley Hall when it was full of our richers and betters would be too tempting for her, no matter what she might tell me about how much she really loved me and how she was mine for ever. She'd have made a nuisance of herself. Probably a fool of herself too, and me, and ended up getting hurt.

Worst of all, of course, she just might have succeeded, skipping off with some doolally trustafarian and leaving me ditched, looking like a wanker. Couldn't have that either, could I?

It was through touching on this sort of stuff over a game of billiards late on the Saturday night that I got to know Mr Noyce. It was just us two by this time. Everybody else had gone off to bed. All done without chemical aid on my part, too. Billiards is what the toffs play instead of snooker.

"You really see it so coldly, do you, Adrian?" he asked, sketching the tip of his cue with green chalk. He blew the excess off and smiled at me. Mr N was a biggish, twinkly sort of guy, light on his feet for a portly gent. He had greying straw-coloured hair and bushy black eyebrows. He wore the big-framed glasses that were still just about fashionable at the time. Give him a cigar and he'd have looked like Groucho Marx. We'd both hung our proper dinner jackets over chairs. He'd loosened his bow tie. I'd unclipped mine. I'd made a mental note to buy a proper bow tie. Even if I couldn't be bothered going through the whole rigmarole of tying it up at the start of the evening I could keep it in my pocket, wear the clip-on and just replace the fake one with the untied real one at the end of the evening, leave it hanging. Looked much classier. Like Mrs N, Barney's dad had that way of looking perfectly relaxed in the sort of ultra-formal gear most of us feel dead awkward in.

The rich love dressing up, I'd realised that weekend. It has to be within a strict sort of framework, though. They have specialist clothes for morning, afternoon, eating dinner, riding, hunting (actually different sets of clothes for different sorts of hunting, not to mention fishing), boating, general tramping around the country, popping into the local town and for going up to London. They always went up to London, even if they'd started far north of it. Something to do with trains, apparently. Seen in this light, even their casual clothes became like Casual Clothes rather than just stuff you liked knocking about in or that made you feel comfortable.

"What, relationships, Mr N?"

"Please, call me Edward. Yes, relationships." He had a soft, deep voice. Posh but not fruity. "That's a terribly unromantic outlook, don't you think?"

I grinned at him, cued up, whacked a white ball around a bit.

I'd picked up the rules of billiards easily enough, though it still seemed a pretty pointless game to me. "Well, they say everything's a market, don't they, Edward?"

"Hmm. Some people do."

"Didn't think you'd disagree, in your position," I told him. Mr N was senior partner in one of the City's best-known stockbroking firms and allegedly worth a mint.

"I treat the market like a market," he agreed. He took a shot, stood admiring it for a moment. "Perverse to do otherwise." He smiled at me. "Probably expensive as well, I imagine."

"Yeah, but life's like that too, isn't it?" I said. "Don't you think? I mean, people tell themselves all these fairy stories about true love and stuff, but when it comes right down to it, people have a pretty good idea of their own value on the marriage market or relation-ship market or whatever you want to call it, know what I mean? Ugly people know better than to go up to beautiful ones and expect anything else but a knock-back. Beautiful people can grade them-selves and other people, spot the pecking order. Like a squash ladder." I grinned. "You know where you are and you can challenge some-body a bit above you or be challenged by somebody a bit below, but it's going to end in embarrassment if you outreach yourself. Bit like that."

"A squash ladder," Mr N said. He sighed, took his shot.

"Point is," I said, "people start from whatever social level they get born into but they can trade up with looks, can't they? Or a bit of looks and a lot of face, a lot of self-confidence. Or some sort of talent. Footballers do that. Film stars. Rock stars. Superstar DJs, whatever. Gets you money and fame. But the point is that looks are liquid, know what I mean? Specially for girls. Looks can take you anywhere. But only if you use them. A girl like my Lysanne, she's very aware of her looks. She knows how to use them, and she does use them, bless her. She thinks she can do better than me. Better than where I am at the moment, anyway. So she'll take any chance she can to trade up, do a bit better for herself. Well, fair play to her.

Though there are risks, obviously. It's a bit like mountaineering. The trick for somebody like her is checking out the next hold's firm before you leave the security of the one you've been depending on until now."

"That is a lot of face, indeed."

I grinned, to show I'd got the joke, obscure though it might have been. "Can't blame her for it, though, can I? I mean, if I found somebody better-looking or as good-looking but better educated, a bit more sophisticated than Lysanne, I suppose I'd ditch her for them." I shrugged, gave him my cheeky-chappie grin. "Fair's fair."

"And 'up' always means up to more money, I take it?"

"Course, Edward. Money's what it's all about in the end, isn't it? Life's a game and whoever dies with the most toys wins. Don't ask me who said that, but it's true, don't you think?"

"Well," Mr N said, drawing the word out. "You have to be careful. One of the wisest things anybody ever said to me was that if all you ever care about is money, money is all that will ever care for you." He looked at me. I smiled back. He sighed as he surveyed the table. "Meaning, I suppose, that if you care nothing for people, then, when you're old and fading, only hired carers, and maybe what we used to call gold-diggers, will still be around to look after you."

"Yeah, well, I'll worry about that when it happens, Edward."

Mr N went to the side table where our drinks were and sipped from his whisky. "Well, I suppose as long as you both know where you stand." He tipped his head to one side. "*Do* you both know where you stand? Is this something you've talked about, together?"

I grimaced. "It's . . . tacit."

"Tacit?" Mr N smiled.

I nodded. "It's understood."

"And is there no room for love in this terribly transactional view of human relationships, Adrian?"

"Oh, yeah, of course," I said breezily. "When it comes along. Kind of thing there's no allowing for. Another level. Boss level. Who knows?"

He just smiled, took his shot.

"Thing is," I said. "With all due respect, Edward, you can afford to think the way you think and feel the way you feel because you've kind of got it all, know what I mean?" I smiled broadly to show there was no edge here, no jealousy involved. Just an observation. "Lovely wife, family, important job, country estate, flat in London, skiing in Klosters, sailing in the Med, everything you could ask for. You have the luxury of observing the rest of us from your Olympian heights, haven't you? Me, I'm still scrabbling up the foothills. Knee-deep in scree down here, me." He laughed at that. "Most of us are. We need to be clear-sighted, we need to see things the way they really are to us." I shrugged. "Looking after number one. It's all we're doing."

"And how are things for you, Adrian?"

"They're fine, thanks." I took my shot. Lots of aimless clacking and movement.

"Good. I'm glad for you. Barney talks very highly of you. What is it you do again?"

"Web design. Got my own company." Which was nothing but the truth without being remotely like the whole of it.

"Well, I hope you do well, but you ought to know that no amount of success frees you of all problems." He stooped, evaluating.

"Well, we all have our crosses to bear, Edward, no doubt about that."

He took his shot, stood up slowly. "What do you think of Barney?" He watched the balls click and clack across the baize, not looking at me. He rechalked his cue, brows furrowed.

Ah-ha, I thought. I didn't reply too quickly. Took a shot in the meantime. "He's a great guy," I said. "Brilliant company." I put on a slightly pained expression. When Edward looked at me I took a breath and said, "He could choose some of his friends better." I laughed lightly. "Present company excluded, obviously."

Mr N didn't smile. He bent to size up another shot. "I worry that he's enjoying himself a bit too much. I've talked to the people at

Bairns Faplish." This was the broking company Barney worked for, Mr N having thought it would look bad to bring the boy straight into his own firm after graduation. Barney had told me himself that he'd needed intensive tutoring to blag his way from Eton into Oxford and had barely scraped a 2.2. Whatever that is. I thought it was an airgun pellet. "They're a little concerned," Mr N continued. "He's not bringing in what he might. They can't let that situation go on for ever. It's not like the old days. Once, any idiot could be a stock-broker, and a lot were. Not good enough these days." He flashed me a mouth-only smile, no eyes involved at all. "There's a family name at stake, after all."

"We're all a bit wild when we're young, aren't we?" I suggested. Edward looked unconvinced. "He'll pull straight in time," I told him, looking serious. I could say this sort of shit fairly convincingly on account of being a bit older than Barney. I put my cue down on the table, folded my arms. "Look, Mr N, Edward, it's always more pressure on a guy when he's got a successful father, know what I mean? He looks up to you, he does. I know that. But you're, you know. You're a lot to live up to. It's bound to be intimidating, being in your shadow. You might not see it, but that's you being up in your Olympian heights again, isn't it?"

He smiled. A little sadly, perhaps.

"Well, as you say, he could do with some better friends," he said, leaning on his cue and surveying the table. "I don't want to sound like some Victorian paterfamilias, but a little more of the straight and narrow would do him no harm."

"You're probably right, Edward." I picked up my cue. "My theory is that he's too nice."

"Too nice?"

"Had it all too easy, thinks the world's a nicer place than it really is. Expects everybody else to be as relaxed and good-natured as he is." I shook my head. I bent to my shot. "Dangerous."

"Perhaps you'd care to instruct him in life according to you. Oh, good shot."

"Thanks. I could," I agreed. "I mean I have, already, but I could make more of a point of it. If you liked. Don't know that he'll listen to me, but I could try."

"I'd be very grateful." Mr N smiled.

"It'd be my pleasure, Edward."

"Hmm." He looked thoughtful. "We're off to Scotland next month, shooting. Barney and Dulcima have said they'll be there for the first week, though I expect he'll find an excuse not to come at the last minute again. I think he finds us boring. Do you shoot, Adrian?"

(Great, I think. I can make Barney come along by promising him the whole week's my treat coke-wise and then I'll be right in with Mr N!) "Never tried, Edward."

"You should. Would you like to come along?"

Madame d'Ortolan

Mr Kleist thought the lady took the news remarkably well, considering. He had done something he'd never thought to do in the several years he had been employed by her, and disturbed her while she was at her toilet. She had called him in and had continued to apply her make-up while she sat at her dressing table with him standing behind her. They looked at each other via the table's mirror. Madame d'Ortolan had donned a peignoir before receiving him; however, he found that if he let his eyes stray downwards he could see rather a large portion of both her breasts. He took a half-step backwards to save both their blushes. There had never been anything of that nature between them. Nevertheless, when the cat called M. Pamplemousse unentwined itself from beneath the stool its mistress sat upon and gazed up at him, it was with what looked like an accusation.

Madame d'Ortolan sighed. "Harmyle?"

"I'm afraid so, ma'am."

"Dead?"

"Quite entirely."

"Our boy has jumped the rails, then."

"Indeed, ma'am, he might be said to be on the opposite track, heading in precisely the wrong direction, and at some speed."

Madame d'Ortolan regarded Mr Kleist with a look of desiccated withering that most men would have flinched at. Mr Kleist was not the flinching sort. "He's still being tracked?"

"Just. Two of the five report they managed to hang on by their fingernails, metaphorically. However, his next transition ought to be much easier to follow, apparently."

"Bring him in," she told him. "Hurt but unharmed." Mr Kleist nodded, understanding. "And address all the correct targets individually and concurrently." He nodded. "Immediately," she told him, taking up her hairbrush.

"Of course, ma'am."

Mr Kleist did his best to kick M. Pamplemousse accidentally on purpose as he turned away, but the creature easily avoided his foot and mewed with what sounded like self-satisfaction.

The Transitionary

I sniff, blow my nose, look round. I am in another version of the building which housed the Perineum Club, back where Lord Harmyle is – at this very moment, I should think – lying on the floor, kicking and gurgling his way to a rather bloody death.

In this reality, the Vermyn Street building contains a parfumerie. The dark wood panels are mostly hidden by exquisite wall rugs and creamy, gently glowing light panels illuminating a smattering of tear-shaped perfume bottles arrayed on glass shelves. The air is laced with enchanting female scents and no one looks in the least surprised that I have just sneezed. The well-heeled clientele is composed mostly of ladies. One or two are with gentlemen, and there are a couple of other unescorted men besides myself. It is the men I find myself looking at. The shop assistants are mostly very good-looking young men. One especially chiselled specimen, tall and dark, smiles at me. I smile back, a little thrill running through me.

Ah well. I never fully appreciate being gay, but at least I haven't hit the ground counting the cracks in the parquet flooring. I seem to have left the OCD behind, for now at least. My languages are English, Spanish, Portuguese, French, German and Cantonese, plus smatterings.

I quickly review my attire in a full-length mirror. I am dressed similarly to the way I was with Lord Harmyle (I wonder if he is the *late* Lord Harmyle yet). My hair is long and dark and ringleted in what would appear to be the fashion here, though it looks particularly good on me, I must say. No wonder the young assistant favoured me with a smile. I check my hands for any signs of blood. It would be unusual and alarming if there were any, but one always looks. Spotless. I have very pale hands, beautifully manicured and sporting two silver or white gold rings on each hand.

I have no time to dally. One further regretful smile at the handsome young assistant and I make for the door, checking my wallet, papers and ormolu pill box as I go. I am Mr Marquand Ys, according to my British passport. That is all in order. The wallet is full of large white banknotes and several important-looking bits of plastic with silvery chips embedded.

Into the street. Still no airships. *Dommage*!

However: above the relatively low-rise buildings a very large aircraft sails serenely overhead, heading west. I wave my cane at a cab – a whirring, hunchbacked-looking thing which I'd surmise runs off electricity – and order the lady cabbie to take me to the airport.

In the mirror, the woman's brow creases. "Which one?"

Ah, a *large* London; Londres grande! How splendid. "Where's that aircraft heading?" I ask, pointing with my cane.

She cranes her neck out of her window, squinting. "Eafrow, I should fink."

"There, then."

"It'll cost ya."

"I'm sure. Now do drive on." We set off. "Plyte, Jésusdottir, Krijk, Heurtzloft-Beiderkern, Obliq, Mulverhill," I mutter. It feels pleasing to me, just saying it. It has a become a mantra, I suppose. The girl cabby glances askance at me in her mirror. "Plyte, Jésusdottir, Krijk, Heurtzloft-Beiderkern, Obliq, Mulverhill," I repeat, smiling.

"Wottevah, mate."

I sit back, watching the relatively quiet traffic and rather loud architecture glide past. My heart has been beating rather rapidly since my transition – well, since Lord Harmyle's murder, I suppose. Now it begins to slow, allowing me the luxury of reflection.

Of course I think about whatever poor wretch I've left behind to deal with the aftermath of my actions, especially when it is something as dramatic and unpleasant as a murder. What must it be like for them, I wonder? Allegedly they know nothing about what has happened until after I have gone, though I always wonder if this is really true. Might they not be aware of what I am making them do, even as I do it? Are they not perhaps along for the ride when I take over their body, observing – doubtless terrified and frustrated – as I perform whatever actions I deem to be necessary to fulfil whatever orders I have been given?

Or are they genuinely oblivious, and effectively wake up to be suddenly confronted with – in the case of the operation just concluded – a dying man, blood on their hands and the stares of shocked witnesses? What could one possibly do in such circumstances? Flinch back, horrified, exclaiming, "But it wasn't me!"? Scarcely supportable. One would do best to run, I'd imagine. It might be better for the poor bastards to collapse, quite dead, the instant I leave them. I have asked about this kind of thing, but the Concern is by its nature very conservative and secretive and even the researchers, technicians and experts whose business it is to know of such matters are not inclined to divulge the relevant answers.

There are those who assuredly do know the answers to all these questions and more. Madame d'O would know; Mrs M would too, and Dr Plyte and Professore Loscelles and all the others on the Central Council. There is in all likelihood an entire division of the . . . hmm, for some reason I don't want to think of it as the

Concern. This is one of the worlds where it is thought of as l'Expédience.

Anyway, indeed. There is an entire cadre of experts who have studied what happens when someone like myself takes over a previously existing person in another reality and then leaves them again, but l'Expédience does not deem me to be one of those who needs to know the results of their research. I'd love to know. I have carried out my own modest experiments, attempting to rummage round in the memories I find or the feelings I discover, trying to find some trace of the personality I have displaced, but so far such vicarious introspections have produced nothing except a lingering feeling of foolishness at having undertaken them in the first place.

Plainly I inherit something of the character of the person whose being I usurp. That must be where the OCD comes from, and one's sexual inclination, as does the taste for, variously, coffee, tea, chocolate, spiced milk, hard liquor, bland or spicy food, or prunes. I have found myself, over the years, surveying the reality I find myself in with the eyes of somebody who is plainly a general medical practitioner, a surgeon, a landscape designer, a mathematician, a structural engineer, a livestock breeder, a litigation lawyer, an insurance assessor, an hotelier and a psychiatrist. I seem to be at home amongst the professions. Once I was a sewerage system designer who was also a serial killer. (Yes, I know, but I would beg the indulgence of being regarded, rather, as an assassin. I will even accept Paid Killer, so long as it is understood that I do what I do through informed choice rather than due to some grubbily psychotic urge. Though I'll allow that the importance of this distinction might escape my victims.) On that occasion I had to suppress the urge to strangle prostitutes in order to carry out my mission, which was to track down and kidnap (ha! You see? Not kill) my quarry.

On the other hand, I have never been a woman, which is slightly odd and even a little disappointing. Obviously there are limits.

And are these bodies I inhabit ever used more than once? I have never visited the same body twice – indeed, I rarely visit the same reality twice.

These taken-over persons will have had perfectly full lives before I invade them. They have pasts, careers, networks of relationships both personal and professional; all that one would expect. I have had "my" wives, partners, girlfriends, "my" children and "my" best friends greet me without a trace of discomfiture or any sign that I am behaving oddly or out of character. I seem to know how to behave when I am somebody else, as naturally as the most gifted actor, and when I search my/their memories I find no trace of earlier exposure to the Concern – or whatever it might be called locally – or preparation for what has happened.

I extract my little ormolu pill case from my coat and study it. I shall probably next take one of the tiny capsules it contains while ten kilometres above the Atlantic, or over the Alps, or while looking down at the Sahara. Or I could wait until I arrive wherever it is I decide to go. In any event, how do these little white pills – small enough for one to fit three or four on the nail of one's smallest finger – actually work? Who manufactures them, where? Who invented them, tried and tested them? I work the sweetener case conventionally, causing it to produce a perfectly normal sweetener such as any diet-conscious person might slip into their tea or coffee (while often, of course, tucking one's snout into a glistening cream bun). It is almost identical to the special pills, lacking only a tiny blue dot – scarcely visible to the naked eye – in the very centre of one face. I slide open the end of the ormolu case and replace the sweetener.

The little case itself is quite an exquisite piece of work. Used as one would expect it to be used it will happily dispense sweeteners and nothing but sweeteners all day until they run out; only by holding and pressing it just so may one access the small compartment concealed within that contains its real treasure, so that it releases one of the little pills which lead one to flit, bringing about a transition, flicking one into another soul and another world.

Questions, questions. I know how I am supposed to think. I am supposed to think that one day I might rise to the level of Madame d'Ortolan and her ilk, and discover some of the answers. Eliding everybody on the list my orders contained might well be quite enough by itself to ensure just such an elevation, and I should think so too; such a close-packed sequence of elisions would require my best work, and success would by no means be assured.

Anyway – sadly, as far as Madame d'Ortolan's purposes are concerned – I have no intention of killing the people on the list. On the contrary: I will save them if I can (with any luck, in a sense I already have). No, I intend to go quite diametrically off-message in this matter.

I already have, of course; Lord Harmyle wasn't even on the list.

5

Patient 8262

A h, our profession. Mine, and those who will now be looking for me. My peers, I suppose. Though I was peerless, if I say so myself. There was – especially at the more colourful end of the reality spectrum – an insane grace to my elisions, a contrived but outrageous elegance. As evidence, the fiery fate of one Yerge Aushauser, arbitrageur. Or perhaps you would prefer the brain-frying exit of Mr Max Fitching, lead singer of Gun Puppy, the first true World Band in more realities than we cared to count. Or the painful and I'm afraid protracted end of Marit Shauoon, stunt driver, businessman and politician.

For Yerge, I arranged a special bubble bath at his Nevada ranch, replacing the air feed to the nozzles in his hot tub with hydrogen. The cylinders, hidden under the wooden decking around the tub, were controlled by a radio-activated valve. I was watching from the other side of the world through a digital camera attached to a spotting scope, a sunlight-powered computer and a proprietary satellite uplink, all sitting disguised by sage bushes on a hillside a mile away. A motion sensor alerted me that the hot tub was in use while I was asleep in my hotel in Sierra Leone. When I gazed, bleary-eyed, into my phone I saw Yerge Aushauser striding up to the tub, alone for once. I swung out of bed, woke the laptop for a higher-definition view and waited until he was sitting there in the frothing water, all hairy arms and furious expression. Probably another expensive night at the gaming tables. He usually brought home a girl or two to knock around on such occasions, but perhaps this morning he was tired. The view was quite clear through the cool morning air, untroubled by thermals. I could see him put something long and dark to his mouth, then hold something to its end. A spark. His fat fingers would be closing round his Gran Corona, his throat exposed as he put his head back against the cushion on the tub's rim and blew the first mouthful of smoke into the clear blue Nevada sky.

I punched in the code for the valve controlling the feed from the hydrogen cylinders. Seconds later, half a world away, the water frothed crazily, briefly seemed to steam as though boiling, hiding first Yerge and then the tub in a ball of vapour. This erupted almost immediately into an intense yellow-white fireball which engulfed the tub and all the nearby decking. Even in the early morning sunshine it blazed brightly.

Amazingly, after a few seconds, while the pillar of roaring flame piled towards the heavens like an upside-down rocket plume, Yerge stumbled out of the conflagration and across the decking, hair on fire, skin blackened, strips of it hanging off him like dark rags. He fell down some steps and lay there, motionless, minus his cigar but still – in a sense – smoking.

Until the decking itself caught fire – Yerge's servants had run out from the house and dragged him away by then – there was little smoke; oxygen and hydrogen burn perfectly, producing, of course, only water. Most of the initial burst of smoke, now drifting and dissipating in the cool morning breeze and heading towards the distant grey sierras, would have come from Yerge himself.

He had ninety-five per cent burns, and lungs seared by flame inhalation. They managed to keep him alive for nearly a week, which was remarkable.

Max Fitching was a god amongst mortals, a man with the voice of an angel and the proclivities of a satyr. I killed Max while he sat in a seriously pimped open-top half-track in Jakarta, waiting for a roadie to return with his drugs (Max never did get the hang of dressing down. Or going incognito). The Israeli laser weapon was originally an experimental device designed to bring down Iranian missiles while they were still over Syria, or, better still, Iraq. I fired it from a container truck a block down the street from Max's idling half-track. Even attenuated to the minimum it was grossly over-powered for the job and rather than drill a neat hole straight through Max's fashionably pale, heavily sunglassed, wildly dreadlocked head, it blew it to smithereens. Windows shattered three storeys up.

This was not elegant – far from it. The elegance came from the fact that the laser burst was not a single brutally simple pulse but one which had been precisely frequency-modulated to mirror the digitalised information of a high-sample-rate MP3 signal, compressed into a microsecond. What hit Max was effectively an MP3 copy of "Woke Up Down," Gun Puppy's first worldwide hit and the song that had made Max truly famous.

Marit Shauoon was a populist politician in the Perón mould, and, like the others, I had been reliably informed that he would, if left alone, take the world to a Very Bad Place, in his case starting with South and Central America. (As if any of this really mattered to me. Craft, my trade, was all. I let those who handed me my orders worry about the morality of it.) He had been a motorcycle stunt rider, the most famous in Brazil and then in the world. He crashed a lot but that just added to the excitement, anticipation and sense of jeopardy in the crowd. All four of his major limbs were pinned and strengthened with extensive amounts of surgical steel and even without those there were enough metal implants in the rest of his body to set off airport security scanners while he was still walking stiffly from the car park.

I found an induction furnace for him. He heated up, quite slowly, from the inside, to the sound of vastly thrumming magnets all around him, and his own screams.

. . . What? Why, why, and why? I would have had no idea if I had not been told, and even once I was told frankly I still didn't care. (I am mildly surprised I recall any of the reasons given below at all.)

So: Yerge would have started a political party to rid the USA of non-Aryans, bringing chaos and apocalyptic bloodshed. Max would have given all his hundreds of millions in royalties to an extremist Green movement who – taking an arguably rather drastic approach to harmonising the planet's natural carrying capacity with the size of its human population – would have used the windfall to design, manufacture, weaponise and distribute a virus that would kill ninety per cent of humanity. And Marit would have used his vast communications network to . . . I can't remember; broadcast pornography to Andromeda or something. As I say, it didn't really matter. I had by then entirely stopped enquiring why I might be committing such terminally grievous acts. All I cared about was the artistry and elegance involved in the doing, the carrying out, the commission.

The execution.

The Philosopher

Screams. Too many screams. They have kept me awake at night, woken me from dreams and nightmares.

I do not enjoy what I do, though I am not ashamed of it, and it would not be an exaggeration to say that I am proud of it. It is something that has to be done, and somebody has to do it. It is because I do not enjoy it that I am good at it. I have seen the work of those who do enjoy our mutual calling, and they do not produce the best results. They get carried away, they indulge themselves rather than stick to the task in hand, which is to produce the results which are desired and to recognise them when they are produced. Instead, they try too hard, and fail.

I torture people. I am a torturer. But I do no more than I am told to do and I would rather that the people I torture told the truth, or revealed the information that they carry and which we need to know, as quickly as possible, both to spare themselves and to spare me the unpleasantness of the task because, as I say, I take no pleasure in what I have to do. Nevertheless, I do all that I am asked to do, and will always work long hours and take on extra duties if required. This is conscientiousness, and a sort of mercy because at least when I do it only the minimum is done. I have had colleagues – the ones mentioned above who enjoy what we do – who have been impatient to cause the maximum amount of pain and damage. They are, in the end, inefficient.

The clever ones pretend not to be psychotic and only indulge themselves rarely, opting for routine efficiency for the majority of the time. They're the dangerous ones.

My favoured techniques are electricity, repeated near-suffocation and, hard though this may be to believe, simply talking. The electricity is the crudest, in a sense. We use a variable step resistor attached to the mains and a variety of common-or-garden car jump leads. Sometimes some water or conducting gel. The crocodile clips on the end of the jump leads hurt quite a bit without any current flowing through them. The ears are good sites, and fingers and toes. The genitals, obviously. The nose or tongue with the other terminal inserted into the anus is a favourite with some of my colleagues, though I dislike the resultant messiness.

Repeated near-suffocation involves gaffer-taping the subject's mouth and then using a second small piece of tape to close the nostrils, removing it just before or just after the onset of unconsciousness. This is a useful technique for low-level subjects and for those who must be returned to some other department or security agency, or even to normal life, without any signs of injury.

Talking involves telling the subject what will happen to them if they do not cooperate. It is best done in a perfectly dark room, talking quietly and matter-of-factly from somewhere behind the chair they are secured to. First I describe what will happen to them anyway, even if they tell us everything, because there is a certain minimum, a kind of call-out fee level of torment that we have to inflict once people have been referred to us. This is to maintain our reputation and the sense of dread that must be associated with us. Fear of being tortured can be a highly effective technique for maintaining law and order in a society and I believe that we would be in dereliction of our duty if we did not do our bit.

Then I describe what I might do to them: the voltages used, the symptoms of suffocation and so on. I have studied the relevant physiology in some depth and am able to elucidate with the use of copious medical terminology. Then I describe some of the other techniques used by some of my colleagues. I mention the man whose code name is Doctor Citrus. He restricts his torture instruments to a sheet of A4 paper and a fresh lemon, using numerous – usually several dozen to start with – paper cuts distributed all over the subject's naked body which then have a drop or two of lemon juice squeezed into them. Or salt, sometimes. Like repeated near-suffocation, this does not sound so terrible to most people, but, statistically, it is one of the most effective torture techniques that we employ. Of course our friend Doctor Citrus does not use just one sheet of paper, as any single sheet will grow moist with sweat and small amounts of blood, over time. He always has a box of paper to hand.

There are colleagues who prefer to use the tried and trusted tools of torture: thumbscrews, pincers, pliers, hammers, certain acids and, of course, fire; flame or just heat, supplied by gas burners, blow-torches, soldering irons, steam or boiling water. These are sometimes the techniques of last resort when others have failed. The subject will usually be scarred for life should they survive, and the survival rate, even if full cooperation is achieved, is not high.

Another of our colleagues likes to use cocktail sticks: hundreds of wooden cocktail sticks inserted into the soft tissues of the body. He talks too, softening the subject up psychologically by sitting in front of them and using a small penknife to slit the cocktail sticks, producing little barbs and curls of wood which will increase the pain caused both when they are inserted and when – and if – they are removed. He sits there for an hour or more with a big pile of sticks, using the tiny knife on these hundreds of little wooden slivers and detailing to the subject precisely where they will be placed. He too has some medical training and describes to the subject the thinking behind his technique as being in some ways the opposite of acupuncture, where the needles are inserted with the aim of causing little or no pain on entry and alleviating pain thereafter.

This preparatory dialogue can in itself be sufficient to produce full cooperation from the subject, though, as I say, there is a minimum level of pain which has to be inflicted in any event, just to be sure that full cooperation really has been achieved and to ensure that we, as an agency, are taken seriously.

My own talking technique is in some ways my personal favourite. I like the economy of it. I have found it is especially useful on artistic people or those of an intellectual persuasion as they tend to have their own very active imaginations and thus this technique lets these imaginations do my work for me. Over the years, some of them have even mentioned said phenomenon themselves, though this recognition would appear to make the process no less effective.

I do not like to question females. The rather obvious reason would be that their screams remind me of those of my mother when my father raped her on that never-to-be-forgotten night following her return home after the birth of my sister. However, I would prefer to think that it is simply good old-fashioned manners. A gentleman simply does not wish to subject a female to anything unpleasant. This does not stop me torturing women; it is still something that has to be done, and I am a professional, and conscientious, but I enjoy the process even less than I do when working with a male subject and I am not ashamed to admit that I have on occasion begged – literally begged – a female subject to exhibit full co-operation as quickly as possible, and I am also not ashamed to reveal that I have felt tears come to my eyes when I have had to work especially hard with a female subject.

The use of tape across the mouth, regardless of what other technique is being employed, is good for cutting down the sound of screams, which must then all exit the subject via the nasal passages – more than somewhat reduced in volume, I am relieved to be able to report.

I do draw the line at children. Some of my colleagues will happily oblige when a child must be tortured to force a parent to talk, but I think this is both morally objectionable and suspect in principle. A child ought not to have to suffer for the follies or beliefs of his or her parents, and to the extent that the techniques we employ on the subjects are in themselves a kind of punishment for subversion, treachery and lawbreaking, they ought to be applied to the guilty party, not visited upon their family or dependants. Everyone talks eventually. Everyone. Using a child to shorten the process is, in my opinion, sloppy, lazy and simply bad technique.

Largely due to this scruple and perhaps also because I find it interesting and illuminating to discuss or at least attempt to discuss with my colleagues subjects such as those enumerated above, my code name within the department is The Philosopher.

The Transitionary

I live in a Switzerland. The indefinite article is germane.

The particular Switzerland I live in is not even called Switzerland, but it is a recognised type, a place whose function and demeanour will be familiar to all those we number amongst the Aware. "Aware" means being au fait with the realities of the realities. "Aware" is a term applied to those who understand that we live not in one world – singular, settled and linear – but within a multitude of worlds, forever exponentially and explosively multiplying through time. More to the point, it applies to those who know how easy it is to travel between these disparate, ever-branching and unfolding and developing realities.

My home is an old lodge in the pines, on a ridge looking out over the small but sophisticated spa town of Flesse. Beyond the town, to the west, is high rolling ground, clothed with trees. To the east, behind my lodge, the hills rise in craggy increments, culminating in a serrated massif of mountains high enough to hold snow all the year. Sufficiently compact for one to take all of it in with a single glance from my terrace, Flesse nevertheless boasts an opera house, a railway station and junction, a medley of fascinating and eccentric shops, two superior hotels and a casino. When I am not on my travels, working for Madame d'Ortolan or some other member of l'Expédience – the Concern – I am here: reading in my library during wet weather, walking in the hills on the finer days and, in the evening, frequenting the hotels and the casino.

When I am, as it were, away, flitting between other worlds and other bodies, I still have a life here; a version of me remains, living on, inhabiting my house and my body and going through all the appropriate motions concomitant with existence, though by all accounts I am, in the shape of this residual self, quite astoundingly boring. According to my housekeeper and a few other people who have encountered me in this state, I never leave the house, I sleep a great deal, I will eat but not cook food for myself, I am reluctant to get dressed properly and I show no interest in music or conversation. Sometimes I try to read a book but sit staring at the same page for hours, either not really reading it or reading it over and over again. Art books, paintings and illustrations appear to pique my interest as much as anything, which is to say not very much at all, as will a television programme, though only if it is visually arresting. My conversation becomes monosyllabic. I seem happiest just sitting in the loggia or staring out of a window at the view.

I'm told that I appear drugged, or sedated, or as though I have had a stroke or been lobotomised. I maintain that I have met several allegedly normal persons and not a few students who exhibit a lesser degree of day-to-day animation – I exaggerate only slightly. However, I have no cause to complain. I don't get into trouble while I'm away from myself (well, I don't get into trouble *here*) and my appetite is not sufficient to cause me to gain weight. Perish the thought that I might go for a walk in the hills and fall off a cliff, or head for the casino and incur vast debts, or start an ill-advised affair while my back is turned on myself.

The rest of the time, though, I am entirely here, living fully, attention undivided, in this world, this reality, on the seemingly singular version of the Earth that calls itself Calbefraques. My name – in what is for me at least this base or root reality – is nothing like the ones I usually end up with when transitioning. Here I am called Temudjin Oh, a name of Eastern Asian origin. The Earth I came from is one of the many where the influence of the Mongolian Empires, especially in Europe, was more profound than the one in which you are reading these words.

I live an orderly, even quiet life, as entirely befits somebody who spends potentially highly disorienting amounts of time flitting between one world and the next, too often for the unfortunate purpose of killing people. Murder is not all that I do, however. Sometimes I will be a positive angel, a good fairy, an imp of the benign, showering some unfortunate who is down on their luck with money or granting them a commission or pointing them in the direction of somebody who might be able to help them. On occasion I do something almost unbearably banal, like trip somebody up in the street, or buy them a drink in a bar or – once – fall down in front of them while apparently suffering a fit.

That was one of the few times when I glimpsed what I might really have been doing. The young doctor – hurrying to an appointment but who nevertheless stopped to tend to me – was thereby prevented from entering a building that promptly collapsed in a great burst of dust and mortar and smashed wooden beams. Lying there in the gutter, seeing this, just a few dozen strides down the street, I feigned a partial recovery, thanked him and insisted that he hurry to treat the many wailing unfortunates injured by the tenement's collapse. "No, thank *you*, sir," he muttered, face grey, not just with dust. "I believe your fit saved my life." He disappeared into the growing crowd while I sat there, trying not to get fallen over by those rushing to help or gawp.

I have no idea what that young fellow then went on to do or achieve. Something good, I trust.

Sometimes I simply introduce one person to another, or leave a particular book or pamphlet lying around for them to discover. Sometimes I just talk to them, generally encouraging them or mentioning a particular idea. I relish such roles, but they are not the ones I remember. They are certainly not the ones that keep me awake at night. Perhaps this is simply because geniality is conventionally a little insipid. Havoc rocks.

Most of my colleagues and superiors choose to live in cities. It is where we are most at home and where one can most easily make the transition from one reality to another. I do not pretend entirely to understand either the theories or the mechanics – spiritual mechanics, if you will, but still mechanics – behind such profoundly disconnected travellings, but I know a little regarding how these things work, some of it gleaned from others and some of it the result of simply working matters out for myself, practically, rather as I was able to work out what the true purpose of my appearing to faint in front of that young doctor was when the building he had been about to enter fell down.

Flitting from here to there to any-old-where requires a deep sense of place, and some sort of minimum level of societal complexity, it would seem. It is as a result of this that cities are by far the easiest places in which to slip between realities.

Aircraft work too, though, if one has the skill. Something about the concentration of people, I suppose. I sip my gin and tonic and look down at the clouds. The peaks of some of the higher mountains in the Norwegian coastal range protrude like jagged ice cubes floating in milk. I am taking a direct Great Circle route from London to Tokyo, cosseted within a giant aircraft coasting high above the weather where the sky is a deep, dark blue.

I may flit from here, within the plane. I may not. It is not an easy thing to do – many of us have wasted our drug by trying to effect transitions from remote places or – especially – moving start points. The way it appears to work is that if a successful flit cannot be made then nothing at all happens and one remains where one is. There are rumours, however, that people who have tried such manoeuvres have indeed ended up in another reality, but without the benefit of whatever mode of transport they left behind in the source reality being there to greet them in the target one. One pops into existence over open water if one flitted from a liner, splashing into an empty ocean to drown or be eaten by sharks, or – if the attempted transition is from an aircraft like this – one materialises in mid-air twelve thousand metres up with no air to breathe, a temperature of sixty below and a long way to fall. I have had successes flitting from aircraft, and failures; obviously failures where nothing happened.

I take the little ormolu case from my shirt pocket and turn it over and over on my fold-down table. To flit or not to flit. If I do vacate the aircraft then I will cover my tracks more completely than if I wait until my arrival. However, I could waste a pill. And I just might discover the hard way that the rumours are true, and find myself blast-frozen and gasping my way to unconsciousness as I start the long fall to the sea or the land. There is also the well-documented complication that sometimes one ends up in an aircraft going somewhere quite different to the destination of that one started from.

Usually there is a reliable commonality between a roughly aligned group of worlds regarding the placement of continents, major geographical features such as mountain ranges and rivers and hence big cities and therefore the air routes between them, so that leaving one aircraft results in a transition to a similar craft on a parallel course, but not always. There appear to be limits to the maximum displacement in space and time that people have made in such circumstances – a few kilometres up or down, a few dozen later-ally, and some hours later or earlier – and it is as if some aspect of

one's will or visualisation is guiding one to the nearest approxima-
tion it's possible to find, but sometimes the influence of this ghostly
presence goes quite awry, or just accepts something that it hopes
will do, but which will not.

Once, flitting while flying over the Alps bound for Napoli from
Dublin, I ended up on a flight from Madrid to Kiev. That's practically a right-angle! It took me a day and a half to repair the damage
to my itinerary, and I missed one appointment. I had and have no
idea why this happened. When I mentioned this little adventure to
someone from the Transitionary Office – the primary body of
l'Expédience, which at least in theory oversees all the actions of those
like myself and Madame d'Ortolan – the bureaucrat concerned just
blinked behind his rimless glasses and said how interesting this was
and hastened to record a note! I mean, really.

The drug we take to effect our travels is called septus. Some take
theirs in liquid form, from tiny vials like medical ampoules. Others
prefer to snort their travellers' medicine, or inject it. Some like it
to be in the form of a suppository or pessary. Madame d'Ortolan
was always said to have favoured the latter option.

I tap the little ormolu case gently on one corner, rotate it a quarter
turn, tap it again, and repeat. Most of us take septus in pill form;
it is simply less of a bother. I regard most of the other methods as
being rather like showing off.

A clear patch of sea gleams up at me. A ship, made tiny by the
vertical kilometres between us, slides slowly north across the ruffled
grey surface, drawing a feathery white wake after it. I imagine somebody on that ship looking up and seeing this aircraft, a bright white
dot leaving its own thin trail inscribed across the blue.

Perhaps some of those who are said to have disappeared are gone
to other Earths entirely, where Pangaea still holds, Man never evolved
and sapient otters or insectile hive-minds rule in our place – who
can say?

When we flit we go to where we imagine, and if – distracted,
disoriented – we imagine something too far away from what we

know and where we wish to go to, we may end up somewhere it is somehow impossible to imagine one's way back from. I don't know how that could be – what saves people like myself, sometimes, is how intensely we long for our home – but you never know.

I have quizzed the theorists, technicians and general functionaries of the Transitionary Office regarding just how all of this works and have yet to receive a satisfactory answer. I am not supposed to know because I have no need to know. Still, I would like to know. My being sent to save that young doctor from being crushed in that collapsing building in Savoie, for example: does that not imply foresight? Must we – I mean the Concern – not have some ability to look ahead in time, or be able to use realities otherwise similar to another but separated only by being slightly displaced in time so that – having observed what has happened in the leading one – one is able to affect events in the trailing one? This would amount to the same thing.

Of course, maybe it was complete happenstance that the tenement collapsed, pure chance. I find this unlikely, however. Chance is rarely pure.

It was at the casino that I encountered Mrs Mulverhill again, for the first time in a long time – or at least so I thought. Not that I realised immediately.

Cities are, as I've said, the best places to flit between realities; nexuses of transportation in our multiple existence just as they are in any given single world. The principal embassy of l'Expédience in the world I have tended to travel to and within – partly though chance and partly through some affinitive predisposition on my part, I dare say – is in what is called variously Byzantium, Constantinople, Konstantiniyye, Stamboul or Istanbul, depending. It is an ideal focus for our interests and abilities, straddling continents, linking east and west and evoking the past and its manifold legacies in a way that few other cities do on this meta-Earth I deal with. Ancient, modern, a furious mix of peoples, faiths, histories and attitudes, poised above and threatened by myriad fault lines, it exemplifies both heritage, jeopardy, division and linkage all at once. We have another office in Jerusalem.

There used to be another, in Berlin, but that city has, perversely, become less attractive for our purposes since the fall of the Wall and the reunification of Germany (one of those distributed, straggling meta-events that resonated through the sheaved realities for all the many worlds like some coordinated spawning phenomenon). So the office was closed. A shame, in a way; I liked the old, divided Berlin, with its wall. The greater city was a vast, open, airy place enfolded with lakes and sprawling tracts of forest on both sides of the divide but still, at its core, there was always a forlorn air about it, as well as a faint feeling of imprisonment, on both sides.

And a slowly spinning plate, if you know what I mean. We look for spinning, wobbling plates; places where it feels that matters could go either way, where another spin, another input of energy might restore stability, but where, equally, just a little more neglect – or even a nudge in the right/wrong place – could produce catastrophe. There are interesting lessons to be gleaned from the wreckage that results. Sometimes you cannot tell everything about a thing until you've seen it broken.

There ought to be a certain point in one's training for the post of transitionary (our official job title – clunky, I know; I prefer the sobriquet "flitter" – or "transitioner" or "transitioneer," at a pinch) when one realises that one has discovered or acquired an extra sense. It is in a sense the sense of history, of connection, of how long a place has been lived in, a feeling for the heritage of human events attached to a particular piece of landscape or set of streets and stones. We call it fragre.

Part of it is akin to having a sharp nose for the scent of ancient blood. Places of great antiquity, where much has happened over not just centuries but millennia, are often steeped in it. Almost any site of massacre or battle will have a whiff, even thousands of years later. I find it at its most pungent when I stand within the Colosseum, in Rome. However, much of it is simply the layered result of multifarious generations of people having lived there; lived and died, certainly, but then as most people live for decades and die just the once, it is the living part that has the greatest influence over the aroma, the feel of a place.

Certainly the entirety of the Americas has a significantly different fragre compared to Europe and Asia; less fusty, or less rich, according to your prejudices.

I'm told that New Zealand and Patagonia appraise as terribly fresh compared with almost everywhere else.

Myself, I love the fragre of Venezia. Not the fragrance – at least, not in summer, anyway – but very much the fragre.

I prefer to arrive in Venice by train, from Mestre. As I disembark at Santa Lucia station I can, if I declutch my senses and memory, fool myself into thinking that I have arrived at just another big Italian railway station, one more terminus amongst many. One walks between the towering trains, crosses the indifferent commercialism of the rather brutalist concourse and expects to find what one would find anywhere: a busy road or square, another bustling vista of car and truck and bus – a pedestrianised piazza and a few taxis, at best.

Instead, spreading beyond the sweep of steps and the scatter of people – the Grand Canal! Light green choppy water, the churning wakes of vaporetti, launches, water taxis and work boats, reflected light slicing off the waves to dance along the façades of palazzos and churches; spires, domes and inverted-cone chimneys ranged against a sky of cobalt shine. Or against milky clouds, their mirrored pastel tones softening the restless waters of the canal. Or against dark veils of rain cloud, the canal flattened and subdued under a downpour.

The first time I visited the place was for the carnival in February. I discovered mist and fog and quietness, and a chill in the air that seemed to rise from the water like a promise. My name was Mark Cavan. My languages were Mandarin, English, Hindustani, Spanish, Arabic, Russian and French. The Berlin Wall was already history, though still mostly standing.

It was your world.

Some way down the Grand Canal, on its west bank, sits an imposing near-cubical palazzo. Its walls are a glacial white, the shutters shielding its many windows matt black. This severely formal and symmetrical building is the Palazzo Chirezzia, once the home of a Levantine prince, later that of a cardinal of the Roman Catholic church, then for a hundred and fifty years an infamous brothel. It belonged, then as now, to Professore Loscelles, a gentleman who knew about and was sympathetic to the Concern. Back then, he simply made himself, his money and connections useful to us, and, equally, gained much through the association. He has since risen to join the ruling Central Council, though on that cold February morning twenty years ago this was still an ambition of his.

I had been invited to the city and the carnival as a reward for my services, which had lately been energetic if not onerous. There were no other transitionaries present, though there was a gaggle of Concern apparatchiks and officials, all of whom were polite to me. Despite the rather generous amount of blood I had on my hands even then, I was still not yet used to the idea that people who knew of my role within l'Expédience might find my presence intimidating, alarming or even frightening.

Professore Loscelles is a modest figure of a man, verging on short, though with a stately bearing which belies this. He is one of those who grow in isolation. Alone, one might swear he is as tall as oneself; in a small group he seems to shrink by comparison and in a crowd he disappears entirely. He was balding then, losing thin brown hair like seaweed dropping back from a rock with a receding tide. He has a splendid hook of a nose, prominent teeth and eyes of a frosty-looking blue. His wife was dramatically taller than him, a statuesque Calabrian blonde with a large, honest-looking face and a ready laugh. It was she, Giacinta, who taught me the dances which would be required at the series of balls to which we had been invited. Happily I am a quick learner and apparently I move well.

The palace contained a ballroom where one of the great masked balls of that year's carnival was to be held. This took place the day after I arrived. I was appropriately entranced by the fabulous masks and costumes and by the sumptuous decor of the ballroom itself; a hymn of ancient, polished woods, glossy marble and extravagantly gilt-framed mirrors, all lit entirely with candles, imparting a distinct mellowness to the light and a smoky scent to the air, like incense. It mingled with the odour of perfumes and the smoke from cigarettes and cigars. The men were peacocks, the women whirling, dazzling belles in glittering gowns. A small orchestra in antique dress filled the space with melody. Three enormous chandeliers of red glass oversaw it all – great swirling, abstract shapes looking like vast surges of glistening blood caught in the act of spinning within an unseen whirlpool – but were reduced to mere pendulous sculptures reflecting candle flames, their bulbs unnecessary and unlit.

Breathless, gripping a glass of Tokaj, I stepped out onto a little terrace bounded by fat white marble balustrades shaped like tears. A small crowd of partygoers stood quietly watching snow descend against the lights of the few passing boats and the light-flecked buildings on the canal's far side. The spiralling chaos of flakes appeared from the darkness overhead as though created by the lanterns of the palazzo and disappeared silently into the oily blackness of the gently moving waters before it.

I went out early the next morning into that cold, encasing whiteness, my breath spreading into the dark narrow spaces in front of me, and found some untrodden stretches on the Sestiere Dorsoduro. I strolled the ancient, hidden stones, breathing in the cool, clear salty scent of the place and soaking up the world's fragre. It tasted, of course, of all the things that all the other worlds taste of, but the identifying highlights spoke of a kind of seductive cruelty, an orchidaceous venality, so infinitely sweet it could only be redolent of corruption and decay. Here, in the eternally sinking city, with that odour of glamourous savagery filtering through my mind like mist off the lagoon into a room, it all felt spent here but only paused elsewhere, like something waiting to resume.

The snow lay across the city for the next few days, creating a starkness beneath those sea-wide skies, draining colour from the passing clouds, water and buildings and promoting the views of that city of Canaletto and fractious colour to a ravishing monochrome.

The final ball was held in the Doge's Palace in a vast and splendid room built half a millennium ago to house two thousand milling princes, merchants, ambassadors, captains and dignitaries. An airstream originating in Africa had pushed up over the heel of Italy and the Adriatic, melting the snow and bringing mists and fog as it collided with and was slowed by contesting winds spilling down from the mountains to the north. The city seemed to submerge beneath the resulting vapours, cloaking itself in veils and shrouds of moisture.

I met my Masked Woman there, then.

I wore the costume of a medieval Orthodox priest, topped with a mirror mask. I had danced some dances, sat at the Loscelles' table and taken part in some slightly stilted conversations with my fellow house guests and the Professore, who was too interested in the details of my assignments for the health of either of us, had I answered him honestly. One of the non-Concern guests of the Loscelles – a tall, pretty brunette who was a distant relation of the Professore and whose lissom form had been squeezed most attractively into the garb of a renaissance lady – had rather taken my eye that evening. However, she seemed to be equally captivated with a dashing cavaliere and so I had put any thoughts involving her to one side.

I took a break from the eating and drinking and dancing and talking and sought to explore what I could of the palace, strolling through some of the lesser chambers, being shooed out of others and finally ending up back in the Hall of the Great Council while a dance processed like a gaudy vortex in the centre of the vast room. I stood staring up at the frieze of paintings depicting the sequence of Doges, my gaze eventually fastening on one which appeared to be missing, or at least covered by a black veil. I wondered if this was some tradition of the carnival, or just of this particular masked ball.

"His name was Doge Marino Faliero," a female voice announced at my side, in lightly accented English. I looked round to discover that I was being addressed by a pirate captain. Chunkily high-heeled boots brought her almost to my height. Her jacket hung, attached like a hussar's, from one shoulder. The rest of her uniform appeared motley, arranged to look thrown together: baggy breeches, brass-buttoned, an extravagantly frilled blouse, a half-undone waistcoat worn like a bodice, a tricolour sash plus beads and various chains and some sort of brass plate like a half-moon slung around her neck, which looked pale and slender. Her mask was black velvet, misted with what looked like tiny pearls set out in spirals. Beneath the mask her mouth looked roseate, amused. A few locks of black hair escaped a crumpled cap of navy blue surmounted by a cocky burst of gaudy feathers.

I glanced back up at the veiled space in the succession of Doges. "Is it now?"

"He was Doge for a year in the mid thirteen hundreds," my informant told me. Her voice sounded young, melodious, confident. "He's covered up because he's in eternal disgrace. He tried to make a coup to sweep away the republic and have himself declared prince."

"But he was already Doge," I said.

She shrugged. "A prince or a king would have had more power. Doges were elected. For life, but with many restrictions. They were not allowed to open their own mail. It had first to be read by the censor. Too, they were not allowed to conduct discussions with foreign diplomats alone. A committee was required. They had much power but they were also just figureheads." She gestured with one hand (black-gloved, silver rings over leather). Her sword – or at least a scabbard for a sword – swung at her left hip.

"I thought perhaps he was only veiled for the ball," I said.

She shook her head. "In perpetuity. He was condemned to Damnatio Memoriae. And mutilated, and beheaded, of course."

"Of course." I nodded gravely.

She might have stiffened a little. Was I talking to a local? "The republic took such threats to its existence seriously," she said.

I executed a fraction of a bow, smiling and tipping my head. "You would appear to be an authority, ma'am."

"Hardly. Merely not ignorant."

"I thank you for relieving me of some measure of my own ignorance."

"You are welcome."

I nodded to the swirl of people. "Care to dance?"

She moved her head back a fraction, as though appraising me, then bowed a little further than I had. "Why not?" she said.

And so we danced. She moved with a lithe grace. I sweated beneath my mask and robes, and understood the wisdom of having masked balls in winter. We talked over the music in the rhythm imposed by the dance.

"May I ask your name?"

"You may." She smiled slightly, fell silent.

"I see. Well, what is your name?"

She shook her head. "It is not always the done thing to ask someone's name at a masked ball."

"Is it not?"

"I feel the spirit of the late Doge looks down upon us and demands due reticence, don't you?"

I shook my head. "Probably not even if I knew what you were talking about."

This appeared to amuse her, as the soft lips parted in a smile before she said, "Alora." For a moment I thought she was telling me her name, but of course it is simply an Italian word, nearly identical to the French "alors." I found her accent impossible to place. "Perhaps we come to names later," she said as we danced around each other. "Otherwise, ask what you will."

"I insist; ladies first."

"Well then, what do you do, sir?"

"I am a traveller. And you?"

"The same."

"Indeed. You travel widely?"

95

"Very. You?"

"Oh, extraordinarily."

"Do you travel to a purpose?"

"A series of purposes. Yourself?"

"Always only with one."

"And what would that be?"

"Well, you must guess."

"Must I?"

"Oh yes."

"Let me see then. Your pleasure?"

"I am not," she said, "so shallow."

"Is it shallow to seek pleasure?"

"Exclusively, yes."

"I know people who would disagree."

"So do I. May I ask what you're smiling at?"

"The scorn in your voice when you mention those people."

"Well, they are shallow," she said. "This proves my point, no?"

"It certainly proves something."

"You are smiling again."

"I am aware that my mouth is almost all you can see."

"Do you think it is all I need to see of you?"

"I would hope not."

She tipped her head to one side. "Are you flirting with me, sir?" she asked curtly.

"I'm fairly sure I'm trying to," I said. "How am I doing?"

She appeared to think, then moved her head side-to-side, like a nod rotated ninety degrees. "It is too early to tell yet."

Later – the music echoing down stairwells and through chambers and corridors – we stood in front of a great wall-wide map of the world. It looked reasonably accurate and therefore late, though of course in some ways I would be the last to be able to judge. We stood close, both a little breathless after the last dance. We still wore our masks and I still did not know her name.

"Does it all look present and correct to you, sir?" she asked as I gazed up at the configured continents and cities.

"We return to my ignorance," I confessed. "Geography is not my strongest subject."

"Or does it then look wrong to you?" she asked, then seemed to drop her voice a little. "Or too limited?"

"Too limited?" I asked.

"It is, after all, just the one world," she said calmly.

I looked at her, startled. She returned her gaze to the map. I recovered my composure. I laughed, gestured. "Indeed. A starry vault or two would not go amiss."

She stood still, looked at the map, said no more.

For some time I divided my attention between her and the map while various individuals, couples and groups of people passed to and fro, chattering and laughing. Then, in a lull, I reached out to take her gloved hand. She moved away and swivelled. "Walk with me, would you?" she asked.

"Where to?"

"Must it be to anywhere? Might we not just walk?"

"I think you'll find that when you stop walking you'll have arrived somewhere."

She fixed me with a stare. "I thought geography wasn't your strong point."

We collected our cloaks. Outside, in the Piazzetta and then the Piazza, a misty rain was falling, blurring the lines of lights set high on the great square's walls between the lines of dark windows.

She led me north through a succession of narrow, twisting calles and across small bowed bridges over dark narrow canals, quickly leaving behind the scatter of people in and around San Marco, our steps echoing from overhanging buildings, our shadows – unbearably dramatic in our out-belling cloaks – dancing around us like ghostly partners, sometimes ahead of us, sometimes behind, to one side, or just a pool of darkness at our feet.

She found a tiny bar off an ill-lit calle which would have been too narrow for us to walk down side by side. The establishment was shady, almost empty save for a couple of workmen sitting near the back nursing beers – we were given slightly contemptuous glances – and a diminutive blonde bar girl in jeans and a baggy jumper. My companion ordered a spritz and a bottle of still water. I accepted a spritz as well.

Our hostess disappeared into a storeroom, clutching a clipboard and pen. We remained standing at the bar. I took off my mask, faced my pirate captain and smiled expectantly. "There," I said.

She merely nodded, made no move to remove her own mask. She did take off her hat. The moment might have called for a shake of the head, coquettish or not, but she just let her long black curled hair fall about her shoulders without ceremony. The workman facing us glanced up, nodded to his fellow, who turned. Both eyed her for a few moments. She put her head back and glugged half the bottle of water in one go, exposed throat moving. She wiped her mouth with a couple of fingers, then sipped delicately on her spritz, back to ladylike. Dim though the bar was, the angle of a light above the gallery of bottles gave me the best view I'd had so far of her eyes behind the almond-shaped piercings in the black mask. They glittered, hinting at lightness; pale blue or green or a delicate hazel.

"Would it be time for names yet?" I asked.

She shook her head.

"I could tell you mine," I said. "Like it or not."

She put one finger to my lips, very carefully and gently. Her finger was warm and smelled of a dark, oily perfume. I hadn't even seen her take off her glove. The finger pressed my lips very briefly, then withdrew. I might have made to kiss it, equally gently, but there had hardly been time. She smiled.

"Do you know the word 'emprise'?" she asked.

I sighed, thought. "I don't believe I do."

"It means a dangerous undertaking."

"Does it?"

98

"It does. Do you partake of dangerous undertakings, sir?"

I leant forward, my gaze going to one side then the other. "Am I partaking in one now?" I asked quietly.

She tipped her head forward. "Not yet," she murmured. "No more than you would usually. Less so. You would be off duty now, yes?"

"Off duty?" I asked, confused.

"Not travelling."

"Ah, yes. In that sense, then, I suppose so."

One of the workmen walked up and stood behind her, rapping his knuckles on the bar's wooden surface. The blonde girl reappeared from the back room. My companion seemed to be about to say something, then checked herself. She turned and looked at the workman behind her, who had just asked the barmaid for two beers. His mouth was still open.

The workman and the barmaid looked straight at each other. Then she shivered and he twitched. And that was that; they were changed. Their bodies and their faces appeared identical, but were not. Their stance, balance, body language – what you will; that changed, in an instant and almost more than I'd have believed possible, as though every muscle in their bodies had flicked instantaneously to a completely different setting, carrying their skeletons and organs with them.

I was still in the process of realising what had just happened when my pirate captain stepped back, away from me, the bar and the workman, just as the barmaid grabbed at something under the bar and the workman kicked out savagely. My companion folded back from the man's kick, which roundhoused past and would have caught me on the thigh if I hadn't jumped away too.

The sword was in her hand with a noise like the wind through a fence, flashing in the light as she lunged forward. The workman was still turning from the momentum of his kick; the sword's blade seemed to slip into his neck and his own rotation opened a line across his throat in a pink spray as his booted foot finally connected with the bar. His right hand started to go up to his throat as the masked girl swung one leg to knock both of his from under him. He started to fall to the floor, clutching his neck.

The barmaid brought the club up only a little too late. A scything stroke from the thin sword caught her laterally across both breasts and one arm, making the baggy jumper flap like wet rags as her face screwed up with pain and she thudded back against the gallery, bringing bottles crashing down. My pirate captain, meanwhile, was stamping one heavy heel into the groin of the workman, who had just hit the floor, shoulders first. She barely glanced at him as he rolled into a ball. She did glance at the other workman, who was sitting where he had been all the time, open-mouthed. She peeked over the bar where the barmaid was lying, also curled up, blood spreading from an arm slashed to the bone, bottles and glasses still falling and crunching and settling around her.

I had stepped back from all this mayhem, closer to the door. My pirate captain glanced again at the remaining workman, who looked like he was trying to decide whether to rise from the table or not. I was guessing he'd decide not. She sheathed her sword and went to take me by one arm. "Time to go, sir."

I moved to take her by the arm instead and started to move with her to the door. Then I was hit by a sudden feeling like a kind of sideways vertigo, a sensation instantly identifiable to any transitioner as *slew*, the result of one's consciousness having been dragged into a fractionally different world. Nothing visible had altered and the fragre of the place seemed the same, but something had effectively changed around us, something small but concentrated, hard and important. During my field training I'd been particularly bad at identifying slew, but it was one of those skills that had improved with experience and I'd never had it as strongly as now. Something told me that whatever it was had changed, it was behind us. I felt the hairs on the back of my neck start to rise. My little pirate captain stiffened and jerked as though she had felt the same thing. Her hand darted to her sword as she began to turn.

The shot filled the small room in an instant, ending all other sound but for ringing in the ears. The flash, from the table where the other workman sat, seemed almost to come after the noise. My pirate captain was spun round, thudding into my chest. She started to go limp as I went to hold her. I tried to grasp the pommel of her sword, glancing at the man who had shot her. The workman who had been sitting in the back all this time carried himself quite differently now. He held a small, flat-looking gun and was rising from the table, his free hand spread out to me as he shook his head.

"Hunting in packs now," the dying girl in my arms muttered. "Motherfuckers." I looked down into her eyes. She was a dead weight now and her sword was unreachable as the workman started towards us. Weakly, she brought one hand up and for a moment I thought she was about to remove the mask. It looked as if moving that arm and keeping her head from flopping forward was taking all her remaining strength. Then I saw that she held something like a tiny gun in her hand. She put it under her jaw near her neck. "Another time, Tem," she murmured. The second workman had almost reached us.

"Don't—" I had time to say. Then something clicked and hissed and a second later she went perfectly slack, sagging in my arms.

"Fuck!" the second workman said, kicking the tiny device from her hand.

I caught the heel of his boot and swung him round and down so that he whacked into the floor even more heavily than his comrade. I rolled the pirate captain's body on top of him, unsheathing her sword as I stood. I had one foot on her bloody back, so pinning him beneath her, and the sword's tip just breaking the skin of his wrist on the hand still clutching the gun, ready to skewer him to the floorboards if necessary before he got his breath back.

"Cavan!" he gasped. "Your name is Mark Cavan. We're on your side! We're Concern!" The bar girl made a sound that might have been meant to be a confirmation of this. The other man, foetal on the floor, just moaned. "We're Concern!" the man with the gun repeated. "L'Expédience! We were sent!"

My little pirate captain – or whoever's body she had inhabited for the evening – bled to death on top of him while I thought about this.

Perhaps inspired by such memories, I squeeze the little ormolu box just so, releasing a tiny white pill. I swallow it with the last of my G&T and promptly order another, for the sport of seeing whether it'll arrive in time for me to take a first sip.

I look down, watching for more breaks in the cloud – going dark as the horizon seeps to oranges and reds above the sinking sun now – but the cloud is unbroken. I start to slip into the transitioning trance, already half disconnected from this world. The steward is approaching with my gin and tonic when I feel the sneeze coming on. I *ach-oo!*

When I open my eyes my first thought is, I was in seat A4: that is a type of paper in Europe, a class of steam locomotive from mid-twentieth-century Britain and as far as the white player's queen's rook's pawn can travel on its first move, though it blocks an obvious diagonal for the queen or the queen's-side bishop to apply pressure on the centre of . . .

Pressure. Yes, pressure. I feel pressure. Pressure on my knees and on each shoulder.

The interior of the plane is darker and it is full night; the windows are all either black or closed by plastic shutters. The airy spacing of first class is gone; I am crammed in with ranks and rows of people, mostly sleeping in slightly reclined seats. A baby is crying. The engines sound a little noisier and I have a lot less leg room, my knees touching the tilted seat back in front. I look to each side, already knowing that something is wrong. The pressure on my shoulders is coming from two very large tanned Caucasian men, one on each side of me, each half a head taller than me and much broader. They both have crew-cuts and wear dark suits over white shirts. The one on my right encloses both my wrists in one gigantic hand. Under his grip, I am wearing handcuffs.

"Gesundheit, Mr Dise," the other one says. "Welcome to wherever you think you are." He reaches into my jacket pocket and removes the little ormolu pill case before I can do anything about it.

"What the—" I splutter.

"We'll take that," he tells me smoothly, sliding the pillbox into a shirt pocket.

My wrists remain crushed inside the other one's locked fist. I try to lift my arms, even though I would still be handcuffed. To no avail; I am strong, but I feel like a small child gripped by an adult.

"Who the hell do you—" I have time to say, before the one who has relieved me of my pills brings an absurdly massive fist sailing up into my face.

6

Patient 8262

B eyond the beginning, nothing. At the beginning, a torrent of universes in a single timeless blink that is the mother and father of all explosions and is the opposite of an explosion, destroying nothing – destroying nothing but Nothing – but purely creating; snapping into existence the first semblance of order and chaos and the very idea of time, all at once. This takes both the entirety of for ever and precisely no time whatsoever.

After the beginning, all else.

Expansion beyond expansion; an explosion that does not dissipate or slow or lose energy but instead does quite the opposite, bursting out for evermore with increasing power, intensity, complexity and scope.

We were taught to envisage it.

"Close your eyes," we were told, and we did. I lie here, eyes closed, listening to the sounds of the clinic – a clank of pans, a patient in a distant room coughing, the tinny gabble of the radio at the nurses' station down the echoing hall – and I think back to that day and that lecture hall, my eyes closed along with those of everybody else in the class, listening, imagining, trying to learn, attempting to see.

From far enough away, it would look like a sphere, like a world with a troubled, ever-changing and expanding surface, or a vast, growing star. Within the limits of our understanding, it was simply the idea of roundness, in as many dimensions as you fooled yourself into thinking you could imagine.

This is the true Universe, the universe of universes, the absolute beyond-which-there-is-nothing foundation of all. Utterly ungraspable, of course, though if you had envisaged it, as above, you had in a sense already transcended it because you'd thought of looking at it from outside, when there is and could be no outside. Which could be seen as a victory of sorts, though the idea of clutching at straws always came to my mind when that was suggested.

Some things mean too much to matter. This was the exemplar of that. For any sort of usable meaning you had to look closer at the surface of that unstoppably burgeoning immensity.

"Keep your eyes closed. Envisage this," our tutor told us.

We sat in a lecture theatre in the Speditionary Faculty of the University of Practical Talents, in the city of Aspherje, Calbefraques. Our tutor had instructed us to close our eyes, to remove distractions and make the envisioning easier. There were a few giggles, yelps and hisses as those students not taking the matter entirely seriously used the fact that those nearby had their eyes closed to tickle, prod or grope.

Our tutor sighed theatrically. "Yes, my apologies to the rest of you; there may be a delay while the last percentile present mature beyond primary-school behaviour." She changed her voice, became more businesslike. "Just keep imagining that ultimate roundness," she told us. "And think yourself closer to it. Imagine a surface: highly complex, wrinkled, ridged, fissured, with continually growing structures like trees, bushes, covered in tendrils and filaments."

"Ma'am," a male voice said, already amused with itself, "I'm looking at a giant crinkly hairy ball."

"You're looking at a punitive essay if you speak again, Meric. Be quiet." Another loud sigh. "Keep looking closer," she told us. "Closer still," she said, sounding amused and serious both. "Those of you with memories and imaginations beyond the insect stage may wish to invoke the idea of fractals at this point, because that would help. Assuming that you have successfully imagined a maximally complex surface on Mr Meric's giant hairy ball –" she paused for a smatter of amusement "– you need to keep on imagining just more of the same no matter how much further in you zoom. The tiniest hair, the most microscopic tendril reveals, on closer inspection, that it too has a surface composed of ridges and wrinkles and tree shapes and filaments and so on, effectively identical to what you were looking at before you zoomed in. That'll be your fractals made real, that will. The closer you go, the deeper you look and the higher you turn your magnification, the more of the same you see. Only the scale has changed."

"I'm struggling to imagine this, ma'am," said one of the girls.

"Good. If you're struggling you're still trying, you haven't given in. Keep trying. You'll get there. And do try to keep in mind that this is not really happening just in three dimensions or even four, but many more."

"How many more, ma'am?" asked one of the boys.

"A lot."

"Just 'A lot', ma'am?"

"Yes. For now, just 'A lot.'" She paused. You might almost have called it a hesitation. "This is one reason that extremely wise, intelligent and knowledgeable people like myself bother to teach unutterably ignorant and callow people like yourselves when we could be happily feet-up in front of a big log fire reading a book, or talking urbanely amongst ourselves about the latest exciting idea or faculty gossip. There is, despite all the many, many appearances to the contrary, just a sliver of a chance that one of the better minds in this class might answer one of the questions that no one of my generation – despite the aforesaid wisdom, intelligence, et cetera – or any previous generation has been able to answer definitively, like why is Calbefraques unique, why is a transitioned soul unique, where is everybody, where did septus come from originally and precisely how does it work? That sort of question."

A few people quietly went, "*Ooo!*"

"Yes, do let it go to your heads," she said drily. "You're not here to learn how to memorise stuff, you're here to learn how to—"

"Think!" a few voices chorused.

You could hear the smile in her voice. "Well memorised," she said, then raised her voice. "Of course, if you're really smart, you'll be imagining all this complexity that you're looking at zooming out to meet you as you zoom in to meet it, the surface growing explosively, exponentially, all the time."

"Excuse me, ma'am, I was already imagining that."

"And I imagine your handwritten essay on, oh, the history of fractal theory will contain spelling mistakes, Meric. In fact, probably the closer I look, the more I'll find."

"Aw, ma'am . . ."

"Aw, ma'am, nothing. Fifteen hundred words. On my desk by tomorrow morning. What do we say, Meric?"

"We say thank you, Mrs Mulverhill."

"Just so."

Adrian

Scotland is wet and dreary. Don't let anybody tell you different. Even the hills are mostly just big mounds, not proper mountains like the Alps or the Rockies. People will tell you it's all romantic and rugged but I've yet to see the evidence. Even when it's nice it's covered in a cloud of these bastard little insects called midges so you have to stay inside anyway. Plus it's full of Scots. Case rested.

I endured the week we spent in Glen Furquart or whatever it was called. That's what I did, I endured it. I did not enjoy it. Even the shooting was a bit shit. I don't know why but I thought we'd be shooting rifles at deer or moose or Highland cattle or something, but no, it was shotguns, at birds. Shotguns. Like we were in a fucking Guy

Ritchie movie or something. They were very nice shotguns with scrolling or whatever and engravings and stuff and they were heirlooms and blah blah blah, but still just shotguns. Shooters for the hard of aiming. And we were shooting them at birds. Lots and lots of birds. Pheasants. If there's a stupider bird on the fucking planet I wouldn't like to see it. Pig shit would get an honours degree by comparison.

When we were driving up there we saw a pheasant standing on the grass on our side of the road, halfway up a long straight on the A9. Few hundred metres ahead of us. There was this long stream of cars heading the other way towards us, just coming level with the bird. Suddenly the pheasant ran across the road, almost like it was aiming for the front car. We were all convinced the silly fucker was going to get hit. Miraculously, it didn't. Maybe the driver braked – though he couldn't brake hard, not with that line of traffic behind him – but anyway the bird got across to the other side with about a millimetre to spare. When it skidded to a stop on the grass verge on the far side you could see it get rocked sideways with the slipstream of the car passing. Then once the first car had whooshed past it the stupid fucker of a bird changed its mind and started running back across the road in the direction it had just come! The third or fourth car in the big line of traffic hit it full on and the thing exploded in a cloud of feathers. Everybody just drove on, obviously. But I mean. How stupid can you get?

Anyway, they breed them just to shoot them, which also seems a bit shit, though whether they do the same with the deer too I don't know. Can't imagine the deer are as stupid as pheasants, though.

I'd taken plenty of coke with me for the week but I was actually trying to pull Barney off it. I was wanting to get well in with Mr Noyce senior and being his boy's dealer maybe wasn't the best long-term position to be in. Barney wasn't a cunt but he was a bit of a fuckwit, know what I mean? Sooner or later he'd have used my dealing him stuff against me. Threaten to tell his dad on me, basically. I couldn't be having that. I had plans. Mr Noyce was part of them. Barney wasn't.

We drank well. I was letting Mr N teach me about wine, and I did develop a taste for single malts, properly watered. So at least something good comes out of Scotland. We ate well, too. Not too much pheasant, thank God. The house was a sort of fake castle, a Victorian take on what they thought the Scots ought to have been building, with decent plumbing and no-nonsense central heating. I was definitely with the Victorians there.

Once again I hadn't brought Lysanne, the girl friend, along. She'd have hated it. All that rain and no shops. Dulcima, Barney's girl, hated it too, but I think she just wanted to keep close to Barney. At the time I thought it was cos he might be having second thoughts about her and his eyes had started roving again but later I decided she just liked that he always had lots of drugs and never asked her to help pay for them.

Dizzy bint even tried it on with me once in the back of a Land Rover coming back from a shoot, can you believe it? Hand on me tackle through me moleskin plus fours or whatever they're called and whispered did I want her to come to my room that night after Barney had conked out, her wearing a pair of waders and nothing else?

I mean, she's a gorgeous girl, and I'd certainly had thoughts about her, and my cock definitely liked the idea – this was towards the end of the week and it was getting to know my palm like the back of my hand, know what I mean? But fuck me, really. Dangerous ground. Too dangerous. A complication I devoutly didn't need. I told her I thought she was the most humpable thing I'd seen all year and if I wasn't such a good friend of Barney's . . . She took it pretty well, all told. Maybe just after a bit of reassurance that she was still lusciously fuckable. Some girls are like that.

Long week, but worth it. We escaped eventually, back down the long long road to civilisation. I'd got on extremely well with Mr N. I'd dropped a hint that I was looking to take on a proper job, something serious, like what Mr N did. Nothing too obvious, but still a hint.

Next time I saw Mr and Mrs Noyce I took Lysanne. We went up to his family's place in Lincolnshire on the coast near Alford. The place was called Dunstley but they called it D'unstable because it was right on the edge of the sea, standing at the end of a road on a sort of sandy cliff above a wave-washed beach. They were on their third garden fence because the other two had disappeared into the North Sea during storms and the garden had shrunk by two-thirds – nearly ninety feet, according to Mr Noyce – in the last forty years.

This time Barney and Dulcima weren't there. Other things to do. So it looked like I'd made it to friend, not just friend of son. En route to protégé, with a bit of luck. Excuse my French.

Mr N thought Lysanne was a laugh, which was a relief. I could see her weighing him up soon as we arrived and could almost spot the point at dinner on the first night when she looked from him to Mrs N and realised that there was no opening there for her to exploit. That was a relief, too. No play that a girl like her could have made for a guy like him could have lasted longer than a night, but she could have messed things up for me. Mrs N exchanged a look with me over coffee that made me think she'd had pretty much the same feeling re Lysanne as I'd had.

The house was young compared to Spetley Hall; Edwardian, built at the turn of the last century. Whitewashed brick and painted wood compared with mossy stone and polished panel. Great big salt-streaked draughty windows instead of tiny little leaded draughty windows. Very light by comparison, full of morning sunshine coming in from the sea and sparkling.

"It's all about confidence," Mr N told me. We were standing in the garden after dinner looking at the latest fence while the waves breaking on the beach below glowed in the last of the evening night. Lysanne and Mrs N were further down the garden. I could hear Lysanne shrieking with laughter at something Mrs N had said. Mr N was slurring his words just a little and at first I thought he'd said "conference" but actually it was "confidence."

"What, like a trick?" I asked.

Edward laughed. "Maybe. A little harsh, but maybe. Confidence is what keeps the whole show on the road. You need confidence – faith, even – to keep putting one foot in front of the other. Arguably, if you just stopped the whole edifice would collapse." He glanced at me. "It's also about value, but there's the rub. What is value? Value is what people think it is. A thing is worth what somebody will pay for it. But then somebody pays what everybody thinks is an outrageous price for something, a price everybody 'knows' is idiotic, and yet if they can offload it for even more to somebody else then it really was worth at least what they paid for it, wasn't it? The profit is the proof. Though of course if they get caught with it, when it becomes horribly clear that it wasn't worth anything like what they paid, then they were wrong and everybody who 'knew' they were wrong gets proved right." He sipped his whisky. "The difficult thing is to spot reliably who's right and who's wrong by buying in before a stock gets too expensive and get out before it becomes clear it's actually like somebody in a cartoon who's just walked over the edge of a cliff and only doesn't fall because they haven't realised yet. You know, like Tom and Jerry."

I'd been thinking Road Runner myself, but I knew what he meant. We both watched the waves for a moment. "Is that the Invisible Hand holding them up, then?" I asked.

Mr N laughed again. "The Invisible Hand. Well, that's just an article of faith. That's another myth. Like we're a twenty-four-hour society. No, we're not; the markets aren't. They close at teatime every day in whatever city they're in, there's nothing between New York and Sydney and they're shut the whole of the weekend. And holidays. Just as well too or I'd never get any time off. What do you think of the whisky?"

I shook my head, frowned. "I'm not sure. It's quite sweet and a bit peaty. I sort of want to say an Islay but I don't think it is. Could be a Talisker that I haven't had before but I'm still thinking about it." I shrugged and looked bashful. "Leave it with me?" Mr N grinned and nodded, looking almost proud of me. This uncertainty was all bollocks by the way. It was a Highland Park from the Orkney Islands. I knew cos even though Mr N had poured it while I wasn't looking I'd spotted the bottle on the sideboard with the dribbly bits running back down the inside when he'd handed it to me, so I knew. But I needed to go through the charade to make it look good, didn't I?

"It is a confidence trick," Edward said, staring out to sea again. "All banks are technically insolvent and all PLCs are one-way bets, or they bloody should be if you handle them right. If they work you keep the profits and if they don't you close them down and the money they owe to other companies or other people is just left hanging. *You* don't go bankrupt, not if you've arranged things right. Shareholder, director, MD. That's what the Limited bit of Public Limited Company means, you see? Limited liability. Not the same as a partnership, or being a Name at Lloyd's." He waved his arm at the waves, spilling a little of the whisky. There had been quite a few G&Ts and bottles of wine before the whiskies.

"Really?" I said. I wasn't sure this sounded right. I guess I must have looked dubious.

"There you are, you see?" Edward said. "A civilian, a very naive person, might think that if a group of people got together, borrowed a lot of money to start a business, ordered lots of plant and equipment and raw materials without paying for them and then made a complete mess of it and lost everything they would somehow still owe all that money, but they don't. If what they started was a PLC then the company becomes a sort of honorary person, do you see? *It* owes the money, not *them*. If it goes under then it goes into administration and its assets are sold off and if those don't cover what was owed then that's too bad. As long as they stayed within the letter of the law throughout you can't touch the directors or the shareholders. The money's just gone. Of course, if it's all a great success, then hurrah. All shall have prizes. See what I mean? One-way bet."

"Jesus, Edward, you're starting to sound like a commie."

"Right-wing Marxist, Adrian," Mr N said briskly. He nodded once, still staring out to sea. "As a matter of fact I did flirt with Socialism, in my youth."

"That when you were at university, was it?"

He smiled. "Yes. University. But then I saw how much more comfortable life could be as one of the exploiters rather than one of the exploited. Plus I decided that if the proles were so stupid as to let themselves be exploited, who was I to stand in their way?" He smiled at me, his sparse, sandy hair ruffled by the wind. "So I went over to the Dark Side. Cheers." He drank.

I laughed. "That must make Barney Luke Skywalker."

He shook his head. "I'm afraid I don't know *Star Trek* well enough to say who he'd be. Not Doctor Spock, that's for sure."

I almost didn't correct him. But it was such an obvious one he might say it to somebody else who would and then I'd look like I was being what do you call it? Obsequious or something. So I said, "You're getting your stars tangled" and explained.

"Yes, well," he said airily, waving his glass again. He turned to me. "And which side are you on, Adrian?"

"I'm on me own side, Mr N. Always have been, always will be."

He looked like he was studying me for a moment. "Best side to be on." He nodded, and drained his glass.

(Ensemble)

It began with Dr Seolas Plyte. The good doctor was asleep in the with-drawing room off his study in the Speditionary Faculty of the University of Practical Talents in Aspherje when it happened. His favourite mistress, still lying on top of him on the chaise longue in a haze of post-coital torpor, jerked once, exactly as she might have had she too been in the act of falling asleep. She reached down, took him purposefully in her arms and before he could properly wake they were both gone.

Ms Pum Jésusdottir was hiking in the Himalayan Hills when they came for her. A long-laggard world this one, where the Indian subcontinent had barely begun its slow crash into Asia. Here, the highest point in the Himalayas was tree-covered and less than thirteen hundred metres above sea level. She was walking alone along a recently blazed trail beneath tall plane trees dripping from a recent shower, stepping from side to side of the track to avoid the stream of water that it carried, reflecting that if you made a path in an environment of high precipitation without also making ditches then really you just made a stream bed, when she saw the girl sitting – hunched, hugging her knees, staring ahead – a short way up the path.

She couldn't have been more than thirteen or fourteen; one of the native tribal girls, dressed conservatively ankle to neck in a black caftanne, her hair gathered in a net, fingers glittering with rings. The girl didn't look at the older woman as she approached. She just sat staring straight ahead, across the path. From a few metres away, Jésusdottir could see that the girl was shaking, and had been crying.

"Hello?" she said. The girl looked at her, sniffing, but did not reply. Ms Jésusdottir tried Hindic. The girl's expression changed. She rose, standing, unfolding herself, and smiled at the older woman, who only then felt the first pang of fear in her gut. "Oh, Ms Jésusdottir, I have some bad news."

Brashley Krijk disappeared from his yacht while cruising in the Eastern Middlearthean, off Chandax, on the isle of Girit.

Der Graf Heurtzloft-Beiderkern heard somebody come into the opera box behind him. He assumed it was one of his sons returning; they had both left earlier to indulge their cigar habit in the corridor outside and to flirt with any young ladies they happened to encounter. Whoever it was, they slipped in while the coloratura soprano was just launching into her final and most heart-rending solo. But for that, he might have looked round.

Commandante Odil Obliq, peril of the Orient as an admiring enemy had once described her, was dancing with her new lover, the admiral

115

of her ekranoplan assault squadron, in the moonlit ruins of New Quezon while a blindfolded orchestra did their best to out-voice the Howler Orangs that were ululating from the tumbled stones and twisted metal frames of the most recently destroyed buildings. Across the plaza, from which the wreckage had been cleared by chain gangs of defeated Royalists, came a waiter carrying a tray with their champagne and cocaine.

They stopped dancing, both smiling at the fat old eunuch waddling towards them with the tray.

"Commandante," he wheezed. "Admiral."

"Thank you," Obliq said. She picked the silver straw from the tray. At the ends of her long ebony fingers, her nails were painted in swirling green camouflage, as a joke. She handed the straw to the admiral. "After you."

"We shall never sleep," the admiral sighed, bending slightly to the tray and the first two lines of powder, glowing white in the moonlight.

She handed the straw to the commandante, who had taken the opportunity to sip some of the champagne. Then the admiral's expression changed. She gripped Obliq's hand and said, "There's something wrong . . ."

Obliq stiffened, her hand dropping the silver straw and going to her holstered pistol.

Her earpiece crackled. "Commandante!" her ADC radioed, his voice desperate.

The eunuch waiter hissed, twisted his hand under the tray so that it began to fall, taking the champagne flutes and the rest of the cocaine with it while the pistol revealed underneath pointed straight at the commandante. Obliq had already started to drop, going limp in the admiral's arms and falling as though in a faint, but it meant only that the chest shot the eunuch had aimed at her became a head shot. The admiral stared on blankly as the first shot was followed by two more before the nearest guards finally woke up and started shooting.

* * *

The assassination teams sent after Mrs Mulverhill could find no recent trace of her anywhere.

The Transitionary

When I wake, I am in some pain and tied to a chair. Altogether, this is not a satisfactory turn of events.

I underwent some training to cover such situations, and know enough to wake slowly without, one would hope, giving any sign of having woken. This is the theory. In practice I have never been convinced that this is really possible. If you're unconscious you're unconscious – so by no means in full control of what your body is doing – and if you're unconscious you're probably unconscious for a good reason, like some gorilla in a suit smacking you so hard in the face that your nose seems to be broken, you cannot breathe normally, you have bled copiously down your naked chest, two of your front teeth feel loose and the whole forward portion of your face feels swollen and suffused with bruised blood.

I am hanging forward in the seat as far as my bonds will allow, my chin nearly on my chest, my gaze falling naturally on my own lap. I'm naked. My thighs are bloodstained, brightly lit. I become more fully aware, wallowing my way to consciousness like a nearly waterlogged lump of wood rising slowly to the surface of a cold and sluggish stream. I have taken the most immediate and rudimentary stock of the situation and am just starting carefully – without giving any outward signs of movement – to flex the appropriate muscle groups to test precisely how tightly I am tied to the chair, when a male voice says, "Don't bother, Temudjin, we can tell you're awake. And don't waste your time testing the wires and the chair, either. You're not going anywhere. We know what you're doing because it was us who taught you to do it."

I think briefly about this. My captors seem to know exactly how I am trained to react in such a situation, and they appear to be claiming that they are my own people, or at least that they helped to train me. The individual addressing me is probably not of first-rank education.

I bring my head up, stare into the darkness between a pair of lights pointed at me from a couple of metres away and say, with all the fluency I can muster, "It was *we* who taught you to do it."

I'm expecting a "What?" or a "Huh?" but he just pauses and then says, "Whatever. The point is we'll know what you're trying to do at every stage. You'll save us both a lot of time and yourself some pain if you drop the tradecraft stuff."

An ominous phrase. "At every stage of what?" is the obvious question. I can see nothing beyond the lights. As well as the two to each side of straight ahead there are two more I can see, one level with each shoulder, and from the shadows beneath my chair I guess there are another two behind me. I am encircled with brightness. The voice talking to me is male and I do not recognise it. It might be that of the wide-shouldered man who talked to me on the aircraft, but I don't know. His voice is coming from directly behind me, I think. Listening to it, I get the impression that I am in a large room. I don't seem to be able to smell anything, except my own blood: a sharp, metallic scent. The fragre of the place, the information from that extra sense that people like myself have, indicates a world I have not visited before, and a place which feels confused somehow, full of clashing, competing historical and cultural sensations. I check my languages. English. Nothing else.

That is unprecedented. I do not have even the language of my home or my base reality in the house in the trees on the ridge looking out over the town with the casino, where my original self wanders round the place dead-eyed and monosyllabic.

Now I feel fear.

"At every stage of this interrogation," the man's voice says, as though in reply to my earlier thought.

"Interrogation?" I repeat. Even to my own ears it sounds as though I have a heavy cold. I try to snort back some of the blood blocking

118

my nose but succeed only in producing a sensation akin to somebody having just stuck a large metal spike in the centre of my face.

"Interrogation," the man confirms. "To determine what you know, or what you think you know. To discover who is controlling you, or who you think is controlling you. To find out what it is you think you're doing—"

"Or what I think I think I'm doing," I offer. Silence. I shrug. "I was spotting the pattern," I tell him.

"Yes," he says, sounding tired. "Be clever about it, give cheek, be defiant and even insult the intelligence of the interrogator, so that when you are put to the question your collapse will be all the more abject and your apparent degree of cooperation all the more complete. As I said, Temudjin, we did train you, so we know how you'll respond."

I let my head drop so that I am looking at my bloodstained thighs. "Ah, the infinite cowardice of the torturer," I mutter.

"What?" he says. I did mutter very quietly.

I raise my head again. I try to sound tired and world-weary. "How easy it is to be so confident and to sound so in charge when the person you're talking to is tied down, utterly helpless and at your mercy. None of that annoying freedom of action for the other party that might let a person fight back, or just leave, or speak as they want to speak rather than as they hope – in their desperation and terror – you want them to speak. Does all that make you feel good? Does it give you that sensation of power people always denied you in normal life, so unfairly? Does it give you what you always missed when you were growing up? Did the other children bully you? Did your father abuse you? Overly strict potty training? Really, I'd love to know: what's your excuse? What aspect of your upbringing fucked you up to the point that doing this seemed like such a promising career? Do tell."

I didn't really expect to get to the end of this speech. I thought he'd appear out of the shadows and start laying into me. That he's done no such thing may be a very good sign or a very bad one. I have no idea. I've somewhat gone off-piste here.

119

"Oh, Temudjin, you must have made that bit up yourself," he says, sounding amused. My heart sinks. "Are you *trying* to get beaten to a pulp?" He gives a snorting laugh. "What in *your* past made you such a masochist?"

It may be time for a change of tack. I sigh, nod. "Hmm. I see your point. Serves me right for extemporising."

"That's another thing we're going to be asking you about."

"Extemporising?"

"Yes."

"Ah ha."

I have not been entirely open with you, I suppose. There should be a way out of this. A way that they don't know about, a way that this faceless, unseen interrogator doesn't know about. But I think it might have been taken from me. I have hardly dared to make sure until now, and it has not been as immediately obvious as it would have been had I not been punched so hard in the face. I put my head down again and move my tongue around in my mouth, probing.

There is a hole in my lower left jaw where a tooth has been removed. It feels gaping, and very fresh. That would be my last hope of escaping with a single bound, gone.

"Yes," the man says. I suppose he saw some movement about my mouth or jaw. "We took that too. Thought we didn't know about it, didn't you?"

"So did you know about it?"

"We might have," he says. "Or maybe we just found it."

It was a partially hollowed-out tooth, the space within concealed beneath a tiny hinged ceramic crown. I kept one of my little transitioning pills in there; an emergency dose of septus in case I ever miscounted and ran out of them, or had the little ormolu box stolen, or it failed to make a transition with me. Or I found myself in a situation like this.

Well, so much for that.

I lift my head up. "Okay. So, what do you want to know?"

*   *   *

I had been here before, in a minor key. I hadn't been tied to the chair with wire, and the light hadn't been in my eyes but there had been a chair and a man asking me questions, something had certainly gone wrong and there had been at least one death.

"Didn't you suspect?"

"Suspect what? That she might be one of us?"

"Yes."

"It crossed my mind. I thought—"

"When did it cross your mind?"

"When we were standing in front of a map of the world in the Doge's Palace. She said something about it being just the one world, and that being limiting."

"What did you think then?"

"I thought she was one of the guests staying here, somebody from the Concern I just hadn't happened to bump into; late arrival, maybe." We were back in the Palazzo Chirezzia, the black and white palace overlooking the Grand Canal.

"You didn't think to ask her this outright?"

"I could have been wrong. I might have misheard or misunderstood. Trying to discover whether she was Aware or not by just asking her would have been an unnecessary risk, don't you think?"

"You were not intrigued?"

"I was very intrigued. Masked ball, mystery woman, the back alleys of Venice. I'm not sure how much more intriguing something can get."

"Why did you leave the ball with her?"

I laughed. "Because I thought she might want to fuck me, of course."

"There is no need for coarse language, Mr . . . Cavan."

I sat back and put my hand over my eyes. "Oh for fuck's sake," I breathed.

I was talking to the man who had shot and killed my little pirate captain. He was called Ingrez and did not appear to have forgiven me for getting the better of him in the bar an hour or so earlier.

He wore a neat bandage over his right wrist, where I'd punctured it with the pirate captain's sword. He was no longer in the workman's clothes. He'd changed into a black suit and grey polo neck. He certainly didn't carry himself like a workman now. He looked like somebody used to giving rather than taking orders. He also had to be something of a specialist transitioner, a real adept, if he was able to take something as substantial as a gun between worlds with him; few of us could do that. I could, just, but it took a lot of effort. It was his effort, doing just that, that had been responsible for the hit of slew I'd experienced a second or two before he'd shot the girl. He had a broad, tanned, open-looking face with a lot of laughter lines that looked possessed, haunted by something much darker and without humour.

After I'd withdrawn the sword from his wrist and helped him to his feet there had barely been time for any explanations before two of Professore Loscelles's larger servants had burst through the door of the bar, their right hands rather ostentatiously inside their jackets. They had looked like they were spoiling for a fight and seemed disappointed that they had arrived too late, having instead to act as nurses to the two injured members of the team. Ingrez got one of them to walk us to the canal a minute away where the launch that had brought them sat idling, its engine loud in the narrow spaces between the darkened buildings. It sat lightless, its driver wearing what looked like a pair of binoculars strapped to his head. It brought Ingrez and me back to the Palazzo Chirezzia, then sped away again. It kept its light on while it was on the Grand Canal.

I was asked to wait in a second-floor bedroom. There was a stout black grille over the window and the door was locked. No telephone. So that when I was escorted here, to the Professore's study, I was still wearing my priestly fancy dress.

Ingrez cleared his throat. "Were there any other points at which you thought she might be Aware?" he asked.

"Just before you arrived," I told him, "when she said something about not travelling, about me being off duty."

"Any other points?"

"No," I said. "She mentioned the word 'emprise.' Said it means a dangerous undertaking. Does that mean anything to you?"

"I know the word," Ingrez admitted, after the tiniest of hesitations. "What does it mean to you?"

"I'd never heard it before. Now I'm not sure what it should mean. Is it important?"

"I couldn't say. But she did not try to recruit you?"

"Into what?" I asked, mystified.

"She made you no offers?"

"Not even the one I was hoping she might make, Mr Ingrez." I tried a regretful smile. I might have spared myself the effort.

"What offer would that have been?"

I sighed. "The one involving she and I having sex," I said quietly, as one might explain something obvious to an idiot. I paused. "For fornication's sake," I added. Ingrez just sat looking blankly at me. "How did you know about all this?" I asked him. "Who was she? What was she doing? Why did she want to contact me in the first place? Why were you trying to stop her, or catch her or . . . what?"

He looked at me for a while longer. "I am unable to answer any of those questions at this moment in time," he told me. It didn't even sound like he was trying to keep the tone of satisfaction out of his voice.

Madame d'Ortolan and I walked amongst the tombs and tall cypresses crowding the walled cemetery isle of San Michele, in the Venetian lagoon. The bright blue sky was strewn with ragged clouds, in the south-west already turning pale red in the late-afternoon sunset.

"Her name is Mrs Mulverhill," she told me.

I sensed her turning her head to look at me as she told me this. I kept my eyes on the path ahead between the rows of marble tombs and dark metal grilles. "She was one of my tutors," I said. I tried to say it as matter-of-factly as I could. Inside, I was thinking, It was *her*! Something sang within me.

"Indeed," Madame d'Ortolan said, pausing to pick a lily from a small vase attached to the wall of one of the tombs. She handed the flower to me. I was about to say something grateful but she said, "Remove the stamina, would you?" I looked at her, puzzled. She pointed into the heart of the flower. "The stamens. Those bits with the orange pollen. Would you pinch those out for me? Please? I'd do it myself but this body's fingers are so . . . chubby."

Madame d'Ortolan was inhabiting the body of a middle-aged lady with bright auburn hair and a tall, powerful body. She wore a two-piece suit of pink with purple edging and a white silk blouse. Her fingers did look a little thick. I reached into the bell of the flower, trying to avoid the pollen-laden ends. Madame d'Ortolan leant in, watching this intently. "Careful," she said, almost whispering.

I removed the stamens. Two of my fingertips were turned orange by the operation. I presented her with the flower. She snipped the stem with two long fingernails and inserted the bloom into a button-hole in her jacket.

"Mrs Mulverhill has been many things in the Concern," she told me. "An unAware enabler, an arrangements officer, a theatre-logistics supervisor, a transitionary, a lecturer – as you have pointed out – a transitioneering theorist in the Speditionary Faculty itself and now, suddenly, a traitor."

No, I thought, she was always a traitor.

"What is it that you think we do, Temudjin?" she asked me quietly, stroking my belly with one slow and gentle hand.

"My God," I breathed, "is this a heavily disguised tutorial?"

She pulled at one of the light brown hairs that grew in a fluted line beneath my belly button. I drew a breath in through my teeth, smacked at her hand. "Yes," she said, raising one dark eyebrow. "Do answer the question."

"Okay, then," I said, and stroked the stroking hand. "We are fixers." I was talking very quietly. The room was bathed in shadows, lit only by the embers of a near-dead fire and a single candle, still burning.

The only sounds were our voices and the soft susurration of rain on a window slanted into the ceiling. "We fix what is broken," I said, trying to paraphrase, trying not to repeat what she had told me, told us, told all her students. "Or stop things about to break from breaking in the first place."

"But why?" She tried to smooth down the hairs on my belly.

"Why not?"

"Yes, but why? Why do this?" She slicked her palm with saliva and attempted to make the hairs stay flat like that.

"Because it's worth doing," I said. "Because we feel it's worth doing and we can act on that feeling."

"But, all else aside, why is it worth doing when we are only so many and there is an infinitude of worlds?" She rubbed my belly as though it was a puppy and then gently smacked it.

"Because there might be an infinitude of people like us too, an infinite number of Concerns; we just haven't met them yet."

"Though the further we expand without encountering anybody else like us, the less likely the chances of that being true become."

"Well, that's infinity for you."

"Good," she said drily, and traced a circle round my belly button with one finger. "Though you skipped a bit. Before that, you are supposed to say that it is still worth doing some good rather than choosing to do none simply because it seems of so little significance."

"'Futility is self-imposed.'"

"Ah, so you weren't asleep after all." She cupped my balls. Very gently, she began to knead them, working her hand round them in a soft, continuous, curling motion.

"Ma'am, you always had my full attention." It had been an enjoyable if strenuous few hours, here in her dacha. I'd thought we were finished for the evening, and I'd have guessed so did she, but maybe not; under her hand's caress, I began to feel the first stirrings, once again.

"There is a grain to the fabric of space–time," she said. "A scale on which there is no further divisible smoothness, only individual, irreducible quanta where reality itself seethes with a continual effervescence of sub-microscopic creation and destruction. I believe there to be a similarly irreducible texture to morality, a scale beyond which it is senseless to proceed. Infinity goes in only one direction; outward, into more inhabited worlds, more shared realities. In the other direction, on a reducing scale, once you reach the level of an individual consciousness – for all practical purposes, a single human being – you can usefully reduce no further. It is at that level that significance lies. If you do something to benefit one person, that is an absolute gain, and its relative insignificance in the wider scheme is irrelevant. Benefit two people without concomitant harm to others – or a village, tribe, city, class, nation, society or civilisation – and the benefits are scalable, arithmetic. There is no excuse beyond fatalistic self-indulgence and sheer laziness for doing nothing."

"Absolutely. Let me do this." I reached over the golden scoop of her back and slid my hand down between her legs. She shifted, bringing herself a little closer so that I didn't have to stretch. She opened her legs a little, scissoring across the crumpled bedclothes. My thumb pressed lightly on the tiny dry flower of her anus while my fingers caressed her sex, already half lost in its moistness and heat.

"There you are," she said, sounding amused. "I am experiencing some benefit already." She became quiet for a while, moving her backside rhythmically up and down a little and pressing back against my exploring hand. She brushed some hair from her face, shifted up the bed to kiss me, fully, luxuriantly, one hand behind my head, cupping, then settled back again, her head down, hair veiling her face as I worked my fingers further into her. Her other hand closed round my cock, thumb stroking its glans, side to side.

"The question," she said, a little breathless now, "is who determines what is done, and to whom, on whose behalf, and precisely why; to what end?"

"Perhaps," I suggested, "we are working up to some sort of climax, a consummation."

Her body trembled, in what might have been a silent laugh. Or not. "Perhaps we are," she said, then caught her breath. "Ah. Yes, do keep doing that."

"That was my intention."

"Who benefits?" she murmured.

"Perhaps more than one group does," I suggested. "Perhaps those producing the benefit for those most in need also benefit. Why should it not be mutual?"

"That is one view," she said. She brought the hand not supporting her upper body, the one that had been stroking me, up to my mouth, half cupped. "Spit," she said through her dark fringe of hair. I drew more saliva into my mouth, raised my head and let it dribble into her palm. She brought the hand carefully down to her own mouth and did the same, worked the fingers into the glistening fluid on her skin – just seeing that made me harder still, when I'd have thought I couldn't be – then she set her hand around my cock once more, gripping it more firmly, moving her hand more forcefully now. I did the same, watching the sweet mounds of her buttocks shake as my fingers moved in and out of her.

"There is another view?" I asked.

"There might be," she said, each breath a gasp now. I was impressed that she could still concentrate on speaking at all. "With sufficient knowledge, if we were able to delve deeper into matters."

"One should," I said, swallowing, "always explore as thoroughly as possible." I cleared my throat. "You taught me that."

"I did," she agreed. Through her hanging fringe of hair, I could just make out that her eyes were tightly closed. "We do some good," she said, her voice raw now, her words clipped, bitten off, "but do we do as much as we might? Is not some of any good we do merely . . . collateral benefit created as we follow – unwittingly at our level, perhaps . . . perhaps quite deliberately by those in possession of more knowledge and power – some other and greater . . . greater . . . greater agenda?"

"Such as?"

"Who knows?" she said. "The point is . . . that by now we might be blind to such subterfuge. We trust our own forecasting techniques so fully that those in the field charged with doing the . . . doing the dirty work . . . blindly obey orders without a second thought, even though there is no obvious immediate or even medium-term benefit to be observed, because they have come to trust that genuine good will always accrue in the fullness of time; that's what's always happened and that's what they've been taught to expect, so it's what they accept and what they believe. Thus they do less than they think but more than they know. It is, if I am right, an astonishing trick; to conjure the symptoms of zealotry from those who believe they are being merely pragmatic, even utilitarian."

(When I first saw her, she was half sitting on a stone parapet, one slim trousered leg extended in front of her, the other drawn up beneath her rear, her face and body turned to one side as she talked to one of a group of men all but surrounding her. She held a glass in one hand and was in the act of laughing as she raised her other palm towards the chest of the tall man standing, also laughing, by her side. She was slim, compact and still seemed – even sitting, seemingly cornered, her back to the drop beyond the terrace edge – to dominate the company with a confident ease.

This was on a wide balcony of the Speditionary Faculty main building on the outskirts of central Aspherje. The view led the gaze out across the exquisitely terraced valley beneath to the forested undulations of the Great Park on the far side and then, over the encircling outer reaches of the city – hazily indistinct in the low evening rays – to the misty foothills guarding the still snow-bright peaks of the far Massif. It turned out that from her dacha in the hills you could see the University's Dome of the Mists on a clear day, though you had to stand on the cabin's roof to see over the trees.

I didn't know that on the evening when we first met, of course. Then it was close to sunset, the gold-leafed Dome shining like a second setting sun and the blond stones of the building and the multifarious skin tones of the faculty members, senior students and undergraduates all appearing rouged with that silky light. She wore a long jacket and a high-cut top, ruched but tight across her breasts.

". . . like an infinite set of electron shells," she was saying to one of the surrounding academics as I approached. "The set is still infinite but there are measurable, imaginable and innumerable spaces in between that can't be occupied."

She grasped my hand when we were introduced.

"Mr . . . *Oh?*" she said, one eyebrow flexing. She wore a small white pillbox hat with an attached veil, which seemed an absurd affectation, though the material was white, light as gauze and showed her face within. It was a face of some beauty; broadly triangular, with large, hooded eyes, a proud nose, dramatically flared nostrils and a small, full mouth. The expression was harder to read. You could have believed it was one of charmingly casual cruelty, or just a sort of amused indifference. She was maybe half as old again as me.

"Yes," I said. "Temudjin Oh." I could feel myself colouring. I'd long got used to the fact that my Mongolian-extraction surname could cause some amusement amongst English speakers determined to extract a toll of discomfiture from anybody whose name was not as banal or as ugly as theirs. However, there was something about the way she pronounced it that immediately brought a blush to my cheeks. Perhaps the sunset would cover my embarrassment.

I was no innocent, had known many women despite my relative lack of years and felt perfectly comfortable in the presence of my supposed superiors, but none of this appeared to matter. It was frustrating to feel reduced again, and so easily, to such callowness.

The handshake was brief and firm, almost more of a squeeze. "You must make many a partner jealous," she told me.

"I . . . yes," I said, not entirely sure what she was talking about.

I wanted her immediately. Of course I did. I fantasised about her outrageously over the next year and I'm sure I did significantly worse in my finals because I spent so many lectures distracting myself imagining all the things I wanted to do to her – there, draped over that lectern, against that blackboard, across that desk – when I should have been listening to what she was telling us. On the other hand I tried especially hard to impress her in tutorials with immaculately researched and devastatingly well-argued papers. So maybe it balanced out.)

"Been thinking about this?" I asked her. Her hand, sliding up and down my cock, was just starting to be less than perfectly blissful, becoming too hot and dry. "Reached any conclusion?"

She let go, raised her head, blew hair from her face and said, breathing hard, "Yes. I think you should fuck me. Now."

Later, we sat at the table, she in a sheet, me in my shirt, sharing some food, drinking water and wine.

"I've never asked. Is there a Mr Mulverhill?"

She shrugged. "I'm sure there is somewhere," she said, tearing bread from the loaf.

"Let me rephrase that. Are you married?"

"No." She glanced up. "You?"

"No. So . . . you were married."

"No," she said, smiling and sitting luxuriously back, stretching. "I just like the sound of the name."

I poured her more wine.

She ran her hand – fingers spread – across the candle flame.

Madame d'Ortolan adjusted her cropped lily blossom until it lay just so on her pink-jacketed breast. We paced the uneven flagstones between the gracefully looming tombs and wanly shining mausolea. The parched, faded flowers, left lovingly to adorn vases in front of some of the sepulchres, contrasted with the motley green scrub of vigorously healthy weeds pushing up between the stones.

"Mrs Mulverhill has gone renegade," Madame d'Ortolan told me. "She has lost her wits and found a cause, which appears to be attempting to frustrate us. She has used that famously imaginative mind of hers to concoct a lunatic theory so deranged that we cannot even grasp exactly what it is. But, at any rate, she thinks we take a wrong course, or some such idiocy, and opposes us. It is irritating, and ties up resources we could employ to more actively beneficial effect elsewhere, but so far she has done little real damage." She glanced at me. "That might change, obviously, should she grow more aggressive through frustration, or recruit any others to her cause."

"Do you think that's what she was trying to do with me?"

"Probably." Madame d'Ortolan stopped and we faced each other. "Why do you think she would approach you, particularly?" She smiled. Not entirely unconvincingly.

"Why, has she singled me out?" I asked. She just looked at me and raised her eyebrows. "Has she approached other people?" I asked her. "If she has, were they all transitioners?"

Madame d'Ortolan looked up at the sky, hands behind her back. I imagined the chubby fingers clasped awkwardly, tight. "It may not be in your best interest to know the answers to those questions," she said smoothly. "We would simply like to know if there is any special reason she may have had to choose to approach you."

"Perhaps she finds me attractive," I suggested, smiling. It was, if nothing else, a more sincere smile than Madame d'Ortolan's.

She leaned closer. A swirl of breeze brought a hint of her perfume to my nose; something flowery but cloying. "Do you mean," she said, "sexually?"

"Or just attracted to my sunny character in general."

"Or attractive in the sense that she thought you one of those more likely to go over to her cause," Madame d'Ortolan suggested, smile gone now, head tipped to one side, evaluating. Her expression was not unkind, but it was intent.

"I can't imagine why she would have thought that," I said, drawing myself up. In her heels, Madame d'O was as tall as me. "I would not expect or appreciate to be under any sort of suspicion just because that lady chose to approach me."

"You can't think why she did?"

"No. For all I know she's working her way through whatever group she's chosen alphabetically."

Madame d'Ortolan looked to be about to say something, then didn't. She snorted and turned. We resumed walking. For a while, nothing was said. A jet stroked a double strand of white across the sky, ploughing heaven.

"You are one of the first," she told me as we approached the landing stage where the Palazzo Chirezzia's launch waited. "We think she is targeting transitioners alone. We have people and techniques able to predict her movements and we have, we believe, been able to prevent her doing any real mischief so far. We shall need the full cooperation of all concerned to propagate that fortunate trend onwards into the future, as I'm sure you are entirely able to appreciate."

"Of course," I said. I left a pause, then said, "If the lady's cause is so arcane and her threat so trifling, why is it necessary to oppose her with such force?"

She stopped suddenly and we turned, facing each other. Our eyes never truly flash, of course; we are not the luminously grotesque inhabitants of the deep sea (well, I certainly wasn't. I wouldn't vouch for Madame d'Ortolan). However, evolution has left us primed to notice when somebody's eyes widen suddenly, showing more white, due to surprise, fear or anger. Madame d'Ortolan's eyes flashed. "Mr Oh," she said, "*she* opposes *us*. Therefore she must be opposed in return. We cannot let such dissent go unchallenged. It would look weak."

"You could try ignoring her," I suggested. "That might look more confident. Stronger, even."

An expression crossed her face that might have been exasperation, then she smiled briefly and patted my arm as we resumed walking. "I dare say I could tell you more of the lady's corrupting theories and you would be both more horrified at her and more understanding of our position," she told me, with what sounded like forced amusement. "Her accusations are more alarming and damaging than it is necessary to reveal, but centre, as far as we can gather, on the whole course and purpose of the Concern's activities. She fantasises some vast ulterior motive in all we do, and so takes issue with us existentially. Such madness absolutely requires treatment. We cannot let it pass. Her charges against us must be defended, her argument broken." She flashed, this time, a smile. "You must trust us, as your superiors – those with a broader, more knowledgeable and encompassing view – to do the right thing in this."

She was watching me as we walked. I smiled at her. "Where would we be," I asked, "if we did not trust our superiors?"

Her eyes might have narrowed a tiny fraction, then she smiled in return and looked away. "Very well," she said, sounding like somebody who had just made her mind up about something. "There may be another debriefing." (There was not.) "You may be under moderately enhanced surveillance for a short time." (It was occasionally highly intrusive enhanced surveillance and it lasted a long time; a couple of years at least.) "Your career, which we are happy to note has already met with some success – precocious success, in the eyes of some of my more conservative colleagues, though I hope we may dismiss their opinions – is still at its beginning. I hope and would expect that this incident has not harmed it in any way. It would be such a tragedy if it did." (It was harmed. I harmed it. Still I became the best and most used of my peers.)

We reached the jetty, coming out of the shadow of the island's encircling walls. Madame d'Ortolan accepted the hand of the boatman as he helped her into the launch. We sat down in the open rear well of the launch. "We hope that our trust in you is both well-founded and reciprocated," she said, smiling.

"Entirely, ma'am," I said. (This was a lie.)

As the boat gunned away from the isle of the dead, Madame d'Ortolan detached the flower from her lapel. "They say these things are unlucky, outside of a cemetery," she said, and let the gelded blossom fall into the restless waters of the lagoon.

133

7

Patient 8262

We change things. For the better, we would hope, obviously. What would be the point of trying to change things for the worse? We do what we can. We do all that we can. We do our very, very best. I cannot see how anyone could disagree. And yet still we encounter disagreement. People take issue with us. Our views and prescriptions are not accepted as being definitive, and correct, and desirable, by certain people.

This has to be regarded as their right, and yet it does seem also to be their conceit, perhaps even their indulgence.

I suppose we have to take these things and these people and their views into account. We are not, however, obliged to indulge them.

We work to make the many worlds better.

There. That's the official line.

The saying goes that Aspherje would be a great city even without the University of Practical Talents, but then so would the UPT without Aspherje. To me, coming from the background I came from, it looked like a crunched, piled-together collection of several dozen cathedrals; all domes, spires, elongated windows and flying buttresses, with the great central dome – extravagantly clothed in gold leaf so that even in dull weather it seemed to shine like something not entirely of that or any other world – plonked on the rough summit of the whole chaotic frozen storm of brick, stone, concrete and clad steel like a gloriously irrelevant yet sublimely triumphant afterthought.

There we learned our trade. First, though, we had to learn ourselves, discover where the mother-lode of our talent truly lay. The Transitionary Office had developed its techniques for detecting likely candidates for training at the UPT over many centuries, and one of the talents that it found most useful was that of rapidly and reliably identifying those with any sort of talent that might prove of subsequent use to itself.

So spotters, as they were generally called, travelled amongst the many worlds, looking for those who might be recruited to the cause. A few could take themselves there; the vast majority could not.

The most widespread talent, or at least the one that it was easiest to find, was the ability to transition, that is, to shift oneself, preferably with a high degree of willed accuracy, between the many worlds. It was unheard of to find somebody already doing this; only the signs of a potential future proficiency were obvious to somebody attuned to such indicators, not naturally occurring instances of the applied talent itself. As far as we knew, that came only once the subject had been trained generally in the techniques of transitioning and instructed specifically in the use of the drug septus.

Beyond that extraordinary but in a sense basic skill, the most useful additional talent was that of being able to take somebody else with you when transitioning. A tandemiser could do that. This meant that the ability to flit became separated from any other talent that it might have been deemed would be useful on the target world.

Rumour had it that the ability to take another with oneself between realities had been discovered fortuitously, if not perhaps entirely accidentally, when a certain transitioning adept had willed the standard transitioning process while in the act of coition with their lover. Adept and lover both discovered themselves in the bodies of another sexually joined couple on another world entirely. This was a shock, obviously, but allegedly not so great a one as to prevent the couple from being able to return successfully to their home world, or complete the act they had been engaged in. Nor was this pioneering transitionary shy about exploring the possibility that they alone had caused the event, rather than it being a function of the specific combination of qualities embodied by that specific first couple.

Further gossip insists that it was some time before our adventurous virtuoso informed the Transitionary Office of this innovation, the individual concerned claiming that they wanted to ensure this novel ability was not the result of some freak, one-off stroke of luck. They had carried out further research and established that the ability was controllable and the process both repeatable and, probably, transmissible: a teachable skill rather than a unique and freakish abnormality.

Allegedly, that same adept discovered how to bring an act of sexual congress to a fully successful conclusion in one world and then transition to another world to experience the whole thing again (in some versions, with or without their partner in the first world).

Most strands of these rumours hold that it was Madame d'Ortolan who discovered this ability, and that she did so some two hundred years ago, thereafter using the influence and power that the discovery of this innovation provided her with both to fulfil her ambition of being elevated to the Central Council of the Transitionary Office and to gain the particular privilege the Central Council granted its most distinguished and illustrious members: that of being allowed to skip back a generation or two every now and again when one's original or presently occupied frame grew old, so that – re-emplaced in a succession of younger bodies – one might never grow truly old, or – save by violent chance – die.

It is said that for those perverse souls for whom the prospect of travelling throughout an infinitude of worlds is somehow not incentive enough to undergo the training that the Transitionary Office requires, the rather more base promise of serial sexual transitioning makes all the difference, even if the practice is both frowned on and made difficult by the Office's tightly controlled monopoly of septus. Equally, for those for whom power stretching across unnumbered realities is not enough, effective immortality helps provide an extra spur to aspire to a place on the Central Council.

Subsequent research has revealed that for most people capable of the technique it is not necessary to penetrate or be penetrated; a tight hug over as much of the body as possible, with a minimal amount of skin-to-skin contact, preferably about the head or neck, is all that's required. A few blessed individuals need only encircle or nearly encircle both wrists, or just one, and an even tinier number need only hold the other person's hand.

Foreseers are those who can see into the future, though usually only for a brief moment as they transit from one world to another, and hazily. It is a highly limited skill, the least well understood of those we know about and the least reliable and consistent of those of interest to us, but it is the most highly prized nevertheless, for its rarity apart from anything else.

Trackers may or may not be a specialised form of foreseer (the foreseers claim this, the trackers deny it). Trackers are those who are able to follow individuals or – more unusually – specific events or trends between the worlds. They are spies, essentially; a semi-secret police force that the Transitionary Office uses to keep its transitionaries under some sort of control.

That the trackers' services are required to the degree that they undeniably are is due to a quality of character shared by most transitionaries. The people who turn out to be capable of flitting amongst the many worlds are almost without exception selfish, self-centred individuals and individualists, people who think rather highly of themselves and exhibit or at least possess a degree of scorn for their fellow humans; people who think that the rules and limitations that apply to everybody else don't or shouldn't apply to them. They are people who already feel that they live in a different world to everybody else, in other words. As a specialist from the UPT's Applied Psychology Department expressed it to me once, such individuals are some lopsided distance along the selfless–selfish spectrum, and clustered close to the latter, hard-solipsism end.

Clearly, if left to their own devices such rampant egoists might misuse their skills and abilities to pursue their own agendas of self-glorification and self-aggrandisement. Such individuals need to be controlled, and to be controlled they need to be watched, and that is what trackers do: they spy on and help to police the transitioners. Trackers and transitionaries are as a result kept as far apart from each other as possible, to prevent them concocting their own little conspiracies or drawing up plans of benefit to them but not to l'Expédience and its aims.

As a result, the general demeanour of the Transitionary Office, the University of Practical Talents, the Speditionary Faculty and the Concern itself – their own collective fragre, if you like – is one of some watchfulness, a degree of suspicion and outright paranoia, both unfounded and entirely justified. An entire Department – the Department of Shared Ideals – exists to attempt to ameliorate this unfortunate and – if only at a low level – debilitating effect and investigate further how it might be both treated and prevented.

The Department's success, however, might be fairly if sadly judged by the fact that the overwhelming preponderance of those it ventures to assist in the course of its duties are absolutely convinced that it is itself simply another part of the whole rigidly proscriptive controlling apparatus whose baleful influence it is supposedly there to mitigate.

There is a smattering of other categories of skills, all of them essentially negative in their effects: blockers, who by their presence – usually they have to be touching – can prevent a transitioner from flitting; exorcisers, who can cast a transitioner out of their target mind; inhibitors, who can frustrate the abilities of the trackers; envisionaries, who can see – albeit indistinctly – into other realities without going there and randomisers, whose skills are almost too wayward to categorise fully but who can often adversely influence the abilities of other adepts around them. Randomisers are severely restricted in what they are allowed to do, where they are allowed to go and who they are permitted to meet – rumours exist to the effect that some of them are imprisoned for life or even disposed of.

Transitioners, tandemisers, trackers, foreseers, blockers, exorcisers and the rest are in effect the front-line troops of l'Expédience (it does have proper troops too – the Speditionary Guard: rarely mobilised and never, in the thousand-year history of the Concern, yet used, thank Fate). They are outnumbered ten or more to one by the back-up grades of support staff who provide all the logistical and intelligence services they need and who plan, oversee, record and analyse their activities. Bureaucrats, basically, and as loved for their activities as bureaucrats everywhere.

These days l'Expédience also has its own transitioneering research facilities – controversially as far as the UPT is concerned, its Speditionary Faculty believing that it ought to hold a monopoly regarding such matters. The Central Council has made noises about the wasteful duplication of effort involved but seems unwilling to act to resolve the issue, either because it believes the competition might be fruitful (plausible if unprovable), the redundancy a safety feature (safeguarding against what has never been made clear) or because it was Madame d'Ortolan's idea in the first place and it provides her and the Central Council with the ability to pursue avenues of transitioneering research as they see fit without having to appeal to – and wait on the approval of – the notoriously staid and conservative Professors and other members of the Research Council Senate of the Speditionary Faculty itself.

Adrian

"Cubbish. Adrian Cubbish," I told her. I grinned. "Call me AC."

"Why, are you cool?"

I was impressed. Usually I have to make the AC/Air-Conditioning thing clear myself. This was a clever one. "Course I am, doll."

"Course you are," she agreed, looking like she wasn't sure she agreed, but still smiling. She was tall and blonde, though her face had a hint of Asian about it that made the tall blonde part look odd and meant it was hard to be sure how old she was. I'd have said about my age, but wouldn't have wanted to swear to it. She wore a black suit and a pink blouse and carried herself like somebody who was even more of a stunner than she actually was, know what I mean? Confidence. I've always liked that.

"So you're Connie?"

"Sequorin. Connie Sequorin. Pleased to meet you."

Sequorin sounded like Sequoia, which is those big trees in California, and she was tall. Or there was that CS gas they use in Northern Ireland. But I thought better of saying anything. Clever ones need careful handling and usually it's better to say nothing and stay silent and mysterious than try to make jokes that probably won't impress them. Probably heard it all before, anyway.

"Good to meet you, Connie. Ed – Mr Noyce – said you wanted a word."

"Did he?" She looked a bit surprised. She glanced over to him. We were at the house-warming party for Ed's new gaff, a loft conversion in Limehouse with views upriver. He'd sold the house on the coast in Lincolnshire after another bit of garden fell into the sea. Still got a tidy price from some Arab he vaguely knew who never even bothered to go and see it. Some sort of investment or tax dodge or whatever. The loft was tidy, all tall ceilings, white walls and black beams and timber walls on the outside like a yacht's deck with stanchions and cables round the balconies. Small-fortune territory. The area was still getting gentrified, but you could smell the smart money moving in.

This would have been mid-Nineties now, I suppose. I was working in Ed's brokerage firm, which was a private company these days rather than a partnership. This made sound business sense according to the lawyers. The boy Barney had been living on a farm in Wales for the last year with some hippies or something but had recently turned up in Goa and was running a bar that his dad had helped him buy. Bit of a disappointment, really, but at least he'd tamed the coke habit, seemingly. I was almost clean myself, just took the occasional toot on special occasions and had stopped dealing entirely. Healthier.

I'd clocked that the real currency involved in making money out of money is knowledge, info. The more people you knew involved in a business, and the more you knew of what they knew, the better informed you were and the better the judgements you could make about when to buy and when to sell. That was all there was to it, really, though that's a bit like saying all there is to maths is numbers. Still enough complications involved to be going on with, thanks.

"Mr Noyce speaks very highly of you," Connie told me. Something about the way she said this made me think she wasn't my age at all, but a lot older. Confusing.

"Does he? That's nice." I moved round her a bit as though making room for somebody passing nearby, but really getting her to turn more fully into the light. No, she really did look quite young. "What do you do yourself, Connie?"

"I'm a recruitment consultant."

I laughed. "You're a *headhunter*?" I glanced over at Ed.

"If you like." She looked over at Mr N too. "Oh, I'm not trying to entice you away from Mr Noyce's firm."

"You're not?" I said. "That's a pity, isn't it?"

"It is?" she asked. "You're not happy there?" She had an accent that was hard to pin down. Maybe Middle European, but spent some time in the States.

"Perfectly happy, Connie. Though Mr N and me think the same way." I glanced over at him again. "He knows if I got a much better offer from somebody else I'd be a fool not to take it." I looked back at her. I did that glance thing, where you sort of flick your gaze over a woman, certainly as far as their tits if not their waist. Too quick to really take in anything you haven't already seen through periph-eral vision, but enough to let them know you're, what's the best way of putting it, alive to their charms, shall we say, without actually ogling them like a classless wanker, know what I mean? "No, I just meant we could all do with a bit of enticement now and again, don't you think, Connie?"

I should explain that Lysanne was history by now. The barmy Scouse bint had stormed out once too often and I'd changed the locks on her. She was back in Liverpool running a tanning salon. I was playing the field, as they say, which meant I was seeing a few girls at a time on my terms. Plenty of sex, no commitments. Fucking Holy Grail, isn't it?

She smiled. "Well then, maybe I can entice you to meet a client of mine." She handed me a card.

"What's it in connection with?"

"They would have to explain that themselves." She glanced at her watch. "I have to go." She reached out and touched my arm. "It was good to meet you, Adrian. Call me."

And off she fucked.

I asked Mr N.

"Some people that I know, Adrian," he told me. He was standing under a really bright light, his white-sand hair shining like a halo. "They've been helpful to me in the past. I'm on a consultancy for them. I hold myself ready to help them if and when they need it. They rarely do, apart from some very trivial matters. Frankly, so far I've been able to hand everything over to my secretary to deal with." He smiled.

I frowned. "What sort of people, Ed?"

"People it's very useful and lucrative to know, Adrian," he said patiently.

"They Italian?" I asked. "Or American? Or Italian-American?" I was already thinking Mafia or CIA or something.

He laughed lightly. "Oh, I don't think so."

"Do you *know* so?"

143

"I know they've been very helpful and generous and have asked for next to nothing in return. I'm quite certain they're not criminals or a threat to the state or anything. Have they asked you to talk to them?"

"I've to call Connie."

"Well, perhaps you should." There was a minor fuss at the door. Ed glanced over. "Ah, the minister, fresh off Channel Four News. Excuse me, Adrian." He went over to greet him.

I think I was supposed to think about it but I called her moby right then.

"Hello?"

"Connie, Adrian. We were just talking."

"Of course."

"All right, I'll see your client. When's good?"

"Well, possibly this Saturday, if that's good for you."

"Yeah, all right."

There was a slight hesitation. "You have the whole day free?"

"Could do. Would I need it?"

"Pretty much, yes. And your passport."

I thought about this. I had a date on Saturday night with a girl who owned a lingerie shop in deepest Chelsea. A proper Sloan. And a lingerie shop. I mean, fuck. I watched Mr N glad-handing the Minister for Transport. "Yeah, why not?" I said. "Okay."

"Let me call you back."

Which was how I found myself at a cold, rainy Retford airport in Essex two days later on the Saturday morning and then in a proper executive jet heading out across the Channel, pointing due east as far as I could tell. Connie had met me at the airport, dressed the same apart from a purple blouse, but she wasn't saying where we were heading. She had a bundle of newspapers with her and seemed determined to read them all, even the foreign-language ones, and didn't want to talk. After I stopped checking out the luxury fittings I started to get bored so I had to read too.

144

I'd dozed off. I only woke when we touched down, the plane slowing along a bumpy runway with a lot of weeds at the edges. Flat country with lots of bare trees which looked like they were ready for winter a bit early. I checked my watch. Four hours in the air. Where the fuck were we?

The place looked deserted. There was a passenger terminal in the distance but it looked run-down and abandoned, concrete all stained. A couple of big dark hangars even further away, streaked with rust. The air here was a bit less chilly than in Essex and smelled of grass or trees or something. No Customs or other officials about, just a big military-looking tanker truck – which started refuelling the plane immediately – and a long black saloon. Both the vehicles looked Eastern European to me and the two guys dealing with the fuelling sounded Russian or something, not that I got much of a chance to listen to them as we were shown straight into the limo and it tore off across the runway and out through a half-collapsed boundary fence in a cloud of dust.

"So, where are we, Connie?"

"You have to guess," she told me, not looking up from the newspaper she'd brought from the plane.

"I give in. Where the hell are we?" I put just a little edge into my voice.

"Set your watch forward two hours," she told me.

"Seriously," I said.

"Seriously," she said, nodding at my wrist. "Two hours."

I gave her a look but she wasn't paying attention. I left my watch alone. I checked my mobile. No reception. Not even emergency numbers. Fucking marvellous.

There was a partition between us and the driver. He looked old. Worn-looking uniform, open shirt, no cap. Connie lifted up what looked like one of those very early mobile phones with a separate handset and looked at a dial on its top surface. Then she put it back on the floor of the limo and went back to the newspaper.

We sped down this weedy highway. No other traffic at all. There was what looked like a big town or a small city off to one side. We turned towards it, hurtling along a four-lane road still with no other traffic. The buildings looked pale, blocky, very Fifties or Sixties and all the same. I caught a glimpse of what might have been a helicopter, low over the horizon.

It was a bit stuffy in the car. There was a big chrome rocker switch by the window that looked like it might lower the glass. I tried pressing it. Didn't work.

"Don't bother," Connie said. She clicked another switch on her side and spoke to the driver via a grille I'd thought was for ventilation. Again, sounded like Russian. The driver's voice crackled back at her and I could see him gesticulating as he looked at us in his rear-view mirror. The car wove from side to side a bit as he did this, which would have been even more alarming than it was if there had been anything else on the road.

Connie shrugged. "The air-conditioning is not working," she told me, and went back to her paper. "The filters are okay."

"Window on your side work?"

"No," she said, not looking up from her paper.

I bent forward, studying the sun roof.

"I wouldn't bother," she said.

I looked out at the deserted city whistling past. Long tall lines of identical apartment blocks, all abandoned.

"Connie, where are we?"

She looked over the paper at me. She said nothing.

"Is this fucking Chernobyl?" I asked her.

"Pripyat," she said, and started reading again.

I reached over and pushed the front of her paper down. She glared at my hand holding the newspaper.

"What-eh-at?"

"Pripyat," she said. She nodded. "The city near Chernobyl."

"What the fuck are you doing bringing me here?" I actually felt quite angry. No wonder we couldn't open the windows to all that dusty air. The big mobile-phone whatsit would be a Geiger counter, I guessed.

"It's where my client would like to see you."

"Why?"

"They have their reasons, I'm sure," she said smoothly.

"Is it one of these fucking oligarchs or something?"

Connie appeared to think about this. "No," she said.

We came up to a big shed of a building that looked like it had been a supermarket once. A wide metal door rolled part-way up and the car drove straight in. We got out inside this brightly lit loading area that held a couple of other cars and a small military-looking truck with big wheels and lots of ground clearance. The air was cool. A couple of very large bald guys in shiny suits greeted us with nods and walked us up some steps, through a couple of those transparent plastic-curtain doorways. Between the two plastic curtains there was a bit with a big circular grating in the ceiling and another in the floor. A blast of air was roaring out of the over-head grating and down into the one beneath our feet. Then we went down a hushed, wood-panelled, soft-carpeted corridor to a door which opened with a sucking noise. There was a very big plush office inside, all bright lights and potted plants and desks and comfy leather sofas. One whole wall was a giant photo of a tropical beach with palm trees, shining sand and blue sky and ocean.

A very pretty round-faced girl with a bit too much make-up smiled from behind a desk with a couple of computer monitors and said something in Russian or whatever. Connie fired something back and we sat down on two of the plush leather couches, facing each other across a glass table covered in the sort of magazines you only seem to see in posh hotel rooms.

Before I had time to get bored there was a buzzing noise from the receptionist's desk. She said something to Connie, who nodded at the wall of beach photo. There was a door in it that had been concealed until now. It was opening, all by itself.

"Mrs Mulverhill will see you now," she told me.

(Ensemble)

A man bursts into a book-lined room. On a chaise longue, there's an old man lying underneath a younger woman. They both look groggy and confused, lying/kneeling on the chaise. The man who has just burst in hesitates because the old man looks like the person he is supposed to kill, but he seems vacant, like a husk or something, and when the old guy's gaze meets his – the man who has just broken into his private study and caught him mostly naked in flagrante with his mistress – the old fellow doesn't seem outraged, ashamed or embarrassed. He just stares up, blinking, at the younger man, and looks confused. The young woman straddling the older man is staring, fascinated but unconcerned, at the gun he is holding. The younger man remembers what he is supposed to be doing and shoots them both in the head, twice.

They found the woman sitting against a tree just off the hill path. She was humming and making little chains of flowers. Three of them held her while the fourth garrotted her. She offered no resistance and they knew something was wrong. There followed some debate regarding how much they ought to tell the people who had hired them.

The body washed up on the beach near Chandax was patently still smiling, despite having been nibbled by various aquatic fauna. A small crowd was gathering on the morning-cool sand. A man standing at the back looked at the expression on the body and frowned. He'd known it had been too easy, on the yacht, the night before. He thought about lying to his superiors.

The woman who'd sunk a razor-chisel between two of the Graf's vertebrae conscientiously reported that her target had stopped humming along with the aria a moment or two before she'd struck, though she was adamant that she had been so silent – and so mindful as she'd entered the box of give-away drafts, not to mention careful of where her shadow might fall and her reflections might lie – that he could not possibly have realised she was there.

It was agreed that the admiral had been staring ahead rather blankly in the instant before she was shot, despite the fact her lover had just been cruelly cut down in front of her. Under pressure, the team agreed that perhaps the admiral had been transitioned just before her death. Under further pressure, they agreed to consider the possibility that so had the Commandante.

The assassination teams still could find no trace of Mrs Mulverhill.

The Transitionary

I set some chips down on a green square, changed my mind and pushed them over to blue. I sat back as the last few gamblers placed their own bets and the croupier looked expectantly, impatiently around. He announced "No more bets" and spun the wheel. It whirled, glittering, forever if banally like a Ferris wheel from a funfair.

Through its whirring gilt spokes I saw the woman approaching the table. The ball inside the wheel clacked and rattled around the vertical spinning cage of spokes, battering off the blurred edges like a fly trapped in a bottle. The woman – girl? – moved with an easy, swinging step, almost like a dance. She was very tall and slim, dressed in flowing grey, and wore a small hat with an attached grey veil. I thought of Mrs Mulverhill immediately, though the woman was too tall and seemed to move differently. Not that that meant anything at all, of course. Veils were just about still common enough at the time for her not to look out of place wearing one, though she still attracted some looks.

It was spring here in the southern hemisphere of Calbefraques. Perhaps five years had passed since that night in Venice when my little pirate captain had tried to talk to me and had died for it.

I had been asked – perhaps twice a year at first, later once a year or so – by my Concern superiors if any other attempt had been made to recruit me to whatever paranoid cause Mrs Mulverhill espoused. I had been able to answer honestly that no, neither she nor anybody else had tried to do so.

I had by now become a trusted agent of the Concern, spending a slim majority of my time in other worlds, doing whatever was asked of me. It was mostly the very banal stuff: the delivering of objects, the couriering of people (not that I was especially good at that), the pointed conversations, the leaving of pamphlets or computer files, the tiny, usually mundane interventions made in a hundred different lives.

I had since made only one other intervention as dramatically salvationary as the one with the young doctor in the street, when the building fell down; I was sent to one of the topmost floors of a tall building in a Manhattan, to buttonhole a young man who was about to step into a lift. He was a physicist and the world was a fairly laggard reality so engaging him in a conversation featuring an idea or two that he – and anybody else there, for that matter – had never heard of was not difficult. This stopped him from entering the lift, which promptly plunged twenty storeys and killed everyone aboard.

There were two other occasions when I was asked to take rather more violent action, once in a sword fight in a sort of unevenly early Victorian Greater Indonesian reality (leaping in to defend a great poet and hack off the limbs of a couple of his attackers) and once when I transitioned straight into the mind of a very brilliant, very handsome but very headstrong young chemist who had made powerful enemies in a Zimbabwean United Africa. I became him for just the few seconds required to turn, aim and fire his duelling pistol – blowing his much more experienced opponent's brains out – before exiting again.

My handlers were most impressed. I got the impression that ever since the affair in the Venetian bar they had had me marked out as a natural thug. I did ask not to have to do too much of that kind of blood-sport stuff in future, but I was also quietly proud to have acquitted myself so well. Still, every now and again I was asked, and I obliged.

Meanwhile, I had been learning. I knew more about the history and organisation of the Concern now and had studied it the way it studied other worlds.

Mrs Mulverhill, I'd learned – through rumour rather than any official channel – was the latest of the very small number of Concern officers who had gone bad, mad or native over the centuries. She had somehow evaded the network of spotters and trackers and foreseers who were supposed to guard against this sort of thing and might even have had her own supply of septus, the transitioning drug, though this probably just indicated that she had access to a stockpile she'd somehow built up while still in the fold, as it were, rather than a way of making it from scratch.

She was regarded as a strange, remote, almost mythical figure, and – given her patent irrelevance and powerlessness – one to be pitied rather than reviled, though of course one was supposed to report immediately any contact with anybody who might be operating in a manner similar to that of l'Expédience but who was doing so outwith its control and oversight, and that would certainly cover her and her behaviour. I was, in any case, still not sure my little pirate captain really had been her.

The woman in grey in the Flesse casino came up to the table and stood watching the play. The ball clicked and clacked inside the slowing wheel and settled into its trap when the wheel finally swung to a stop. Gold. I comforted myself that my first instinct – putting the chips on green – had been no more prescient than my later change of mind favouring blue.

The game went on. She refused a seat when one came free. I tried to see her face but the grey veil hid it effectively. She turned and left ten minutes later, disappearing into the crowd.

I lost fairly steadily, then won moderately and finished a fraction down over the evening.

I tested the air in the outside bar, on the terrace under the trees by the side of the river, the town centre a buzz of music and traffic under the lights on the far side. It was warm enough under the hissing table heaters. I had met some people I knew and sat with them for a drink. The grey-veiled woman was standing by the stone wall a couple of tables away, looking out over the river.

At one point, I was fairly sure, she turned and looked at me as I talked with my friends. Then she turned slowly away again.

I excused myself and went up to her. "Excuse me," I said.

She looked at me. She put the veil up over the front of the little hat. It was a pleasant, unremarkable face. "Sir?"

"Temudjin Oh," I said. "Pleased to meet you." I put out my hand. She took it in one grey-gloved hand.

"And I am pleased to meet you."

I hesitated, waiting on a name, then said, "Would you care to join me and my friends?"

She looked over at our table. "Thank you."

Much talk, all very congenial. She said her name was Joll and that she was a civilian, not part of the Concern, an architect making a submission to the local authorities in the town in a couple of days.

The evening drifted on, people drifted away.

Finally only we two were left. We had got on terribly well and shared a bottle of wine. I invited her to see the town from my house on the ridge and she accepted with a smile.

She stood on the terrace of the house, gazing at the lights. I put my hand on the smooth grey surface covering the small of her back and she turned to me, setting her drink down on the balustrade and removing her hat and veil entirely.

We repaired to bed, with the lights out at her request. We had fucked once and she was still holding me in her arms and inside her when she took me.

Suddenly, I was sitting at the corner of another gaming table in a different casino. She was in the next chair, just round the corner of the table from me so that we could talk easily. The game was under way; the wheel in this version was horizontal, sunk into the table's surface. It was spun by what looked like the top of a giant golden tap. The only colours on the table appeared to be red and black, though the baize was green.

"Hmm," I said. My companion was looking much more glamorous and more heavily made-up than she had been, though the face was not dissimilar. Better cheekbones, maybe. Her hair was blonde where she had been auburn. She wore a lot of jewellery. I appeared to be heavier than I was used to being. Nice black suit, though. I went to smooth my hair down and discovered I didn't have any. There was a polished cigarette case lying by my ice-filled drinks glass, and an ashtray. That would account for the gurgling feeling in my chest when I breathed, and the slight but insistent craving for tobacco. I looked at myself in the reflective metal of the cigarette case. Not a prepossessing figure of a man. My languages were French, Arabic, English, German, Hindi, Portuguese and Latin. A smattering of Greek. "This is, ah, interesting," I told her.

"Best I could do," she said.

"You did say you were a civilian," I reminded her, a little reproach-fully.

She flashed me a look. "So: a lie, then."

The last time somebody else had couriered me, taking me on a transition I was not controlling, had been back in UPT, when I was still being trained. That had been over ten years earlier. What she had just done was impolite at least, though I suspected this was beside the point.

"Have we met before?" I asked. It was time to place bets. We had some plastic chips in front of us; she had more than me. We both chose nearby numbers.

"Most recently, here," she said quietly. "This world, or as good as. Venezia, Italia. Five years ago. We discussed restrictions on power and the penalties associated with trying to evade them."

"Ah. Yes. That didn't end too well for you, really, did it?"

"Have you been shot yet, Tem?"

I looked at her. "Yet?"

"Hurts," she said. "The way the shock of it spreads through your body from the point of impact. Waves in a fluid. Fascinating." Her eyes narrowed fractionally as she watched the horizontal wheel spin, its centre glittering. "But painful."

I looked round some more. The casino was gaudy, over-lit, expensively tasteless and full of mostly slim and beautiful women accompanying mostly fat and ugly men. The fragre was not so much of too much money as of too intense a degree of concentration of it in too few places. It's not uncommon. I'd thought I'd recognised it.

"Can you remember your very last words?" I asked. "From that earlier occasion?"

"What?" she said, brows furrowing attractively. "You want to check it's really me?"

"Really who?"

"I never said."

"So say now."

She leaned right in to me, as though sharing some intimacy. Her perfume was intense, musk-like. "Unless I'm much mistaken, I said, 'Some other time, Tem.' Or, 'Another time, Tem'; something like that."

"You're not sure?"

She frowned. "I was in the process of dying in your arms at the time. Perhaps you didn't notice? Anyway, hence I was a little distracted. However, the interception team might have heard me use those words. More to the point, before my violent but dashing end, I used the term 'emprise.' Only you heard that."

Which was true, I recalled, though I had told the debriefing team from the Questionary Office this fact as well, so that didn't really prove anything either.

"And so you are . . .?"

"Mrs Mulverhill." She nodded forward as we were asked to bet again. I hadn't even noticed we'd lost the last gamble. "Good to see you again," she added. "Had you guessed?"

154

"Soon as I saw you coming."

"Really? How sweet." She glanced at a thin, glittering watch on her honey-tanned wrist. "Anyway, we don't have for ever. You must be wondering why I'm so keen to talk to you again."

"Not just the sex, then."

"Wonderful though it was, obviously."

"Uh-huh. Consider any latent male insecurity dealt with. Carry on."

"Briefly, Madame Theodora d'Ortolan is a threat to more than just the good name and reputation of the Concern. She, with her several accomplices on the Central Council of the Transitionary Office, will lead us all to disaster and ruin. She is a threat to the very existence of l'Expédience, or, even worse, if she is not, and instead represents all that it most truly stands for, proves beyond any doubt, reasonable or otherwise, by her past actions and present intentions that l'Expédience itself is a force for evil that must be resisted, contended with, brought down and, if it's possible, replaced. But in any case reduced, entirely levelled, regardless of what may or may not come after it. In addition, there may well be a secret agenda known only to the Central Council, and perhaps not even to all on it, which we – or, at least, you and your colleagues, given that I am not one of you any longer – are unwittingly helping to carry out. This secret agenda has to stay secret because it is something that people would reject utterly, perhaps violently, if they knew about it."

I thought about this. "Is that all?"

"It's enough to be going on with, wouldn't you say?"

"I was being sarcastic."

"I know. I was seeing your sarcasm and raising you deadpan literalness." She nodded forward. "Time to bet again." We both placed more chips.

"Have you any proof of any of this?"

"None you'd accept. Nothing that would convince you empirically."

I turned to her. "And what was it that convinced you, Mrs M?

155

One instant you're a lecturer; bit truculent, bit misfit, but a star of common room and lecture hall and marked for greatness, according to the rumours; the next you're some sort of bandit queen. An outlaw. Wanted everywhere."

"Wanted everywhere," she agreed beneath a flexed brow. "Unwelcome throughout."

"So what happened?"

She hesitated, gaze flicking restlessly across the table for a few moments. "You really want to know?"

"Well, I thought I did. Why? Am I going to regret asking?"

Another uncharacteristic hesitation. She sighed, tossed a chip to a nearby square on the table and sat back. I placed some chips on another part of the table. She kept looking at the table while she talked quietly. I had to sit closer to hear her, hunched over the giant ball that was my borrowed belly. "There is a facility at a place called Esemier," she said. "I was never privileged with the exact world coordinates, I was always tandemed there by somebody with impeccable security clearance. It's on a large island covered in trees on a big lake or inland freshwater sea. Wherever it is, it's where Madame d'Ortolan used to carry out research and test some of her theories, especially on those transitioners with an abnormal twist to their talents. Both the official line and what you might call the top layer of rumour have it that it's gone now, the remaining research decentralised, distributed, but Esemier is where the important programmes started. Maybe where they're still going on. One day I might go back there, find out."

"I've never heard of it."

"That would please her."

"Go on."

"As you say, I was seen as promising; a future high-flyer. Madame d'Ortolan likes to have such people on her side, or at least brought before her so that she can test them; evaluate them while they think they're the ones doing the evaluating. I was invited to take part in a programme investigating – amongst other things – the possibility of involuntary transitioning; the theoretical possibility that changes in the structure of an adept's mind might let them flit without septus, or at least without a specific pre-enabling dose."

"I thought that was completely impossible."

"Well, quite, and if you ever ascend to the clearance levels that allow you access to the results of the research I'm talking about you'll learn it was this programme that's credited with determining that."

"And did it?"

"After a fashion. It was more thorough and wide-ranging than just that, though. The full programme was aimed at establishing what randomisers were capable of, removing the myths and superstitions associated with their weird-shit powers and giving the field a proper scientific grounding, but septus-free transitioning was the pinnacle, the platinum-standard goal we were never likely to achieve but should never quite lose sight of, either."

"What did it involve?"

"Torture," she said, fixing her gaze on me for a moment. "In time, it involved torture." She looked back at the gaming table as the chips we'd placed were raked away. She reached out, placed another on the same square. I placed some of mine nearby. "The randomisers ranged from the cretinous through the educationally subnormal and the socially awkward to the odd disturbed genius. Initially it was harmless. We were convinced we were helping these misfit people. And it was fascinating, enthralling; it was a privilege to be spending a vacation researching something that was almost certainly impossible but which would be simply astounding if it proved to be a viable technique, the sort of breakthrough that resounds across the many worlds and down the centuries, the kind of achievement that means your name is known for evermore. Even if it proved to be an entirely mythical talent – as we suspected – we were finding out lots of stuff. It was the single most exciting time of my life. When the autumn came and I was supposed to resume work at UPT, I volunteered to take a year's special leave so that I could stay on at the facility and keep working on the problem. Madame d'O herself smoothed away any problems the faculty might have offered. For most people, that was when I disappeared." She looked at me. "I'm sorry I never did say goodbye to you, not properly. I thought I would see you at the start of the new term, then . . . well, I'm sorry." She looked away again.

Quite. I had no intention of telling her how much I had missed her throughout all these years, or that I had felt, at the time, as though my heart had been broken, or that I became a different person thereafter, and became so specifically because of that abrupt abandonment, turning from a prospective career in academia or research to the training required to become a transitionary, an operative, an agent; eventually, an assassin. It would only have sounded maudlin, and what good would it have done?

"I think," she continued, "Theodora mistook my fascination with the theoretical side of the research for outright zeal, a shared passion." She glanced at me and a smile, soon gone, flickered across her face. She stared at the chip on the table again. It was scraped away too and she replaced it with another.

"It was during that year, after the people who'd just been there for the vacation had gone back to their studies, that we started to make real progress. Just the hard core were left. We had our own septus techs on the staff, seconded from wherever they actually formulate the stuff; experts in its manufacture, use and side effects. That was a privilege in itself; you never get to meet these people. Did you know there are trace elements put into septus to make transitioners easier to track?" She glanced at me, long enough to see my eyes widen. "Trackers would have a much more difficult job if those trace elements weren't present. They would have to rely on something like pure instinct. As it is, with the elements there in every standard dose of septus, it's as though they see a puff of smoke left behind where somebody has just transitioned, and can follow a faint line of that discharge to the next embodiment."

"Seriously?" I asked.

"Absolutely seriously." Mrs Mulverhill nodded slowly, still staring at the gaming table. "And Madame d'Ortolan was absolutely serious about what we were doing, too. She spent a lot of time at the facility, directing our research, guiding our enquiries, even helping to refine some of the abstract, speculative stuff. I spent a few evenings doing nothing but talk with her about transitioning theory. She has quite a fine mind, for a psychopath. At the time, I didn't know that was possible. However, she was . . . overenthusiastic. Wanting what she did so much, she took risks, cut corners, overextended herself. She let transitioners and trackers and septus chemists get together properly for the first time in centuries, and some of us learned things we were never supposed to know."

"Like the trace-elements thing."

"Like the trace-elements thing." She nodded again. "I think she assumed my hunger to know was directed solely at the problem in hand: finding out what the randomisers were really capable of and grasping after septus-free flitting. I don't think it occurred to her that I might just have a general urge to find out all I could about everything, especially whatever was being kept purposefully hidden."

More of our chips had disappeared. Some people left the table, to be replaced by others. Mrs M put another chip on the same square. I placed mine on the square next to hers. "The randomisers were troublesome. Socially inept, highly neurotic, riddled with problems and often medically challenged. Continence seemed to be a particular problem. It was possible to grow to despise them, certainly to dismiss them, to forget their humanity. One began to feel that they kept their secrets locked away inside them deliberately, just to spite us. We were encouraged never to fraternise, to treat them as experimental subjects, in the name of objectivity. They were broken, mostly useless people; a threat to themselves as well as society. We were doing them a favour, almost ennobling them, by containing their awkward, undisciplined powers and giving them a purpose, making them a part of a programme which would benefit everybody.

"We began to stress them. It was quite easy to do. They were like uncooperative children: wilful, perverse, often knowingly obstructive, sometimes aggressive. Stressing them – severely rationing their food and water, depriving them of sleep, giving them impossible puzzles while they were forced to listen to painfully intense noise – felt like a necessary discipline, like a sort of small collateral punishment they had already asked for, yet at the same time it seemed perfectly excusable because it was for research, for science, for progress and the good of all, and we weren't enjoying it; in fact we suffered maybe as much as they did because we knew more fully what we were doing. They were something like brutes while we were properly functioning human beings: educated, cultured, sensitive. Only the best could be asked to do the worst, as Madame d'Ortolan liked to say.

"When I went to Theodora with some misgivings, after watching what was basically a torture session when a man strapped to a bed was injected with a mixture of psychotropic drugs and corrosive chemicals, she told me about the menace we were all facing. She'd convinced herself that the Concern and every world it could reach was under some terrible threat from outside, that there was some diabolic force forever pressing at its boundaries – wherever they were supposed to be – and we had to prepare ourselves for onslaught. I pressed as much as I thought I could get away with to get her to be more specific, but whether she was talking about a sort of anti-Concern, some equally worlds-spanning shadow organisation opposed to everything we tried to do, or was hinting at space aliens or supernatural demons from unglimpsed dimensions it was impossible to tell. All that mattered was that it – they – posed an unmitigated and existential threat to the Concern. In that cause, nothing was too great a sacrifice and no action was inexcusable. Our inescapable duty and solemn obligation was to explore without stint absolutely everything that might help us prevail when our time of testing came, entirely regardless of any petty and irrelevant qualms we might feel. We could not afford to indulge our own squeamishness; we had to be brave.

"She talked to me for a long time. During that hour or so I calmed down, I relaxed a little and I realised that I no longer felt quite so distressed. I accepted a handkerchief from her and dried my tears, I took a few deep breaths, I nodded at what she said, I clutched at her hand when she offered it to me and I hugged her when that seemed like the right thing to do. I thanked her for listening and for suggesting that I take the rest of the day off, which I did. I did all this and I felt relieved in that way because I'd realised she was mad and that soon this would all be over, or at least my part in it would soon be over, because I had to get away from that place for my own sanity, my own peace of mind, and if, as I suspected, Madame d'Ortolan would rather have had me imprisoned or even killed than let me go from there while I might be harbouring any doubts about what was being done, then at least making the attempt would bring an end to it one way or the other. It hadn't occurred to me that she was more likely to turn me from one of the investigating to one of the investigated. If she'd caught me I'd have been the one in the padded cell or the strap-down bed. I heard that happened to a couple of other dissenters, later."

Our chips were removed. Mrs M leant forward to replace hers with another, almost colliding with the retreating rake removing the previous one. She hesitated, then she nodded at our two piles of chips. "Shall we put them together?"

"You have more to lose," I pointed out.

"Even so."

"Then, certainly." I used my hand as a blade, pushing my small pile into hers. She took all our remaining chips and stacked them onto the square she had been favouring.

"Theodora had miscalculated," she continued. "I knew people. I'd made friends with some of the trackers and the septus chemists, taken a few as lovers. Some of them had misgivings too. Some just needed somebody to talk to. Some only wanted sex. When I left, very suddenly and without warning – despite the fact that Theodora was having me watched by a team of spotters and trackers brought in specially, immediately after our talk – it was without a trace, without the traditional puff of smoke, and with a plastic drum the size of my head containing a supply of untraceable septus in micropill form that will last me into my dotage, or until Theodora finally captures me or has me killed. I even have enough to share around, Tem," she told me, glancing at me. "I am a bandit queen with a following these days. I have my own small band of outlaws. Care to join?"

I sat back, took a deep breath, put a hand to my bald head and smoothed my hand over my naked scalp. "What would I be supposed to do?"

"Nothing direct yet. Just keep what I've said in mind. Keep your eyes and ears open and, when you're asked to jump, jump the right way."

"Is *that* all? You could have sent a note."

"You'll remember tonight, Tem," she said, with a wintry smile. "I've risked a lot to come and see you like this. That . . . emprise is a signifier of both my seriousness and that of the situation."

"And why me, anyway?"

"You're Theodora's golden boy, aren't you?"

"Am I?"

"Have you had to fuck her yet?"

"No, I haven't."

"Astonishing. She must actually like you."

"So why do you think I would act against her?"

"Because I know that she's an evil old fuck and I hope that you're not."

"What if you're wrong?"

"And you're an evil old fuck too?"

"I meant about her; but either."

"Then we are lost. Because I am *not* wrong about her."

"Hmm?" I said in response to somebody nudging my elbow. I looked round and saw a substantial pile of chips being pushed up the table towards us like an untidily clacking wave of gleaming plastic.

"Isn't that just the way?" she breathed, and swung herself onto my lap, draped herself over my paunch, threw her arms around me and in the midst of a deep kiss, with her legs wrapping around mine under the table, we transitioned back to the dark bedroom of my house just in time for her to slip off me and me out of her.

She placed a single straight finger across my lips and then rose, dressed and left.

She had left two tiny pills on my bedside cabinet. They were exactly like septus micropills except that each had an almost invisibly small red dot, rather than the standard blue one, centred on the top surface.

The Philosopher

I met GF in the doctor's surgery. GF were her initials as well as being what she was. She was one year below me in school. I had seen her a few times in town, at bus stops and in the library. She was tall and skinny and had thin brown hair. She always walked with her head down and shoulders hunched as though she felt she was too tall or was always looking for something on the ground. She wore braces and cheap glasses and always dressed in long dark dresses and long-sleeved tops even on hot days. Often she wore a sort of shapeless hat which looked like it had been pulled down hard over her ears. Her face and nose were both elongated. Her eyes looked quite big until she took her glasses off.

I had left school that spring and was in a training college. Even though I was now a young man I didn't know how to approach girls so I followed her home from the surgery and got up very early the next morning so that I could be waiting at her bus stop when she got the school bus. When she arrived at the bus stop I said hello and left it at that, burying my face in my newspaper. I had intended to engage her in conversation but decided that it would be better to take things more gradually. Two other girls in school uniform turned up but they didn't talk to her. The bus came and they got on.

I couldn't, of course, because it was a school bus and I wasn't in school any more.

The next two days were the weekend and I hung around places in town where I'd seen her before but she didn't show up. At the start of the next week I went back to her bus stop. This time I smiled and said hello and attempted to engage her in conversation but she was very quiet and looked embarrassed. When the other two girls appeared she stopped talking altogether and stood at the far end of the bus shelter. The other two girls looked at me strangely. I took the next ordinary bus that came along even though it wasn't the one I needed.

I returned the next day, undaunted. I spoke to her again. She wore sunglasses even though it was a dull day. I thought perhaps she imagined that I would not recognise her, though this was wrong. The other two girls huddled together and glanced at her and giggled and sniggered. One of them asked if she had walked into a door and she ran away in the direction of her home and appeared to be crying. She missed the school bus, which the two girls boarded.

She had left her school bag behind. I looked in it and found school books, pencils and pens and a girl's magazine as well as some sweets. Something rattled inside her pencil sharpener, which was of the type that comes contained in its own cylindrical waste-shavings bin. I unscrewed it and discovered four spare blades for the sharpener, though no small screwdriver with which to facilitate the replacement of one blade by another. Two of the spare blades had what looked like dried blood on them. I kept one and replaced everything else as it had been, save for a Sugar Cherry, which I ate.

I remained, awaiting my own bus, and she reappeared. I said hello again and handed her the school bag and asked if she was all right. She muttered something and nodded. She got on the same bus as me but sat elsewhere.

The next day she still wore the dark glasses. She stood in the bus stop and stared at me, though she ignored my attempts at polite conversation. When the two other girls appeared – to be joined later

164

by another – she ignored them too. When the school bus came she ignored that also. The driver shrugged and drove off. When my bus came she got on it with me and asked to sit beside me. I of course said yes, and was happy at this unexpected turn of events. I was beside the window, she was by the aisle.

When the bus was moving she turned to me and hissed, "Where's my other blade? What have you done with it? Where is it?"

I was sitting so close to her and the light fell in such a way that I could see that behind the dark glasses she had bruises around her eyes and the top of her nose.

I had meant to study the blade that I had removed from the pencil sharpener, perhaps using an old microscope I knew I still had at the back of a cupboard. However, there had hardly been time. It had been a busy day at the college yesterday. I had forgotten about an exam – which was not like me – and I had been involved in a fist fight with another boy. This was also not a common occurrence, certainly not since mum had left and I'd renounced her idiotic sect and taken up the True Faith. The tiny blade had slipped my mind until that morning. I'd looked at it while walking to the bus stop but this had revealed nothing.

Initially I denied all knowledge of what she was talking about, but she was adamant that the blade had been present before she had left the house the morning before, and she knew that I must have looked in the bag when she had left it behind and removed the blade. She accused me of stealing a Sugar Cherry, too. I remember that I started to panic, realising that she did indeed know what had happened and that I was guilty, but then a strange calmness seemed to descend on me and I thought about what I could say that would be convincing and yet leave me relatively blameless in her eyes. I told her that now I remembered; the two girls had looked inside her bag and had been messing around with the stuff inside for a while and one of them must have removed it then. They had found a dead mouse in the bus shelter and put it in her bag but when they had gone on their bus I had taken the dead mouse out again, though I hadn't wanted to say anything because I felt bad about looking inside her bag even if it was just to search for the mouse and remove it. The girls must have taken the sweet, too; I didn't even like Sugar Cherries.

She frowned, and the bruised skin above her nose trembled. I knew then that I had convinced her, and I felt a sense of great relief and victory. I was especially pleased with the bit about the mouse.

"It was one of them?" she asked, still sounding suspicious.

I nodded.

"Which one?"

I said I didn't know. I hadn't actually seen either of the girls take anything from her bag, but nobody else had touched it so it had to be them. She appeared to accept this.

I introduced myself. She told me her name too. Her initials were GF. I pointed out that if she was somebody's girlfriend then she had the right initials, and she seemed amused at this, though she did not actually laugh. When she smiled she would always put her hand to her mouth to hide her braces and teeth.

I threw the tiny sharpener blade down a drain outside the college.

I started to meet her after school, at a café. I told her jokes and amusing things that had happened at the college. She talked of pop stars and other celebrities and sometimes we listened to the music she liked, sharing one earphone each. She had no brothers or sisters and her mother was dead so she lived alone with her father. I told her she was lucky to have no annoying siblings but she did not seem to share this view. It was very hard to get her to talk about her father or her life at home at all.

GF first let me kiss her at a bus stop while she waited for a bus back home. Her braces proved less of an encumbrance than I'd anticipated, though it still felt odd. We went to a dance for young people at the town Youth Club and danced very close throughout the closing songs of the evening. I think she could feel my erection through our clothes but far from holding back, as I'd feared, she pressed herself amorously against me. Later, in a shop doorway, we kissed very passionately, and I was allowed to put my hand up her blouse to feel her bra and breasts.

One day on a weekend she came to my house when my family were away visiting a dying relation. I had been expected to go as well but I'd claimed I was supposed to go on Work Experience that day. She brought a quarter-bottle of spirits with her and we got a little drunk. She had also brought some of her music and so we danced in my parents' lounge, which felt odd. This time when we danced and kissed she let me undo her bra inside her blouse and put my hands on her behind through her long skirt, allowing me to cup her buttocks and tease them apart and slide my hands as deeply into the space between her legs as the skirt would allow. Her fingers dug into my back through my shirt and she made a cage of her fingers and clutched at my head, ramming my mouth against hers.

"Do you want to fuck me?" she asked. She looked and sounded very serious. I felt extremely nervous. I had meant to say "Nothing would give either of us greater pleasure!," which was a line I'd heard in a film, but in the end I just nodded and said yes, I did.

"Where's your room?" she asked, taking me by the hand. "We'll have to close the curtains."

I had kissed a few girls, and one, since gone away to university, had put her hand into my pants and wanked me off, but I was otherwise still a virgin. I had hoped to see things, to get to look at a girl's body properly, in close-up, in soft sunlight or full moonlight, but she wanted the curtains closed and no lights on. I had a packet of condoms I'd stolen from my mother's bedside cabinet but she assured me there was no need for these. I came very quickly the first time. She wanted to be taken from behind, her holding onto the headboard of my narrow bed, me kneeling behind her. Later she took me in her mouth. I thought this was a bit dirty at first, but she just gave a single snorting laugh when I mentioned this. I had become very hard again and could feel, against the skin of my cock, the braces imprisoning her teeth. I began to pull out as I felt myself approaching orgasm, gasping and telling her this, but she kept me in her mouth and let me come there. Later again we made love face to face, though her eyes remained tightly closed throughout. Her nails drew blood on my back, though I only realised this later. At the time the pain was not so bad and I remember thinking this was interesting. She laughed at the fact that I always wanted to clean up immediately, with tissues.

The room was dim but nowhere near fully dark and I had already noticed the various scars and burn marks distributed over a large proportion of her body. Even if the room had been pitch black or I had been blind, I would have felt the welts of raised scar tissue on her arms and thighs and torso. I had already half guessed, and one or two boys I knew – I would hardly call them friends, but we hung around together sometimes – had suggested that there was a reason she always wore long clothes and was excused gym classes and swimming lessons.

We had sex whenever we could. My dad's garden shed was prob-ably where we did it most, usually at night. It was hidden from the house and it was easy to get the key from near the back door. Sometimes we would pretend to do things to each other with items like the saws and hammers and the heavy vice that sat clamped to the workbench. We were invited to a party at the flat of some of her friends and had sex in a bedroom that had been set aside for just this activity; there was a queue.

GF had long been in a girls' organisation called the Girl Foresters and had risen to the rank of junior officer. One time I got to fuck her while she wore the uniform of this organisation and that felt especially good. I fantasised that one day she would become a police officer and I would get to fuck her while she wore that uniform.

One time, for nearly a week, we had the run of a house belonging to an old lady who she cleaned for sometimes, when the old lady was in hospital. We fucked until we were both sore. She had bruises on her arms and the backs of her legs that I had not caused.

"Of course it's my dad," she said one evening, lying on the floor. If we did lie down to have sex, we always did so on a sheet spread over a quilt on the floor; she would not use the beds in the old lady's house. I had asked her if the bruises came from her father. I had wanted to ask her this for some months now but had never felt the time was right. In all honesty I wasn't sure the time was actually right then and perhaps if I'd thought about it more deeply I'd have realised the time would perhaps never be right, but I did want to know and I felt we were in a relationship of sufficient long-standing and even commitment that I deserved the prerogative of being able to enquire regarding such matters.

I asked whether he had always hit her. "Long as I can remember," she replied. "Ever since mum left."

I said I thought her mum was dead.

"He says she is," she told me. "Won't say where she went or where she ended up before she died. If she *is* dead." She rolled over onto her front. I stroked her buttocks, which were very firm and round and smooth and one of the few places on her body that she had never marked with the various implements she used to cut herself. I wanted to ask her if her father had abused her in other ways, if he had abused her sexually as well. I had already guessed that he had but I wanted to be sure. However, I was worried that this might prove a rather difficult subject. GF could be very nervous and highly strung and was liable, when faced with a conversational subject she felt uncomfortable with or a line of questioning she objected to, to burst into tears, fly into a rage or storm out of a room.

"I know what you're thinking," she said as I gently caressed her behind and she pushed back the cuticle on each finger to inspect the pale moon of nail beneath before biting on the ragged edges of her fingernails. I hesitated, wondering if she really had guessed what I was thinking. I decided, with a disturbed feeling, that she probably had guessed correctly. However, I did not say anything. I kept on stroking the glossy skin of her backside. "It is what you're thinking, about him, isn't it? What else he might have done to me if he does this to me. That's what you want to know, isn't it?" she said. Still I said nothing. She continued to worry at her fingernails, biting them

169

and tearing at them. She still didn't turn round to look at me. "Well, what do *you* think?" she asked.

I could tell from her voice exactly what I should think but I told her I didn't know what to think. I said this partly to be completely sure and partly because I felt that doing so kept me in a better situation.

"Well, he did," she said. "From when I was nine." There was a long pause during which she slapped my stroking hand away from her behind. "He still does."

She turned and stared back at me then, with a fierce and terrible look on her face. She rolled over onto her back, drew her legs up and let them fall apart so that her genitals were fully revealed, still moist and glistening from our last bout of lovemaking ten minutes earlier. "Still want to fuck me now?" she asked, her expression and tone of voice both defiant and desperate. I looked at that raw wound, then into her eyes.

I told her to stay where she was, then got up and went through to the utility room where I found a clothes line. I went back to the room where she lay just as I'd left her. I asked her if she trusted me and she thought about it and then said that she did. I told her to roll back onto her front, which she did. I brought her hands together behind her back and tied them at the wrists. I could hear her crying but trying not to make too much noise about it. I moved an old heavy chair into position and tied each of her feet to its two front legs so that she could not move them, then brought the companion chair round in front of her and carefully raised her by the shoulders and laid her chest and head across the seat.

I told her that of course I still wanted to fuck her, and I did so, though not aggressively or hard. Instead I fucked her very gently and slowly, until I came. Later I untied her and held her while she cried and I told her that she wasn't to let her father fuck her ever again, but that was the wrong thing to say because she went into one of her rages and tried to slap and punch and bite me, screaming that she couldn't stop him.

We tied each other up occasionally after that. I did not enjoy being immobilised, though, and so we stopped. I like to think that she stood up to her father and he abused her less after this time but he did not stop altogether and I always knew when he had done so, either from the bruises or from the reopened cutting sites on her body.

I shall be completely honest and record here that I think people make too big a fuss about incest these days. I'm sure it has always gone on. However I had grown to hate Mr F, GF's father, and this was as much about the physical damage he did to her and the physical damage that he caused her to do to herself as about the fact that he had raped her from the age of nine, taken her virginity, made her distrust everybody and had treated her like a sex toy rather than a person or a daughter. It seemed to me that he had done something quite literally unforgivable, even if GF had been inclined to forgive him.

I rather lost the plot with Mr F. I went too far. I got carried away. It was not so much that I had let it become personal as that it started out as nothing but personal, because I knew nothing else back then.

I broke into their house when GF was away at a camp with the Girl Foresters. She would be absent for a full week. I crept out of our house, took my bike down the lanes and dark back-roads to their house and used the key that I knew lay under a particular flowerpot to let myself in. I had never been to her house but I had a rough idea of the layout of the place. I knew that Mr F would be drunk and fast asleep that night after his weekly Chamber of Commerce dinner. He was in the bedroom, with the light still on. He was lying on top of the bed, face down, half undressed. He was a tall man, gone to fat about the upper chest and belly, but not as well developed as my old man.

I'd grown up and become quite strong. I'd made myself a cosh from a pair of old socks and a load of piggy-bank change. I whacked

171

him on the back of the head and did it again when he started to rear up, roaring. He went down, gurgling, breath spluttering from his mouth as though he was trying to snore.

I gagged him with thick tape, right round his head twice, and tied him up, then dragged him down to the cellar feet first with his head thumping off each step and tied him to the central-heating unit. I made sure he was well secured and properly gagged, then went up to ransack the house so that it would look like it had been a burglary gone wrong. I was wearing charity-shop gloves and a woollen ski mask that looked like an ordinary hat until you pulled it down. On my feet I was wearing a pair of old sneakers I'd found hanging from a tree in the forest a couple of months earlier. I'd padded them with socks because they were far too big for me. In my rucksack I'd brought another pair of shoes, ones my dad thought he'd thrown out and which were even bigger. I changed into them and walked around in them for a bit, opening drawers and pulling stuff out and pulling back carpets and using a crowbar to prise up a few floor-boards. I went into what was obviously GF's room and treated that just the same; I couldn't not. Even that felt oddly good. When I thought I heard a muffled noise below, I went back to the cellar and Mr F.

I would have liked to have done something to him like he'd done to his daughter, but that would have been to leave a clue, so I just used kettles of boiling water, an old-fashioned blowtorch and a hammer. When I used the hammer I covered his feet or his hands – as appropriate – with a towel, so that no blood would splash on me, though there wasn't actually that much. Probably the most blood came when I used a cheese grater on his knees. He screamed through the gag so much that I had to cover his whole head in a sack, and then with a bin bag, just to try to shut him up.

I think that he suffocated because I tied the bin bag too tight.

I hadn't really intended to kill him, not at the start, not until I really got into it, I think, but as I worked on him I think he somehow became less human to me, more just this thing that reacted in a certain way to a certain stimulus, a set of workings that produced a set of noises and a set of muscular contractions and a set of blisterings and discolorations on the skin, according to what I subjected him to. I think also that I started to feel I had done so much damage to him that it would somehow be tidier to kill him off. I don't mean that I wanted to be merciful, to put him out of his misery – his misery was what was interesting to me – but that he was so badly compromised as a human specimen he had stopped being entirely human. I'm not putting this very well. He was all too clearly human, but he was, he had become, less than human. I would even resist the obvious conclusion that it was I who had done this to him. I had the nagging, perhaps illogical, but quite inescapable feeling that he was doing this to himself, that, despite my total and absolute control over him, he was still somehow responsible for his own torment. I'm still not entirely sure why I felt this, but I definitely did. I think that I developed a sort of contempt for him, despite the fact that I knew I had surprised him and left him with no chance of escaping or resisting me. I'd clubbed him while he was asleep (drunkenly asleep, but still). What chance had he had? None. But that's just the way things are sometimes.

In any event, I did kill him, obviously. Partly it was because I got distracted when I found an old car battery at the back of the cellar when I was looking for new things to use on him and I believe he expired from lack of oxygen while I was still trying to get the acid out of it. I thought he might be pretending at first. He was completely limp, and there was no pulse in either wrist or under his jaw, but you could never be sure. I used pliers on his fingernails – the fingers were all loose and granular-feeling because I'd already smashed them with the hammer – but he did not react so I concluded he really was dead. I tied the bin bag back round his head – tied tightly, reckoning that if he was dead I ought to be sure of it.

The thing is, I had thought my heart could not have beaten harder and faster than when I'd been breaking into the house in the first place but I'd been wrong. It thrashed in my chest like something

173

wild as I tortured Mr F and although I won't pretend that I was in any way professional, I felt powerful and in charge and as though I had finally found something that I just naturally knew how to do.

What I had not done, of course, was actually put any questions to him. I hadn't asked him whether he'd raped his daughter, or what he might have done with his wife. I'd thought of it, but in the end I was too frightened that my voice would betray my nervousness, or he'd scream loud enough to attract a neighbour. I suppose I could have got him to respond to questions through simply nodding or shaking his head but that didn't really occur to me. I just wanted to inflict a lot of pain on him for what he had done to GF and, as the night went on, I suppose, yes, I thought I might as well kill him, even though he hadn't seen my face, I hadn't spoken to him and I was fairly sure he'd never be able to identify me. It just seemed like the right thing to do. The tidiest.

I unlocked the front door and put the key back under the flowerpot where I had found it. The last thing I did was break the window in the spare room from the outside to make it look like I'd come in that way. I'd left enough of a clear area on the carpet beneath the window for it not to be obvious this had happened after the ransacking. I got home and back into bed, unseen. I didn't sleep the rest of the night.

The next day I went for a walk in the woods. I took the rucksack with all the clothes I'd worn that night, far into a dense plantation, and burned it. Then I dug a hole nearly a metre deep and buried the ashes.

A business colleague of Mr F found him two days later, the day before GF was due back from the camp. Relatives came to look after her and took her away for nearly a month. The police said they were looking for one or two burglars and announced that it was probably a robbery gone wrong. Everybody in town apart from myself slept very badly for the next few weeks. I slept like a baby. All I had to do to cover my tracks was keep the swagger out of my walk and the sneer from my lips. I knew what I had done, and felt proud and manly and in control. I was even more proud that I had been able to see through to the end what I had done to Mr F than I was of getting away with murder.

When I heard they were fingerprinting all the men in the town I went along to the police station without grumbling; not one of the first to go, but not reluctantly either. I was never even questioned. The police concluded the ghastly crime had been committed by an unknown person or unknown persons from out of town and gradually life returned to normal.

Nevertheless, what I had done had been amateurish and out of control and I had acted like policeman, jailer, judge, jury and executioner. I admit that this did seem wrong to me. I had discovered something that I was good at and even – in a sort of righteous but I hope not perverse way – had enjoyed, but this was not altogether right. There have to be limits, there has to be some sort of apparatus of judgement and rightful jurisdiction, an oversight, if you will, that gives the torturer proper authority.

I had got away with what I had done but if I hoped to do anything like it again then I felt I could not repeat my actions. I certainly was not about to start murdering people in their cellars like some seedy serial killer. Mr F had deserved what had happened to him and I had been the means of delivering justice to him, but that was that. I had to accept that through sound preparation, good judgement and good luck I had succeeded in my mission and been able to walk away.

GF came back and stayed with one of her aunts in a town-centre hotel until the funeral. I left a message and we met in our usual café. She seemed distant and yet relaxed and I realised she was probably on some sort of medication. She no longer wore the braces on her teeth and said that she had missed me and had stopped cutting herself, for now at least.

I didn't go to the funeral; she didn't ask me to.

She started at the same college I attended and got a flat with another girl. I moved into a place nearby with a couple of guys. GF and I started going out again and soon became intimate once more, though neither of us ever again suggested any bondage games.

She never talked about her father, but then she rarely had.

One day we both had time off and had gone to bed in my flat.

"Remember these?" she asked, producing a packet of Sugar Cherries from her bag. "Confiscated them from a Junior Forester." She popped one into my mouth and another into her own. We chewed on them noisily for a while. I tried to remember the last time I had eaten one. "I used to love these," I said.

Then she sat upright in the bed and stopped chewing and looked down at me, her face looking drained. One of her hands stroked her other wrist and forearm, where the old marks were. She got out of the bed and took the sticky mess that was all that was left of the Sugar Cherry out of her mouth and threw it into the waste bin. She started to dress.

I asked her what was wrong.

She didn't answer. She just shook her head. I could tell that she was crying. I kept on asking her what was wrong but she would not reply and left soon afterwards.

We were never intimate again and she refused to engage in any proper conversation thereafter, not quite ignoring me but treating me very coldly.

Had I written this two or three years ago I would have concluded by admitting, genuinely mystified, that I never understood why this happened, why she suddenly left me. However, now I think that I do know why: I was betrayed by a remembered taste. (No, I must be honest; my betrayal was revealed by a remembered taste.) Considering all that I have seen and done, it is remarkable that it is this – such a tiny, trivial thing, so many years ago, before our relationship had even properly begun – that brings a blush of blood to my face when I think about it and makes me feel ashamed. I have done things most people would be ashamed of and watched things done I would be ashamed of, yet it was for the taking of one sweet – not even that, perhaps; for not owning up to that petty theft, and the implication that it had been me who had stolen her pencil-sharpener blade as well – that I was condemned then and still feel soiled now.

I joined the army later that year and was posted abroad, becoming a military policeman after much study. The hardest bit was passing the psychological test. They didn't really want people who had done what I had done to another human being in the force, at least not then, anyway, but I was smart enough to know what they wanted to be told, and told them what they wanted to hear. Knowing how that process works, from the inside as it were, is in itself an important part of my line of work, so even then I was learning, and adding to my skill set.

8

Patient 8262

Most worlds are Closed, a few are Open. Most people are not Aware, a few are Aware. An Open world is one in which most people are Aware and there is no need to dissemble regarding the business of flitting or transitioning between worlds. Where I am now, lying in this bed in this clinic, is a Closed world, a reality where possibly nobody except myself knows that the many worlds exist, let alone that they are connected and that travel between them is possible. This is as it should be, for my purposes. This is what I wanted when I came here. This is my protection.

I opened my eyes to find the fat bald man sitting staring at me; the same man with the bad skin who makes a habit of sitting beside me in the television room during my rare visits there and talking continually in his incomprehensible dialect or accent.

There is mist outside and the weather feels cold for the first time this year, though I am still warm inside my hospital bed. The fat man wears the same white and pale blue pyjamas that we all wear, and a faded blue dressing gown that has seen better days. He is talking to me. It is mid-morning and the usual mid-morning cup of fruit juice is sitting on my bedside cabinet. I was not aware of the orderly leaving it.

The fat man is talking quite animatedly to me, as though he expects me to understand what he's saying. Actually he may be making an effort for me; I get the impression he is trying to talk more slowly, at least initially. Also, his skin condition appears to have improved recently too. He may be talking more slowly than usual, but he seems to be compensating by talking more loudly and with greater emphasis. He gestures quite a lot, too, and his upper body moves as he does so and I can see tiny specks of spittle arcing from his mouth to fall on the bedclothes between us. I am a little worried that some of his spittle might land on my face, even on my lips. I might catch something.

I frown, sit up in bed and cross my arms, enabling me to put one hand up to my mouth so that it looks like I am listening, or at least trying to listen, to what he's saying, but really I'm just shielding my mouth from any errant spit. I frown some more as he jabbers on, I put a pained expression on my face and sigh deeply, generally trying to give the impression of wanting to understand what he is saying, but failing. He doesn't appear to be paying much attention anyway, frankly, just talking away in a machine-gun flurry of sound within which I can barely make out one word in twenty.

I suppose if I concentrated I might understand more, but from the little I can make out he's complaining about another patient stealing something from him, or insulting him, or taking his place in some queue, or all three, and the medical staff either being responsible in the first place or being complicit or guilty of not listening – or all three – and to be perfectly honest I don't care. He just needs to talk to somebody, preferably somebody who might be neutral regarding whatever petty nonsense this is all about, and preferably, I suspect, somebody who is not likely to answer back or ask any pertinent questions or actually engage with him and his concerns at all. He's just offloading. Depressingly, I am the perfect choice.

It's strange, this need to talk, to express ourselves even when we know or strongly suspect that the person seemingly listening isn't really, or can't understand, or doesn't care, or couldn't do anything anyway even if all the above did not apply. Some of us just like the sound of our own voice and most of us need to vent sometimes, to get things out, to release pressure. Occasionally, too, we need to articulate vague but powerful feelings and so make them less frustratingly vague, the act of expressing them itself helping to define what it is we feel in the first place. I suspect the fat man, just now, hovers between the love-of-own-voice and letting-off-steam explanations.

He nods emphatically, falls briefly silent and sits back, hands on knees, having apparently just come to some conclusive break in his oration. He looks expectantly at me, as though I'm supposed to respond. I move my head in a sort of circular motion, something between a nod and a shake, and spread my hands. He looks annoyed at this and I feel I need to say something, but I don't want to attempt anything in his own language as this will just encourage him. I can't let slip that I can speak languages which are quite simply not of this world – vanishingly small though the chance may be that this could materially affect my security or threaten my anonymity – so I decide to make up some gibberish.

I say something like, "Bre trel gesem patra noch, cho lisk esheldevone," and nod, as though for emphasis.

The fat man rocks back, eyes wide. He nods too, enthusiastically, and comes out with a barrage of quick-fire sounds not one of which I comprehend. He looks like he actually understood what I said. But that's not possible.

"Bloshven braggle sna korb leysin tre epeldevein ashk," I tell him when he stops to draw breath. "Kivould padal krey tre napastravodile eshestre chroom." I shrug. "Krivin," I add, with a nod for emphasis, for good measure.

He nods so hard that I expect to hear his teeth rattle. He slaps his knees. "Blah blah blah blah blah!" he replies. Not actually that one repeated nonsense filler word, obviously, but a stream of noise.

181

It is almost as though he does understand me. This is becoming alarming. I can feel myself getting rather hot. I determine to say no more, but he lets loose such a tirade of sound, complete with wild gestures and more spitting, that I feel it is impossible not to respond. If nothing else, at least when I am speaking he is not and so I am in no danger of being splashed with flecks of saliva.

"Lethrep stimpit kra zho ementeusis fla jun pesertefal, krin tre halulavala!" I respond. He nods again, talks quickly and incomprehensibly, then holds up one hand and gets up, grunting, disappearing into the corridor. I would like to think he has gone for the day. Or for good, but something about his last gesture, holding his hand up like that, leads me to believe he is going to reappear all too soon. While he is away I fan my face and flap the bedclothes to cool myself down.

He comes back a couple of minutes later, shepherding into my room another patient, a skinny, slack-jawed fellow I recognise but have never talked to. In fact he's one of those I thought didn't talk to anybody. His thin, worn face looks too old for his body. He has lank black hair, an expression of no expression and a straggly beard that never seems to grow. He shows no sign of acknowledging me. The fat man plonks him down in the seat he has just vacated and gibbers a stream of language at him. I think I catch a word or two about listening and talking, but he is talking too fast for me to be sure. The younger man looks at me and in a low voice says something I do not catch. The fat man, standing behind him, gestures expectantly at me. I signal back, a two-handed *What?* motion. The fat man rolls his eyes and makes a sort of circular hurrying signal with one of his hands while the other taps the younger man on the shoulder and then points at me.

"Skib ertelis byan grem shetlintibub," I say to the younger man. "Bolzaten glilt ak etherurta fisriline hulp." I feel my face grow hotter still and fear that I am blushing. Sweat is gathering on my brow. This is perfectly absurd, but both men now seem rapt, and I feel it is easier to go on talking, even if it is utter gibberish, than it is to fall

182

silent and wait for them to reply, or just burst out laughing. "Danatre skehellis, ro vleh gra'ampt na zhire; sko tre genebellis ro binitshire, na'sko voross amptfenir-an har." Finally I can go on no longer, and – as my throat dries up – I simply run out of nonsense to speak.

The younger man narrows his eyes and nods slowly, again as though he understands this absolute rubbish. He looks slowly away from me to the fat man and says something. The fat man nods and makes a hand gesture that might mean *I told you so*. The young man leans forward and says, quite slowly, "Poldi poldipol, pol pol poldipolpol poldi poldi." He sits back, smirking.

Well, of course, they are simply making fun of me. I smile thinly, look him in the eyes and say, "Poldi poldi polodi plopolpopolpopilploop."

I expect him to smirk again, or laugh, but he doesn't. Instead he sits back as though struck, his expression changes to that of some-body who has just been profoundly insulted, he looks me up and down and then rises smartly to his feet, angrily shrugging off the hand of the fat man who appears to be trying to placate him. The fat man starts to say something, sounding soothing, but the young man interrupts him, shouting him down in what sounds like a stream of invective. The only word I can make out is the nonsense one "Poldi." He turns imperiously, spits at the floor under my bed and storms out, head held high.

The fat man says something plaintive to him, goes to the door and says something after him, then gives a deep sigh, shakes his head and looks in at me, his expression regretful, hurt and dis-appointed. He scratches the back of his head with one chubby hand and expels another resigned sigh. He says something inflected to be a question, I think. I am definitely not saying anything else from this point on, and I just sit there glaring at him.

He shakes his head once more, asks another, similar-sounding ques-tion, then – when I still do not reply, but glare even more pointedly at him – he rubs one thick-fingered hand over his bald pate and stares down at the floor, possibly at where the younger patient spat. I doubt he will have the manners to do anything about that particular outrage.

I bet I shall have to wait for an orderly or the cleaners to clean it up. I suppose I could do it myself, but I feel the gesture was both rude and uncalled-for and I don't see why I should.

He mutters, staring away, as though talking to himself, and rubs his hands together, looking and sounding worried. He sighs theatrically, shakes his head one more time, and leaves, shoulders drooped, still muttering.

He stays away this time. Filled with relief, I reach for my thin plastic cup and the watery fruit juice. As I drink it, I notice that my hands are shaking.

The Transitionary

"Did you kill Lord Harmyle?"
   "Yes."
   "Why?"
   "I was ordered to."
   "By whom?"
   "Madame d'Ortolan."
   "I know that not to be true. Lord Harmyle was not on your list."
   "Really? Must have misread it."
   "Please don't affect flippancy."
   "No? Okay."
   "Now, did you—"
   "Have you seen the list?"
   "What?"
   "Have you seen the list?"
   "Not relevant. Did you have orders to kill anybody else?"
   "Yes."
   "Who?"
   "Dr Seolas Plyte, Ms Pum Jésusdottir, Mr Brashley Krijk, der Graf Heurtzloft-Beiderkern, Commandante Odil Obliq and Mrs Mulverhill the younger."
   A pause. I got the impression this was being written down as well

as recorded. The circle of lights surrounded me. My questioner was still behind me, unseen. "My information indicates that you were asked merely to forcibly transition the people you mention, with the exception of Lord Harmyle, who, as already indicated, we know was not on your list."

"I was given verbal orders from Madame d'Ortolan that all those on the list were to be killed, not transitioned. Quickly as possible."

"*Verbal* instructions?"

"Yes."

"In a matter of such importance?"

"Yes."

"To be confirmed in writing subsequently?"

"No. I asked specifically. Definitely not to be confirmed in writing subsequently."

"That would be unprecedented, I take it?"

"Yes."

"I see."

"I would like to ask a question."

Another pause. "Go ahead."

"Who are you?" We were speaking a version of English which had separate "yous" for singular and plural; I had used the plural version.

"We are officers of the Concern," the calm male voice said. "What did you think?"

"Who do you answer to?"

No pause. "Were your orders delivered to you in the usual fashion?"

"Yes. A one-time mechanical micro-reader."

"Did you question your orders?"

"Yes. As I've said."

"But you still accepted them, including the unprecedented alleged instruction to kill individuals who, according to your written orders, were only to be forcibly transitioned for their own safety."

"Yes."

"Had you received orders to kill so many people before?"

"No."

"Were you aware that they were unusual orders in requiring such a . . . such a glut of killing?"

"Yes."

"And yet you did not think to question them."

"I did question them. And in the end I did not obey them."

"You were not able to. You were captured before you could."

"But I had—"

"Be quiet. Plus, you took it upon yourself to kill at least one more person in addition to the already significant number you falsely claim you had been instructed to kill."

"As I—"

"Be quiet. I take it you were aware of the seniority of the persons you claim you were instructed to elide. Save for the Mulverhill woman, they are all on the Central Council of the Transitionary Office. Answer."

"Of course." (*Are* all on. An interesting choice of verb tense; inadvertently instructive, I hope.)

"And yet still you did not think to question the orders?"

"As we've established, I *did* question them. And I did *not* carry them out."

"I see. Is there anything you would like to add?"

"I would like to know who you answer to. Under whose authority do you operate? I would also like to know where I am."

A pause. "I think that concludes the preliminary part of our investigations," the voice said. There was a hint of a question in the tone and I got the impression that he had turned his head and was talking to somebody else, not to me. I heard another, younger, man speak. Then the voice that had been conducting the interrogation said quietly, "No, we'll call that stress level zero." The young man's voice came again, then the older man's once more, patient and instructive, a teacher to a pupil: "Well, it is and it isn't. Absolute to the level per individual, but individuals differ. So, zero. Provides headroom." I was starting to sweat. The man cleared his throat. "Very well," he said.

I heard him rise from a chair and sensed him walking towards me. My heart had been beating quickly anyway. Now it started to beat even faster. Shadows twisted on the concrete floor. I sensed the man behind me. I heard the deep, rasping, tearing noise of thick sticky tape being unrolled. He reached over me and put the tape over my eyes and right round my head, blinding me. I was breathing short and shallow, my heart thrashing in my chest. More tearing. He put another long line of tape round across my mouth and, again, right round my head. I had no choice but to breathe through my nose now. I tried to calm myself, to take fewer, deeper breaths.

Imagine that you could simply flit away, I thought. Imagine that just by thinking, you could be elsewhere.

Yes, and imagine that you are any different from any other poor, helpless, doomed wretch about to suffer, as poor, helpless, doomed wretches have suffered across the many worlds and down the countless ages an infinitude of times. With no escape and no choice and no hope.

A final, brief noise of a short length of tape being ripped from a roll, then torn. A very short, narrow piece of tape.

I felt him reach over me, his clothed chest pressing on my naked back and sweating head. The last thing I smelled was an antiseptic scent from his hand. He pinched my nose with one pair of fingers, wiped my skin with a paper handkerchief and stuck the tape over my nostrils, smoothing it down.

Now I could not breathe.

Headache. He has a headache.

He is not certain, for a few moments, which way up he is. Indeed, initially he is not entirely certain what "up" even means.

Pressure. There is pressure on one side and not on the other. This reminds him of something and he feels frightened.

He was lying on his left side. His head was on the floor, his arms lay just so, his left side was taking most of his weight, his left leg lay here and his right ankle and foot lay on the floor too, the right knee lying supported by the left knee.

He supposes he ought to get up. He needs to get up. The people who have applied or who might apply pressure to him might be here, might be in pursuit of him. He can't remember why. Then, with a feeling of some astonishment, he realises that he does not know who he is.

He is a person, a human, a man, a male, lying here on this cool floor – wood? – in darkness, with darkness beyond his eyelids. He tells his eyes to open, and they do, with what feels like reluctance.

Still dark.

But with some light. A soft grey light, off to one side. Bars of light, a sort of grating of light, canted across the floor some distance away.

There is a faint breeze. I can feel it on my exposed skin. I realise that I am naked.

I shift, rearranging my limbs. I am that he. He is me. I am the person who woke up but I am still not sure who he is and I am. I feel a sense of me-ness, all the same. I am confident and sure regarding my self now; it is simply my name I am unsure about. The same may be said for my history and memories, but that too is not that important. They will be there. They will come back, when they need to, when they have to.

If the pressure is on this side, then applying increased pressure – reacting against that gravity, replying to it – should lift me up.

I apply that pressure and lever myself up.

Unsteady, trembling. Breathing hard. Breathing fast and shallow, heart thrashing, bringing on a feeling of panic and a sudden shiver. The feeling passes. I force myself to breathe more slowly and more deeply. My arm, supporting me, is still trembling. The floor beneath my hand feels wooden and cool. The grey light spills in from the far end of a long room.

I turn my head as far as I can in both directions, then tip it up and down, then shake it. This hurts but is good. Nothing shiny to look at my reflection in. Languages: Mandarin, English, Hindustani,

Spanish, Arabic, Russian and French. I know that I know these but right now I'm not sure I could muster a word in any of them. I have never had such a rough, disorienting transition, not even in training.

The light seems to increase. The bars of grey laid across the floor in the distance shine. They turn to silver, then a pale gold. I cough. That hurts too.

. . . This is a large room.

And I feel I have been here before. Just looking at it I feel this, but the fragre of the place is familiar too. I know this room, this space, this place. I feel that *of course* I know it. I feel that my knowing it is precisely why I am here.

I feel this, but I do not know why I feel this or what it is I am really feeling.

Ballroom.

Palace.

A sudden rush of sensation as though dry conduits throughout my body are flooded with glittering water.

The palace in Venezia, the unique city in so many worlds. And the ballroom, the great space, a map and a studied beguilement and the sudden flash of seamy violence, leading to interrogation, a chair and a certain Madame . . .

I am in the Palazzo Chirezzia, overlooking the Grand Canal, in Venice. This is the ballroom: quiet, deserted, out of season (or decaying years later or decades later or centuries later or millennia for all I know). I came here from who knows where, as I was about to be tortured.

Did I? Could I have?

It's the last thing I remember. I can still smell the antiseptic scent of his fingers . . .

I shiver again, look around. A great rectangular space. Three enormous shapes like inverted teardrops hang from the high ceiling, covered in grey; wrapped ghosts of chandeliers. Little sign of any furniture, but what there is also appears to be wrapped in dust sheets. The draught is on my back and legs too now. I am quite

189

naked. I touch my mouth and nose, look at my naked wrists. Unfettered.

Using my tongue, I feel for the hole in my gum where a tooth used to be. There is an intact tooth instead. I prise open its hinged cap with one fingernail. It is empty.

It is empty, but it is there. The tooth remains, as though it was never extracted in the first place. Something more than just my sense of self was carried over.

What has happened to me? I raise my head and moan and then force myself slowly up from the floor, going briefly on all fours and then standing, staggering and swaying, unsteady.

This cannot be, I think. I must still be there, still suffocating in that chair. This is an hallucination, a waking dream, or the self-deceiving fantasy of somebody deprived of oxygen because their mouth and nose have been taped up. This is not possible.

I stumble to the nearest tall window and scrabble ineffectually for a while before seeing and feeling how to open the shutters. I barely crack them, just enough to see out.

The Grand Canal stares brightly back at me, grey and cool beneath what looks like an early-morning summer's sky. A water taxi passes, a work-boat laden with bagged garbage creases down the waves in the opposite direction and is narrowly avoided by a clattering vaporetto crossing from one side of the canal to the other, running lights still greasily bright in the half-dawn, a few sleepy commuters sitting hunched on seats inside.

I bite on a knuckle until I make myself cry out with the pain of it, but I do not wake up. I shake my bitten hand and stare out at a place where I have no right to be.

And yet I am here.

Adrian

Bint was wearing a veil. Not a Muslim-type burka veil, I mean an old-fashioned sort of black-lace-with-spots-on-it thing hanging from a tiny little hat. Actually, the hat looked like an afterthought, only there to support the veil. The office was as big as the reception area, lined in very fancy-looking wood panelling that had silver or some other metal inlaid into it. I'd never seen anything like it. She sat behind a big desk. Some sort of computer screen was just sort of flattening itself out of the way and becoming part of the surface of the desk as I went in. She stood up and said hello but didn't offer to shake hands.

She waved me to a seat on the far side of the desk. She wore a sort of weird-looking suit thing, like she'd been wrapped in black bandages. Actually looked quite tasty, especially with the veil for some reason, but still like she'd just paced off a catwalk rather than being in a converted warehouse or whatever in the middle of one of the most poisoned places on the planet. I wondered if this was some sort of radiation-proof suit or something, though it seemed unlikely.

"You're Adrian?"

"Adrian Cubbish. Pleased to meet you."

"I'm Mrs Mulverhill. I am glad to meet you, Adrian."

Another confusing accent. I supposed it was from somewhere round here, Ukraine, Russia, Eastern Europe, whatever. Hints of US English, too. We both sat down.

She opened her mouth to speak but I started first. "Well, Mrs Mulverhill, I really hope you're going to tell me why I'm here, cos otherwise this is just going to be a big waste of my time, and frankly my time is quite precious to me. Plus I don't appreciate being brought into this place – what do they call it? The Zone? No one said anything about this, know what I mean? I mean technically I'm not here against my will cos I got on that plane of my own free will, didn't I? But if I'd been told where we were coming then maybe I wouldn't have, so legally you could be on dodgy ground. If I start growing a second head any time in the next few years there will be lawyers, I'm telling you now."

She looked surprised at first, then smiled. The face behind the veil looked Asian, I thought. Maybe Chinese, though less flat than Chinese faces usually are. Sort of triangular. Eyes too big to be Chinese, too. Cheekbones too high as well. Actually, maybe not Asian at all. You'd need more light, or just that veil off, to tell for sure.

"You should be safe," she told me. "The car's air is filtered and the atmosphere in here is healthier than it would be in a hospital operating theatre. Any dust on your clothes and shoes was removed before you entered here."

I nodded. "Consider me mollified for the moment. Now, about the why bit of me being here in the first place."

"Perhaps Mr Noyce has given you some idea of what we offer and what we might require."

"He said you paid well and didn't ask for much. Not normally, anyway."

"That would be accurate, I'd say."

"Okay. Keep going."

"Let me set out the basics, Adrian—"

"Shouldn't you be calling me Mr Cubbish," I said, "seeing as I've got to call you Mrs Mulverhill? Or would you like to tell me your first name?" So far this was all still too much on her terms, frankly, and I wanted to unsettle or even annoy her. How sensible this was is another matter, of course, as, when you think about it, I was in the middle of a fenced-off nowhere where nobody with any brains wanted to be anyway, a thousand or two thousand miles away from home, having got on a plane and as good as disappeared as far as anybody back in the UK was concerned, with no forwarding address or destination or nothing and with no reception on my moby.

Didn't care. I really was annoyed at them bringing me here, even if it was eventually going to be in my own interests. Who did these people think they were? Anyway; hence the remark about her calling me Mr Cubbish or telling me her first name.

"No," she said, sounding not in the least insulted. "I wouldn't like to tell you my first name. Mrs Mulverhill is what I answer to.

If you're uncomfortable with me calling you Adrian, I'll happily call you Mr Cubbish."

I shrugged. "Adrian is fine. You were saying?"

"That we will pay you a retainer, monthly, plus an extra annual payment, for your services as a consultant and for other services we may occasionally require. You would be free to terminate this arrangement at any time, without notice."

"Consultant? Me?"

"Yes."

"Consulting on what?"

"General cultural, economic and political matters."

I laughed. "Oh yeah?"

"Yes," she said. The veil made it hard to see what was going on with her expression.

"Mrs M," I said, "I'm a trader. I trade stocks. I know a lot about that. Though probably not as much as Mr Noyce. Also I know about some computer games. Oh, and snowboarding, though I'm what they call an enthusiastic amateur, not an expert, know what I mean? I'm not the person to consult on cultural and political matters."

"Tell me what you think about the political parties in your own country."

"Tories are toast. Labour are going to get back in at the next election and people like me may have to leave the country. I should point out that Mr N doesn't think they're going to be so bad – Labour, he means. He's met this Blair geezer and reckons they'll leave us alone to make money, but I'm not convinced."

"There you are," the lady purred. "You've started work for us already."

"Course I have, Mrs Mulverhill. What were the other services you were thinking of?"

"Liaison with individuals. Helping them out if they need help."

"What sort of help?"

"Getting them on their feet. Obtaining funds, documents, the ear of officialdom. That sort of thing."

Now, it so happened that I *could* help with some of that stuff, through contacts I had, some got through dealing and some through trading. But I hadn't thought that Mr N would know much about that, and it must have been him who recommended me to whoever this Mulverhill woman worked for.

"These would be serious, capable people, Adrian, but they would be starting out with very little when they make themselves known to you. Once they have a start they'll rapidly make their own way, but they need that initial boost, do you see?"

"Are you smuggling immigrants?" I asked. "You people-trafficking – is that it?"

"Not in the manner you mean, I suspect. These people would not be foreign nationals as your government would understand it, were they to come to its attention. Which they almost certainly never would. It is quite possible, though, that all you'd ever be asked to do would be to provide guarantees for bank accounts, references, letters of recommendation, that sort of thing. All expenses would be repaid to you and any loans reimbursed expeditiously."

"Expeditiously?" I pretended to be impressed.

"Expeditiously." She pretended she hadn't noticed.

"So," I said, "is this what Mr Noyce does already?"

"That's a good question. Fortunately Mr Noyce has already pre-cleared me answering it honestly. The answer is yes." I could see the smile through the black veil.

"So if it's good enough for him it should be good enough for me, is that the idea?"

"Yes, it is."

"And of course he'll be retiring in a few years, I should think."

"I should think so too." Mrs M tipped her head to one side. "More to the point, so does he."

"And what sort of sums would we be talking about here, for this, um, consultancy and services unspecified?"

"The same as Mr Noyce receives. Eight and one half thousand United States of America dollars per calendar month, paid into a bank account in your name in the Cayman Islands. The extra annual payment would be twice that monthly amount, payable at the commencement of the last month of the year."

"And I can quit any time without notice?"

"Yes."

"And without penalty?"

"Yes. The monies will stop being paid, that's all."

"Call it ten K a month and I'll think about it."

"That is more than Mr Noyce receives."

"Well, if you don't tell him, neither will I," I said. She was silent for a few moments. I spread my arms. "That's my price, Mrs Mulverhill."

"Very well. The first payment will be delivered forthwith. We'll mail you the account details."

"Like I say, I'll think about it." I wanted to talk to Mr N some more. This was too weird to just jump in on, given what I knew so far.

"Of course. Decide in your own time."

"Is that it?" I asked. This had all been too easy. I strongly suspected I'd underpriced myself.

"That's it," she said. She just sat there, didn't go to shake my hand or produce a contract or a letter of agreement to sign or anything.

"Our agreement to be reviewed annually," I said.

"If you like."

"Uh-huh." I nodded for a bit. Still just sitting there. I sat forward in my seat. "So, Mrs M."

"Adrian."

"Tell me who you work for."

"The Concern," she said smoothly. "You can call us the Concern, Adrian."

"And who are you really?"

"We're travellers."

"What, like gypsies?" I said, with a fake smile.

"I don't think so. Well, maybe a little."

195

"Russian?"

"No."

"No?"

"Definitely. No."

"CIA?"

"No."

"Some other American . . . organisation?"

"No."

I took a breath. This time she jumped in on me before I could speak. "Don't bother, Adrian. You'll never guess."

"You reckon?"

"Oh, I'm pretty certain." She flashed the veiled smile again. "We should celebrate," she said, "that you're thinking of joining with us. Would you like that? Where shall we go?"

"I can't imagine there's much happening in this Pripyat place."

"It *is* a little quiet," she agreed. "Shall we go to Moscow? The plane will have been refuelled by now. Yes? I want to show you something."

Seemingly my watch had to go forward yet another hour, though I still left the Rolex alone.

"Adrian," Mrs M said as we settled into the jet's plush seats, "Connie and I have much to talk about. Can you amuse yourself?"

"Certainly. No, wait a minute."

"What?" Connie asked.

"What if you keep me up past my bedtime?" I smiled.

Connie looked at me. "I understand there are hotels in Moscow."

"What a relief," I said.

They started talking some language I couldn't even begin to unscramble. I left them to it and watched the ground slide by beneath. I'd hoped to see Chernobyl itself – from a safe height, obviously – but didn't. It was only another hour's flight but by the time we arrived in Moscow it was almost dark. Outside, on the tarmac of the airport, the wind felt cold enough for snow and smelled of jet fuel. A big black Merc was waiting. This time the driver had a cap and tie and everything. We went straight to a tall wire gate with a small guardhouse. A uniformed Customs/Immigration guy took the briefest look at our passports, exchanged a few words with Connie S. and waved us through to join chaotic traffic on a packed four-lane road.

My moby was happy again, reconnected to civilisation. I texted a couple of pals back in the big smoke to say where I was, and felt happier too.

The Novy Pravda was a club housed in a new-build block within sight of what I guessed was the Red River or whatever big river it is that runs through Moscow. Frankly I had no idea where we were. In something called the Central Administrative Okrug, which was not a vast amount of help. If we hadn't driven through what was obviously Red Square with the big Disney church and stuff I'd only have had Mrs M's word for it that we were even in Moscow.

The club was in a big black cube of a building. Lots of UV and dark purple lights on the outside, outlining it. The air shook with muffled music. Valet parking. Front of the line, two big bouncers with armpit bulges. Straight in, greeted by some guy in a very flash suit who took Mrs M's long fur coat, fake-kissed Connie on both sides and gave me a small bow. I was in what I'd been wearing since I'd got up: black Converse, black 509s, a purple Prada shirt and a peach-soft thin black leather jacket. I felt underdressed for the first time that day.

"Kliment, how are you?" Connie said as the guy kept pace with us down a broad corridor lined with mirrors and what looked like blobs of mercury running down bronze mazes behind plates of glass.

"I am well, madam," Kliment said, sounding very Russian. "You are well too, I hope."

"Very. This is Mrs Mulverhill, my employer," she told him.

"An honour, madam."

"And this is Adrian. He's from London."

"Adrian. Welcome. I love London," he said.

197

"Smashing," I said.

"This is Kliment's club," Connie told me.

I looked round. The sounds were getting loud and the light level dropping as we entered a big space with slowly flashing lights on the ceiling. A flunky came up, bowed to Kliment and took Mrs M's coat and Connie's jacket as well as my own to a coat-check counter staffed by two astoundingly beautiful girls, all high cheekbones, long black hair and sultry, unimpressed looks. The thudding music and faster flashing lights were coming from a big fluted archway ahead. "Tasty," I said, smiling at Kliment. He nodded appreciatively, I think.

"Please," he said. "We have your table."

Vodka and champagne, caviar and blinis. We proceeded to get very drunk in our semicircular table facing a giant multi-level dance floor. I danced with Connie, then with Mrs M, who had a weird all-over-the-place way of dancing. In her black-bandages outfit and veil – yep, still with the veil – she got a lot of looks. Appreciative ones, too, and I could see why. She danced like she could move bits that other women didn't even have. Connie was a lively bopper too. The two of them kept turning away bottles of bubbly from distant tables.

Connie leant over as they were opening our third bottle of Salon. "Come to the toilets. We'll do some coke, yeah?"

By this time I'd drunk enough for this to seem like a good idea, and for the prospect of some white stuff to have taken on a sort of sensible, even medicinal quality, i.e. if I took some it'd sober me up a bit. Not to mention the fact that both Connie and Mrs M had only got even better-looking and more devastatingly attractive as the evening had gone on, and here was one of them inviting me to the loos. Well, why not? I looked from the gorgeous, blondely shining Connie to the shadowy Mrs M. Connie grinned and shook her head.

Mrs Mulverhill must have overheard, or guessed. She waved one hand. "Enjoy," she said, watching the mass of people pulse and surge around the dance floor.

No eyelids were batted when we entered an extremely posh Ladies and commandeered a cubicle. We took turns snorting from a handily placed glass ledge. Good gear, almost uncut.

We stood up, grinning from ear to ear at each other. "Another dance?" Connie suggested.

I leant back against the wall, gave her a long look up and down. "We in a hurry?"

She laughed, shook her head. "Too sordid. Let's away."

I thought she might have meant *Let's away to somewhere quieter*, but she just meant back to the dance floor and then the booth and the table where Mrs M was knocking back another deep-chilled vodka and looking as sober as when we'd walked in. She nodded at me. "We dance now," she told me, rising.

"Can I catch my breath?" I asked.

She shook her head and took my hand.

It was quite a sexy dance. There were slow bits in the tune and she moved round me, curling and uncurling and rising and falling, circling about me like she was caressing my personal space. I'm not a bad dancer – many compliments received, know what I mean? But Mrs M was something else. Maybe it was the booze and toot, but I seriously felt I was in the presence of bopping royalty.

She sidled up, pressing herself against me. I felt the heat of her body through her black-bandage outfit and my own clothes. She was half a head shorter than me. She put her veiled lips close to my ear as I leant down to her. "Adrian," she said loudly, just audible over the music, "I want to take you somewhere. Will you come with me?"

I pulled back, showed some amused, pleased surprise and then bent to her ear. "Really?"

"Really," she said. Then added, "Yes, that's a way of putting it." Which seemed unnecessary. "Follow me."

"To the ends of the Earth, Mrs M," I said as she took me by the hand. She laughed. Strange noise, almost like a bark. Her hand was very warm but perfectly dry. We slunk through the press of dancing people. She let go of my hand once we were clear of the dance floor and were heading for some cordoned-off steps. Not the loos again, then. Another pair of bouncers, nodded to. Down some wide, spiralling steps.

"This is called the Black Room, apparently," she said as a large door was opened for us by another wide-shouldered gent, this one in dark glasses. Fair enough, it was nearly black inside. From what I saw as we walked through it was a fuck club. Lot of humping and humping-watching going on in/around/on/over tables and big comfy seats. Warm, it was.

We walked on through to the far wall and another door. Yet another bouncer. Lady, this time. She was much bigger and wider than me. She handed Mrs M a key. We entered what looked like a dark hotel corridor. Mrs M let us into a dimly lit bedroom and closed the door behind her.

"People come here to have sex, Adrian," Mrs Mulverhill said.

"You don't say," I said. From the way she'd said what she just had I was already starting to guess that wasn't why *we* were here. I felt some disappointment, and just a tiny bit of nervousness. Still, I've always had, right from the first days when I started dealing, a completely reliable alarm system in my head for situations that might be about to turn genuinely nasty and threatening, know what I mean? And so far the alarm bells hadn't gone off.

"I do say. But you and I are not here to have sex. I hope you are not disappointed if that was what you were expecting."

"Devastated, Mrs M."

"You are, I think, joking."

"Not entirely."

From somewhere in those bizarre clothes Mrs M produced two little pills. Smaller than any E pills I'd ever seen; nearer to sweeteners or something. She popped one herself, held the other out to me. "Please, take this."

"What is it?"

"It is a form of lifebelt."

"Well, that's a new one." I shrugged, popped it.

200

She watched my neck to see me swallow. Again, just a little worrying. She reached up and put her veil up at last. The light wasn't great but I could see a little more of her face. A very beautiful, strong, semi-Asiatic, semi-I-couldn't-tell-what face, with big, wide eyes. And with catlike slits for pupils, not round ones. Ah-ha. I'd heard you could have contacts like that and a few weirdos had even had eye surgery to get the same effect. Music thudded very distantly. She looked into my eyes and said quietly, "Nothing should go wrong, Adrian, but if we become separated I want you to think yourself back to here, to this room." She waved one hand. "Take a good look round."

I looked around the place, humouring her.

"Do it for real, Adrian," she said, as though guessing I was only pretending to. "Look at it, remember its visual details, remember the smell and the sound of this place. Will you be able to envisage it accurately again?"

The light in the room was amber, like sunset, subdued. The bed was queen- or king-size, with black satin sheets. There was a black couch, one ornate chair of red and gold, a mirror on the ceiling, a TV set into the wall and in one corner a black cube with the one word MINIBAR on it in blue neon. There was one other door, presumably leading to a bathroom. The bed had those unnecessary bedposts that are handy for tying people to with furry handcuffs or whatever.

"I guess," I said. Separated? What was she talking about? Still no actual alarm bells, but I was starting to think that I needed a second set to go off to tell me when the first lot had mysteriously stopped working.

Now Mrs M produced what looked like a tiny cigarette lighter.

"I shall apply this to myself first, then to you. It must happen in rapid succession," she said, bringing the device up to her neck and putting her free hand behind my head, fingers spread over my sweaty hair like some giant spider. "Please try not to flinch when I apply it to you. Then I will hug you tightly. Do you understand?"

"Got you." Must confess, my mouth was dry. The music stopped briefly, its thud-thudding gone, leaving only my heart.

"Then here we go."

She stepped up to me, her body tight against mine. I could feel her small, firm breasts pressing into my chest and smell a scent somewhere between antiseptic and a musky perfume. She pushed the lighter up into her lower jaw and it clicked. A hiss. Her hand swooped from under her chin and came up to my neck. Pressure, another click and a hiss and a cold sensation in my neck and jaw like an infusion of ice. She wrapped her arms tight around my back, then wrapped her legs around mine too, rising a little on her feet and pressing her head side to side against mine. I put my arms around her. She felt good. There were stirrings down below. I was getting wood. I wondered if she could feel it. She would soon if she hadn't already. Then, very suddenly, it felt like my head turned itself inside out.

I must have closed my eyes. I swayed and staggered as I opened them again. There was a grey light all around us and the air was suddenly chill and fresh. Mrs M was releasing me from her grip but holding one of my hands so I didn't fall over and saying over and over, "It's all right, Adrian, it's all right, it's all right . . ."

But it wasn't all right, because not only was there was no dark, amber-lit room around us, there was no fucking *building* around us.

The Novy Pravda was gone and here we were in the grey light of a dawn that was hours too early on a low hill surrounded by marshes with a big river coiled across the landscape in the direction of the still-cloud-obscured rising sun. Great. Not just the room, not just the Novy Pravda. The whole of fucking Moscow had gone.

Scattered all about, stretching to the horizon, lay ruins.

I felt like I was going to keel over and we did a bizarre dance for a few seconds as Mrs M still held my hand and tried to stop me falling onto my bum and I sort of staggered and revolved around her, trying to get my balance back and gasping as my shoes slipped on the tussocky grass on the cold hilltop. Finally I got my legs spread far enough apart to stop gyrating and Mrs M pulled me to a stop, taking me by both shoulders while I bent, breathing hard and fast and not believing what I was seeing whenever I took a look out across this deserted landscape of grey marshes and black ruins.

"I'm okay," I said. "I'm okay."

I straightened up. She kept one hand on my elbow.

·I took a few deep breaths, holding them a handful of seconds each. I looked around. Couldn't see another soul. There was a dot on the distant river under the light patch of sky where the dawn was. It might have been a boat. The ruins spread in every direction. A few were on the horizon, darkly jagged. Towers and bits of domes; bitten, slumped-looking squared things that might once have been tower blocks or big office buildings.

There were some dressed stones sitting half-overgrown by longer grass a few steps away down the slope towards the nearest marsh.

"Let's sit," Mrs M said. She sat me down on the cold hard stones.

"Where the fuck is this?" I asked when I had my breathing back to something like normal.

"Another Earth, another Moscow," she said. She sat beside me, half turned to me. The veil was down again, had been ever since we got here.

I rubbed my neck. "Was that the pill did this, or—?"

"This did this," she said, showing me the little lighter gadget. "The pill was for if something went wrong. You had to visualise the room we left from, remember?" I nodded. "That was your way back. You shouldn't need it now, though. We can go back together. The first transition is always the most problematic. We're well attuned." She smiled, patted my arm reassuringly.

"Fuck," I said, shaking my head and standing up again and looking desperately around. I found a fist-sized lump of stone and threw it as hard as I could towards the still-rising spread of light where the dawn was. It disappeared into the grass downhill with a barely audible thud. I turned back to Mrs M. "No, just give me a minute, okay?"

"I'll stay here," she said, smiling behind the veil and clasping her hands over one raised knee.

I ran down the slope, skidding in places, jumping over a few more of the piles of dark brown stones lying in heaps within the grass. When the slope levelled out the marsh began and I squelched into muddy water. I put my hand down, brought up some grey-brown mud, stared at it then stared out over the grey landscape and let the mud dribble back through my fingers. A bird made a lonely mewling cry in the distance and another answered from even further away.

It all looked and felt and smelled real as fuck. The surface of dark water pooling between my shoes – black slip-ons! What happened to my Converse? – was going still. Looking at my face reflected in it, I didn't even look like myself. My trousers felt coarser, and were more like very dark brown than black. No Nokia; nothing in the pockets at all. No Rolex on my wrist, either. I studied my hands. They looked a bit different too. They had freckles. I didn't have freckles, did I? Suddenly I wasn't sure any more. Fuck me, it turned out that I didn't even know the back of my hand like the back of my hand. I turned and saw the small black figure of Mrs Mulverhill sitting where I'd left her. I trudged back up.

"I am able to tandem," she explained as we sat side by side on the stones. A hint of pale yellow-orange sun had peeked out between two layers of cloud to the east. "Some people can. A tandemiser can take one other person with them when they transition. Usually just one. Most people can't transition at all, but of those who can, few can take anything other than themselves from world to world."

"Transition?"

"From one world to another."

"Uh-huh. And you need a pill or something?"

"There is a substance called septus, both in the pill you took and in the spray in here." She brandished the little lighter thing, then secreted it away in the black bandages again somewhere under her ribcage.

I closed my eyes, rubbed my face. When I looked out again, everything was just as it had been. Grey skies, rising sun gleaming all watery, wide marshes, distant black ruins. "So is this like another dimension or something?" I asked. Fuck, I was struggling. I almost wished I'd paid attention in physics lessons.

The whole total bizarre weirdness of this was still affecting me in waves of dizziness, unless it was the drugs I'd swallowed or been injected with. Had there really been no blackout phase? We seemed to have come here from the Novy Pravda between heartbeats, with only that rush of head-turning-inside-out to lead up to it, and that had felt like part of the experience itself rather than something properly separate from it. But had there really been no time to get me properly drugged and able to be shipped out to wherever we were now? It didn't feel like it, but it still had to be more likely, I mean logically, than what Mrs M was telling me.

She shrugged. "This is one of the many worlds," she said. "There are infinities of them. The people I represent travel between them. Sometimes they might need help. Transitioning – travelling between worlds – is not a perfected process. We would like to employ you to be there to help any travellers blown off-course into your world, as it were, or who would otherwise need help in it. Minor help. Would you do that for us?"

"What exactly do you do? Why are you doing all this travelling, anyway?"

Mrs M made a clicking noise with her mouth. "Nothing that bad, but nothing I can tell you about, either. Nothing that we are doing ought to get you into any legal trouble with your authorities, in the highly unlikely event that they ever find out. You must have heard of the idea of need-to-know?"

"Yeah."

"Well, you don't need to know, so it's best for you not to." A pause while she looked out over the chilly landscape before turning back to me. "Though I suppose I should say that it's not unknown for people to start out doing what we're asking you to do and them then

205

going on to become more actively and operationally involved and even eventually becoming transitioners themselves." That smile behind the lace and dots again. "Not unknown. But one thing at a time, eh? What do you say? Do you think you might accept our offer?"

I stared at her. "I was going to need time to think anyway," I said. "Now, I . . . I think, I mean . . . This has given me . . ." I thought she looked disappointed behind the veil. I sighed. "Oh fuck, who am I trying to kid? Sure. Yes, of course. Either I've gone fucking nuts or you've got the keys to the universe in a pill. Or now in a handy spray version."

"Well, the keys to different versions of Earth," she said.

"No other planets?"

"Not as such, yet," she said. "No true time travel, either."

"What about untrue time travel?"

"There is an apparent phenomenon called lag – though I suppose it could equally justly be called lead – where otherwise near-identical worlds differ only in one being ahead or behind the other, by any interval up to several million years, but it's not a real phenomenon, any more than a celestial constellation is. They remain intrinsically separate and nothing occurring in one directly affects the other."

"Sorry I asked. No aliens?"

"We're still looking."

I paused. "You look a bit alien yourself, Mrs M. No offence."

"None taken. You ready to go back?"

"I think so."

"You may still feel a little disoriented."

"You reckon?"

"You will be finding out something about yourself over the next few days, weeks and months, Adrian."

"Oh yeah?"

"What I said about the pill you took was true, but its other purpose is to give you an excuse to dismiss this as some sort of drug-induced hallucination."

I must have looked sceptical.

Mrs M spread her arms. "Right now you know that this is real and all this has definitely happened. But when you're back in your own body and back in your own world and country and house and job and so on, with life going on as usual, you will start to doubt that any of it was real at all. You may well determine that it did not happen, in which case that is probably what you need to believe to protect your sanity. Or you may accept that it did. Either way this will tell you something about yourself."

"Can't wait." I paused. "Anyway, so long as the money's real. Know what I mean?"

She laughed. A high, tinkly kind of laugh this time. "We try to choose pragmatic, selfish people for such positions, Adrian."

"Selfish, am I?"

"Of course. You know you are. It's not high praise, Adrian, but it's not criticism either. It's just an acknowledgement. All our best people are highly self-centred. It's the only thing that holds them together in the chaos." She grinned. "Anyway. I think you will do very well. Time to go back."

We both stood up. A low breeze ruffled my hair and some of her black bandages. I took a last look round this landscape of watery ruins.

"What happened here, anyway?" I asked.

She looked round briefly. "I don't know," she said. "Something terrible, I should think."

"Yeah," I said. "I should think so too." Even I knew enough history to think of Napoleon and Hitler, and what might have happened in a Third World War.

"Oh," she said, clicking her fingers. "I should warn you."

"What?"

"The selves we left behind, back at the Novy Pravda."

I stared at her. "They're still there?"

"Oh yes. On standby, if you like. Our minds, our true selves are in these bodies, the ones that we happened to find here, but the husks remain where we left them."

I looked at my freckled hand again, then at her. "But you look just like you did."

She smiled behind the black veil. "Well, I am very good at this. And there are infinitudes of worlds to work with. There are even an infinite number where we are having exactly the same conversation as this right now, worlds differing only in one tiny detail – which might be an atom of uranium in a deposit deep underground in Venezuela decaying a microsecond earlier than it did here, or a photon in the University of Tasmania taking one slit, not the other, in another running of the two-slit experiment. There may even be an infinite number which are utterly indistinguishable from this one and which are taking place precisely contemporaneously, where the divergence has yet to occur. Though there may not. Partly it depends how you look at it." She gave me a big smile. I'd been looking at her blankly, I guess. "Further research is required," she said. "Anyway, about our other selves, the barely aware husks we left behind."

"Yeah?"

"We may get back to find they are having sex."

I stared at her. "Seriously?"

"When you leave two physically healthy adult humans of each other's preferred gender alone in such close proximity, and they're effectively morons, it tends to happen."

"How romantic."

"Yes. Though it depends. Was it something on your mind before we left?"

"What, you and me having sex?"

"Yes."

"The idea had crossed it."

She tipped her head to one side. "Well, you're not my usual type, but I was finding you moderately attractive, possibly due to the disinhibiting effects of alcohol."

"Don't you get carried away there now, know what I mean?"

She shrugged. "There are couriers who can only take another person with them when they are penetratively conjoined. I have to embrace my fellow traveller. One or two can co-transition just by holding the other's hand. Anyway. We'll see. All I'm saying is, don't be alarmed if we flit back and that's what we're doing."

"Okay," I said. "I'll try not to be alarmed."

She stepped up to me. "Now we embrace, yes?"

My brain felt like it was turning inside out again. Or outside in this time. Whatever. But when we got back I was lying curled up on the floor of the amber-lit room and Mrs M was sitting cross-legged by my side, patting my shoulder and making sorrowful, comforting noises and I had tears in my eyes and a sick feeling in my gut, nursing what felt like a pair of badly bruised testicles, exactly as though somebody had kneed me in the balls a few minutes earlier.

"Ah," she said. "Sorry. Sometimes that happens, too."

9

Patient 8262

I nfinities within infinities within infinities . . .

The human brain quails when confronted with such prolif-
erating vastness. We think we have a grasp of it, brandishing our
numbers – natural, rational, complex, real, unreal – in the face of
all that's inestimable, but truthfully these resources are mere talis-
mans, not practical tools. A comfort; no more.

Nevertheless, the doorways into that inexhaustible wilderness of
forever multiplying worlds had been opened to us, and we required
the means to at least try to understand as much as we could of
their hidden mechanisms and how they might be comprehended
and navigated.

Learning about the many worlds occurred, appropriately, in layers.
One was history. In at least three categories.

There was history that we knew we were allowed to know, history
that we knew we were not allowed to know, and history that allegedly didn't exist but that we – that is, the students of this effectively measureless subject – suspected did exist but was never talked
about, not at our level and perhaps not even at the level of the
people who taught us.

We were aware from the beginning that the Concern had many more levels than were immediately visible from the lowly strata where we existed in its tortuously convoluted hierarchy, and it was hard even to guess at how far beyond us it extended, given both the irredeemably complex nature of the many worlds themselves and the seemingly quite deliberate opacity of the organisation's structure.

We knew there were various levels and classes of executives within l'Expédience with, at the apparent pinnacle of this structure, the Central Council itself, composed of people who knew all there was to know about the Concern's provenance, internal configuration, extent, operational methods and aims, and some of us were of the opinion – always perverse, in mine – that there might be one central authority figure at the head of all this tiered knowledge and power, a kind of organisational autocrat to whom everybody else was obliged to defer. But for all we knew that final, single, near-godlike Emperor of the realities – if he or she did exist – was little better than a foot soldier in a still greater grouping of other Concerns and meta-Concerns extending further and higher out across and through the furiously expanding realities and numbered in millions, billions, trillions . . . who knew?

For us lowly foot soldiers, though, mere trainees that we were, the centre of our world – the centre of all our many worlds – was the Speditionary Faculty of the University of Practical Talents, Aspherje, on an Earth that – almost uniquely – did not call itself Earth, but Calbefraques.

Calbefraques was the ultimate Open world, the mirror image of one of the numberless perfectly Closed Earths where nobody knew about the many worlds; a place where possibly every single adult soul who walked its surface knew that it was merely one world within an infinitude of worlds, and a nexus at that, a stepping-off point for as much of that infinitude as it was possible to imagine.

And a world, an Earth that was close to unique. Logically there had to be other versions of this Earth that were close to the

Calbefraques that we knew, but we seemed to be unable to access them. It was as though by being the place that could act as a gateway to any other version of Earth, Calbefraques had somehow outpaced all the other versions of itself that would otherwise have existed. It seemed that in the same way that the true consciousness of a transitioner could only be in one world at a time, there could only be one world that was perfectly Open, and that world, that unique Earth was this one, called Calbefraques.

It was here that almost all the transitioners lived when they were not on missions to other worlds, and here too that the vast majority of theorists of transitioning, experts in transitioning, researchers into transitioning and experimental practitioners of transitioning both made their home and plied their trade. In its globally distributed factories and laboratories all the multifarious paraphernalia of transitioning was manufactured, and – somewhere, allegedly – the ultimately precious substance we called septus, the drug that made flitting possible in the first place, was brought into being. Exactly how and where this was done and exactly what septus really was, nobody seemed to know. The secrecy surrounding the drug's creation was of an order more intense even than that associated with the severely security-conscious operations of the Transitionary Corps. Naturally, this meant that the speculation regarding this piece of arcana was, to put it mildly, unrestrained.

There were strict rules about the use and exposure of septus within this world or any other, restricting its use to its flitting-enabling purpose and absolutely nothing else. But it was rumoured that, if one did try to have some of it analysed, in the most advanced laboratories one could find, the sample itself simply vanished, or appeared on inspection – by chemical analysis, mass spectrometry, microscopes working on a variety of wavelengths or any other technique available – to be nothing more complicated than pond slime, or even pure water.

Here, in the university that was a city within a city, within its piled pyramids, ziggurats, towers and colonnades, and in the profusion of outlying buildings distributed all across the greater city – an ever-multiplying number, in a fit image of what was studied within them – millions of students like myself had, over the years, learned as much of that proportion of the truth as it was thought appropriate for us to be allowed to comprehend. What some of us really wanted to know, naturally, was the size of that proportion, and what was concealed in the fraction of it being denied us.

The Transitionary

It was the septennial Festival of Death in Aspherje, Calbefraques, and the Central Council of the Transitionary Office had arranged a particularly extravagant party and ball to celebrate both the formal cultural event and the latest expansion and reconstitution of the Council.

Guests arrived on a specially constructed narrow-gauge railway which ran in a loop round the closed city centre, picking up guests from a variety of temporary stations – manned by servants dressed as ghouls – which were dotted around the periphery of the cordoned-off area, where the guests' own transport had deposited them. The track was lit by tall, smokily guttering torches and by burning braziers hanging from gibbets and made to look like ancient roadside punishment cages, the skeletons of starved miscreants visible through the smoke and flames inside.

At the Final Terminus, the station – seemingly made entirely of dinosaur bones – where the guests were deposited, a wide moat had been dug across the park in front of the entrance to the University's Great Hall. Beneath the water lay a system of pipes which fed marsh gases and flammable oils to the surface, where they were lit or detonated by floating bundles of burning rags containing clockwork mechanisms that made them jerk and move and appear briefly human.

Guests proceeded across a bridge bowed out across this waste of sporadic conflagration and entered the Great Hall through a recently

214

constructed ill-lit tunnel of soot-blackened stone. Enormous iron doors creaked open to admit guests to a tall circular space containing another, near-circular moat of unpleasant-smelling water lying at the foot of a great steep bowl of curved walls running with liquids. Across a bridge ahead stood a great wall of what appeared to be slate, its slick surface running with water cascading down its imperfectly vertical surface in fast, hissing waves. Beyond the far end of the bridge, where one might have expected to see a door, there was only this wall of water, nothing else.

The great iron doors behind swung shut on each batch of two dozen or so guests, leaving them looking nervously round, unable to see a way out. Streamers of fire appeared twenty metres above them, all around the top of the vast bowl they found themselves trapped within, while the small bridge that had led them from the tunnel behind was drawn quickly back up to clang and echo against the rust-pitted surface of the doors.

The burning oils quickly covered most of the bowl's curtain wall and started to pool on the surface of the water at the foot, spreading slowly towards the low island of dry stone in the middle where the now-fearful group of guests huddled, beginning to wonder if something had gone wrong with one of the various mechanisms – large parts of the university had been closed for months while all this had been set up and there had been rumours of cost overruns, technical problems, project delays and last-minute panics – or if it was all some horrendously complicated and involved plot directed at them personally and they were to be cruelly put to death for some real, exaggerated or entirely imaginary crime.

Just when the guests could feel the heat from the wall of flame around them starting to become uncomfortable and were genuinely beginning to fear not just for their costumes but for their lives, the vast wall of slate covered in spilling water ahead of them cracked vertically to reveal itself as a pair of enormous doors which began to open with a crushingly ponderous grace, their burden of water still crashing down their faces undiminished while a broad tongue of stone levered smoothly down between them to provide a bridge over the encircling noose of fire.

Servants dressed as ghosts and the risen dead – a few of them equipped with fire extinguishers, just in case – beckoned the by now usually highly relieved and indeed cheering partygoers over the stone bridge and into the throat of another dark tunnel which led via almost disappointingly conventional cloak- and restrooms into the main body of the Great Hall, where the ball was to be held under a vast black tent of a roof studded with high and distant lights arranged in starlike constellations.

A short walk away down a corridor lined with skulls gleaned from catacombs across the continent another only slightly smaller hall held a collection of circular drink, food, drug and smoking bars around which people milled like magnetic particles ricocheting within some colossal game. Further away, up some wide steps turned into an uphill slalom slope by dense wavy lines of antique funeral urns, the way led to the great circular space underneath the Dome of the Mists itself.

This space too had been waterproofed and filled with a little artificial sea a metre deep; a circular lake over a hundred metres across was covered with fragrant floating plants and dotted with tiny islands covered in food and tinkling fountains of wine. Skiffs, rowing boats and barges rowed by exotically uniformed children plied the placid waters while, above, tumbling and high-wire acts were performed, surrounded by make-believe shooting stars composed of great fireworks raining sparks and running on lines suspended across the darkly glittering lake. An orchestra on the largest island, situated in the centre of the waters, filled the space with music while the wildly decorated lantern-lit vessels sailed serenely around.

A porcelain coracle rowed by a preposterously dressed dwarf bumped very gently into the rushes-bundle fenders lining the wooden quay near the hall's entrance. The miniature man toked on a tube sticking out from a frill on one of his sparkling concentric collars. "Mr Oh?" he asked in a helium-high voice.

"Good evening."

"Madame d'Ortolan awaits, sir." He nodded at the other man's shoes. "Boat's a bit delicate, squire. You'll have to take those off." Oh undid his shoes. He had dressed conservatively in his old Speditionary Faculty dress uniform, having no particular intention of joining in the ball and – slightly to his own surprise – no desire to dress in a fancy costume. "You can leave them with the quay master, sir," the dwarf said when Oh went to take his shoes with him. "You won't be needing them on the barge."

Oh handed his shoes to the cadaverously dressed man in charge of the little pier. He stepped carefully into the fur-lined interior of the bizarrely fragile craft. The ceramic hull was so thin that, where the furs did not cover it, you could see the shadow of the waters lapping around its waterline from inside. The dwarf took a breath from a different tube and said in an unfeasibly deep voice, "Off we go, sir. Please do sit still and don't touch the sides."

Oh sat patiently where he was, legs and arms crossed, and let the dwarf row him slowly out over the gently chopping water towards the most extravagantly decorated vessel on the whole lake. It was made of ice and glided unhurriedly across the waves in its own surrounding skirt of curling mists. It was sculpted to look like an ancient royal barge: its carriage-like superstructure was covered in gold leaf and it bore at its centre a great square sail on which was projected a filmed performance of a famously sensual and erotic ballet.

The air grew noticeably colder as the dainty coracle approached the ice barge; the dwarf used one oar to prevent his frangible craft hitting the larger vessel's hull. Servants dressed like skeletons helped Oh up to the deck and the dwarf rowed slowly away again. The barge's deck covering looked like some form of dark skin, and felt as warm.

Madame d'Ortolan reclined with a few other members of the Central Council in a nest of glistening blood-red cushions inside the main cabin of the craft, surrounded by canted gilt poles holding furled curtains of gold-threaded purple material. The tented ceiling of the enclosure appeared insubstantial, made from thousands of little black and white pearls threaded on silver wires.

The raised, airy cabin afforded views out across the lake, its tiny jewel-like islands and the flotilla of slowly swirling vessels. Oh recognised the others of the Council who were present and greeted them individually: Mr Repton Bik, Madama Gambara-Cilleon, Lord Harmyle, Professor Prieska Dottlemien, Comptroller Lapsaline-Hregge, Captain Yollyi Suyen and of course Madame d'Ortolan herself, who, with the latest changes to the Council, was now its acknowledged if unofficial head.

She was dressed in some ancient wildly complicated costume, all frills and ruffles and floaty films of material, the outer layers of which which seemed barely heavier or less transparent than the air. Jewels glittered on the lacy extremities of her pooled skirts and on her fingers, ears, throat, forehead and nose. She had lately been accorded the privilege of moving from her earlier, aged body – already her second since she had been invited to join the Council – and was now a curvaceously beautiful white-skinned creature, raven-haired, with icy blue eyes and fabulously near-spherical breasts which she had chosen to reveal in all their considerable glory. Her extravagant costume stopped at her amazingly thin waist and only resumed again at her shoulders, where a little lacy thing like a volup-tuary's idea of a bed-jacket covered her shoulders and arms.

A ruby nestled in her belly button and her breasts were strung with lines of tiny diamonds. A diamond choker encircled her long, slim neck.

"Young Mr Oh," she said, patting a plump of pillows beside her. "Do come and sit."

Two other Council members – like the others, fabulously attired, though in no case as opulently or as revealingly as Madame d'Ortolan – adjusted themselves where they lay to accommodate him. Oh kissed her hand when she offered it. "Madame, I feel underdressed," he told her.

"To the contrary," she said. "I am so, and you are positively swaddled in your schoolboy uniform. Ah. I see your feet are naked. That is something." A tray held outstretched by one of the skeletally dressed servants appeared between them. Madame d'Ortolan waved her hand at it and Oh lifted a globular glass with a double skin and several tiny fish swimming in the watery space surrounding the drink itself, which was warm and highly spiced. "I am some opera costumier's version of a slave girl," she told him, looking down at herself and spreading her arms. "What do you think?"

"It's very spectacular."

She cupped her diamond-rashed breasts in her hands as though weighing them. "I'm particularly pleased with these."

"I imagine everybody else is too, ma'am."

She looked up at him and smiled exasperatedly. "Mr Oh – Temudjin, if I may – you sound like an old man. Listen to yourself!" She nodded at the globular glass. "Drink up. You obviously need it."

He drank.

Oh wondered at Madame d'Ortolan's startlingly young and vivacious new body. It was generally held that one had a physique one had grown up with and grown accustomed to and that trying to stray too far from this template when transitioning – or, even more so, when re-embodying, as Madame d'Ortolan had done – was both difficult to accomplish and disagreeable to maintain, especially over extended intervals.

He knew from his own transitions that unless he made a particular effort to avoid doing so he tended to end up in quite plain, rather averagely sized bodies, whereas his own real body, this body, the one that stayed in Calbefraques in the house on the ridge overlooking the town of Flesse, was taller, more pleasingly proportioned and altogether better-looking than those he naturally gravitated towards in the course of his missions for the Concern.

Of course, expressing oneself into quite plain, unremarkable forms was a positive benefit in his line of work as it made it easier to slip in and out of situations and worlds without attracting undue attention, but he had always wondered why his transitionary selves always seemed to be so short and bland without him intending them to be so. Maybe deep down that was just his physiology of choice, though he could not see why.

They did say that for those with transgender issues, transitioning into bodies quite different from that one had grown up within was a positive boon, almost a treatment and solution in itself.

Madame d'Ortolan had always been a slightly dumpy if still elegantly turned-out lady, according to both gossip and the photographic records of the Concern; to have chosen the body she was displaying so luxuriantly before him now must indicate she was prepared to make a considerable sacrifice of her own future comfort – taking on that very feeling of not being happy in one's own skin that sufferers found so objectionable – for the sake of looking like she had obviously convinced herself she ought to look. It indicated a single-mindedness and determination that many people would find admirable, Oh supposed, but also a sort of ruthlessness against the self that did not speak of a wholly healthy and untroubled personality.

She made an all-embracing gesture with one arm. "What do you think of the party?"

He made a show of looking all around. "I have never seen anything quite like it," he told her truthfully. "I can't imagine what it must have cost. Or how long it must have taken to arrange."

"A fortune," she told him, smiling broadly. "And for ever!" She produced a corded mouthpiece joined to a giant water pipe situated some metres away and carefully tended by another of the skeletally dressed servants. She took a little sip of the smoke, passed the mouthpiece to him. "Do, *do* be careful," she told him archly, putting one ring-heavy hand on his knee and leaving it there. "It's frightfully strong."

Oh put his lips to the mouthpiece. She had left it a little moist. He drew in a mouthful of the grey-pink smoke, which smelled and tasted like a cocktail of different drugs. He let the fumes touch just the top of his lungs and then blew them decorously out again rather than hold them in and get too stoned. He got the impression that Madame d'Ortolan had already smoked quite a lot. She was still smiling fixedly at him. One of her hands played with one of the strings of diamonds curved over her breasts.

"I do hope you're here quite determined to enjoy yourself, Tem," she told him. "It would be such a terrible waste of time and resources otherwise."

"Madame, I feel entirely obliged to."

"Please, call me Theodora."

"Thank you, Theodora. Yes, I intend to enjoy myself." He held up the half-drained glass of warm liquor and presented the hookah mouthpiece back to her. He did his best to smile with all the warmth he could command. "Indeed, I have already begun to."

She tapped his knee. "So," she said, for a moment slightly more businesslike. "How did the Questionary Office treat you after your meeting with Mrs M?"

Oh had told the Concern about his encounter with Mrs Mulverhill at the casino in Flesse, their subsequent flit and something of their conversation.

"Quite humanely, Theodora." There had been a lot of questions and they had – hilariously, he thought – tried to hypnotise him, plus he was sure they had people listening and watching him while he answered their questions who would be attuned to any degree of falsity or evasion. But there had been no threat of unpleasantness and he had been as open as he felt he could.

"And Mrs M herself," Madame d'Ortolan purred. "Did she treat you humanely?"

"She certainly treated me like a human."

Madame d'Ortolan tapped his knee with one ringed finger. "I heard," she said, seemingly addressing his knee or her finger, "that she took you to another world while you were inside her." She looked up at him, wide-eyed. "Is that true?"

"It is, Theodora."

221

"Ah," she said, with what sounded like wistfulness. "The transport of delight."

"Just after, actually."

"I hope it was worth it."

"That would be impossible to judge," he said, aware he was being gnomic. Still, it seemed to satisfy her.

She stroked his knee. "Tell me, Tem, what did she say about me?"

"Well, Theodora, I can't entirely remember."

"Really?"

"Really."

"Are you sure you're not just trying to be gallant?"

"Fairly sure."

"I think you are. You are trying to be gallant." She brought herself confidentially closer to him, leaning so close that one of her nipples pressed gently against his jacket, level with his heart. "You are trying to be gallant!"

"Well, it's just that, having talked about it all at such length with the Questionary people, the recollection feels worn. Stripped out, if you like. As though I have the memory of a memory, not the memory itself."

She looked at him unsteadily, as though dazzled. "I do hope you're not trying to be *too* gallant, Tem," she said, her voice quite firm. "There's nothing you need spare me."

He was sure that Madame d'Ortolan had either read the transcript of what he'd told the Questionary Office or seen a recording of his interview. At the very least she would have had full access to any records so could have learned all she needed to know from those.

"Mrs Mulverhill," he began, and instantly sensed the three faces nearest to them flick their attention in his direction. He brought his mouth closer to Madame d'Ortolan's ear and lowered his voice accordingly, "said that you would lead the Concern to disaster and ruin," he told her. "And that you – or some part or faction of the Central Council – might have a hidden agenda. Though she was not sure what that might be."

Madame d'Ortolan was silent for a moment. Beyond her feet, two of the other Council people, who had not overheard what he'd said earlier, were sharing a hookah mouthpiece and a joke. The two men laughed suddenly and uproariously in a spluttering cloud of grey-pink smoke. "You know," Madame d'Ortolan said quietly, and there was a steely edge to her voice that made him think that she had not been drunk or stoned in the least, "we have tried so hard to protect you, Tem." She looked steadily up at him. He chose to say nothing. "We have watched you so very, very carefully, and surrounded you with so many people charged with making sure that you come to no harm from this woman, and put our best people onto the job of monitoring all your flits, and every world you go to and everything you do there. We have been so impressed with every-thing you've done, but so disappointed that we seem unable to stop this woman finding you, or prevent her taking you wherever she wants once she has, or backtracking where you've been with her subsequently. I find it almost unbelievable that she can do that all by herself. Don't you think it's unbelievable?" She played with a strand of her curling black hair, twisting it round one finger, again looking up at him wide-eyed.

"No, Theodora, I don't," he told her. "It happens to me. I take no part in it, but it happens nevertheless. So I find it perfectly believ-able. You would too." He drank from his fishily inhabited glass.

She took the mouthpiece of the water pipe and used it to stroke his leg lightly, from upper thigh to mid-calf. "I believe you, Tem, of course," she said absently, as though not paying attention to herself. "However, there are those who feel that we may be being a tad too lenient in all this. It does just seem so very strange that she can do what she can so terribly easily, and all without any help or cooper-ation from you. Perhaps we need to check how . . . how easy it is to flit with you like that."

"You mean, so embraced, so contained?"

"Well, yes." She was still watching her hand holding the hookah mouthpiece.

He waited until she brought the mouthpiece back up and then took it from her and sucked on it. "If you are saying what I think you are, Theodora, then it would be both a pleasure and an honour."

She looked up with an open, vacant expression. "I do beg your pardon, what was it you thought I was saying?"

"I may have misinterpreted, ma'am," Oh said on an in-breath, waving the mouthpiece through a grey-pink cloud. "Perhaps you ought to say what it was you were actually saying, to spare the blushes of us both."

She looked at him knowingly and took the mouthpiece back, sucking daintily on it. "I think you know exactly what I was saying, Tem."

He bowed as best he could, given that he was reclining. "Ma'am, I am at your disposal."

She smiled. "You are amenable, Temudjin? You consent?" She reached out and took hold of one of his hands. "You see, I ask your permission rather than just take you. I think to do that is simply rude. A violation, even."

"I am entirely amenable, Theodora."

She gave a little tinkling laugh. "Still so formal!" She squeezed his hand. "Come then. Let us do this."

Without further ado they were suddenly somewhere else. She was dressed just as she had been. He was not. Now he wore fancy dress; some sort of blue-and-silver-striped puffed-out outfit with shoes whose toes turned up and a giant hat shaped like an onion. Everything else felt very similar. Same fragre, same languages. They appeared to be lying on a collection of pillows and cushions similar to those they had just left, but situated on a little circular island surrounded by a wide pool of water lit from below by slowly changing lights of green and blue. The walls and ceiling were dark or invisible. The air was warm and smelled of strong, heady perfumes. There was nobody else within sight.

Madame d'Ortolan moved herself closer to him. "There. We are just beneath the floor of the Dome of the Mists. Our vacated selves

are floating somewhere just overhead. This seems agreeable to you?"
There was a kind of slightly delayed natural amplification behind
her voice that made him suspect they were right in the centre of a
perfectly circular space, her words echoing off the totality of the
circumference around them.

Oh felt round the perimeter of his giant hat. "I'm not sure about
this," he said, and took it off. His voice, too, sounded strange, the
echoes overemphatic, lagging behind his words just enough to clash
with them. "But otherwise, yes, it's perfectly agreeable."

She smiled, smoothed a hand over his hair. "Let us make it more
agreeable," she whispered, and slid to him, embracing him, bringing
her mouth up to his.

He had wondered if this would prove awkward or difficult, but
it did not. He remembered Mrs Mulverhill asking him if he'd fucked
Madame d'Ortolan yet (or had she even expressed it as her fucking
him? – he couldn't recall) and deciding at the time that his pride
would not let that happen. Even that he ought to feel some sort of
loyalty, some fidelity to Mrs Mulverhill, both sexual and – what?
ideological? – despite feeling even at the time that this was preposterous, almost perverse. At the very, very least, he'd thought over
the last few minutes, he would be cold, or difficult to persuade or
rouse, or perfunctory and hinting at contemptuous.

But, faced with such flattering attention from on high, confronted
with such a powerful regard from somebody who had taken such
trouble to make themselves so formidably if ostentatiously attractive,
there was no part of him that was not responding enthusiastically.
There might, he supposed, have been something in the drug smoke
or the drink, but probably, he admitted to himself, not.

Madame d'Ortolan was a highly capable lover; dextrous, smooth
and with a sort of restless, almost impatient touch, forever moving
her hands and mouth and attention from one place on his body to
the next, as though, while never exactly dissatisfied with what she
had uncovered already, she was still searching for something even
better.

Both their costumes seemed to have been designed to provide easy sexual access without having to take any part of them entirely off. When he entered her, she let out a great satisfied sigh and hugged him tightly to her with all four limbs, throwing her head back to expose her long white neck and giving a sort of growling laugh. "Ah, now," she said, half to herself. "Just there, just there."

There was a virtuosic skill in what happened a few minutes later, when they both achieved orgasm at once. This was such a cliché in itself, and so relatively unusual, that Oh found, even in the course of it, time to be unashamedly impressed. As the sensation was beginning to ebb – the echoes of his cries and hers starting to fade around them – she took him, transitioning them together into another pair of coupled bodies. Then, moments later, into another, and another, and another. He had no time to evaluate each passing body and world, was barely aware of more than a riffling sequence of fragres, glimpses of different amounts or qualities of light – eyes open or not – and the feel of larger or smaller spaces around them. Cooler air, warmer air, varying smells of perfumes and bodily musks, even their physical state in the shape of different sexual positions; all flickered past him in a strobe of elongated ecstasies.

He did recall, despite the pulsings of such concentrated, extended pleasure, that there were people who existed in a state of perpetual sexual arousal, coming to orgasm continually, through the most trivial, ordinary and frequent physical triggers and experiences. It sounded like utter bliss, the sort of thing drunk friends roared with envious laughter over towards the end of an evening, but the unfunny truth was that, in its most acute form, it was a severe and debilitating medical condition. The final proof that it was so was that many people who suffered from it took their own lives. Bliss – pure physical rapture – could become absolutely unbearable.

Mrs M was right; in everything a leavening.

But it finished, the final few transitions into other heaving, sweating, trembling bodies taking longer and longer in each, each time, and synchronised so that it was just the last few spasms on each occasion, then the exhausted dregs of climax that were experienced, and finally a long, extending afterglow, the sum of it like some absurdly exaggerated romanticised ideal of perfect physical and spiritual lovemaking.

When it was finally over and Oh was able to open his eyes, clear his head and take stock of his surroundings, he was still inside her, and they were sitting together, facing each other in some sort of tall V-shaped love seat, its velvety components and cut-outs arranged just so to offer the occupying lovers access, support, purchase and leverage.

They were in a great flat desert of pale golden sand, beneath a plain black canopy flapping in a steady wind, the air warm as it flowed across their entirely naked bodies. There was nobody else around that he could see. Beneath them, his feet were just touching the surface of a thick abstractly patterned carpet. A small table nearby held some decorated ceramic pots and a tall elegantly worked jug. A pile of their clothes lay folded on a wide footstool. A short distance away, a couple of large tawny-pelted animals that he didn't recognise lay asleep on the sand. Little fragre to sense. Languages as before. This body was leaner and more muscular than his own. Thinking about it, they all had been. Looking down, he saw that he was as shaved as she was.

Madame d'Ortolan yawned and stretched. She smiled at him. She looked just as she had, though bereft of her clothes and jewellery. She ran a hand through his hair, her gaze flicking about his face.

"So, Tem," she said lazily, and gave a little shiver, squeezing him inside her.

"Your investigations are complete, I take it," Oh said. His words sounded a little more cold than he'd meant.

She gazed levelly at him. "I suppose they are, Tem." It was hard to read her voice. She stroked his face. "And very pleasant they were to perform, too. Wouldn't you say?" Her smile appeared engagingly tentative.

He took one of her hands and kissed it gently with dry lips. "I would," he said, but stalled there, and could not even look her in the eye. Confused, he felt a need to say more, to make light of this, or, perhaps, instead, to behave in an overtly and overly romantic, grateful manner, to reassure her even, to compliment and flatter her and declare his admiration and appreciation, yet at the same time he wanted to dismiss her, deflate her, hurt her, just get away from her.

He felt caught, poised between these conflicting urges, as balanced on their cusp as he was on this absurd fucking chair.

"I trust something of the lady's spell might now be broken, yes?" she asked, bringing her mouth close to his ear as she stroked his cheek with the back of her fingers. "I'm sure she has her own naive charms, but further experience offers us greater richness, don't you think? It offers us some extra perspective. We compare, contrast, measure and judge. Initial impressions, however enchanting they may have seemed at the time, are evaluated again in the light of something more accomplished. What might have seemed matchless becomes . . . re-valued, hmm?" She levered herself away a little and smiled, her hand still stroking his cheek. "The young wine serves its purpose and seems well enough when one knows no better, but only the fine wine, brought patiently to the summit of fruition where it may reveal all its complexities and subtleties, satisfies all the available senses, wouldn't you say?"

He stilled the stroking hand, folding it in his own. "Well," he said, forcing himself to stare into her eyes. "Indeed. There was no comparison."

He felt her gaze pierce him, and knew immediately that the remark, which had been meant to deceive, which he had thought cunning and which was supposed to mean one thing to her and another entirely to him, had failed to mislead her.

He felt something in her change. She pursed her lips, said, "We'll go back now."

And they were back, back to the ice yacht and the corpuscular landscape of pillows and cushions they shared with the others, she just letting go of his hand and looking away, her expression bored. She lifted the mouthpiece for the hookah and drew deeply on it, then glanced back at him. Her face looked closed, composed. "Fascinating, Mr Oh," she said. She waved one hand dismissively. "I'll let you get back to the party. Good night."

He felt silenced by his own clashing emotions as much as by her. He hesitated, then decided that there was nothing he could say or do that would not make the situation worse. He nodded, rose and left.

A drunk, singing dwarf in a spun-sugar dinghy rowed him back to shore, breaking off a bit of gunwale as they approached and offering it to him. "Tastes of rum, sir! Go on! Try it! Try it! Try it!"

The Philosopher

I must concede that I was lucky in a sense. On my return from abroad and my quitting the Army I found employment immediately during a time of high unemployment, having been recommended to the national police force by one of the special-forces liaison officers I had worked with overseas. My skills and abilities had been recognised at quite high levels and I will not pretend that I did not feel a degree of pride on realising this.

I met with some ill feeling from a few of my new colleagues in the police force at first, perhaps because I had been brought in at a relatively senior level. However, I like to think that I soon won the respect of almost all of them, though of course there will always be those in any organisation who will find something to be resentful about and one simply has to live with that fact.

I found myself in the civilian police, albeit the more senior and serious national police force, at a moment in time when the full extent of the Christian Terrorist threat was just beginning to become clear even to those, not least our own government, who had persuaded themselves that such people could be dealt with effectively by negotiation and the occasional slap on the wrist.

I think the first airport massacre ended that policy of folly. The CTs sent in a small suicide team of big, well-trained men who simply overpowered one of the two-man armed police teams who patrolled our ill-defended airports at the time. The two officers stood no chance; they were bundled to the ground by three or four fanatics of substantial physical size, their throats were cut without mercy and their machine guns and ammunition clips taken from them and turned on the nearest check-in queue. The members of the suicide team not firing the guns set about slashing at as many of the screaming, fleeing holidaymakers as they could, chasing down women and children and slitting their throats too, without mercy. Nearly forty innocent people of all ages were butchered in this orgy of violence.

When the machine guns ran out of ammunition everyone in the team was meant to kill themselves but two of them were over-powered by angry citizens before they could take that coward's way out. One did not survive their summary justice but the other did and it was on him that I had what I will freely confess was the pleasure of working subsequently, with the aim of discovering as much as possible about the organisation and aims of the CT organisation.

I felt intense pride that I had been chosen to conduct this inter-rogation. I took it as a compliment both to my technical skills but also to my reputation for the measured and considered application of my techniques. Such was the national outrage at the attack at the time that a more hot-headed operative might have botched the assignment. It is a myth that the police and other security personnel are immune to emotion, both their own and that of the law-abiding populace at large. We may be trained to combat the deleterious effects of acting on such emotions, but we are not inhuman.

I too felt a cold fury towards the wretched individual who had carried out such a cowardly attack, but I would not let that emotion, however understandable, cloud my professional judgement regarding the task in hand or allow any rashness or overreaction so caused to effectively offer this animal of an extremist an overly quick escape from the torments he so richly deserved.

The specific operational details of the interrogation need not detain us here. The desire to know of such things can be almost prurient at times, in my opinion. My colleagues and I are paid to do such things and are trained to cope with the psychological fallout of our actions and there are good reasons why a veil is drawn over such matters to protect the general populace, who do not deserve to have to confront the realities that we have to face every day to keep them safe.

Suffice to say, despite the subject's attempts to convert me to his bizarre, perverted and cruel religion with its emphasis on martyrdom, cannibalism and the alleged ability of their holy men to forgive all sins no matter how horrendous and barbaric, I did not reconvert to become a Christian! And let me just say that I do not even concede that he was displaying any real bravery or strength of will in trying to do so. Fanatics are driven purely by their own fanaticism, and anyway it is a common technique used by subjects trained to resist interrogation to try to turn the resultant discourse back upon the questioner, not so much in any realistic hope of altering their views or causing them to cease or go easier in what they are doing, of course, but simply as a way for the subject to take his mind off the process itself.

In any case, I am satisfied that while the cell system of the terrorist organisation sadly protected the identities of its other members apart from the six in the suicide team itself, I, along with my colleagues, extracted all that there was to be extracted from the subject and, thanks to our restraint, we were able to deliver him alive if not intact, and certainly not unbroken, to the Justice Ministry for his trial and subsequent (well-deserved in my opinion) execution.

Adrian

I made a lot of money for Mr Noyce. Not like that dingbat son of his. Barney lost Mr N a lot of money. Soaked it up, pissed it away and snorted it. He would reappear from his bar in Goa every couple of years and announce he was coming back to stay in London and do something useful but he never did. Always ended up going back to the bar. He thought his dad ought to bail him out by giving him a job with his own firm, but Mr N wasn't having it. Blood might be thicker than water but it's no match for liquidity, know what I mean? Money is serious. You fuck about with it at your peril.

Barney was always at Mr N to give him the bar, too, to turn it over to him legally but Mr N was too clever for that as well. He knew Barney would just sell it or lose it in a poker game or use it as collateral to fund some shitwit scheme that he'd make the usual unholy fucking mess of and be back at Mr and Mrs N's with the begging bowl shortly after.

Frankly, I think Ed found his boy a bit of an embarrassment. He was glad he was mostly arm's length away in sunny Goa. Barney and me weren't getting on so well any more either. I found him a bit of a moaner, always on about how tough things were for him when this was clearly a load of bollocks. Little cunt had had a charmed life with all the advantages, hadn't he? Not my fault or his dad's that he'd fucked it. And I mean, running a bar on a beach? That's the fucking jackpot prize for most people, that is, that's what your average geezer would regard as a brilliant retirement. Hard done by, my arse.

And he had the nerve to blame me for this, at least partly. Good as told me this when we were drunk together once during a weekend at Spetley Hall. Like it was all my fault because I'd replaced him in Mr and Mrs N's affections. So what if I had? I was a better friend to them than he was a son. I mean, the soft git.

But I was the golden boy, wasn't I? Never mind that the Noyces were like a second family to me, Mr N's firm was like the first national bank of AC. I made a fucking mint. Most of it went to the firm but a lot came back to me in the way of a decent salary but especially in bonuses. Mr N and I had some heated discussions on the subject of bonuses on a few occasions but we always came to an agreement in the end.

I suppose we both always knew I'd be leaving and going else-where eventually, but in the meantime the good times rolled with no hard feelings.

Bought a bigger flat in delightful Docklands and a succession of less and less practical cars. Thought about a yacht but decided they just weren't me – you could always charter if you really needed to. Took me hols in Aspen, the Maldives, Klosters, the Bahamas, New Zealand and Chile. Not to mention Majorca and Crete, doing a bit of old-fashioned raving in the big hot loud clubs.

And the girls. Oh, bless their little cotton gussets, the girls: Saskia and Amanda and Juliette and Jayanti and Talia and June and Charley and Charlotte and Ffion and Jude and Maria and Esme and Simone. There were lots of others, but those were the non-casual ones, the ones I took the trouble of remembering their names and was happy to have stay over more than once. I loved them all in my own way and I guess they returned the favour. Most of them wanted to take things further but I never did. There's no "us" in commitment, I'd tell them, there's just a "me." They couldn't complain. I was generous and if there were ever hard feelings then it wasn't my fault.

And every month that 10K in US greenery appeared in my main spending account, and every time I saw it on the statement I got a little leap of the heart, remembering what had happened or what had seemed to happen that night in chilly Moscow, at the Novy Pravda.

After our visit to the room with the black furniture and the amber light, Mrs M and I went back to the table where Connie Sequorin was chatting to two large Russian guys. They didn't look very pleased to see me and Mrs M, especially me, but they left their cards and a bottle of Cristal and fucked off soon enough. We ate more blinis and caviar, drank more champagne and Mrs M and Connie both danced with me. I was still in a daze, though, not really paying atten-tion to very much at all. Soon enough Mrs M paid the bill, we got our coats and walked straight to the waiting Merc that had brought us here. Snow was swirling from the orange-black sky. We went to this massive, very bright and warm hotel and I was handed the key to my own room. Mrs M said she'd be in touch and pecked me on the cheek. Connie said the same and did the two-cheek pretend-kiss thing. They had a suite and I wondered, as I padded down a very broad tall corridor to my room, if they had something going together.

I slept till mid-afternoon the next day and found an envelope had been shoved under my door with a thousand roubles in it and a first-class BA ticket to Heathrow on a flight leaving four hours later. The room had been paid for. Mrs M and Connie had checked out hours earlier. A note left behind reception by Mrs M just said, "Welcome abroad. Mrs M." Welcome abroad. Not Welcome aboard. Welcome abroad. I couldn't tell if this was a mistake or a bit of cleverness.

I went back. Back to Moscow and back to the club, the following month. I made friends with the manager guy Kliment (after a bit of suspicion – he didn't really remember me or Mrs M or Connie Sequorin and probably thought I was police or a journalist or something) and got to have a look round the place one day. I found the room, the bedroom where Mrs M had taken me and we'd seemed to go on the weirdest of weird trips to a marshy wasteland where there was no Moscow, just ruins.

It hadn't occurred to me at the time to bring back a flower or a pebble or something – I'd been too fucking freaked out, I suppose. Not that that would have proved anything anyway. I knew something bizarre had happened but I didn't know exactly what. I had the use of the room and the run of the place for the afternoon, until the staff arrived in the early evening to make the club ready for the night's fun, and I had a good look round the room, the rooms on either side and even the cellar underneath and the little private bar directly above but it all looked plain and kosher, just slightly seedy in the cold strip light of day and I couldn't see how the trick, assuming it was a trick, obviously, had been pulled. Drugs, I supposed. Or hypnosis. Suggestion and all that, know what I mean?

No, I didn't know what I meant either. It had just been too fucking real. I left the place no wiser than when I'd arrived and even turned down the offer of VIP entry, a nice table and a free bottle of bubbles from my new friend Kliment. Tired, I said. Some other time. Flew straight back to dear old fuck-off Blighty that night.

I looked into travelling back to the Zone, around Chernobyl, but it was properly difficult to arrange and I never really felt happy with the whole idea. The more I thought about it the more sure I was I'd go back, at some risk to my future health, find the place where Mrs M had been hanging out and discover, oh wow, it was empty and deserted and it was as if it had all never been. No office, just an old supermarket or warehouse or whatever the fuck.

Tried asking Ed about it but he claimed he knew nothing. Never met or heard of a Mrs Mulverhill. Connie S was just a woman he'd vaguely heard of recently at the time when she asked to be introduced to me. He swore he'd never heard of anything called the Concern and he certainly wasn't getting any mysterious dosh every month, eight and a half K or otherwise. I'd have pushed further but he was just on the edge of getting annoyed with me, I could tell, and I was pretty sure I knew when Mr N was telling the truth by now. I hadn't told him any more than I'd needed to but he was obviously intrigued just from the little I had said and started asking me questions. I stonewalled him, told him he didn't want to know any more.

Connie herself seemed to have disappeared off the face of the fucking Earth. Phones disconnected, business address a briefly rented office in Paris, unheard of by anybody who might have known somebody in her line of work.

Checked the account, saw the money, waited for the call that never came. All that happened was that a couriered letter arrived from a C. Sequorin in Tashkent, Uzbekistan with a bunch of weird-looking names that were codes, apparently. I was to commit them to memory if I could, otherwise just keep the letter safe for future reference. I put it in my safe. (I hired a private eye in Tashkent, because you can do that sort of thing these days in the wonderful new globalised world, providing only that you have access to piles of dosh. Nothing. Another deserted office. No joy tracing the source of the funds in the Cayman Islands either. Well, of course not. If governments can't trace anything in tax havens, how the fuck was I supposed to? When I thought about this it was actually highly fucking reassuring.)

A week after the letter with the codes, a padded envelope arrived with something the size and weight of a brick inside. It was a black box of thick plastic and inside that was a steel box with a sort of dial on the top made of seven concentric rings of different metals arranged around a very slightly concave button in the centre. These rings circled round and back with a sort of smooth clickiness, if you know what I mean, and if you looked carefully they had lots of little patterns of dots on them but they didn't seem to do anything. There was a thinner-than-hair fine line around the middle of the box, like it was meant to open, maybe if you got the dials on the top arranged just right, like a combination lock on a safe, I suppose, but with the box came a note from Mrs Mulverhill saying I was to keep this metal box safe, guard it with my life and only give it to somebody who knew the codes from the letter.

I tried having it X-rayed via a pal who works in airport security at City, but the box wasn't having it. In fact, my mate thought his machine must be broken cos the thing didn't show up at all. How fucking weird is that? If you could make a gun out of this stuff you could saunter onto any plane in the world totally tooled up. My guy pointed this out and I told him it'd be very unhealthy indeed for both of us if he breathed so much as a syllable about it. I'd barely finished telling him this when I got a very terse text message on my mobile telling me never to X-ray the box again or even think about trying any other method of looking inside.

Keep it hidden; keep it safe. That was all.

How the fuck had they known?

Anyway, I lobbed the fucker into the back of the safe with the

letter and did my best to forget about both of them, quite successfully.

Months, years passed. Left Mr N's firm when he retired in 2000,
became a hedgie working out of an ultra-smart property in Mayfair
with another dozen or so guys, left NYC the day before the towers
came down and was never sure if I'd had a narrow escape or had
missed something it would have been worth being there for, despite
all the nastiness of it, just to be able to say I'd been there, know
what I mean? Anyway, I was on a beach in Trinidad so it didn't
matter. Didn't see much of the Noyces after Ed retired, though they
kept inviting me to Spetley Hall for years afterwards.

Made more money. Lost some of it opening a restaurant with a
couple of mates when each of us thought one of the others must
be the one who actually knew what he was doing. Still, live and
learn, eh? Me and half a dozen other guys broke away from Tangible
Topiary (that was the name of the hedge fund) and started up a
new one a few doors down from our old office. We called it FMS.
It was registered at Companies House and in the Cayman Islands
as just FMS Ltd with no further detail though we told people who
insisted on knowing that the letters stood for Financial Merchant
Securities or Future Market Superstars or some such tosh, but really
it stood for Fuck Me Sideways. As in Fuck Me Sideways, Look At
The Amount Of Money We're Making.

Our Mayfair office was even grander than TT's, deliberately. We
had a pool put in in the basement, a gym in the attic, and a games
room with wraparound monitors for driving and shoot-'em-up games.
Oh, and a flotation pod each. All tax-deductible, as you'd expect.
Even the computer games were there to help us work off all that
testosterone and aggression, weren't they? The place usually
contained more people there to advise us or tutor us on stuff than
it did us actual hedgies. We had personal trainers, an in-house masseur,
fine-wine advisers, bespoke personal-scent consultants, grooming and
presentational experts, lifestyle and diet gurus, yacht brokers, fencing
instructors and personal shoppers arriving from Harrods or Jermyn

Street every couple of hours or so with stuff they thought would suit us (no time or inclination to actually go to the shops or mix with the plebs).

Not to mention an account with a very discreet top-of-the-range escort service based a couple of streets away for when all that testosterone needed another sort of outlet. We had a special room for that too that we called the canteen, though the joke was some guys took it at their desk. I was slow to start using that particular service. Never paid for it before, so it was like a pride thing? Only there'd be times when you'd be sitting there in front of the screens and feeling suddenly horny and knowing a fabulous-looking girl who needed absolutely no chatting up or dining or alcoholic lubrication or talk of *Where do we think this is going?* or even cuddling was only a phone call and maybe ten minutes away and even though it was a week's wages for some wanker it was only petty cash given what we were making. Daft not to really, know what I mean? Like fast food, only really quality fast food.

Lot of toot taken too. Not so much by yours truly but the other guys got wired into it. I was like the sommelier of the office, though, know what I mean? We had very good contacts though mostly the dealers weren't people I'd mixed with, the turnover being what it is in the industry, but I was always the one they came to to check it was good stuff, which it almost always was. Stamp of authority, me. I should have issued certificates, charged.

When Chas, the other senior guy from TT who'd left with me to set up FMS in the first place retired to raise kids and thoroughbred racehorses I realised I was actually the oldest of the people in the office, and I was only in my early thirties. FMS indeed.

And we had our own financial advisers, believe it or not. We could make it and we could spend it (with a bit of help – see all the above), but putting it to best use, saving for a rainy day, that was another area of expertise. I mean, obviously we had a pretty good idea what to do with the loot, hundred times better than your average Joe Mug in the street, but there were people who specialised in that sort of stuff, so you listened to them. Tax shelters, write-offs, offshoring all you could, putting stuff in trusts which in theory were controlled elsewhere and just doled out what you needed if you asked nicely (ha ha). Cayman Islands, Bahamas, Channel Islands, Luxembourg, Liechtenstein, Switzerland . . .

In the end we were paying less tax than our Paki cleaners. I'd drive through the clogged and teeming streets of west London and look at all those passing faces thinking, *You mugs, you fucking mugs*.

Some of us were genius mathematicians. Not me, obviously. We split into two lots, really. There were the instinctive hedgies like me who just had a feel for what was going on and put ourselves about, keeping eyes and ears open and calling in and doing little favours here and there, and the Quants, the pure numbers guys, the mathematics wizards who in another stupider age would have been mouldering away in some ancient pile of stones in Oxbridge, inventing new numbers and burbling on about fuck knows what and doing nothing useful for society. We put them to work and paid them more money than even they could count. Then there were the programmers. They were a sort of subset of the maths guys, working on stuff that none of the rest of us even started to understand but that made everything work even more efficiently and let us make even more money.

The lease on the property next door came up. We bought that, knocked through, upped the numbers. Place became a computer centre. Had to install industrial air-conditioning plant to get rid of all the heat that the machines produced.

Guess what? Made even more money. Cars, flats, Mayfair townhouse, a nice little eight-bed new-build in Surrey, lots of hols, and girls girls girls. Still no call to make me start earning that 10K a month. Not that I needed the money, of course, but it was sort of a tradition by now, know what I mean?

Still, it always gave me an ever so slight funny turn whenever I saw it on the statement.

10

Patient 8262

I think it was our Philosophy tutor at UPT who said something which I took for granted (or, just as likely, didn't bother to think about) at the time and have only lately begun to find worrying, now that I have had all this time to think about it. It was this: Any argument or point of view that makes solipsism look no less likely may be discounted.

Solipsism, he told us, was in a sense the default state of humanity. There was, arguably, a kernel of us that always believed that we personally, our own individual consciousness, was the only thing that really existed and that nothing else mattered. That feeling we have – certainly that behaviour we exhibit – of utter selfishness as a child, absolutely demanding (beginning as an infant, when we are para-doxically all-powerful due to our very helplessness), transfigures into the common adolescent intuition that we are invulnerable, almost certainly marked out for something special, but in any event simply not capable of dying, not in our present gloriously fresh state of youthful primacy.

Armed forces at war, our tutor pointed out, are full of barely mature individuals who are perfectly convinced by the proposition

It Won't Happen to Me, and that, significantly, this applies to many who have no serious religious faith predisposing them to such wildly optimistic and irrational self-centredness. This is not to say that there aren't plenty of others who know perfectly well that It Can Happen to Anybody, or that somebody who started out feeling special and invulnerable cannot change into somebody who is rightly terrified by the randomness and capriciousness of fate – especially military fate – but the vast majority are convinced, despite the evidence all around them of that essentially uncaring arbitrariness, that nothing bad will happen to them.

It might be said that we never entirely shake off this feeling, no matter how many of our illusions we lose in later life or how let down, abandoned and irrelevant we may feel as age extracts its various tolls from us. Of course, this persistence did not in any way mean it might actually be true. We had to assume that solipsism was nonsense because otherwise everything else around us was nonsense and irrelevant, and the result of a kind of self-inflicted deceit.

The tutor's point, though, was to provide a kind of check on the wilder excesses of philosophical investigation. Of course it was always interesting and sometimes worthwhile to speculate on highly outré propositions and explore exquisitely rarefied and unlikely ideas, but that ought not to distract one overmuch from the mainstream of philosophical thought, or indeed reality.

Whenever one was struck by a previously unlikely-seeming idea that had come to appear plausible or even sensible, one ought to apply that test: was it inherently any more likely than solipsism? If solipsism seemed to make just as much sense, then the idea could be dismissed.

Of course, the proposition that nothing – or at least nobody – else in the universe really existed could never be disproved from first principles. No evidence that might be produced was capable of convincing somebody fully and determinedly holding this idea that they were not the only thinking, feeling thing in existence.

Every apparently external event could be consistently accounted for through strict adherence to that central hypothesis, that only one's own mind existed and that one had therefore made up – simply imagined – all apparent externalities.

Now, our tutor pointed out that there was a weakness in the hard-line or extreme solipsist's position which came down to the question why, if they were all that existed, they bothered to deceive themselves so? Why did it appear to the solipsistic entity that there was an external reality in the first place, and, more to the point, why this one specifically? Why did the solipsist appear to be constrained in any way by that supposedly physically non-existent and therefore utterly pliable reality?

Often, in practice, one would be talking to the solipsist concerned in a sheltered institution or outright lunatic asylum. Why did they appear to be there, with all the restrictions such establishments tended to involve, rather than living some life of maximally efficient hyper-pleasure – a god, a super-heroic master-figure capable of any achievement or state of bliss through the simple act of thinking of it?

How this argument affected the individual solipsist apparently depended entirely on their degree of self-deception and the history and development of their delusional state, our tutor informed us, but the depressing truth was that it pretty much never resulted in a eureka moment and the solipsist – now happily convinced of the existence of other people – returning to society as a rational and useful part of it. There was inevitably some underlying psychological reason why the individual had retreated to this deceptive bastion of selfish untouchability in the first place, and until that had been successfully addressed little real progress towards reality was likely.

But do you start to appreciate my concerns? Here I am, lying in my hospital bed, relatively powerless and certainly obscure, unheeded by almost everybody, of merely passing interest even to those charged with my care, and yet I am convinced that I am merely hiding, biding my time before I resume my rightful place in the world – indeed, in the many worlds! Before this I had a life of adventure and excitement, of great risk and even greater achievement, of unarguable importance and prominence, and yet now I am here, an effectively bed-bound nonentity who spends a lot of the time asleep, or lying here with my eyes closed, listening to the banality of the clinic going on all around me, day after almost unchanging day, remembering – or imagining – my earlier life of dashing, daring feats of elegance and style, and positions of importance and great power attained.

How likely, really, is it that these memories are real? The more vivid and spectacular they are, the more likely, perhaps, that they are dreams, mere notions, not the set-down traces of actual historical events. What is most likely? That these things happened, threaded through my life like some charged conducting wire spun through the drab fabric of my existence? Or that – doubtless under the influence of some of the drugs prescribed by the Clinic seemingly as a matter of course – I have used a febrile, undemanded-of mind with too much time to think and too little happening in the common weft of reality to distract it to conjure up a theatre of colourful characters and exciting events that flatter my own need to feel important?

I could easily believe that I am mad, or at least self-deceiving, or at the very least that I have been so, and that only now am I beginning to grasp the reality of my situation, my plight. Perhaps these very thoughts are the start of the process of me dragging myself out of this pit of lies that I have dug for myself.

And yet, where did all these traces come from? Where could they have come from? Whether they are genuine memories of actual events which occurred in the real world, or even several real worlds, or whether they are stories I have told myself, where must they have come from? Could I really have made them all up? Or is it not more likely that their very variety and dazzle indicated that they must genuinely have happened? If I am so banal and ordinary, where did these absurd fancies appear from? I must have had some life before I ended up here. Why should it not be as I appear to recall?

I think I can remember a common enough upbringing in a world no more exotic than any might appear to an outsider. A city, a house and home, parents, friends, schooling, jobs, lusts and loves, ambitions, fears, triumphs and disappointments. All seem present and correct (if a little vague, perhaps due to their very ordinariness). All in a minor key, though. All humdrum, everyday, unremarkable, that's all.

Then my true life (as I think of it) commenced; my entry into the many worlds and l'Expédience, my dealings with persons and events that were anything but ordinary. That was when I became the me I was, even if I am, temporarily, a pale reflection of that person now.

I shall be that person again. I know it.

But you can see why I might be worried. You, who might be a part of me, or a future self.

The Transitionary

Did I do what I think I just did? Surely not. If I did, I'd be the first. (Or not, of course. Maybe it happens all the time but they keep it secret. This is the Concern we're dealing with here. Secrecy comes as standard. But wouldn't there be rumours?)

Could I have just flitted without septus? That isn't supposed to be possible. You must have septus, the drug is absolutely necessary, even if it is not entirely sufficient, if an individual is to transition between realities. I was out of the stuff. They'd taken the emergency pill out of my hollow tooth and taken the tooth itself for good measure. I was unconscious but it must have happened because the tooth was gone.

Or, it occurs to me, I swallowed the pill in a lucid interval – between the smack in the face in the plane and waking up tied to the chair – which I don't remember. Or maybe it went down my throat by pure chance when they punched me. The punch in the face could easily have dislodged it; I swallowed it and they didn't know I had. They'd have needed a bulky piece of kit like an NMR scanner or something to have a chance of locating the pill inside my body, so even after they found the hollow tooth . . .

But they said they *had* found the hollow tooth, and removed the pill. Why lie about that? Didn't make sense. And why the post-flit hangover? I didn't even know who I was for the first few seconds, and my head still hurts. Never had that before, not even in basic training.

Still, even with bits that didn't add up right, that was a far more plausible explanation than somebody accomplishing a septus-free flit. I had to go with the must-have-swallowed-it-by-accident scenario; I'd just got lucky, once again.

Anyway, whatever: I am naked, hardly presentable to the outside world, so the first thing to do is find some clothes. I try the light switches by the door as I pad out of the great ballroom, but nothing happens. Pausing at the tall double doors to the anteroom beyond, I listen for any sound that might indicate I am not alone in the Palazzo Chirezzia. Quiet as a tomb. I shiver as I cross the anteroom and hall, making for the central staircase. The air is cool but it is the air of ghostly desolation – all these rolled-up carpets, this sheet-wrapped furniture and gloomy light and smell of long abandonment – that truly affects me.

I try one of the grand bedrooms on the first floor, but the wardrobes and cupboards in the dressing room are empty save for mothballs sitting in little nests of twisted paper, or rolling around with dull and lazy clicks in drawers. My reflection stares back at me through the shuttered gloom. Another bland-looking man of generally medium build, though reasonably well-muscled.

On the second floor, one room holds a wardrobe with various sets of clothing, some of which might be my size, but the clothes look antique. I go to the window, crack the shutters and look out. The people I can see in the calle running along the side of the palace look to be dressed in colourful, relatively slim-fitting, moderately heterogeneous clothes.

I would guess I am in a fairly standard late-twentieth or early-twenty-first-century Degenerate Christian High-Capitalist reality (a Greedist world, to use the colloquial). The fragre certainly feels right. Probably the same Earth I visited before, when my little pirate captain tried to recruit me, or near as dammit. If I did flit away from torture, without septus, through sheer desperation, then a familiar world, one I'd visited before and felt comfortable in, but not one they'd expect me to resort to, is where I would head for automatically.

Calbefraques might have seemed the obvious destination; you might think, why didn't I just wake in my own body, in my own house in the trees looking out over the town beneath? Because for years I have known I might turn traitor in deed as well as thought, and prepared for it mentally, telling myself that in any transition under duress or in a state of semiconsciousness, the place I thought of as home would be the last place I ought to aim for.

All the same, I would not have thought I'd end up here.

The clothes in this wardrobe are fancy dress, I realise; ancient costumes for balls and masquerades.

Three rooms later I discover men's clothes of the appropriate era and that fit. Just dressing makes me feel better. There is no hot water in the Palazzo Chirezzia; I wash myself from a bathroom cold tap.

There is no electric power either, but when I remove the sheet from the desk in the Professore's study and lift the telephone I hear a dialling tone.

But what to do next? I stand there until the phone starts making electronic complaining noises at me. I replace it on the cradle. I'm here without money, connections and a supply of septus; conventionally the first thing I ought to do is establish contact with an enabler or other sympathetic and Aware, clued-in soul, to put myself back in contact with l'Expédience and to locate a source of septus.

But I'd only be putting myself in jeopardy, handing myself back to my earlier captors and my gently talking friend with his sticky tape, if I do. I have been faced with the choice Mrs M always said I would be faced with and I have made my decision. It is a big thing that I have done and I am still not entirely certain I have jumped the right way, but it is done and I must live with the consequences.

However, the point here is that I will play into the hands of those I oppose if I take the most obvious route and attempt to contact a normally accredited agent of l'Expédience in this world.

The most important thing is to get my hands on some septus. Without that, probably, there's little I can do. Certainly I appear to have flitted, once, without the aid of the drug. However, it was in extremis, uncontrolled, impromptu (a surprise even to me when it happened), it was to a semi-random location and it resulted in considerable discomfort as well as a state of profound confusion – I did not even know who I was initially – that lasted quite long enough to have made me extremely vulnerable in the immediate aftermath of the flit. Had there been anybody who wished me ill present at that point, I would have been in their power, or worse.

For all I know I had that one spontaneous flit in me and no more – perhaps some residue of septus had built up in my system that allowed me to make that single transition, but is now cleared out, exhausted – and even voluntarily putting myself in another situation as terrifying and threatening as being suffocated while tied to a chair would fail to result in anything more remarkable than me pissing my pants. So, I need septus. And the only supplies of it in this world, as in all worlds, are supposed to be in the obsessively wary and inveterately paranoid gift of the Concern.

However, there ought to be a way round this.

I run my hand over the sheet covering the seat by the telephone. Very little dust.

I sit and start entering short strings of numbers at random into the telephone keypad until I hear a human voice. I have forgotten almost all the Italian I learned last time so I have to find somebody who shares a language. We settle on English. The operator is patient with me and finally we establish that what I require is Directory Enquiries, and not here but in Britain.

The Concern has bolt-holes, safe houses, deep-placement agents and cover organisations distributed throughout the worlds it operates most frequently in. As far as I was aware I knew about all the official Concern contacts in this reality, though of course it would be naive to assume there would be none that had been kept from me.

However, I also knew of one that wasn't an official Concern contact because it had been set up by somebody who wasn't part of the Concern proper at all: the ubiquitous and busy Mrs M. So she had assured me, anyway.

"Which town?"

"Krondien Ungalo Shupleselli," I tell them. I ought to be remembering the name correctly; we are solemnly assured in training that these emergency codes should be so ingrained within us that we ought still to remember them even if we have, through some shock or trauma, forgotten our own names. This one has been thought up, probably, by Mrs Mulverhill rather than some name-badged Concern techies in an Emergency Procedures (Field Operatives) Steering Group committee meeting, but, like the official codes, it ought to work across lots of worlds and languages. It will probably sound odd in almost all of them, but not to the point of incomprehensibility. And it should be far enough removed from the name of any person or organisation to avoid accidental contacts and resultant misunderstandings with possible security implications.

"Sorry. Where?"

"It may be a business or a person. I don't know the town or city."

"Oh."

I think about it. "But try London," I suggest.

There is indeed a business answering to that name in the English capital. "Putting you through."

". . . Hello?" says a male voice. It sounds fairly young, and just that single word, spoken slowly and deliberately, had been enough for a tone of caution, even nervousness, to be evident.

"I'm looking for Krondien Ungalo Shupleselli," I say.

"No kidding. Now there's a name I haven't heard in a while."

"Yes," I say, sticking to the script. "Perhaps you might be able to help."

"Well, that's what this is all about, isn't it?"

"May I ask to whom I'm talking?"

A laugh. "My name's Ade."

"Aid?" I ask. This seems a little too obvious.

"Short for Adrian. What about yourself?"

"I assume you know the procedure."

"What? Oh, yeah. I'm supposed to give you a name, that right? Okey-doke. How about Fred?"

"Fred? Is that common enough?"

"As muck, mate. Common as muck. Trust me."

"Indeed I do, Adrian."

"Brill. Consider yourself sorted. What can I do for you, mate?"

Madame d'Ortolan

Madame d'Ortolan sat in the rooftop aviary of her house in Paris, listening to the flurrying of a thousand soft wings and looking out over the darkening city as the street lights came on. The view, graphed by the bars of the aviary, showed deep dark reds and bruised purples towards the north-west, where a recently passed rainstorm was retreating towards the sunset. The city still smelled of late-summer rain and refreshed foliage. Somewhere in the distance, a siren sounded. She wondered how big a city had to become, and how lawless and dangerous in this sort of reality, for a siren always to be heard somewhere. Here, the siren was like an audible signature of fragre.

Madame d'Ortolan took a breath and said, "No, he must have had another pill hidden somewhere."

Mr Kleist stood in the shadows, behind and to one side of her seat, which was an extravagant work in bamboo with a great fan-shaped top. He looked about at the various birds still flying within the aviary. His head jerked as one flew too close and he ducked involuntarily. He shook his head.

"He did not, ma'am, I am sure."

"Nevertheless."

"He was fully restrained, ma'am. It could only have been in his mouth, and that was checked very thoroughly, both before the interrogation began and afterwards. Even more thoroughly, subsequent to his apparent transition."

Madame d'Ortolan looked unconvinced. "Thoroughly?"

Mr Kleist produced a little transparent plastic bag from one pocket and placed it on the small cane table standing at the side of her seat. She leant over, looked at the thirty or so bloodstained teeth inside.

"They are all present," he said. "They are just teeth."

She looked at them. "The false one with the cavity. Was there room inside it for two pills?"

"No, and the septus pill was removed from it and the tooth itself extracted while he was still unconscious."

"Some residue of septus left with the mouth or throat?"

"I have already asked our most knowledgeable experts. Such an effect is next to impossible."

"Send these to be analysed, all the same."

"Of course." Mr Kleist picked up the plastic bag and replaced it in his pocket.

"Some sort of osmotic patch, or a subcutaneous implant?"

"Again, ma'am, we did check, both before and after."

"Perhaps up his nose," Madame d'Ortolan mused, more to herself than to Mr Kleist. "That might be possible. Ill-bred people sometimes make that ghastly snorting, pulling-back noise with their noses. One might ingest a pill in that manner."

Mr Kleist sighed. "It is a theoretical possibility," he conceded. "Though not in this case."

"Did he make such a noise?"

"No, ma'am. In fact he was probably incapable of doing so or of performing the action you mention because his nose and mouth were both tightly secured by tape. No air movement would have been possible."

"You checked for some infusionary device? Perhaps something concealed within the rectum, activated by . . ." She could not think how you would activate something like that.

"We checked the subject's clothing and performed a second internal examination. There was nothing."

"An accomplice. The septus delivered by a dart or some such thing."

"Impossible, ma'am."

"You were alone with him?"

"No. An assistant was present."

"The assistant . . ."

"Is completely trustworthy, ma'am."

Madame d'Ortolan turned to him.

"Then, unless you were somehow complicit yourself, Mr Kleist, it could only be that he was able to ingest a slow-release pill some time before."

Mr Kleist displayed no reaction. "The arresting interception team assure us this would not have been possible. Also, we took blood samples before and after and there was no sign."

"They must be wrong, all the same. The results must be wrong. Have everything analysed again."

"Yes, ma'am."

Madame d'Ortolan turned and gazed out over the city as it subsided into darkness, strings of street lights curving into the clear distance of rain-washed air. After some time she put one hand to her lower lip, pinching it.

"And if they are not wrong, ma'am?" Mr Kleist said eventually, when he began to think that perhaps she had forgotten he was there.

"Then," she said, "we would have the most severe problem. Because we would be faced with somebody who can flit without septus, and, if they are capable of doing that, they could be capable of doing almost anything." Madame d'Ortolan stopped and thought for a moment. "That would be a perfectly terrifying prospect even if the individual concerned was utterly loyal." She turned and looked at Mr Kleist. She could hardly see him. "However, I do not believe that to be the case."

"It might be wise to act as though it is," he suggested. "Provisionally, at least." There was a small light on the table by her side. She clicked it on. Mr Kleist still looked dark, dressed in black or something near black, his face paler but still in shade.

"That had occurred to me," she told him. "Have the husk killed and a full – and I do mean full – post-mortem carried out."

"The person is not a husk, ma'am."

"I don't care."

"I understand, ma'am."

"What about the trackers?"

"We have another two teams on him in addition to the one that found him after Lord Harmyle's murder. There has been nothing reported so far."

"Are they optimistic?"

Mr Kleist hesitated. "If they are, they're being unusually reticent about it."

"Well, never mind how we lost him initially. Now that he is lost, what if he stays lost? What will he do next?"

"He may already have warned those who were on the list marked for assassination. We think somebody must have. The back-up teams have yet to report a success."

"Not even Obliq?" Madame d'Ortolan asked, pronouncing her name with the sort of acidic tone she usually reserved for Mrs Mulverhill. "I thought they definitely got her."

"Ah," Mr Kleist said. "The team report they now think she may have been flitted an instant before the hit."

"So he did warn them."

253

"Somebody did. We doubt he had time personally."

She frowned. "Your assistant heard the names on the list, didn't he?"

"As I say, ma'am, he is above suspicion."

"That is not what you said, and nobody is above suspicion."

"Then let me rephrase. I have complete faith in his loyalty and discretion."

"Would you vouch for him with your life?"

Mr Kleist hesitated. "I would not go quite that far for anyone, ma'am. As you say, nobody is entirely above suspicion."

"Hmm. That list, then, the people on it."

"We are watching them as closely as we are able to, waiting for an opportunity, but it is not easy and it is not looking promising. Obliq and Plyte disappeared entirely, untrackable, and the rest are awkwardly located, or staying too firmly in the public eye for us to strike. The relevant teams are still primed and in place, ready to resume action on your command the moment we have a clear shot." He left a pause. "Though of course we have lost the advantage of surprise and concurrency. Even if we are able to pick one off, the rest will become even more suspicious and hard to get at, the moment they hear."

Madame d'Ortolan nodded to herself. She took a deep breath. "Thus far, this has not worked out as we intended."

"No, ma'am."

She was silent for a few moments. A bird cooed somewhere overhead, and wings rustled. Sometimes, when one of the birds in the aviary was unwell or had been injured and was hopping about on the floor of the structure, broken-winged or too ill to fly, Madame d'Ortolan would let the cats in, to dispose of the creature. She always enjoyed the resulting kerfuffle, brief though it usually proved to be. She twisted in her chair and looked at Kleist. "What would you do, Mr Kleist? If you were me?"

Without hesitation he said, "We find ourselves fighting on two fronts, ma'am. That is not supportable. I would indefinitely postpone the actions against the Council members and withdraw all but the basic tracking teams involved. Throw everything at Oh. He's the greater threat."

Madame d'Ortolan narrowed her eyes. "Mr Kleist, I have worked for decades to get to just this point with the Central Council. If we don't act now there is every chance they will approve the sort of invasively damaging policies that the Mulverhill woman has obviously been insinuating into the vacuous heads of an entire generation of students, technicians and agents for a decade or more. There are too many Mulverhills out there and their influence is growing. I can't keep swatting them away from all positions of influence for ever. We have to act now. We may not get another chance."

Kleist looked unimpressed. "Ma'am, I think the moment has passed, for now. Another may present itself in time. In the meantime, nobody seems to have any proof that you were behind the actions against the other Council members, or be prepared to speculate openly on the matter, so we have established, as it were, a stable front there. Mr Oh, especially if he is allied with Mulverhill, is an immediate and dynamic threat. Also, once he's dealt with, we may be able to make it look as though he and Mulverhill were behind the attacks on the Council members."

Madame d'Ortolan unwound herself in her seat to sit forward again, looking away from him. She released a long, deflating sigh. "Sadly, annoyingly," she said in a quiet voice, "I think you're right."

Mr Kleist was silent for a few moments. His expression did not change. He said, "Shall I issue the relevant orders?"

"Please do."

He turned to go.

"Mr Kleist?"

He turned back. "Ma'am?"

Madame d'Ortolan had turned to look at him again. "I take this very personally, and very ill. I shall expect Mr Oh to pay for this, in person. Once he has served whatever other purposes we require of him, I think I might ask you to tutor me in some of the techniques you employed in your earlier profession, so that I might apply them to him. And Mulverhill, for that matter. I severely doubt she's innocent in all this."

Mr Kleist gave a small bow. "I am at your disposal, ma'am."

There was a small smile on Madame d'Ortolan's thin lips. Her paper-cut smile, as he thought of it. The image brought with it, as it always did, the memory of the scent of lemons and the echo of long-faded screams. She waved one hand. "Thank you. That'll be all."

He turned again and had walked more two steps when she said, "Mr Kleist?"

He turned and looked back, still untroubled. The lady was known for using this little technique. "Yes, ma'am?"

The birds were almost silent now, settled in for the night.

"What was it they used to call you? The Moralist, was it?"

"The Philosopher, ma'am."

"Ah, yes. So, was it agreeable, to be taking up your old profession again?"

He looked at her for a moment. "Why, ma'am," he said quietly, "we barely began." He regarded her a moment longer. "But no, not especially." He bowed and walked away.

The Pitcher

Mike Esteros is sitting at the bar of the Commodore Hotel, Venice Beach, after yet another unsuccessful pitch. Technically he doesn't know it's unsuccessful yet, but he's developing a nose for these things and he'd put money on another rejection. It's starting to get him down. He still believes in the idea and he's still sure it'll get made one day, plus he knows that attitude is everything in this business – if he doesn't believe in himself, why should anybody else? – but, well, all the same.

The bar is quiet. He wouldn't normally drink at this time of day. Maybe he needs to adjust the plot, make it more family-oriented. Focus on the boy, on the father–son thing. Cute it up a little more. A dusting of schmaltz. Never did any harm. Well, no real harm.

Maybe he's been believing too much in the basic idea, assuming that because it's so obvious to him what a beautiful, elegant thing it is it'll be obvious to everybody else and they'll be falling over themselves to green-light it and give him lots of money.

And don't forget Goldman's Law: nobody knows anything. Nobody knows what will work. That's why they make so many remakes and Part Twos; what looks like lack of imagination is really down to too much, as execs visualise all the things that could go wrong with a brand new, untested idea. Going with something containing elements that definitely worked in the past removes some of the terrifying uncertainty.

What Mike's got here is a radical, left-field idea. The central concept is almost too original for its own good. That's why it needs a generous helping of conventionality slathered over it. He'll rework it, again. It's not a prospect that fills him with joy, frankly, but he guesses that it has to be done and he has to struggle on. It's worth it. He still believes in it. It's just a dream, but it's a dream that could be made real and this is the place where that happens. Your dreams – not just of your idea but of your future self, your fortunes – get turned into reality here. He still loves this place, still believes in it.

Mike leaves the bar, goes outside and sits on a bench, watching the ocean, watching the people pass on the tarmac strip and on the sands themselves, roller skating, boarding, strolling, playing Frisbee, just walking.

A girl comes and sits on the bench too. Well, woman. She might be Mike's age. He starts talking to her. She's cute and friendly and smart, rangy and dark, nice laugh. Just his type. A lawyer, on a day off, just relaxing. Monica. He asks does she want a drink and she says maybe a herbal tea and they sit in a little café still within sight of the beach. Then they go for dinner in a little Vietnamese place a short walk away. Mike gives her the pitch because she's genuinely interested. She thinks it's a great idea. It actually seems to make her thoughtful.

Later they walk on the beach in the light of a half-moon, then sit, and there's some kissing and a modest amount of fooling around, though she's already told him she doesn't go any further on a first date. Him too, he tells her, though strictly speaking that's nonsense and he guesses that she guesses this but doesn't care.

Then, in the middle of a tight, embracing kiss, something changes. He feels it happen, and when he opens his eyes the moon has gone, the air feels cooler and the beach looks narrower and steeper and leads down to a sea that's much calmer than the one that was there just seconds ago. There are islands out there, dark shapes under the stars, covered in trees. He shakes his head, looks at Monica. He starts back instinctively, crabbing away from her on all fours. She's changed completely too. White, blonde, shorter, face quite different. There are a couple of guys – the only other people on the beach – standing massively about ten feet away, watching them.

She dusts her hands and rises, standing in front of the two men. "Mr Esteros," she says, "welcome to your new home."

11

Patient 8262

I have been violated! My worst nightmares have come true. Well,
not my worst, but some pretty bad ones. Fondled, grabbed,
molested in my own bed. Thankfully I woke in time and was
able to defend myself and shout and scream to summon help. But
all the same.

It was day; afternoon, an hour after lunch and I was in that state
it pleases me to remain in for much of the time now, neither awake
nor asleep but lying with my eyes closed, listening a little and thinking
a lot. I heard somebody come into my room and though I did not
hear the door close I noticed a diminution of the sounds from outside
in the rest of the clinic. That ought to have alerted me, but I suppose
I had grown complacent.

Since the bizarre turn of events with the nonsense-talking and so
on, I have spent less time traipsing the corridors and day rooms of
the institution and more time in bed. It seemed to me that the other
patients and inmates were looking at me oddly, and a few even tried
to engage me in conversation in what certainly sounded like the
start of more of that gibberish language, often with big smiles on
their faces that obviously meant they were in on the joke and just

wanted to join in and make fun of me. I would turn aside from them and walk away with all the dignity I could.

When that fat fellow came into my room a couple of days ago – the one who brought the skinny young man in when I was making words up – I hid under the bed sheets and wrapped the pillow over my head. He spoke to me gently, trying – I could tell from the tone of his voice – to get me to come out, but I wouldn't. When he tried to lift up the sheets to look in on me in my little impromptu tent, I slapped his hand away and hissed. He sighed heavily, one of those very-much-for-public-consumption sighs, and left shortly afterwards.

The medical staff continue to care for me. They make me get out of bed each day and have me sit by the side of it and once or twice they have insisted that I accompany one of them on a walk up and down the corridor, though I draw the line at entering the day room with them. They seem happy enough that I am still mobile. I suppose I shuffle a little more than I did, not really picking my feet up prop- erly, but that is all part of my disguise as well. The less fit and able and the quieter I appear, the more I seem like just another patient. I fit in better.

The doctors still call in occasionally, and the lady doctor who has shown interest in me before came and sat with me for almost half an hour last week. She talked slowly to me – I understood most of what she said, I think – and shone bright lights into my eyes.

Then today the violation. I did not open my eyes to see who might have come into the room. I felt the bedclothes being shifted and thought that perhaps a doctor was going to examine me, though whoever it was didn't smell like a doctor. Probably not an orderly or a cleaning assistant either, for the same reason. They sometimes tidy me up if I've eaten messily or I've slumped awkwardly in my bed. If I'd had to guess, I'd have said it might be another patient, though not one of the more unpleasantly scented ones. I foolishly thought that whoever it was might take the hint that I was asleep or pretending to be asleep and therefore did not want to be woken up, but then I felt the sheets being pulled out somewhere down near my hip. I could feel air enter the warm mustiness of the bed just there. What was going on, I wondered?

Then a hand touched my hip, the fingers seeming to prod at first, then lifting and clutching at the material of my pyjamas as though trying to tug them up. What did they think they were doing? Did they think I was wearing a nightgown? I still did not open my eyes, thinking that whoever this incompetent was it would only embarrass them if I confronted them (one ought always to keep the medical staff on one's side and so should avoid making them feel awkward). The hand gave up the vain attempt to pull my pyjama bottoms up and reached out over my crotch. And slipped into the open fly of the pyjama bottoms, fumbling for and closing on my manhood, squeezing it once and then reaching down to hold my testes!

I opened my eyes an instant after the light clicked out. It was not afternoon at all. It was dark now with the light out; late evening or night. I felt confused, disoriented. The hand withdrew immediately from my private parts and the shadowy, barely glimpsed figure at the side of my bed rose hurriedly with a grunting, distressed noise and was gone before I could glimpse who it might have been, leaving the door swinging still further open as they ran down the corridor. Slippers. They were wearing slippers, from the sound of it, and they could not run very fast. I thought of getting up and giving chase but it would have taken too long.

I shouted for help instead.

But the cheek, the nerve, the banal sordidness of it!

Is this what I'm reduced to – being the sexual plaything of some drooling, sub-sentient inmate of a benighted cretin depository like this? The shame of it. With my past, my achievements, my status and – I swear – my still unfulfilled promise.

The Philosopher

There was only one occasion on which I intervened when technically I should not have. I used my seniority to take a subject from the operative they had been assigned to. He was, supposedly, just Subject 47767 to us, but I had seen his name and details on the system and had been intrigued. It was partly because of him that I had offered my services to the police and security service when I'd left the army. He was something of a hero to me and a lot of other people. What was he doing in our clutches?

His case file spoke of an assault on a prominent person and suspected membership of a terrorist group or a related organisation. The second part of the charge might mean almost nothing; some wit in our office had pointed out that the law regarding "related organisations" and having some sort of connection to terrorist groups was so vaguely and widely drawn that technically it included us. It was the sort of thing you charged people with when you didn't know what else to charge them with but didn't want to let them go, when you just suspected them generally.

This man, 47767, had been in the police ten years ago, when the terrorist threat was just starting to become serious. He'd been in a unit that had captured a couple of terrorists who had been planting bombs in various public places, in litter bins in railway and bus stations and in busy thoroughfares, killing a few people and injuring dozens. When they were picked up there had been some sort of breakdown in communication between different parts of their terrorist cell and detailed warnings had been sent for the latest batch of bombs before all of them had been planted. A quick-thinking officer had sent police to the sites relating to the warnings and both men had been caught, though not before they had already planted at least one other bomb not covered by the original warning.

The suspects were split up, and one was questioned conventionally. The other one, who had been in the charge of the police officer who was now our Subject 47767, had been questioned rather more forcefully by him and had revealed the location of the bomb that he and his accomplice had already planted. Police officers dispatched to the location were able to evacuate the area and prevent any deaths or injuries when the bomb detonated just a quarter-hour later. It was one of the few unqualified successes of those early years.

The identity of the officer who would become our Subject 47767 was discovered by the press and he was acclaimed as a hero both in the papers and by the mass of the public as a man who had done something distasteful but necessary. The means he had employed to produce the life-saving results were also discovered; he had been tearing out the terrorist's fingernails with a pair of pliers (there was no detail on how many he'd had to remove like this before achieving cooperation). This is one of those amateurish but fairly effective techniques you hear about sometimes.

Despite the fact that lives had been saved and the terrorist himself was still very much alive, certain sections of the press and some politicians nevertheless wanted the man to be prosecuted and thrown out of the police force for what he had done. Eventually, as I recalled, he was hounded out of the force and was charged with criminal assault. He refused defence counsel, saying he would defend himself, then at the trial he said nothing. He was jailed for only a couple of years, but things went badly for him in prison and he spent nearly ten years inside. In that time his children grew up and his wife divorced him, moving away and remarrying.

He had slipped from public consciousness in the intervening decade, filled as it was with so much violence and treachery. He had been released earlier this year and now had ended up in the hands of the police again, scheduled to be questioned. I felt there was an untold story here, and there were puzzling details that I had never heard had been cleared up. I was unable to contain my curiosity and took over the case myself. This was not actually against regulations but it was highly irregular, the sort of thing you could get away with once or twice but which, done consistently, would be noted in your file.

He was an ordinary-looking man. Medium build, pale skin, short receding brown hair and a resigned, beaten look on his face. There might have been some defiance in his eyes, though perhaps that was just my own prejudice. He had been beaten up at some point in the last few days, judging from the bruising on his face. He was still dressed and his hands were handcuffed and chained to the floor behind him, though he was otherwise unrestrained and was seated normally.

I sat in front of him in another chair. I even put myself within kicking distance of his feet with nothing in between, which I would never normally do. A junior officer sat to one side monitoring the recording equipment but took no part in the subsequent proceedings.

I began by asking Subject 47767 if he was who I thought he was. He confirmed that he was. We used his real first name throughout. It was Jay. I asked him why he thought he was here.

He laughed bitterly. "I hit the wrong person."

I asked who that might have been.

"The son of the Justice Minister." He gave a sour smile.

I asked why he had hit him.

"Because I'm sick to the back teeth of vicious, ignorant dickheads telling me what a fucking hero I am."

I asked him if he meant because of what had happened with the terrorist he had tortured to discover the location of the bomb.

Jay shook his head and looked away. "Oh, let me guess. I'm a hero figure to people like you, would that be right?"

I said that many people admired what he had done, amongst them, certainly, myself.

"Yeah, well, you would, wouldn't you?" he replied.

I asked if he meant because of what he obviously – and correctly – took to be my role.

He nodded. "Because you're a torturer," he said. He looked straight into my eyes as he said this. I am well used to staring people down, but he would not look away.

I told him that even if I was not, I would still admire him because of what he had done.

"You and every other idiot," he said. He said it more with resignation than defiance, thought there was an understandable hint of nervousness too. He swallowed conspicuously.

264

I asked if he didn't feel proud of what he had done.

"No," he said. "No, I fucking don't."

But he had saved lives, I pointed out.

"I did what I thought I had to do," Jay said.

Would he do the same thing again, knowing what he did now?

"I don't know."

Why not? I asked.

"Because I don't know what might have happened differently if I hadn't done it. Probably nothing would have been any different so I suppose I might as well have done what I did. A few people may still be alive who wouldn't have been otherwise, but who knows? We haven't got a time machine."

What did he think might have happened differently?

"We might not live in a society where people live in fear of people like you," he told me. He shrugged. "But, like I say, probably it would still all have worked out just like it is now. I don't kid myself that what I might have done differently would have made any difference."

I said I thought he was wrong to assume the current state of our society was somehow his fault. The fault lay with the people who threatened our society: terrorists, radicals, leftists, liberals and other traitors – those who would like to tear down the state either through direct action or through using words and propaganda to influence the more gullible sections of the masses to do their dirty work for them.

"Yeah, you would think that, too." Jay sounded tired.

I told him I thought it was tough that he'd ended up in prison. He should never have been prosecuted in the first place and certainly should never have been found guilty. He should have been given a medal, not sent to prison. That had probably ruined his life. Especially as they had kept him in for so long.

"Here we go," he said, sounding tired again. "You don't understand anything, do you?"

If he thought that, I said, perhaps he ought to tell me what he thought I ought to understand.

"I insisted that I should be prosecuted. I demanded that I be prosecuted. I refused a defence because I'd wanted to plead guilty but they wouldn't let me. They threatened my family. So I had to plead innocent. But then I offered no defence and so I was found guilty. They sentenced me to two years but the correct sentence, the least anybody else would have got would have been nine years, so I made sure I stayed in prison for that amount of time. Having time added is not difficult." Jay smiled without humour. "And when I got out I told anybody who accused me of being a hero that they were an idiot, and people who said I should have got a medal to fuck off. Finally, when one guy got too insistent about how big a hero I was and how he could make sure that I did get a medal, I hit him. Only it turned out he was the son of the Justice Minister, like I said. And that's why I'm here."

I told him I didn't understand. Why had he wanted to be prosecuted? Why had he wanted to be found guilty? Why had he wanted to be locked up for nine years?

Jay sounded animated at last. He held his head up. "Because I believe in justice." He spat that word out. "I believe in the law." That word too. "I did something wrong, something against the law, and I needed to be punished for it. It was wrong that I was going to be let off for it. Even more wrong that people wanted to give me medals for it."

But he hadn't done something wrong, I suggested. He had saved innocent lives and helped defeat those who would bring society down.

"It was still against the *law*!" he shouted. "Don't you see? If the law means anything then I couldn't be above it. Not just because I was a police officer or because my breaking it had resulted in some lives being saved. That's not the point. Torture was illegal. I'd broken the law. Can't you *see* any of this?" He shook his the chair, rattling the chains attaching his handcuffs to the floor. "It's even more important to prosecute police who've broken the law than it is to prosecute anybody else, because otherwise nobody trusts the police."

I pointed out that the forceful questioning of suspects was now entirely if unfortunately legal, even if it hadn't been then.

"'Forceful questioning.' You mean torture."

If that was what he wanted to call it. But why hadn't he made his feelings clear to all these newspapers that wanted to talk to him? Or at his trial, where, of all places, he was guaranteed a fair hearing?

Jay looked at me scornfully. "Do you really think the papers print what people actually say? I mean, if it's not what their proprietors or the government want everybody to hear?" He shook his head. "Same at the trial."

I said that I still thought he was being too harsh on himself. He had done the right thing.

He looked tired and defeated now, and we had, as I have made clear, applied no physical pressure whatsoever to him up to this point. "The thing is," he said, "maybe in the same situation, even knowing what I know now, I'd still do the same thing. I'd still tear that Christian bastard's nails out, get him to talk, find out where the bomb was, hope that the plods got the right street, the right end of it, the right fucking city." He looked at me with what might have been defiance or even a sort of pleading. "But I'd still insist that I was charged and prosecuted." He shook his head again. "Don't you see? You can't have a state where torture is legal, not for anything. You start saying it's only for the most serious cases, but that never lasts. It should always be illegal, for everybody, for everything. You might not stop it. Laws against murder don't stop all murders, do they? But you make sure people don't even think about it unless it's a desperate situation, something immediate. And you have to make the torturer pay. In full. There has to be that disincentive, or they'll all be at it." He raised his head and looked about him, his gaze obviously being meant to take in not just the room we were in but the whole building; maybe even more than that. "Or you end up with this." He looked at me. "With you. Whoever you are."

I thought about this. It seemed to me that the fellow's mind had been broken in prison, probably, but that he had also probably always been an idealist. He certainly sounded like one now. Almost like a fanatic. Nevertheless, had it been up to me I'd have released him, frankly. However, it was not up to me. There was high-level interest in this case, for one thing, and an accusation of having aided terrorist groups could not simply be ignored. He was right in that; the law had to be obeyed. I thought of handing him over to one of the younger people who would not have heard of him, but decided on reflection to question him myself, determining that I would be more lenient than they, given that I knew the unfortunate circumstances that had led him here.

Accordingly, we employed the gagging tape/suffocation method. Jay admitted nothing regarding membership or support of clandestine or illegal organisations or even any sympathy with them or indeed any outright criticism of the state until approximately the average degree of pressure had been applied, whereupon, displaying all the standard and expected signs of distress, he informed us that he'd admit to anything, of course he would. This was what he'd meant, he claimed. People would admit to anything. The only real truth that torture produced was that people would admit to anything to get the torture to stop, even if they knew that the admissions they were being called upon to make would eventually prove fatal for them, or others. The whole process was pointless and cruel and a waste, he claimed. A state that allowed or condoned torture lost part of its soul, he said. He then pleaded directly with me to stop and reiterated that he would admit to anything we wanted him to admit to, and sign anything we put in front of him. I chose not to point out that what he had just endured was not true torture by my definition as it had not involved any actual pain or physical damage, just great discomfort and distress.

That notwithstanding, I terminated the interrogation at that point, with, I will own, no small degree of relief, before he could admit to anything specific that we might be obliged to follow up.

Jay was released the following day. I filed a report that implied we had been considerably more severe with him than we had in fact been, guessing that this was all that had been desired by the powers that be in the first place, and our skills and facilities had in effect been used as a means of punishment rather than as they were supposed to be, to discover the truth – a use of our time and resources concerning which, I need hardly emphasise, I was in some disapproval, if, of course, powerless to prevent.

Sadly, a month later, we read that Jay, our Subject 47767, the one-time police officer who had been a hero to many of us, had taken his own life, throwing himself underneath the wheels of one of the trucks that deliver giant rolls of paper to newspaper printing presses. One of my colleagues pointed out that suicide, too, was technically illegal, which to me seemed ironic as well as very sad.

Subject 7

Only one person was ever truly kind to her. It was one of the brush ladies. There were various brush ladies. They were all small and dark and hunched. They had brushes that sucked at the air or that swallowed dust from the floor. And from lights overhead. The brush ladies only came at night. A man who was taller than them came with them and told them what to do.

She liked the brush ladies because they did not hurt her. They left her alone. She had been afraid of them at first, because everything that happened here hurt her or confused her and they obviously belonged to this place and so she was scared of them. But in time she stopped being frightened and started to look forward to seeing them because they were not like the others.

The others hurt her. The others had clipboard things and electrical things and torches they shone in her eyes and small hard heavy things they spoke into. They had glass things that they used to put liquids into her. These were called syringes. Also they had wires that they attached to her. Lots of wires. Some tubes too. Mostly wires. The tubes hurt more than the wires but the wires could hurt as well. They all wore white coats or pale blue uniforms. The hurt came from fire in her veins, usually. Though they had other sorts of pain they could make her feel. It depended.

Some of the others did not wear white coats or pale blue uniforms but dressed like ordinary people did. These ones just sat around and stared at her. She got the impression that they could do things inside her head. This was because when she tried to think herself away from here – to escape the way she had escaped from things before, before she had been brought here – the sitting people would close their eyes or bunch their fists or sit forward suddenly and she could feel them in her head, pulling her away from anywhere she might find safety or at least a temporary numbing of the pain.

Even when she was awake she heard voices and saw ghosts. When they put the liquids into her at night she went to sleep and had bad dreams as well. At first there had been little time to watch the brush ladies or try to talk to them before sleep rose up within her and dragged her down to where the nightmares waited. Then, she had thought that the brush ladies were a part of the bad dreams. But gradually she found that, each night, she stayed awake a little longer before falling asleep.

Or perhaps the brush ladies came earlier – she wasn't sure.

Sometimes, after they had put the night-time liquids into her, one of the others would come to check on her. She would pretend to be asleep. The next morning, when they wanted her to wake up and be washed and fed before they started to do things to her, she would pretend to stay asleep. Gradually they put less liquid in the syringe each night before the lights were dimmed. She still pretended to be asleep in the evening but she woke up on time in the morning. They seemed satisfied with this. She was happy because now she got to watch the brush ladies.

She tried talking to them but they ignored her, or – when they did come over to talk to her – they did not speak the same language.

But then one of them seemed to change, and appeared to understand her, and talked to her. The brush lady who talked to her always wore a grey cloth tied round her head. She was sure that this brush lady had been one of the ones who had not been able to talk to her in her own language, so she was surprised that now suddenly she could. Still, that was good. Even so, she still didn't understand everything the brush lady said. Sometimes it sounded as though she was talking to herself, or using the sort of complicated, mysterious words that the others did, the ones who hurt her.

Sometimes the brush lady with the grey cloth went back to not talking to her, or seemed not to be able to understand her again.

That was confusing.

The grey-cloth brush lady seemed different on the nights when she did talk to her compared to the nights when she didn't. She walked differently, stood differently. She was the same all the time when the man who shouted was there, then – when he had definitely gone – she became slightly different, if she was going to talk to her. Perhaps nobody else would have noticed what changed in the brush lady with the grey cloth, but she did. She was able to see these things. She was special and could see things other people didn't. That was just one of the special things that she could do, one of the things that had made her different and worse compared to everybody else. These things had made her a Problem Child and Educationally Special and Developmentally and Socially Challenged, before they'd decided she was Disturbed and a Delinquent and A Danger To Herself And Others (the others would always try to protect themselves – she understood that).

Finally these things had caused her to have a Breakdown and so she had to be Committed Into Indefinite Non-Elective Long-Term Institutional Care With Immediate Effect and so here she was in this long-term care. It had led to a hospital like a prison. And then to another one which was the same but different. And then to this place, which was worse than either of the hospital-prisons because here even the people supposed to be looking after her hurt her. Worse, she couldn't even use the things that made her special to get away from the being hurt.

Also, she couldn't retaliate. She could not hurt people who

271

hurt her because they had these people in plain clothes who sat around her, the ones who sat watching her and did the eye-squeezing, fist-pumping, hunched-over thing. Or maybe it was because they put the liquids into her, using the syringes. These things put her to sleep, or made her just too woozy to think or aim straight.

Here are some of the things that the grey-cloth brush lady said to her:

"Hello. How are you? What have they got you on? What do they call you? Subject Seven. Well, that's caring. Remember me? How are you? What have they done to you? Evening. Me again. I don't even recognise this, what the hell is it? Oh. Hey, Subject Seven. Been a while. How's things? Shit, what are they pumping . . . Are you with us, Seven? Are you? Anybody left in there? Fuck, you poor kid. Yes, they've seen something in you, haven't they? Something they think they can use. Mm-hmm. Fate help us all . . . What? Oh, I wish I could. What are they doing to you now? You poor . . ."

And so on and so on.

She replied by saying things like these:

"I spy Monty's video. Rent me a Sunder. I'll have that child frashed, so elp me. Crivens, Mr Givens, you'll be the deaf of me. Swear I never heard of such a thing. On me muvver's grave, there's a thing. Oi sat in a satin stain. Spot of block and truckle never hurt nobody. Alignment? I'll show you alignment, you arrant plopinjay; bend over. So help me. Hold fast there, bothers and cistern, we shall not face such girlsterous times alone! Clunch."

". . . Can you? Can you hear me? Listen, I can't get you out of here, Seven, not in any way, physically or otherwise. Minor miracle I'm here. Never thought I'd work so hard to get back in. I don't think you can understand a damn thing, can you? But for the record – in case you somehow can, or one day will – you've made it worth it, all by yourself, just to get to see what they'll do, what they want, what risks they'll take, how low they'll stoop. But look, maybe things will change. Now listen, kid. You do whatever you need to do to make things easy on yourself, okay? Go along. Do you understand?

Do something of what they want but keep a true core inside you, a soul of rebelliousness; an anger, not a fear. One day you'll be free, and then we'll see what we can do. I might be there then. If I am, remember me. Good luck."

"Well met by sunlight. We'll greet by sinlight. Stroke me a clyper!"

The grey-cloth lady often touched her; she would stroke her hand or pat her arm or smooth her hair off her forehead. She did that again now, brushing hair from her brow.

Liquid.

In the light, she could see that there was liquid on the grey-cloth brush lady's cheek. Tears.

That was strange. For some reason she'd thought that only she made tears, not anybody else.

Then the grey-cloth brush lady went away with the rest of the cleaners.

She never came back.

The Transitionary

After the great septennial extravaganza under the Dome of the Mists, I was no longer Madame d'Ortolan's golden boy. I was not at all sure that I ever had been, despite what Mrs Mulverhill might have believed, but certainly I was no longer. I must have passed whatever test she had arranged around that consummately bizarre serial two-person orgy she took me on, because I survived in the immediate thereafter and there were no further interrogations, but she felt that I had insulted her, obviously, and now I would be made to pay.

I was still convinced that the whole point of the exercise had been to test how easily I could be couriered and to give the trackers, spotters and foreseers who were undoubtedly in attendance nearby something to work on – like handing a sniffer hound a piece of clothing belonging to the person you wanted to track – and if there had been any personal component – Madame d'Ortolan feeling some

curious form of jealousy regarding myself and Mrs Mulverhill, perhaps
– then surely that had been entirely subordinate to the infinitely
more important business of ensuring the security of the Concern.

Nevertheless, I knew I had insulted her and she had taken it very
badly. I had not reacted as I had been expected to, required to. I
had shown some distaste, even arguably some disgust. Certainly not
the awed, stunned, perhaps embarrassed, perhaps humbled respect
I believe she had anticipated and was convinced should be right-
fully hers.

In the end, on any absolute scale it had been no great hurt; the
average person must endure, absorb and forget a hundred equivalent or worse insults and denigrations each year. But for a person of
Madame d'Ortolan's unparalleled importance and continually
reinforced pride, the very unexpectedness of it had magnified the
offence and made it loom all the larger, set against the otherwise
smoothly functioning progressions of her remorselessly flourishing
life.

For a few months afterwards I was rested and given no assignments at all, but from then on I was sent on gradually more difficult
and hazardous missions for l'Expédience. I was allowed to spend
less and less time in my house in the trees on the ridge above Flesse.
I spent my days instead spread serially far across the many worlds,
engaging in feats of derring-do, close-quarter assassination and
outright thuggery. Gradually even the house at Flesse stopped
seeming the sanctuary it had been and when I had discretionary use
of septus I would holiday, if that is the right word, in the world
containing the Venice where I had met and lost my little pirate
captain, wandering like a lost soul across its history-scorched face,
becoming familiar with that single embodiment of a world crippled
by its legacy of recent cruelties and a self-lacerating worship of the
proceeds of selfishness and greed. Again, this was your world, and
I guarantee that in many ways I know it better than you.

There is a saying that some foolish people believe: what does not
kill you makes you stronger. I know for a fact, having seen the

evidence – indeed, often enough having been the cause of it – that what does not kill you can leave you maimed. Or crippled, or begging for death or in one of those ghastly twilights experienced – and one has to hope that that is entirely not the right word – by those in a locked-in or persistent vegetative state. In my experience the same people also believe that everything happens for a reason. Given the unalleviatedly barbarous history of every world we have ever encountered with anything resembling Man in it, this is a statement of quite breathtakingly casual retrospective and ongoing cruelty, tantamount to the condonation of the most severe and unforgivable sadism.

Nevertheless – as much through chance, I am sure, as through any innate skill or other natural quality – I survived these trials and did indeed grow more skilled, more capable and more adept at all the arcane, ethically dubious, technically overspecialised and frankly disreputable techniques required.

I did, however, grow more frightened too, because with every new mission and each required high-risk intervention, attack or killing, I knew that my gradually perfecting skills would not save me when my luck ran out, indeed that they would stand for precisely nothing when the moment came, as it surely must, and that with every new mission I upped the chances of this one being my last, not through any lessening of my preparation, creativity, vigilance or skill but due to the simple working-out of statistical chance.

I had already long forgotten most of the interventions I had taken part in, then later could not recall how many people I had harmed or injured, or left disabled or terrified for life.

Eventually, to my shame, I even lost count of those I'd killed.

I think there is a kind of queasily mixed emulsion of guilt and fatalism that settles on a man or woman engaged in such deadly, fatal work. I mean deadly to those we target; fatal only potentially to ourselves, but still, eventually, if we keep going long enough, always guaranteed to be terminal.

We come to know that the end cannot be evaded for ever, and

the terror of that knowledge – the increasing certainty that every successful mission and every triumphant side-stepping of death this time only makes it more likely that the next risk we take could be the one that finally takes us – makes us more and more nervous, neurotic, unbalanced and psychologically fragile.

And, I believe, if we are involved with the business of killing others and have any sort of conscience at all – and even if we know that we fight the good fight and do what we do for the best of motives – a part of us, if we are honest with ourselves, comes to look forward to that end, begins even to welcome its increasingly likely arrival. If nothing else it will bring an end to worry, an end to guilt and nightmares, both waking and sleeping.

(An end to tics, neuroses and psychoses, too. An end to seemingly always finding myself in the body and mind of somebody with OCD, and that being the one trait that transfers.)

I might have said no, I might have resigned, but stupid pride, an urge not to be beaten or cowed by anybody, including Madame d'Ortolan, even if she was now the undisputed head of the whole Concern, kept me going until, when that initial impetus fell away and I might have justly claimed I'd made my point and stepped away, the resigned fatalism and thirst for it all to end – and end as it had taken place so far, as though only that could somehow justify and make sense of everything I'd done – took over, enabling and diseasing me at once.

So by the time I might have thought myself able to relinquish the role I had played, it was too late to do so. I was another person. We all are, anyway, with every passing instant, even without the many worlds, changing from moment to moment, waking to waking, our continuity found as much within the context of others and our institutions, but how much more so for those of us who jump from soul to soul, world to world, mind to mind, context to context, husk to husk, leaving who knows what behind, picking up who knows what from whom?

I thought my time had come on a few occasions, most recently when I was chasing a disgraced caudillo out of his estancia, down the steps and into the man-high grasses of one of the great blue-green fields that stretched to the horizon. He fumbled the revolver as he plunged, nearly falling, down the broad stone steps, trying both to hold his trousers up as he went and to avoid tripping over the broad red sash that was supposed to secure them. (I'd surprised him both in flagrante and on the toilet, both bucking and straining under a straddling slave girl. I swear people's sexual predilections never cease to astound me, and you'd have thought by now that I could reasonably claim I'd seen it all: wrong again.)

He'd thrown the girl at me and so bought himself enough time to start running, once he'd tripped over the still twitching bodies of his two guards in the hall outside. I disentangled myself from the screaming girl, then had to punch her with my free, non-cutlass-heaving hand when she came flying at me, nails out (the local gods alone knowing why). Finally I set off in pursuit, roaring for effect. I don't even know where the pistol came from. I stooped and plucked it from the ground as the caudillo disappeared into the grasses, screaming hysterically. Not loaded. Well done. I pushed it into my waistband anyway and followed the trail of tall broken grasses, slackening my pace a little, then a lot. Ahead of me the caudillo had the hard job, pushing into and trampling over the finger-thick stalks, leaving me with a path that a one-legged blind man could have followed and still gained on his quarry.

The wind sighed across the tops of the grasses somewhere over my head, and for a moment I was back in a banlieue just beyond the Périphérique, vaulting a burned-out car and chasing after the two young Maghrebis who'd thought to try and rape the girl in the tower block we'd just left. All gallant stuff, and she would allegedly turn into either a cowed, failed little thing who'd jump with her baby from the roof of this very block before she was twenty, or a noted authority on psycho-semantics – whatever that was – at the universities of Trier and Cairo, according to whether the mooted violation took place or not.

The boys had a bottle of nitric with them. I was supposed to use it to do to them what they'd been going to do to her after they'd fucked her (otherwise they'd try again), but before I could catch them they leapt a wall and fell ten metres into a newly dug hole for a Métro line extension. One had time to scream before he hit the concrete. The other didn't – scamp must have been between breaths. Parkour ninjas only in their PlayStation avatar forms, they'd both tumbled as they went and so hit head first. I'd just got to the wall. I still think I heard both necks snap, though it could have been their skulls popping, I suppose. The smashed bottle of nitric pooled around their bodies, raising fumes.

Except this time they both scrambled up a chain-link fence into an electricity substation and started running across the top of the humming machinery, leaping equipment like hurdlers. They disappeared together inside a single titanic blue flash that wrecked my night vision and produced a concussive bang that left my ears ringing. I bounced to a stop against the fence.

Wait, this hadn't happened . . . I'd almost jumped the wall too, not been about to go geckoing up some chain-link and start dancing across the busbars.

And then I was back in the blue-green field of giant grass again, still pacing heavily after the increasingly desperate caudillo. I could hear his panting breaths mingled with gasped, gulped pleas for mercy somewhere ahead. The path he was leaving was curved; he might be trying to circle back to the buildings, having worked out that he stood no chance while having to blaze the trail for both of us through the stiff, resistant crop.

But no; I was charging down a hillside favela in Bahia, jumping empty oil cans and screaming at the departing back of another skinny young kid blurring through the crowds of shouting people. This one I just had to scare. I was supposed to be mistaken for an undercover cop and she was supposed to become a famous violinist, not a drug courier. She ran into the first big street at the bottom of the hill and missed getting flattened by a truck by about a centimetre. The truck swerved, half toppled, a man on a motorbike went full speed into the side of it, nearly taking his head off, flopping dead. The girl disappeared down an alley on the far side of the traffic and I stopped, stooped, hands on knees to get my breath back.

I felt dizzy, staggered to one side and then the stagger turned into a run; I was still pelting down the alley after her. I shouted her name and she half turned immediately before she reached the street, long brown hair flung out to the side just for a moment. The truck hit her full on and tossed her into the oncoming stream of traffic, sending her spinning doll-loose under a bus, making it bounce on her body like it had gone over a speed bump. I skidded, stopping so fast against a corner that my sunglasses fell off. What the fuck was going on?

I hesitated as I paced after the caudillo, then kept on going, cutlass raised, shaking my head to loose the bizarrely vivid feeling of having just relived the recent past.

Cutlass they wanted, cutlass they would get. It had some historical meaning, apparently. At any rate, there would be no comeback now, no triumphal return no matter how undeserved. (Ask not. Oh, ask then. The answer is: a corrupt press, the manipulations of a foreign power and rich, influential families bribing thugs and judges: any incompetence, any evil can be washed away with sufficient muscle and money.) But not for our boy here; not for this version in this iteration of the world. The trail was still curving back round through the grass. It was a little narrower now, too, less wasteful. The caudillo must be getting half clever, trying to slip between the stalks rather than batter and stumble his way over them. I upped my pace to a normal walk, still puzzling over what was happening with these not-quite/more-than flashbacks.

I found the caudillo's scarlet waist-sash first, scribbled like a trail of rather too neat blood on the flattened grass. And then the man himself, lying in the grass, chest heaving, tears streaming, pants still at three-quarter mast, air whistling in and out of his gaping mouth, his hands clasped in front of him as though in prayer while he pleaded with me and offered rapidly increasing sums to let him go.

I swivelled the cutlass in the most economical of backstrokes – the grass constricted matters – and the bastard twisted, rolled and suddenly had a tiny silvery two-shot up-and-over pistol in his quivering hands, pointed right at my face. In that instant, I had time to see that the gun might be small but the barrels each looked wide enough to stick a little finger down and not get it wedged, and the range was laughable.

How slowly my arm seemed to be moving as it brought the cutlass round and down. Had I time to flit away? Not quite. But I could start the process. You never knew.

So, those flashbacks that were not quite and rather more than flashbacks had been some sort of premonition of things going terminally wrong. That was what they'd meant; they'd been a warning. How foolish of me to ignore my own subconscious, I thought, though it did also occur to me that a simple but very strong urge to take off after the caudillo and his girly cries waving a high-powered handgun might have been a still simpler and less ambiguous hint. But a cutlass they had wanted, and where would people like me be if we didn't even have the weaselly excuse of just obeying orders?

This was taking too long. I thought I could hear the swish of the cutlass edge tearing through the air as it accelerated, and feel its tip connecting with a couple of the closest stalks of grass as it passed, a blade amongst blades . . .

The caudillo's fist, the one holding the gun, jerked once.

There was a click.

No more.

Gun jammed or safety still on.

Or also not loaded, of course – precedent the fumbled pistol dropped on the steps. (The man had made an unholy mess of running the country – why expect him to be competent with a gun?)

Didn't particularly matter.

The scimitar's curved blade hit the blubbering caliph on one arm then the other, slicing all four bones and sending two halved fore-arms and the gun tumbling into the rushes. Wait a minute—

The return stroke took the shrieking man's head off. I was already flitting away, though whether from sighing blue-green grass in Greater Patagonia or tall rushes within the sunlit marshes of New Mesopotamia, I was no longer sure.

12

Patient 8262

I must have made myself understood to the medical staff somehow. Initially I did no more than blow off steam to the nurse who came, grumbling, to investigate my shouting in the middle of the night. The fellow looked like he had just woken up despite the fact he was meant to be fully awake during his night shift.

He gave no sign of understanding what I was saying – I was talking in my own language and so I did not expect him to. He made soothing noises in between his yawns and tucked my bed sheets back in. Then he patted my hand, took my pulse, put a hand on my forehead and then, after scribbling something on my notes, left.

I stayed awake for some time, heart beating fast, mentally daring the pervert who'd tried to interfere with me to come back (I have a weapon I can use). Eventually I must have fallen asleep and only woke up, later than usual, as breakfast was served.

But one of the trainee doctors appeared later that morning and asked me slowly in the local language what had disturbed me during the night. I told her what had happened, or what had nearly happened, as best I could with my still rudimentary vocabulary and she made some notes and left.

Another doctor I haven't seen before arrives after lunch. She is a solid, square-set woman with no-nonsense glasses and a mass of bleached blonde hair swept up and gathered in a bun from which a variety of curled wisps have escaped. Caught in the afternoon sun flooding into the room, they look like solar flares.

She treats me like an idiot. She speaks very slowly and carefully and asks me – I am pretty sure – did something bad happen to me? I think I am right in nodding, indicating that it did. She asks me if I would like to come with her so that we can talk about it some-where else. I try to make it clear that right here in the security and comfort of my own room is just fine but she looks very concerned and talks over my halting attempts at her language and says we'll go to her office.

I try to protest but eventually she calls on an orderly and, over my protests that this is tantamount to another assault, I am helped into a wheelchair and taken along the corridor, down to the ground floor in a large, creakily protesting lift and along the corridor under-neath the one we just left until we get to what I assume is her office, situated, if my navigational skills have not entirely deserted me, somewhere close to the day room where the usual cast of droolers, slack-jaws and incontinence-pad habitués will be congre-gating about now to argue over the choice of afternoon TV channel.

She thanks the orderly, closes the door behind her and after some smiles and soothing words she sits me to the side of her desk while she moves her chair so that we are sitting quite close together at the corner of the desk. She produces two dolls from a drawer. The dolls look as though they have been knitted from vaguely flesh-coloured wool. One is dressed like a girl, one like a boy and they both have blank faces. She hands me the girl doll for some reason and seems to want me to use it to indicate where I might have been touched when the interfering miscreant came to my room last night.

I sigh, lift up the skirt of the girl doll – at least it is not embar-rassingly anatomically correct, with only a little sewn line to indicate the female genital area – and point at its crotch. She holds the male doll up and asks do I want it as well? I nod and she hands me the male doll.

I indicate on it as well where I was touched, which seems to confuse her. She leans forward and seems as if she wants to take the dolls for herself and show me what she thinks must have happened, but then stops herself. I begin to use the two dolls to show her what actually occurred, then hold up the girl doll and ask – as slowly as she has been talking to me – if she has another male doll. She looks uncertain at first, then takes the girl doll away, swapping it for another male doll.

I use a box of handkerchiefs on her desk as a makeshift bed for one of the dolls and point from it to me a couple of times so that there is no ambiguity about what is going on; that's me asleep in my bed. I even mime sleeping. Then I use the second male doll to indicate it walking along, entering my room and approaching the bed. At this point it occurs to me that I am not absolutely certain that the person who did the attempted interfering was indeed male. I did not see them clearly enough and could not tell from the touch of their hand, the feel of their skin or their smell what gender they might have been. I just assumed it was a man.

I show the second male doll reaching over the first, sleeping one and briefly touching it around its genitals, then the bed-bound one sitting up quickly and shouting while the second doll startles and runs away. I lay the second doll down on the desk and spread my arms, indicating that the little show is over.

The broad lady doctor sits looking thoughtful and makes some more soothing noises. She appears to be thinking. I pick up the second doll and sit it on my knee, crossing its legs as it sits there.

From what I can tell, the lady doctor seems to be questioning my version of events, although on what authority I am at a loss to tell. Is there another, conflicting account? I wouldn't have thought so!

I take the doll on my lap in both hands. Is the doctor saying what I think she is? Is she saying that this did not, could not have happened the way that I say that it did? How dare she? Who does she think she is? She wasn't there! I had hoped that at least I might be believed. Does she think I would bother to make something like this up? An injustice upon an assault! I can feel my hands tightening into fists.

Meanwhile, above our heads, there is the sound of some commotion: shouting and a series of small thumps followed by a large, ragged one. More distant shouting. It is a warm day and the window of the doctor's room is lying half open. Outside, I can hear birdsong and leaves rustling in the wind. That and the shouting coming from upstairs.

You are sure it was another person doing this? the doctor appears to be asking. I nod and say "Yes!" with some considerable emphasis. Above our heads, some sort of alarm is going off and I can hear running feet. The doctor appears oblivious.

You know not who it was? she asks.

"No!" I tell her. "I know not!"

You might have dreamed it, she suggests.

"I might have but I did not! It happened!"

"You know not who it was?"

"No! No! How many more times? No!"

"Or could have been?"

"Anyone. Any person it could have been."

"Not nurse," she begins, then I lose the rest. Possibly something about duties, which would make sense.

"Not nurse," I tell her. (Upstairs, more thumping.)

The broad doctor looks down at the doll in my hands. I am holding it rather tightly, squeezing its chest as though trying to throttle it by the lungs. She reaches over and takes it gently from my hands, placing it beside the other one, which is still reclining in its handkerchief-box bed.

Upstairs, the rhythmic thumping ceases and a weak cheer sounds.

"There is (something something) of doll," the doctor says.

"What?" I ask.

Above our heads, the sound of something scraping, probably chair legs on the wooden floor of the day room. Is that clapping?

The male doll I was holding earlier slides off the edge of the desk and flops to the floor. There is a scream from somewhere outside and a white-clad body falls from above, past the window, hitting the ground outside the window with a thump and a roar of pain. I seem to feel that pain. I shiver, half closing my eyes. The room around me starts to dim.

I watch the doctor recede in my gaze, seeming to fall slowly horizontally away from me as the office disappears hazily around me, starting with the outskirts, spreading to the wall behind the desk and the desk itself and ending with just the doctor, an indeterminate dot somewhere in the far distance, looking round in horror at the window and then starting to her feet and dashing towards it.

I see no more. It is as though I am falling down a great dark pipe away from everything and eventually I'm too far away to make out anything at all.

Upstairs: more shouting, again. It too sounds like it is being heard from one end of a long pipe, very distant and echoey and strange. It fades quickly away to nothing.

Finally, I think, I faint.

Adrian

What? Kennedy? Man on the moon? The Wall comes down? Mandela walking? 9/11? 7/7? Notable dates for your diary, end-of-an-era stuff like that? I'll tell you one:

"What, to each according to their greed, is that it, yeah?"

"Yeah," I said, thinking about this. "Yeah, that's a pretty fair what-do-you-call-it. Summation. Yeah, I should think."

"Ho ho!" The girl just widened her eyes and shook her head and took a drink. "You are so fucked up." She flashed a shit-eating smile and added, "Dude."

We were in the Met bar, when it was still cool. I'd already seen one Gallagher brother. I was meeting some mates there; we were off to watch the F1 race the next day at Brands Hatch or Silverstone or wherever. The girl was there with a couple of old school friends, though the other two had gone off to the Ladies, one looking unhealthily pale and the other to hold her hair, I was guessing. Leaving this one. Called Chloë. Chloë with the diaresis, which is the two-little-dots thing, apparently.

The girl who was probably doing the hair-holding by now had volunteered their names earlier. In all the noise I didn't think Chloë had caught my name and she hadn't asked either. She was cute. Young enough to be a student, maybe: curly black hair, cheeky little face with big eyes. Nice top, great tits, designer jeans, red heels. Tasty, in other words. And a challenge. Patently.

"Greed gets a bad press," I told her.

"Yeah. What, like fascism?"

I winked. "You're an idealist, aren't you?"

"I have ideals," she agreed. Her voice was western Home Counties. Girls' school. She was trying a bit too hard to sound bored. "Plus I'm human, so I'm a humanist."

"And feminine," I said. I'd got better at seeing how this sort of stuff worked.

"You're catching on."

I drank my lager, smiled. "Doing all right, am I?"

She raised her eyebrows. "I wouldn't get too optimistic. I don't fuck guys like you."

"What sort of guys *do* you fuck?" I asked her, resting one elbow on the bar and leaning just a little closer to her, taking up more of her field of vision. I'd already got a semi. Just a girl using the f-word like that was usually enough. To be talking about fucking with a girl even when she was basically saying no, or at least was telling you she was saying no, was enough. Promising, know what I mean?

"Nice guys."

"Nice," I said, looking sceptical.

She winked at me. It looked like a what-do-you-call-it, a parody of the way I'd just winked at her. "They finish last." She drank from her cocktail glass, looking pleased with herself.

I laughed. I put my glass down and held out my hand, looking tentative about it. "I'm Ade?" I said, quite quietly, head lowered slightly in that Let's-start-again? kind of way. She looked at my hand like it might be contaminated. "Adrian?" I said, and gave her the first-level cheeky smile, which has been known to melt many a girl's heart and other parts and which I am not ashamed to admit I have practised in the mirror, to get the effect just right. Hey – it's for them in the end. But then she took my hand, gripped it for about a nanosecond.

"Chloë," she told me.

"Yeah, your mate said."

"So, what, you're in the music biz, Ade? Or films?" It was like she was trying to sound sarcastic when there was nothing to be sarcastic about.

"Nah, money."

"Money?"

"Hedge fund."

"What's a hedge fund?" she asked, frowning. To be fair, not many people outside the industry had heard of them then – this was pre-LTCM folding, sort of in between the Asian crisis and the Russian crisis.

"Way of making money," I told her.

"Hedging your financial bets?"

"Something like that."

"Sounds . . . totally parasitic." Another insincere smile.

"Nah, honest, we make a lot of money for a lot of people. We make money work. We make it work harder than anybody else. That's not parasitic at all. Your *banks* are parasitic. They just sit there, absorbing stuff from the people actually making the money. We're out there, we're predators. We're operators. We make the profits happen. We make money perform. We make money work." I'd already said that, I knew, but I was getting enthusiastic. Plus I'd taken a toot in the Gents five minutes earlier and it was still hitting me.

She snorted. "You sound like a salesman."

"What's wrong with being a salesman?" I asked. She was starting to annoy me. "I mean, I'm not, but so what if I was? What do you do, Chloë? What's your business?"

She rolled her eyes. "Graphic design," she sighed.

"That any better than being a salesman?"

"Bit more creative, maybe?" she said in a bored voice. "Slightly more meaningful?"

I put both forearms on the bar. "Let me guess, Chloë. Your dad's loaded. You—"

"Fuck off," she said angrily. "What's he got to do with me?"

"Chloë," I said in mock horror. "That's your dad you're talking about there." I snapped my fingers. "Trust fund," I said. "You're a Trusty."

"No, I'm fucking not! You don't know anything about me!"

"I know I don't!" I protested, pretending to match her in general upsettedness or whatever. "And you're not making it easy for me, quite frankly!" You never want to overdo that kind of thing, though. I made a sort of deflating motion, dropping my shoulders and my voice. "What have you got against me, Chloë?" I asked, trying to sound just a little hurt but also being careful not to overdo the plaintiveness.

"The thing about money, maybe?" she suggested, like it ought to be obvious. "The whole greed thing, yeah?"

"Look," I said, sighing. I was already thinking this wasn't a chat-up situation any longer. I just wanted to say stuff that I'd been thinking about, stuff that I'd sort of wanted to say to people like her before but never got round to. Plus, of course, there are some women that when you stop trying to chat them up and start treating them like a bloke you're arguing with, they really like that and *that* can get them into bed where trying to chat them up normally never would. So, definitely worth trying.

"The greed thing," I say to her. "Everybody's greedy, Chloë. You're greedy. You might not think so but I bet you are. We're all out for number one. It's just that some of us don't kid ourselves about it, know what I mean? We all want everybody to think the same as we do and we think they're stupid if they think any different. And when it comes to love and relationships, we're all looking for the right person to worship us, because that'll make us happy, aren't we? Wanting to be happy – that's selfish, isn't it? Even wanting there to be no more poverty or violence – I mean, it's all bollocks cos there always will be: both. But that's us being selfish cos we want the world to be the way we personally think it ought to be, know what I mean? You can dress it up as wanting other people to be happy, but in the end it comes down to you and your own self-ishness, your own greed."

Chloë held a hand up, almost touching my mouth. "Greed and selfishness aren't the same thing," she said. "Close, but not the same. And they're both different from self-preservation and general self-interest."

"Still, close, like you say."

She sighed, drank. "Yeah, close." She looked like she was studying something behind the bar.

"There's nothing wrong with a bit of greed, Chloë. It's what makes the world go round. Wanting to get on, wanting to better yourself, being ambitious, know what I mean? Wanting the best for yourself – what's wrong with that? Wanting the best for your family – what's wrong with that, either? Eh? It's great having the luxury of thinking about other people, the poor and the starving and all that, but you only have that luxury cos somebody's been thinking for themselves and their family."

She turned to me, big eyes wide and bright. "You know what? You remind me of somebody, Ade," she said.

"Somebody nice?" I asked. Sarcastically, if I'm honest about it.

She shook her head. I liked the way her hair moved, though I was resigning myself to never running my fingers through it or breathing in its perfume or using it to pull her head back towards me while I fucked her from behind. "No," she said. "He's one of those men who was packed off to public school when he was just a little kid—"

"Yeah, well, I wasn't."

"Ssh." She looked stern. "I heard you out. The point is, because of that or not, he decided that everybody's out for themselves and nobody really cares for anybody else, though some people pretend to. He's looked after 'Number One'" – she did that finger-waggly inverted-commas thing – "exclusively ever since and he can't see there might be something wrong with that. In fact, he can't even see that what he's got there is just a single point of view, and a pretty perverse one at that; as far as he's concerned it's some great truth about people and life that only he and a few other realists have worked out. Thing is, he's got a problem. Maybe he's still infected with some tiny remnant of human decency or something, but he can only *really* be content with himself and his despicable egotism if he's satisfied that his self-centred attitude doesn't make him a freak. For his own peace of mind he needs to believe that it's not just him, that anybody who claims to care for others is lying; maybe because they're frightened to admit they only think of themselves too, or maybe because they actively want to make people like him feel bad about themselves."

I was starting to think that Chloë had been on the marching powder too, though somehow it didn't look like she had, know what I mean? She wasn't speaking the way you do when you're coked up. But, fuck me, she was still speaking:

"Socialists, charity workers, carers, people who volunteer to help others; they're all – and he's quite convinced about this – they're all in reality mean-spirited bastards, either self-deceiving bastards or – for their own filthy left-wing reasons – deliberately trying to destroy the self-esteem of normal, healthily ambitious people like him. Because if only everybody looked after their own interests everything would be fine, see? Level playing field, with everybody nakedly ambitious and selfish; everybody knows where they are. If some people aren't totally selfish, or, even worse, *pretend* not to be selfish, then it messes up the whole system. It makes it more unfair, not fairer, the way they'd claim. He calls people like that do-gooders, and they make him angry. I think he would actually prefer do-badders, which is a pretty fucked-up attitude when you think about it. He feels quite strongly that these charlatans needed to be unmasked. Always on about them. Never misses an opportunity to complain that they're liars and frauds. Frankly, Ade, altogether, it makes him sound like – and I firmly believe he actually is – a complete cunt."

Funny, isn't it? The c-word has no discernible effect on me. Wood-wise, I mean. You'd think when a woman uses the term it'd be quite sexy, but it isn't. Weird.

I nodded. "Ah-ha," I said. "Old boyfriend?"

"No, Ade. My dad. You remind me of my dad." Chloë drained her drink and patted me on the arm. "Sorry, dear." She nodded. "Now, here are my friends, coming back from the loo, looking a bit more sorted, thankfully." She slid daintily off her bar stool. "I think we'll be moving on. Interesting to talk to you, Ade. You look after yourself, yeah?"

And off all three of them fucked.

Her fucking *dad*? I fucking wanted to slap the bint.

The Philosopher

I have always had nightmares. Long before I became a soldier or a policeman, long before I killed GF's father or became a torturer, I would have unpleasant, threatening, frightening and distressing dreams. Perhaps they became worse for a while, on a few occasions maybe, especially just after Mr F. However, I believe that my decision not to pursue any further personal vendettas, and to act only when I felt I had the backing of some greater authority and that there existed a viable legal and moral framework supporting my professional actions, helped, as it were, to clear my conscience. At any rate, my nightmares decreased in severity afterwards.

293

They did not disappear. They would still haunt me. People did, faces did, sounds did, screams did especially. Some were very recent in origin: the latest subject, their roar of initial defiance, the following howls of agony and the eventual, inevitable pathetic whimperings and pleadings for mercy, sometimes accompanied by the information required in the first place, more often with nothing of use because the subject knew nothing useful to begin with.

I became a little disillusioned, I suppose, though that had nothing to do with the nightmares. It was just that our job never seemed to end, never seemed to achieve very much. There were always more subjects, and gradually a greater overall number of subjects at any given time, from a greater spread of ages and from more and more backgrounds and professions. Society seemed to be collapsing around us. The Christian Terrorist threat seemed only to increase despite the best efforts of the government, the security services and ourselves, and the real terrorists or terrorist suspects appeared to be joined by those who had fallen foul of the increased security measures and laws which the initial increases in terrorist activity had made necessary in the first place.

My colleagues and I comforted ourselves with the thought that however bad things might be or even might get, just think how much worse everything would be without our dedication and professionalism.

I finally received some long-deserved promotion and began to take on more administrative duties, taking me away from the front line, as it were, though not entirely. In busy periods I would help out and when colleagues were unexpectedly absent I would fill in for them. Both situations seemed to occur rather more often than the department expected or I'd have liked. I began to see a department-approved counsellor, and my doctor put me on some medication that worked relatively well, at first at any rate.

I established a mutually pleasing relationship with a lady police officer and found some solace in that, as I believe she did as well. We had decided to go on holiday, looking for some winter sun.

This was required, certainly in my case. I had lately started to have increasingly distressing nightmares that centred around being killed in my home, waking up to find ex-subjects, especially deceased ex-subjects, standing at the foot of my bed, still in the state we had left them when my department had finished with them. They would stand and stare at me in the darkness, silent but filled with accusation. I could always smell the bodily fluids and sometimes semi-fluid solids that subjects were prone to evacuating either right at the start of the interrogatory episode or when they were under especially pronounced pressure. I would wake up in a sweaty knot of sheets, terrified that I had myself wet or soiled the bed.

Just the prospect of such unpleasantly interrupted sleep was bad enough. My doctor put me on some more pills, to help me sleep. I found that a nightcap of whisky helped as well.

I might claim that I had a premonition regarding what happened at the airport. Though I think, in retrospect, that it was simply a memory of the CTs who had attacked the airport some years before, taking the weapons off the police guards and running amok with them. In any event, I was surprisingly nervous as my fiancée and I arrived at the airport. Nobody had attacked this airport for several years, nor had anyone succeeded in bringing down an aircraft either, despite a few near things, so I kept telling myself that there was nothing to worry about, but my hands were shaking as I locked the car door and picked up our luggage trolley.

Part of my nerves was due to the fact that I had, over the last year or so, begun to worry that I might bump into an ex-subject in a social situation or in a large crowd, and that they would attack me or even just shout and scream at me, or just quietly point me out to their friends and family as their erstwhile interrogator. I must have interrogated thousands of people over the preceding decade-and-a-bit and they were not all dead or in prison. There must be hundreds still at large, those whose crimes had been relatively minor or who had bought their release by turning informer, or who had been the victim of malicious denunciation. What if I encountered one of them? What if they fell upon me or embarrassed me in front of other people? This had preyed on my mind more and more recently. Statistically, it had to happen eventually.

Nowadays, all too often, I thought I did indeed see such people. I tried never to memorise or even casually remember the faces of any of my subjects – as my dreams showed, they proved all too memorable without any effort being made on my part – but nevertheless I had started to see faces in the street or in parks or shops – or anywhere else where there were other people, really – which I felt certain I had last seen tear-streaked, contorted in agony, mouth open in a scream or sealed with tape, their eyes popping, faces turning red.

I had stopped going out quite so much as I had used to. I entertained more at home, had groceries delivered.

We entered the terminal building. I found the beady-eyed gaze of the expressionless border police, paramilitaries and soldiers intensely reassuring. Nobody would be surprising these fellows and stealing their weapons. They took a family just in front of us to one side for a luggage spot check.

We went to the bar after the rather long-winded and laborious check-in process. I claimed I needed a stiff drink after that, and also that I was a slightly nervous flyer. We spent half an hour there before we thought we ought to go through the main security barrier. I drank three or four glasses to my fiancée's one, which she did not finish.

There was a long queue for the security barrier. I had guessed as much from the latest internal security services threat-level alert and had allowed for such in our schedule for the day so far, despite some complaints.

We shuffled forward. I was trying to read a newspaper. Police and soldiers walked up and down by the side of the line, looking at people. I started to worry that I might look suspicious just because I was trying so hard to look as though I was reading the paper, and was so obviously sweating. I could think of a few psychological/physiological parameters that I was fitting into all too neatly.

I put the newspaper down and looked around, trying to appear normal, unthreatening. At least, if I was taken out of the line my identity cards and especially my security forces special police pass would secure a speedy end to any suspicion and doubtless an apology. The line still stretched twenty metres ahead of us. Two desks out of three working, scanning passports and checking tickets before admitting people to the main security area where the hand luggage would be sniffed and scanned.

The coloured family a couple of metres ahead of us would probably attract extra attention. A young man just beyond them carried a kitbag he'd be lucky to get checked as hand luggage. He was an army draftee, judging by his uniform, but even so. We shuffled forward some more.

My fiancée took my hand and squeezed it. She smiled at me.

My most disturbing feelings recently had been something close to treacherous. I had come to think that the CTs had a point, even that all terrorists had a point. They were still wrong, still evil and still had to be resisted with all the means at our disposal as a society, including emergency measures, but the question that had started to occur to me was: were we any better? I put this down to the depressing realisation that people were all the same. They all bled, they all burned, they all begged, they all screamed, they all reacted in the same ways. Guilty or innocent; that made little difference. Race made none. Sex, little. CTs were more fanatical, certainly, but I had begun to doubt they were any more fanatical than the extremists on "our" side who firebombed their congregations or crucified whole families in remote farms.

Ordinary Christians, caught up in the trawls of their areas and families and friendship groups, were just the same as ordinary people. We all were. Almost without exception we human beings were weak and dishonest and cruel and selfish and dishonourable and desperate to avoid pain and torment and incarceration and death even to the point of implicating those we knew full well to be completely innocent.

And that was the point. We were all the same.

There was no difference. We reacted in the same ways to the same actions against us; I'd seen it a thousand times – many thousands of times. So what had driven the CTs to such desperate acts, to such mad fanaticism? Any society, any large group, any substantial creed contained sub-groups of people who would crack first under pressure and turn to violence and extremism. But what had created that pressure in the first place? Who had created it?

And would we, the ordinary, decent people, the security services, my own department for that matter – swapped at birth in the cradle; I don't know – have reacted any differently?

I was still sure we were doing the right thing, but such questions had come to plague me.

At the head of our slowly shuffling queue, between the two open desks, there was a big hip-high transparent plastic bin which contained all the knives, tweezers, pocket knives, metal toothpicks and tools and other bits and pieces which had been confiscated from absent-minded or ignorant people unaware of the relevant restrictions. It looked nearly full. I wondered if the bin's contents would be sold as second-hand pieces, or melted down, or thrown away.

The young trainee soldier ahead of us walked out of the line when he was about five metres away from the bin and waved at the surprised-looking border police official scanning the passports. The young fellow was saying something, sounding amused or jocular, not angry or frustrated. I imagined that he was late for a flight, perhaps liable to be posted AWOL if he didn't get through ahead of the rest of us. I looked back. The nearest police officer, behind us, shook his head and started to head for the front of the queue, where the young man had reached the big bin and was starting to talk to the border control official. He put his heavy-looking kitbag down and stretched his back, putting his hands behind his neck in an unconscious parody of the position the approaching policeman would soon be asking him to assume if he persisted in this attempt to obtain priority. I heard people around us tutting.

The big heavy kitbag was lying right behind the giant plastic bin full of sharps.

To this day I don't know exactly what made me react the way I did. I started to cry out, then somehow knew that there was no time, and pulled my fiancée to the side, throwing her down towards the wall and trying to throw myself on top of her.

That is all I can claim to remember.

The young soldier was a CT, a suicide bomber. The kitbag contained a blast bomb. The explosive charge it held could be made larger than it would have been otherwise because it required no shrapnel; the transparent bin provided that.

Thirty-eight died, not counting the bomber. Both border control gate officials perished, as did the policeman who had been on his way to find out what was happening. Everybody ahead of us in the queue died instantly or within seconds, save for one baby asleep in a backpack cradle. For three or four metres behind where we had been standing, almost everybody died. My fiancée lived for five days. I was on the critical list for about the same amount of time and in intensive care for a further month. I had lost my left eye and left leg and both eardrums.

What I thought most tragic and somehow hopeless was that the young CT suicide bomber had not murdered a real soldier for his uniform or even just stolen it; he really was an army draftee, and one who had come from a good, well-off, well-educated family of unquestionable loyalty and social credentials and who had passed all the relevant weeding-out stages and psychological tests with flying colours. He had only converted to Christianity, in secret, a few months earlier. A kind of conclusive despair settled within me when I learned that, and I had not, being quite frank about it, been in the best of spirits beforehand.

I was in a private room at the hospital, still in some pain a couple of weeks after leaving the Intensive suite, when a lady came to see me while I was snoozing. I got the impression of a short, bustily attractive woman, well dressed and strongly perfumed. I didn't recognise her, and wondered – a little groggily due to the painkillers – if she was one of my ex-subjects, arrived to inflict a bruise upon a bruise. She held my wrist as though about to take my pulse, then encircled it, her hand a bracelet, and with that, and no further ceremony, suddenly I was somewhere else.

The Transitionary

My new friend Adrian insists that he must be personally present to be of the most help, so is on his way. However, it will take most of the rest of the day for him to get here.

I wander the abandoned palace for a while, imprisoned within all this luxury and space, reluctant to show signs of life in case anybody is watching and equally reticent about leaving it. I feel safe here, even as I fret at the feeling of confinement and the prospect of presenting an unmoving target for the next five or six hours. I stand looking at a walk-in freezer on the ground floor. The freezer is switched off, dark, dry, its thick, stepped door wedged open by a shrink-wrapped case of Coca-Cola. I shiver, suddenly remembering the time I came here when it snowed, when I met my little pirate captain, and the very first time I came to this world, when I tasted its unique fragre.

During the initial moments of that original visit, knowing nothing of the place save for that first hint of its true essence, I'd happily have bet somebody else's bottom dollar this was a Greedist world, a world where the untrammelled pursuit of material wealth and the virtues of money itself were extolled, venerated and even worshipped. Not as an original act of faith of course; we always give ourselves more credit than that. Accidentally, rather. Perdition awaits at the end of a road constructed entirely from good intentions, the devil emerges from the details and hell abides in the small print.

I claim no moral superiority here. People like me get to see this more clearly than most only because we are privileged to witness lots of non-unique examples spread across a variety of worlds, not because we are intrinsically wiser or more ethically refined. And even I – knowing full well that the technicalities profoundly matter – have to accept that it is precisely from the details, from the clutter and the turmoil of existence, that the fatal blow inescapably arises, like a freak wave, overwhelming, from the distributed chaos of the ocean.

The specifics will claim me one day; the details always deliver in the end.

There are as many types of capitalism as there are types of socialism – or any other ism for that matter – but one of the major differences – a major difference founded on what appears to be a minor detail – between whole bundles of ostensibly fully capitalist societies centres (indeed, depends) on whether commerce is governed by private firms and partnerships, or by limited companies.

I'd lie if I claimed I possessed any congenital interest in economics, but – from what I've gathered over the years – the invention and acceptance of the limited company means people can take big risks with money not their own and then – if it all goes wrong – lets them just walk away from the resulting debts, because the company is somehow regarded as being like a person in its own right, so that its debts die with it (not the sort of fairy story a partnership is allowed to get away with).

It's a piece of nonsense, really, and I used to wonder that legislatures anywhere bought into this blatant fantasy and agreed to give it legal house room. But that was just me being naive, before I realised that there was a reason why it always dawned on all those ambitious, powerful gents in all those various legislatures that this ludicrous hooey might actually be quite a good idea.

Anyway, limited company worlds often progress faster than other types, but always less smoothly and reliably, and sometimes disastrously. I've looked into it and frankly it just isn't worth it, but you can't tell that to anyone caught up within the seductive madness of the dream; they have the faith, and are forever relieved by the invisible hand.

I kick the case of Coca-Cola aside, letting the freezer door thud closed.

There is a generously sized kitchen in the Palazzo. It also has no electricity, of course, and no other sort of power I can get to work, but it does have drawers full of cutlery and cupboards full of tin cans. I eat cold peas by candlelight.

As I begin to relax, I discover a need to know how many peas are on the spoon I am eating with. Oh dear. I thought I'd shaken that weakness off.

I try to ignore this absurd compulsion and just keep on eating, but it is as though there is an elastic band joining the plate and the spoon, or a membrane in front of my face, physically preventing me from bringing the spoon to my mouth. Preposterous as it may be, it is actually easier to give in and count the peas. I cannot arrive at an accurate figure just staring at the slowly collapsing pile on the spoon, of course (though I'm sure an estimate would be pretty close to the final figure), so I have to spoon the load onto the plate and count them there. In the dim glow of the single candle, this is harder than it sounds. I have to sort them into files of five to ensure accuracy. Having arrived at a figure it proves impossible to pick all the peas up again. I push them back into the mass of peas on the plate and take up another spoonful. That first spoonful was a pretty typical one, I reckon. This one poised before me now is also pretty typical, so ought to have the same number of peas.

But does it? I am growing annoyed at myself and my stomach is growling at me, still mostly empty, but I need to know. Was that first spoonful typical? Did I arrive at a reliable number before? I let this latest sample slide onto the side of the plate and count them as well. Slightly more than the first spoonful. I take an average of the two. Though even as I do this I realise that two just seems an inadequate number. One more sample ought to do it. Three is the number required for triangulation, after all.

There, this third spoonful contains a number in between the first two spoonfuls; a straddle, a sure sign that we are zeroing in on the right number. I decide to take no more nonsense from myself and just eat this spoonful. This works and I am able to sit back again. I sigh through my nose as my teeth and tongue quickly convert the mass of peas into a single lump of paste inside my mouth. I swallow and sit forward, scooping up the next mouthful of *piselli picolli*. On the table the candle flame flickers, as though shivering.

I stop and let the spoon fall back into the plate. I stare at the candle, remembering.

And then, suddenly, I was not merely remembering. I was—

I watched her move her hand above the lit candle, through the yellow flame, fingers spread fluttering through the incandescing gas, her unharmed flesh ruffling the very burning of it. The flame bent this way and that, guttered, sent curls of sooty smoke towards the dim ceiling of the room where we sat as she moved her hand slowly back and forth through the gauzy teardrop of flame.

She said, "No, I see consciousness as a matter of focus. It's like a magnifying glass concentrating rays of light on a point on a surface until it bursts into flame. The flame is consciousness; it is the focusing of reality that creates that self-awareness." She looked up at me. "Do you see?"

I stared at her.

I was here, here with her, in this place, right now.

This was not a memory, not a flashback. Certainly we had taken drugs and we were still at this point under their influence, but this was definitely not some addled consequence of their effects. This was startlingly immediate and unquestionably vivid. Real, in a word.

She put her head to one side a little, flexed an eyebrow. "Tem?" she said softly. "Are you listening?"

"I'm listening," I said.

"You look distracted," she told me. She pulled the sheet that was all she wore a little tighter about her, as though she was cold. She took a breath, went to speak.

I said, "There is no intelligence without context."

Her brows flicked momentarily into a tremulous frown.

"That's what—" Still frowning, she sat back, removing her hand from the candle flame; it curled out after her fingers in a long flexing trail of glowing yellow, as though reluctant to let go of her. "Have I said this to you before?" she asked.

"Not really," I said, watching the candle flame restore itself. "Not as . . . No."

She looked at me with what could have been either suspicion or bafflement. "Hmm," she said. "Well, it's like a magnifying glass, and the partial shadow it casts around its focus. The halo of reduced light around the bright spot at its centre is the debt required to produce that central concentration. In the same way, meaning is sucked out of our surroundings and concentrated in ourselves, in and by our minds."

(*Her hair—*)

Her hair, a brown-red spill of curls across her shoulders and along her slender neck, formed a quiet nimbus around her canted head. Her deep orange-brown eyes looked almost black, reflecting the poised stillness of the candle's flame like some image of the consciousness she had been talking about. They looked perfectly still and steady. I could see the minuscule spark of the flame reflected in them, unwavering, constant, alive. She blinked slowly, languorously.

I recalled recalling that the eyes only see by moving: we can fasten our gaze on something and stare intently at it only because our eyes are constantly consumed with dozens of tiny involuntary movements each second. Hold something perfectly and genuinely still in our field of vision and that very fixity makes it disappear.

"I love you," I said.

She sat forward suddenly. "*What?*"

The word, so emphatically pronounced, was enough to blow out the candle's little flame and plunge the room into darkness.

The candle sitting on the table in front of me, here in the kitchen of the Palazzo Chirezzia, blows out, caught in a sudden draught

I can feel on my face, bringing a chill that lifts the hairs on the back of my neck. The spoonful of cold peas I was about to eat remains poised halfway to my mouth, exactly where it was the instant before I relived, replayed and changed those moments from a room a dozen years and an infinitude of worlds away. But I thought the spoon fell—

A door thuds somewhere in the building. Here in the kitchen, things click and buzz and motors start turning, fridge and freezer compressors sighing into life as a light comes on in the hallway outside and I hear distant footsteps.

13

Patient 8262

Last night I left this bed and this room and this level and I took me down to the floor below, the ground floor, where I witnessed something I found most terrible just yesterday. I found the silent ward. I was there, I was in it, I lay there with them for a time. It did not last long but it was long enough. I found it terrifying.

It happened after I fainted in the office of the broad-shouldered lady doctor. I still don't know quite what happened there. It ended up as some sort of bizarre hallucinatory experience, a lucid nightmare of voodoo cause and effect that ended with a keeling-over that I was frankly thankful for at the time and, despite the fact it meant it makes it harder to work out what did happen, that I am still thankful for.

Usually, I've found, there is a distinct point when one realises that one is asleep and dreaming. I can't remember one in what happened – what seemed to happen – yesterday. Was it all a dream? It can't have been. At the very least, I went or was taken somewhere else yesterday, out of my room.

I was brought back here on a trolley after my time in the silent ward (we're coming to that). I am certain I was as awake at that point as I am now. Though, when I think about it, I felt just as awake at the start of the experience with the broad lady doctor as I do now. Well, we must leave that aside. There is a continuum of banal experience between waking up in the silent ward and now. No manipulated dolls causing people to have breathing difficulties or heart attacks or whatever and then to throw themselves out of windows. I imagined all that anyway, so I'm told.

This needs thinking about, obviously. That is why I am thinking about it. I am lying here, eyes closed, concentrating. I may have to get up and carry out further investigations in the day room amongst the droolers and perhaps ask further questions of the nursing staff, but for now I need to lie and rest and think without distractions.

Having said that, I am very aware that the door to my room is closed and I will open my eyes the instant I hear it open, just in case my assaulter from the other night has the audacity to attempt a repeat visit during daylight hours.

Two things. First, I cannot see where the visit to the broad lady doctor went from rational to absurd. It appears seamless in my memory. This is most vexing. Like not being able to see how a simple trick is performed in a magic show, or the join in a piece of mending where it ought to be obvious.

The second thing is what happened after I regained consciousness.

I woke flat out in a gurney, a trolley bed. It was dark; only a couple of soft glows from night-lights illuminated a large space the size of the day room at the end of my own corridor, maybe bigger. The ceiling looked higher than in my room or the day room. I felt groggy and sleepy but in no pain, unharmed. I tried to shift a little, but either the sheets were very tight or I had temporarily lost a lot of strength – I was too groggy to tell which – and I had to remain lying flat out. Listening carefully, I could hear gentle snores.

I turned my head to one side, then the other. I was at one end of a large open ward, the kind of thing you see in old photographs, or poor countries. My trolley was at the end of a line of beds, lying conveniently near the set of half-glazed double doors. On the other side of the room, beneath tall windows, was another line of beds. To see more, I tried again to raise my upper torso, attempting to bring my arms up so that I could support myself on my elbows, but without success.

Whatever sense we possess that informs us of such matters was busy informing me that I was not exhausted or hopelessly weakened; my muscles were working normally and were simply being physically prevented from accomplishing their allotted tasks. Something was stopping me from moving. I forced my head up as far as I could, to the point where my neck muscles were quivering, and realised, as I looked down the length of the sheet covering my body, that I was strapped in.

Strapped in! I felt a moment of panic and struggled to release myself. There were four straps: one across my shoulders, another over my belly, pinning my arms to my flanks, a third securing my legs at my knees and a fourth gripping my ankles. None of them seemed prepared to release me by as much as a millimetre. What if there was a fire? What if my attacker from the other night came back to find me helpless? How dare they do this to me? I had never been violent! Never! Had I? Of course, obviously, yes, ha, I had been extremely violent in my earlier life as a famously inventive ultra-assassin, but that was a long time ago and far far away and in another set of bodies entirely. Since I'd been here I had been a lamb, a mouse, a non-goose-booing paragon of matchless docility! How dare they truss me like a psychopathic lunatic!

All my struggles were to no effect. I was still tied tightly to the bed. The straps were as tight as they had been when I'd started and all I'd done was raise my heart rate, make myself very hot and sweaty and half exhaust myself.

At least, I thought, as I tried in vain to find any sort of seam or opening or purchase with my wriggling fingers, if the person who had tried to interfere with me in my room the night before did discover me lying helpless here they would be faced with the same problem of absurdly tight sheets as I was. I had to hope that it would be as impossible to squeeze a stealthily insinuating hand into the bed as my hands were finding it going in the opposite direction.

Nevertheless, I was still terrified. What if there was a fire? I'd roast or bake or burn to death. Smoke inhalation would be a mercy. But what if my attacker did return? Perhaps they couldn't get a hand under my sheets without undoing me, but they could do anything else they wanted. They could suffocate me. Tape my mouth, pinch my nose. They could perform any unspeakable act they wanted upon my face. Or they might be able to undo the bedclothes at the foot of my bed and gain access to my feet. There were torturers who worked on nothing but feet, I'd heard. Just being severely beaten on the feet was allegedly excruciating.

I continued to try to free my feet, and to work my hands towards the sides of the bed where it might be possible to find some weakness in the confining sheets and straps. The muscles in my hands, forearms, feet and lower legs were starting to complain and even go into cramp.

I decided to rest for a while.

Sweat was running off me and I had a terribly itchy nose that I could not scratch or move my head enough to relieve against any part of the sheets. I looked around as best I could. There must have been two dozen people in there at least. Still not much detail visible, just dark shapes, lumps in the beds. Some were snoring, but not very loudly. I could just shout, I thought. Perhaps one of these sleepers would wake, arise and come to my aid. I looked at the bed next to mine, about a metre away. The sleeper appeared to be quite fat and to have his – her? – head turned away from me, but at least there were no straps securing them to their bed.

I was surprised that my struggles to free myself hadn't woken anybody up. I must have been quiet, I supposed. There was a funny smell in the ward, I thought. That terrified me too for a moment or so. What if it was burning? Electrical burning! A mattress burning!

But, when I thought about it, it wasn't a burning smell. Not very pleasant, but not the smell of burning. Perhaps one of the people in the ward had had a little night-time accident.

I could shout. I cleared my throat quietly. Yes, no problem there; everything felt like it was working normally. And yet I was reluctant to shout out. What if one of these people was the person who had attempted to assault me? Even if that wasn't the case, what if one of them was of a similar proclivity? Probably not, of course. Anyone dangerous would be in their own room, wouldn't they? They'd be locked away, or at least restrained as I had been, erroneously and absurdly.

Still, I was reluctant to shout out.

One of the other patients in the ward made a grunting noise, like an animal. Another one seemed to answer. That smell wafted over me again.

An appalling thought insinuated its way into my mind. What if these were not people at all? What if they were animals? That would account for the lumpen misshapenness of so many of the shapes I could see, for the smell, for all the grunting sounds they were making.

Of course, over all the time I had been here, there had been no hint that the clinic was anything other than a perfectly respectable and humanely run establishment with impeccable medical and caring procedures. I had no reason beyond whatever my highly constrained senses could supply to my already terrified mind and feverishly overactive imagination to believe that I was in anything other than a ward full of ordinary patients, asleep. Nevertheless, when a person has a completely bizarre experience, faints, and then finds themself strapped helpless to a bed in an unknown room full of strangers, at night, it should come as no surprise that they start to imagine the worst.

The corpulent figure looming dimly in the bed next to mine, from whom it now occurred to me there was a good chance that the strange smell had been coming – as well as some of the grunting

311

noises – made motions as though they might be about to turn over, bringing them face to face with me.

I heard myself make a noise, a sort of yelp of fear. The thing in the bed stopped moving for a moment, as though having heard me, or waking up. I decided I might as well make more noise. "Hello?" I said loudly. With a tone of authority, I trusted.

No reaction. "Hello?" I said again, raising my voice somewhat. Still nothing. "Hello!" I said, almost shouting now. A few snores, but the shape in the bed next to mine made no further move. "Hello!" I shouted. Not a soul stirred. "HELLO!"

Then, slowly, the shape in the next bed started to turn round towards me again.

Suddenly, a noise outside, on my other side, forcing me to look in that direction. There was a shape advancing on the barely lit glass of the half-glazed doors as someone or something came down the corridor. A figure, backlit, and then the doors swung open and a male nurse padded in, humming softly to himself, walked up to my gurney and looked, squinting, for a moment at the notes attached to the footboard. I took advantage of the slightly increased light and looked briefly round at the man in the nearby bed. I saw a dark, fat but entirely human face with a week's worth of beard. Asleep, dumb-looking, mouth and facial muscles slack. He snored. I looked back and saw the young male nurse stepping on the wheel brakes, releasing them.

He wheeled me out into the corridor and let the double doors swing closed themselves, seemingly careless of the noise. He unclipped my notes from the end of the trolley and held them up to the light. He shrugged, replaced them and started pushing me up the corridor, whistling now.

He must have seen me looking at him because he winked at me and said, "You awake Mr Kel? You should be asleep. Well, don't (*I didn't understand this middle bit*) out of those and into bed. I don't know why (*something something*)." He sounded friendly, reassuring. I suspected he was surprised that I'd been trussed up like that in the first place. "Don't know why they put you in there with the . . ." I didn't get the last word, but the way he said it it probably meant something mildly insulting, one of those snappy, honest but potentially shocking terms that medical people use amongst themselves that are not supposed to be for public consumption.

We went up in the big rattly lift. It always went very slowly and he started undoing the straps pinning me to the bed while we made the ascent. Then he wheeled me along to my room, released me from the trolley and helped me into bed. He wished me night-night and I wanted to cry.

The next day, the young mousy-haired lady doctor visited me and asked me questions about what had happened two nights before. I did not understand everything she said but I tried to answer as fully as I could. No insulting dolls nonsense this time, for which I ought to have been grateful, I supposed. No apology or explanation regarding my being strapped to the trolley in a strange ward for the first part of the previous night, either, mind you. I wanted to ask her why that had been done, what was going on, what was being done to identify the perpetrator and what was being done to prevent them trying to interfere with me again. But I lacked the vocabulary to express exactly what I wanted to say, and anyway felt shy in front of the delicate young lady doctor. I should have been able to deal with this sort of thing myself. There was no need to trouble her and risk either of us being embarrassed.

The day passed. I sat up in bed or sat in my chair, mostly, thinking, eyes shut. The more I thought about it, the more I felt there had been something odd about that ward downstairs.

The atmosphere was too placid. The man who turned over to face me looked too out of it. Could they all be sedated? I supposed they might be. Problem patients often are – the chemical equivalent of the restraining straps I was unjustly subjected to. Perhaps the place would have been in uproar if they hadn't all been given sedatives.

And yet it seemed to me more than that. There was something about the place, something almost familiar that woke a half or a quarter or a smaller fraction of a whole memory in me, something that might be important, one day if not now. Was it just the feel of the place, the atmosphere (I feel there ought to be another word, but it eludes me)? Or was it some detail I noticed subconsciously but which slipped past my attentive mental processes?

I resolved to investigate. I was aware that I had resolved the day or the night before to investigate the matter of my attempted assaulter, to ask questions of the staff and the slack-jaws in the day room, but had not done so. However, I decided that perhaps it was all best forgotten about and that so long as it did not happen again we'd say no more about it. It wasn't worth granting the fellow the attention. The mystery of the very quiet people and the silent ward: that seemed more important somehow, more serious. That definitely did deserve a degree of scrutiny. I would take a look down there tonight.

I opened my eyes. I ought to go now. In daylight. The silent ward would tell me more in waking hours than it might at night when everybody was meant to be sleeping anyway.

I got out of bed, donned slippers and dressing gown and made my way down the corridor to the stairwell and the corridor below. The cleaners were washing the floor and shouted at me from near the doors to the silent ward. Mostly from the pointing, I gathered that I mustn't walk on their still-wet floor.

I tried again in the later afternoon and got as far as the doors of the silent ward itself before I was turned back by a nurse. The glimpse I got of the ward through the closing door showed a tranquil scene. Hazy sunshine illuminated sparkling white beds, but nobody sat upright or sat at the side of their beds, and nobody was wandering around. It was, admittedly, a brief glimpse, but I found that very tranquillity disturbing. I retreated a second time, resolved to try again at night.

*   *   *

I slip out of my bed in the depths of the night and pull on my dressing gown. I feel only a little groggy and fuzzy from my usual post-supper medication; I swallowed just one of the pills and spat the other out later. I am allowed a little torch which I keep in my bedside cabinet. It has no batteries but works by being squeezed, a little flywheel whizzing round with a faint grinding noise to produce a yellow-orange light from the little bulb. I take that.

I also have a little knife that the staff do not know about. I think it is called a paring knife. It was on a tray they brought my lunch on one day, hidden by the underside of the main plate. It has a sharp little blade and a nick out of the dense black plastic which forms the handle. There was some slimy vegetable matter adhering to it when I found it, as though it had not long been used. It must have been misplaced by the kitchen staff, ending up on what happened to become my tray.

My first instinct was to report it, summon a member of staff immediately or just leave it lying obviously on the tray to be picked up and returned to the kitchen or thrown out (that nick on the handle might harbour germs). I don't really know why I picked it up, cleaned it on my paper napkin and hid it on the little ledge at the back of my bedside cabinet. It just felt right. I am not superstitious, but the appearance of the knife felt like a little present from fate, from the universe, and one that it would be impolite somehow to turn down.

I take that with me too.

My room is not locked. I let myself out and close the door again quietly, looking down the dimly lit corridor to the day room and the nurses' station. There is a small pool of light there and the faint sound of a radio, playing jingly music. How much more daunting the journey ahead seemed now compared to exactly the same one taken twice in daylight a few hours earlier.

I walk to the stairs, the soles of my slippers making only the quietest of slapping noises. I open and close the door carefully. The stairwell is better lit than the corridor and smells of cleaning fluids.

315

I descend to the ground floor and enter the lower corridor just as silently as I left the one above. Another dim expanse. I approach the two half-glazed doors and the darkness beyond them.

I shut the door behind me. The ward looks just as it did the night before. I approach the fat man lying in the bed nearest the door, the one my trolley had been parked next to. He looks just as he had last night, I think. I walk down past the other beds. They are just ordinary people, all men, a mixture of body shapes and skin colours. All sleeping peacefully.

Something nags at me. Something about the first man I looked at, the fat man near the doors. Perhaps it will become obvious when I look at him again, on my way back out. Near the far end of the ward, I notice that one of the sleeping men has something on his neck. I have to use the torch, shielding it so that it does not shine in his eyes. There is dried blood near his Adam's apple. Just a little, though, nothing sinister. A shaving nick, I suppose.

Ah. That's it. I pad back up to the fat man. He has been shaved. He had a week's worth of beard last night, but now he is clean-shaven. I look back down the ward. They are all clean-shaven. You see men with beards here, and moustaches; there seems to be no particular rule regarding facial hair. Out of over twenty men you'd think at least one or two would have beards. I study the fat man's slack, smooth face. He has not shaved – or been shaved – very well. There are little tufts of hair here and there, and he has been nicked with the razor too. On impulse I put my hand on his shoulder and shake him gently.

"Excuse me?" I say quietly in the local language. "Hello?"

I shake him again, a little more vigorously this time. He makes a sort of grumbling noise and his eyes flicker. I shake him again. His eyes open fully and he gazes slowly up at me, his expression only a little less vacant. There does not look to be much intelligence in those eyes. "Hello?" I say. "How are you?" I ask, for want of anything better. He looks up at me, seemingly uncomprehending. He blinks a few times. I snap my fingers in front of his eyes. "Hello?" No reaction.

I take out my torch and shine it into his eyes. I have seen the medics do this, I'm sure. He squints and tries to move his head away. His pupils contract very slowly. This means something, though I'm not entirely sure what. I stop squeezing the torch's handle. It wheezes to silence and the beam fades to darkness. Within seconds the man is snoring again.

I choose another man at random halfway down the ward on the far side and get the same responses. I have just switched the torch off again and he has just fallen back asleep when I hear footsteps in the corridor. I duck down as a figure approaches the doors, then I crouch out of sight as one of the doors starts to open. I crawl underneath the bed, banging my head on a metal strut, and have to make an effort not to cry out. I can hear the person walking down the ward, and I see a soft light flicking on and off. A pair of legs comes into view: white shoes and a skirt. The nurse passes by the bed I am crouched beneath without pausing. I lower my head so that I can watch her. She goes to the far end of the ward, stopping at a couple of beds, flicking her small torch on and off each time. She turns and walks back down the ward, stops at the door for some moments and then leaves, letting one of the doors swing shut against the other without closing it especially quietly.

I wait a few minutes. My heart calms. In fact I become so relaxed I think I might even drift off to sleep for a few moments, but I'm not sure. Then I let myself out. I negotiate the lower corridor and stairwell without being seen but the light is on in my room when I return. The duty nurse for our floor is in my room, frowning as he looks at my notes on the clipboard. "Toilet," I tell him. He looks unconvinced but helps me back into bed and tucks me in.

As I close my eyes I picture the ward downstairs again, and I realise that one of the things that felt wrong, one of the things disturbing me about it, even though I could not pin it down at the time, was the sameness of it all. The bedside cabinets all looked the same. There were no Get Well Soon cards, no flowers, no baskets of fruit or other items that would personalise the allotment of space each patient is allowed. I can remember seeing a water jug and a small plastic cup on each cabinet, but that was all. I can't recall seeing any chairs by the sides of the beds either. No chairs anywhere in the ward that I could remember.

Husks. I keep coming back to this strangely significant word. Whenever I think about the silent ward and those deeply drugged or in some other way near-comatose men, I think of it. Husks. They are husks. I am not sure why this means so much to me, but it would appear that it does.

Husks . . .

Madame d'Ortolan

"But, madame, is it really such a terrible thing?"

Madame d'Ortolan looked at Professore Loscelles as though he was quite mad. The two of them were squeezed into a dusty study carrel high in a spire of one of the less fashionable UPT buildings, an outskirt adjunctery within sight of the Dome of the Mists but sufficiently distant and obscure for their conversation to stand no chance of being recorded. "Someone *transitioning* without *septus*?" she asked, emphatically. "*Not* a terrible thing?"

"Indeed," Loscelles said, waving his chubby-fingered hands about. "Ought we not, madame, rather, indeed, to celebrate the fact one of our number has, or may have, discovered how to transition without the use of the drug? Is this not a great breakthrough? A veritable advance, indeed?"

Madame d'Ortolan – immaculately dressed in a cream twin-set, an unlined notebook to the olive graph-paper of Professore Loscelles's bucolic three-piece – gave every appearance of thinking fairly seriously about trying to cram the Professore through the unfeasibly narrow window of the tiny study space and out to the sixty-metre drop below. "Loscelles," she said, with an icy clarity, "have you gone completely insane?" (Professore Loscelles flexed his eyebrows, perhaps to signal that, as far as he was aware, he had not.) "If people,"

Madame d'Ortolan said slowly, as though to a young child, "are able to transition without the drug . . . how are we to control them?"

"Well—" the Professore began.

"First of all," Madame d'Ortolan said briskly, "this has not turned up in one of our extremely expensive but – now, apparently – rather irrelevant laboratories, or within the context of a carefully regulated field trial, or constrained by any sort of controlled environment; this has come upon us on the hoof, in the midst of a profound crisis in the Council, *and* in the guise of a previously loyal but now suddenly renegade assassin who, I am nervously informed by those trying and mostly failing to track him, may be continuing to develop other heretofore undreamt-of powers and worryingly unique abilities in addition to this one. As though—"

"Really? But that's extraordinary!" the Professore exclaimed, seemingly quite excited by such a development.

The lady's brows knitted. "Well, *fascinating*!" she shouted, and slammed her palm on the carrel's small desk, raising dust. The Professore jumped. Madame d'Ortolan collected herself. "I'm sure," she continued, breathing hard, "you'll be glad to know that the relevant scientists, experts and Facultarians all share both your enthusiasm and your inability to appreciate what a catastrophe this represents for us." She put her hands on either side of the Professore's ample cheeks and brought them towards each other so as to compress his smooth, perfumed flesh, making it look as though his squashed mouth and ruddily bulbous nose had been jammed between two glisteningly plump pink cushions.

"Loscelles, think! Defeating an individual or grouping of people is easy; one simply brings greater numbers to bear. If they have clubs, and so do we, then we simply ensure that our clubs are always bigger and more numerous than theirs. The same with guns, or symbols, or bombs, or any other weapons or abilities. But if this man – who is now patently not one of us, whose hand, rather, is most forcibly turned against us – can do something that none of our own people can do, how do we combat *that*?"

319

The unyielding firmness of her grip on his face and the concomitant unlikelihood of him being able to form a comprehensible reply led the Professore to believe that this was in the nature of a rhetorical question. She shook his face gently back and forwards in her hands. "We could be in terrible, terrible trouble, thanks just to the threat of this one individual." She jiggled his face in her hands. "And, then – worse, for this can get much worse – what if anybody can do this, just with some training? What if any idiot, any zealot, any enthusiast, any revolutionary, dissident or revisionist can just decide they want to flit into another person's body, displacing their mind? Without planning? Without the necessary safeguards and respect for just cause and proven importance? Without the guidance and experience of the Concern? Where does that leave us *then*? Hmm? I'll tell you: powerless to control what is arguably the single most potent ability an individual can possess in this or any other world. Can we allow that? Can we countenance that? Can we indulge that?" She spread her hands slowly, letting go of Loscelles's cheeks. The Professore's features rearranged themselves into their accustomed alignments. He looked surprised and a little shocked to have been handled so.

Madame d'Ortolan was shaking her head slowly, her expression sorrowful and grave. Professore Loscelles found his own head shaking in time with hers, as though in sympathy.

"Indeed," the lady told him, "we cannot."

"It might, I suppose, lead to anarchy," the Professore said profoundly, frowning somewhere towards the floor.

"My dear Professore," Madame d'Ortolan said, sighing, "we might greet anarchy with an open door, garland its brows, hand it all the keys and skip away whistling with nary a care in our heads, compared to what this might lead to, trust me."

Loscelles sighed. "What do you think we might do, then?"

"Use all our weapons," she told him bluntly. "He wields a new kind of club; well, we have some unusual clubs of our own." The lady glanced to the window. "I can think of one in particular."

She watched clouds drift past in a silver-grey sky before turning back to the Professore's frown. "We have been too cautious, I believe," she told him. "It may even be to the good that something's forced our hand at last. Left to ourselves we might have hesitated for ever." She smiled suddenly at him. "Gloves off, claws out."

The Professore's frown deepened. "This will be one of your special projects, I take it?"

"Indeed." Madame d'Ortolan's smile went wide. She put one hand out to his face again – he flinched, almost imperceptibly, but she only smoothed and patted his right cheek, affectionate as though he were a treasured cat. "And I know you will support me in this, won't you?"

"Would it prevent you if I did not?"

"It would prevent my adoring respect for you continuing, Professore," she said, with a tinkling laugh in her voice that found no echo in her expression.

Loscelles looked her in the eyes. "Well then, ma'am," he said softly, "I could not allow that. It might serve to put me with Obliq, and Plyte, and Krijk, and the rest. There have been . . . narrow squeaks reported; abnormal events."

Madame d'Ortolan nodded, her expression a picture of concern. "*Haven't* there?" She tutted. "We should all be very careful."

Loscelles smiled wanly. "I believe I am being."

She smiled radiantly at him. "Why, I believe you are too!"

The Transitionary

"What is it that we do? What are we for and what are we against? What are we for?"

"This again? I have a feeling that if I say what anybody else in the Concern would expect me to say, you're going to tell me I'm wrong."

"Give it a go."

"We help societies across the many worlds, aiding and advancing positive, progressive forces and confounding and disabling negative, regressive ones."

"To what end?"

He shrugged. "General philanthropy. It's nice to be nice."

They sat in a hot tub looking out across a polished granite floor towards a starlit sea of cloud. She scooped a handful of the warm water and bubbles and let it fall over her left shoulder and upper breast, then repeated the action for her right side. Tem watched the bubbles slide. Mrs Mulverhill, even here, wore a tiny white hat like piled snow, and a spotted white veil. She said, "How do we define the different forces?"

"The bad guys tend to enjoy killing people, preferably in large numbers. The good guys – and girls – don't; they get a buzz when infant mortality rates go down and life expectancy goes up. The bad guys like to tell people what to do, the good guys are happy to encourage people to make up their own minds. The bad guys like to keep the riches and the power to themselves and their cronies, the good guys want the money and power spread evenly, subject to the making-up-your-own-minds thing."

In this world, there had once been an Emperor of the World. He had caused this palace to be built, levelling the top of the mountain that was variously called Sagarmatha, Chomolungma, Peak XV or Mount Everest (or Victoria or Alexander or Ghandi or Mao, or many, many other names). The palace was vast, enclosed by great glass domes which were pressurised and warmed to mimic the conditions of a tropical island. Now, though, after a catastrophe caused by a gamma-ray burster happening relatively nearby by cosmic standards, the world was devoid of humans or almost any other living thing, and was in the slow, eons-long process of changing profoundly as all the processes associated with life, including carbon capture and even most of its plate tectonics, started to shut down.

The Concern had first discovered the world a few years after the catastrophe and had repaired and restored the palace. It had become a place where privileged officers of the Concern could holiday.

Mrs Mulverhill, who now seemed to be able to go anywhere and do anything as long as she stayed away from the Concern proper, had found a version – indeed, a whole unshuffled deck of versions – where this had been done but nobody had yet come to visit. For now at least it was her private world. She had brought him here. This time, she had only needed to hold his hand.

"What is the point," she asked him, "of trying to do any good in the many worlds when there will always be an infinite number of realities where the horrors unfold unstopped?"

"Because one ought to do what one can. Good is good. Specific people and societies benefit. That not all people and societies benefit is beside the point. That a finite number of lives and worlds are better as a result of the actions of the Concern is all the justification that is required, and refusing to do a finite amount of good because you cannot do an infinite amount of good is a morally perverse position. If you feel sorry for a beggar you still give them money even though doing so does nothing for the plight of all other beggars." He let himself slide under the steaming water and the islands of bubbles, resurfacing and wiping water from his face. "How am I doing? I'm paraphrasing here, but it's sounding pretty good to me. I should probably write a paper or something."

"Extremely well. You're a credit to your teachers."

"I thought so." He pushed his fingers through his hair like a rough comb. "So. Tell me where I'm wrong and what the Concern is really up to."

She nodded once. There were times when he thought she lacked any sense of humour, irony or sarcasm. "I think now that the Concern," she said, "exists for a much more specific purpose than simply acting as a multiversal niceness-enforcement agency. It does do some good, but it's incidental, a cover for its true purpose."

"Which is what?"

"That is what I hope you will agree to help me find out."

"So you still don't know?"

"Correct."

"But you suspect they're up to something."

"I know they are."

"How do you know?"

"I feel it."

"You feel it."

"Indeed. In fact I feel certain of it."

"You know, if you're going to convince anybody else about this, including me, you're going to have to do better than just telling them you're certain. It's a little vague."

"I know. But consider this."

Of course, she had a slyly refined sense of humour and appreciated ironies that entirely passed him by. Sarcasm was generally beneath her, but even so.

"I am," he told her, "sitting comfortably."

She put one hand up to the side of her head, so that one rosy nipple surfaced briefly from the white bubbles. She took the little white hat and the veil off, laid them on the black granite at the side of the tub. Slitlike pupils in amber irises narrowed fractionally as they regarded him.

"We have access to an infinite number of worlds," she said, "and have visited some very strange ones. We suspect there are some so strange that we are unable to access them just because of that strangeness: they are unenvisageable, and because we cannot imagine going to them, we cannot go to them. But think how relatively limited is the type of world we do visit. For one thing, it is always and only Earth, as we understand it. Never the next planet further in towards or further out from the sun: Venus or Mars or their equivalents. This Earth is usually about four and a half billion years old in a universe just under fourteen billion years old. Usually, even if it supports no intelligent life, it supports some life. Almost without variance, it exists as part of a solar system in a galaxy composed of hundreds of millions of other solar systems, in a universe composed of hundreds of millions of other galaxies."

As she spoke, she flexed one leg and reached out with it to find his groin with her foot. Her toes brushed against his balls, his cock, stroking them, wafting like the water.

"Wait," he said, opening his legs a little to allow her more room, "this isn't the 'Where Is Everybody?' question, is it?"

"Yes."

"That's easy. There is no everybody. There is only us. There are no aliens. Not a single one of the many worlds shows any sign of alien contact, past or present. Their lack, throughout the multiverse, proves the point. We are alone in the universe." Her toes were gently brushing first one side of his penis, then the other, bringing him erect.

"In all the universes?" she asked, smiling.

"In every single one."

"Then infinity seems to be failing somehow, wouldn't you agree?"

"Failing?"

"It hasn't produced any aliens. It has produced only us. A single intelligent species in all the wide universe does not smack of infinity." She supported herself by stretching her arms out to either side of the tub and reached out now with both feet, finding his erection with two sets of toes and stroking it gently up and down.

He cleared his throat. "What *does* it smack of then?"

"Well, it could simply be due to what the transitioneering theorists call the problem of unenvisionability, as mentioned: we cannot imagine a world that includes aliens – or perhaps, deep down, we don't want to." Mrs Mulverhill raised one hand and blew some bubbles from it to inspect her fingernails before looking at him and saying, "Or it might smack of deliberate quarantine, systematic enclosure, some vast cover-up . . ."

"Why, Mrs Mulverhill, you're a conspiracy theorist!"

"Yes," she agreed, smiling. "But not by nature. I've been forced into it by the conspiracy I'm investigating." She hesitated, uncharacteristically. "I've found some examples. Ones you'll know about. Want to hear?"

"Fire away." He nodded down to where her glistening feet, bobbing rhythmically through the surface of the swirling, bubbling water, were caressing his cock, parenthetical. "Feel free to not stop doing that, though."

She smiled. "The examples are from the more extreme end of the exoticism spectrum," she told him, "but still."

"I've always liked extremities."

"I'm sure. Max Fitching, the singer?"

"I remember."

"The green terrorist explanation was a lie. He was going to give his money to SETI research."

"Uh-huh."

"Marit Shauoon?"

"I still wince."

"He was going to use his network of communication satellites to do a SETI in reverse, deliberately broadcasting signals to the stars. In his will he'd have funded a trio of orbiting telescopes dedicated to finding Earth-like planets and looking for signs of intelligent life on them. You killed him days before he was going to alter his will with just that provision in mind. Glimpsing how it's all heading?"

"You missed out Serge Anstruther."

"Yerge Aushauser. No, he really was a shit. He wasn't really a genocidal racist as such but whenever he's not stopped he ends up causing such havoc he might as well have been. Wanted to buy up a state in the US midwest and build an impregnable Nirvana for the super-rich; Xanadu, Shangri-La. Fantasy made real. A Libertarian." From his expression she must have thought he wasn't entirely familiar with the term. She sighed. "Libertarianism. A simple-minded right-wing ideology ideally suited to those unable or unwilling to see past their own sociopathic self-regard."

"You've obviously thought about it."

"And dismissed it. But expect to hear a lot more about it as Madame d'O consolidates her power-base – it's a natural fit for people just like you, Tem."

"I'm already intrigued."

"Well, you would be."

326

"How do you know all this?"

She waggled her toes over his penis as though it was a flute and her feet were intent on playing it. "I seduce forecasters. I've even turned a few. I have my own now."

"Uh-huh."

"The Concern use you, and others, to do this sort of thing more and more these days, Tem. You still get to kill the genuine bad guys now and again, but that's become little more than cover now, not the main focus of their activities. They've even started going after people who're just thinking about what humanity's true place in the cosmos might be. There's a guy called variously Miguel Esteban/Mike Esteros/Michel Sanrois/Mickey Sants who keeps cropping up across one batch of worlds. All the poor fucker wants to do is make a film about finding aliens but they've started kidnapping him too now. That's one of the few examples we know about. I'm betting there are hundreds of others."

"This is all back to Madame d'O, isn't it?" he said, gripping the rim of the tub and flexing his shoulders to ease his hips forward, closer to her, so that her legs spread a little more, glistening knees appearing out of the surface of the gently bubbling water on either side while her soles and toes still grasped his cock.

"Madame d'Ortolan continues to believe in her imbecilic theories and pursue her sadistic research," Mrs Mulverhill agreed graciously.

"It just always seems more personal," he said, "this thing between her and you."

"I've no particular desire to personalise any of this, Tem, it's just that when you follow the relevant trails she's always what's waiting at the end."

"No doubt." He reached forward, took her ankles in his hands. "And now I think you should come over here."

She nodded. "I think I should, too."

The dawn began to break across the teeth of the eastward mountains, a yellow-pink stain slowly spreading. They stood, bundled in pillowed layers of high-altitude, four-season clothing, on a high circular balcony situated on the summit of the highest dome of the great empty palace. They were in the open air, beyond a small airlock, sucking oxygen from transparent masks over their noses, leaving their mouths free.

Small oxygen tanks in their outer jackets kept them supplied with the life-giving gas and a back-up system of valves dotted round the balcony stood ready to replace those if something went wrong. Even so, one could not simply step from the scented sea-level warmth of the palace into the open air of nine and a half kilometres above the ocean; the pressure difference was so great that a period of adjustment was required in the airlock to prevent discomfort. Before dawn, when the air was most likely to be still, was the best time to be here. Nevertheless, a strong, thin wind was blowing from the north. A movable glass screen linked to a man-high tail of a blade like a giant weathervane had positioned itself to deflect the worst of the blast over the balcony. Glowing figures on a small screen set into the parapet indicated that the temperature was forty below. The air, felt on the lips and the few square centimetres of exposed skin around the eyes, seemed powder-dry, sucking up moisture as much as warmth.

She said, "People will generally make whatever compromises with the world they think necessary still to convince themselves that they are the most important thing in it. The trouble with what we're able to do – specifically the trouble with unfettered access to septus and through it to the many worlds – is that it abets and encourages this delusion to the point of naked solipsism." Her voice, carried over the steady roar of wind, sounded calm and strong, unaffected by the thin air.

"All the same," he said, "it's still an illusion. The world exists without us, whether we like it or not."

She smiled. "A hard-line solipsist would dismiss your words as mere wind," she said. "The point is that to a true solipsist there is no distinction between objective and subjective truth. Subjectivity is all that matters because it is effectively all that exists. And to be a member of the Central Council of the Transitionary Office is to exist in a state that positively encourages such a state of mind. It is not healthy, not for the Office, l'Expédience, or for anything or anybody."

"I'd have thought it was very healthy indeed for those on the Council itself."

"Only in the trivial sense that now they need never die."

"I bet it doesn't seem trivial to them."

"Well, quite." Mrs Mulverhill sat back against the balustrade, its curved top fitting into the small of her back within the puffy layers of insulation. Her outer wear was white. The slowly increasing light to the east washed it with a chilly pinkness. "But one has to ask what this has done to their outlook."

"I cannot wait for you to tell me," he told her.

She smiled. "Unless we have been lied to even more comprehensively than even I suspect, the Concern has existed for a thousand years. In that time, certainly for the first eight centuries, it spent its time investigating the many worlds, researching the properties of septus and the abilities it confers upon people trained to take it, and theorising regarding the metaphysical laws governing the many worlds and the composition of whatever context they might be said to exist within. Until about two hundred years ago, interventions were rare, much argued and agonised over, heavily monitored and subject to extensive subsequent analysis."

"So what happened two hundred years ago?"

"Madame d'Ortolan happened," Mrs Mulverhill said, with a sour smile. "She discovered how a transitioner could take somebody else with them between the realities and that opened up a whole new set of opportunities for l'Expédience; the numbers of worlds investigated soared. Then when she was on the Central Council she pushed for a far more aggressive policy of interference and a still wider spread of influence. She also proposed that the practice of allowing Central Council members to shift down to a younger body when their own body approached advanced old age become the default for all rather than the extraordinary privilege for the most-honoured few, and that the limit of this being allowed to happen only once be lifted."

"I thought that was still just a proposal." It was a rumour throughout the Concern, indeed across Calbefraques, that this might be the case, but there had been no official pronouncement.

"In theory it is," Mrs Mulverhill conceded. She turned and looked out at the nearby peaks starting to shine like vast pink teeth all around them. "But it's being done piecemeal. As each of the other Council members approaches the age when they might start to think that such a proposal does make sense after all – when they have often spent their careers until then decrying and opposing it – the good Madame suggests they might like to reconsider. To my knowledge only two of the Council have resisted her so far, and they might still be persuaded." She looked at him and smiled. "The steps to the grave grow steeper the closer you approach. A degree of urgency can grip people. She might have those two Council members too, in time. And besides, with them gone and with effective control over the Central Council, she can make sure the replacements are more amenable. She has all the time she wants, after all. She can play the longest of games."

"So now the Central Council just goes on for ever?"

"As an entity, it always expected to." She shrugged. "Well, bureaucracies always do, but this one really might, of course. The difference is that in theory the individuals of the Council can now go on for ever. The point is not that the Central Council will never cease to be, the point is that the Central Council will never cease to be exactly the same. It will never change."

"They'll still get older. Their minds will."

"Yes, and it will be an interesting rolling experiment in how much information a healthy and relatively young mind can contain without having to overwrite some of it when it's inhabited by a relatively ancient one, and of course the Council members are quite convinced that they will only get wiser and wiser the older they get in lived years, and that this can only be a good thing. But I think any rational outsider would and should be appalled at the prospect. The old and powerful never want to let go. They always think they're both profoundly indispensable and uniquely right. They are always wrong. Part of the function of ageing and dying is to let the next generation have its say, its time in the sun, to sweep away the mistakes of the previous age while, if they're lucky, retaining the advances made and the benefits accrued." The sunlight was stronger now, picking out her strange dark eyes with their slit pupils. They narrowed, glittering as though frosted.

"It is an insane conceit. Power always drives to perpetuate itself, but this is a phenomenal extra distillation of idiocy. Only people already riddled with the internalised special pleading and self-importance that too much power brings could even start to imagine that this might be in any way sustainable."

He rested one forearm on the parapet, side on, gazing at her. Even bundled so, made comically rotund by the warm clothes, she somehow contrived to appear slim, slight and full of a specifically sensual energy. He had a sudden flashback to the sight and feel and smell of the body contained within all those insulating layers. They had been here for most of a day and had spent a lot of that time fucking. His muscles felt tired and heavy and his legs still felt shaky from their latest bout half an hour earlier, standing, her wrapped around him in the airlock while they waited for the pressures to equalise.

Thinking about her, he half expected some sort of stirring from his cock, but nothing happened. It certainly wasn't the cold so he guessed that this time he really was all done. He had wondered when she had first suggested they come out here onto the balcony if it was some sort of final spectacular site for sex. A risky one, he thought. A chap could risk frostbite. But they had fucked in the airlock instead. He hoped she wasn't expecting more, not for a while – he felt a little sore and absolutely drained.

"You do know so much about it all," he said.

"Thank you. In particular I think I know Madame d'Ortolan," she told him. "I think I know how her mind works."

"I can certainly vouch for how some of her other organs function."

"She has self-belief raised almost to solipsistic levels. It's her weakness. That and a kind of fanaticism for neatness."

"Neatness? Neatness will bring her down?"

"It could be part of it. Having effective control of the Central Council will not be quite enough for her, I think. Even though as a whole it will entirely do her bidding it will annoy her that there are still people on it who disagree with her, just on principle. She will want *everybody* on it to agree with her. It's just neater. And that self-belief, it makes her think that she can do no wrong just because she is who she is. For all her clear-headed cunning and guile and utterly ruthless rationality, there is a kernel of something like superstition in her that tells her any given stratagem, no matter how risky, will work in the end simply because she is destined to triumph; that's just the way the world works, the way all worlds work. And that's how we bring her down, Tem."

"Do we?"

"We keep annoying her, keep opposing her, keep nudging her to riskier and riskier tactics, until she overreaches herself and falls."

"Or keeps winning."

She shook her head. "The longer you keep gambling everything the more certain you are to lose it."

"So don't gamble everything."

"Rational. But if you're absolutely convinced that it is your destiny to triumph, that your victory is inevitable, and gambling everything gets you there quicker than taking it in small steps, why shuffle to glory when you can get there in a few boldly heroic leaps?"

"What if you're wrong?"

She smiled ruefully. "Then we're fucked." She took a deep breath and stared out across the pillowed skyscape of clouds towards the dawn. "But I'm not wrong."

"Something deep inside tells you that, does it?"

She glanced sharply at him, then gave a small laugh. "Yes, quite. Point taken. But we all need to have the courage of our convictions, Tem, if we're not to be just the playthings of the powerful; hordes of falling, clicking balls batted this way and that at their whim in some vast game. And you have yet to say whether you'll help or not. You need to choose which side you're on."

"Mrs M, I'm still not entirely sure what the sides are."

She looked down towards the layer of cloud two kilometres below. "You know," she said, "people at the top of any organisation like to think that they are, metaphorically, on the summit of a mountain in perfect visibility. They're wrong, of course; in fact there's mist all the way down. Organisationally, you're lucky if you can see clearly into even just the next level down. After that it's pure murk, as a rule."

She left a pause, so he said, "Really?"

"Of course, with the Concern it gets even more difficult to see what's going on." She turned to look at him. "There are levels most of us don't even know exist. I was on the level just beneath the Central Council. If I'd kept my nose clean I'd probably be there now; certainly in a decade or so, assuming that one of the hold-outs sticks to their guns and dies rather than keeps going on for ever. You're a level down for that, Tem, fast-tracked for success but, I'd guess –" her eyes narrowed again and her head tipped "– not knowing it. Would that be right?"

"I thought you had to do a lot of committee work and politicking back on Calbefraques. I enjoy working in the field too much. Also, it has been noticed amongst the lower orders that the turnover in the Central Council has slowed down a lot over the last fifty years or so."

"All the same, you're one of the potential chosen ones."

"I'm flattered. Is that why you're trying to recruit me?"

"Not directly. They must see something in you. I do too, though perhaps not exactly the same things. I see a potential in you that

I don't think they know is there. And I think you might choose the right side."

"So do they, I suppose. But this brings us back to the issue of sides. You were about to explain just what they were, I think. I did ask you to."

She moved closer to him, placed one snow-soft white mitten on his. "The Central Council has become obsessed with power before and beyond anything else. The means has become the end. If they are not opposed they will turn l'Expédience into something that exists only for its own aggrandisement and the pursuance of whatever secret purposes the individuals on it choose to dream up. I think that is unarguable. Plus I believe that – at the behest of Madame d'Ortolan – there is something else, some already hidden agenda they're working to – the uniqueness of human intelligent life and the singular nature of Calbefraques itself may well point to the nature of that secret – but I never got close enough to the centre of power to find out."

"What, and I am supposed to?"

"No. It'll take too long for you to be elevated to the Council, if you ever are. It'll be too late by then."

"Too late?"

"Too late because soon Madame d'Ortolan will have the Council exactly as she wants it; full of people who think just as she does and who will do everything she wants them to do, and who will never die, because they will keep repotting themselves into younger bodies as their older ones approach senescence."

"So what do you propose, Mrs Mulverhill?"

Her smile looked defensive. "Ultimately, that the Central Council either ceases to exist or is severely reined in and radically reconstituted. Certainly that it is subject to some sort of democratic oversight. They can even keep their serial immortality, as long as they resign in perpetuity from the Council itself. Long life for long service. An incentive to serve but not to entrench."

"All the same, you're asking a lot of them."

"I know. I don't see them giving up what they have at present without a fight."

"And is the other side just you and your bandit gang?"

"Oh, there are plenty of people who feel the same way, including a few people on the Central Council itself."

"Like who?"

That smile again. A little wary, this time. "First tell me if you've betrayed me, Tem," she said softly. She lowered her head a fraction as she gazed up at him.

"Betrayed?" he said.

"We've talked before. I'm an outlaw. If you were playing by the book you ought to have reported our meetings."

"I did," he said. "Is that betrayal?"

"Not by itself. What else, though? What did they suggest you do?"

"Keep meeting you, keep talking to you."

"Which you have done."

"Which I have done."

"And reporting back."

"Which I have also done."

"Fully?"

"Not quite fully."

"And have you agreed to help catch me?"

"No."

"But have you refused ever to help catch me?"

"No. They did ask. I told them that of course I'd do what was right."

She smiled. "And do you yet know what is right?"

He took a long deep breath of the pure gas and the stunningly cold air. "I think I would find it very hard to help them catch you."

She looked pleased and amused at once. "Is that gallantry, Tem?"

"Perhaps. I'm not entirely sure myself."

"Sexual sentimentality, is what Madame d'Ortolan would call it."

"Would she now?"

"She is a very unsentimental woman. Well, apart from her cats,

335

maybe." Mrs Mulverhill was silent for a moment, then said, "Do you think they're using you to try and catch me even without your consent?"

"I'm sure they are. I've always assumed that when we meet you've taken care of that."

"I do what I can." She shrugged. "I think I'm still ahead of them."

"You think they're in hot pursuit?"

She nodded. "Theodora keeps at least two tracking teams on the lookout for me at all times. And she has her special projects, her wild cards, randomisers whom she's tormented and bent until they form specialist tools for seeking out people like me. She thinks they might be able to work some magic and both find me and then disable me when I'm traced. I suppose I ought to feel flattered to be the object of such obsessive attention."

She looked away at the startlingly bright point of the rising sun. The surrounding peaks shone a bright yellow-white now, the level of illumination dropping down their snow and rock flanks as the sun continued to rise, casting jagged shadows across the steeply sloped snowfields and glacier heads. Just in that moment he thought she looked small and vulnerable and hunted, even afraid. The urge to reach out and take her in his arms, to shelter and protect and reassure her was very strong, and surprising. He wondered for a moment how much of this was deliberate, if he was being manipulated, and in that hesitation the moment passed and she turned back to him, smiling, raising her face. "You need to take care, Tem," she told him. "You can only postpone making up your mind for so long. Perhaps no further, after this. You can seem to cooperate with them and listen to me for now, but sooner or later they'll insist you do something that settles it. You'll need to decide."

"I thought you were trying to get me to decide."

"I am. But I'm not threatening you."

"They're not threatening me."

"Not yet. They will. Unless you take the hints that will be put before you, if they haven't been already, and obviate the need for explicit threats." She looked down towards the ruffled blanket of cloud far below, still in shadow. "The Central Council prefers implied threats, the threat of threats. It's more effective, leaving so much to the individual imagination."

"You're not going to tell me who the people on the Central Council are, are you? The ones who might think the way you do."

"Of course not. You could probably make a fairly accurate guess, anyway. And it's not as though I have signed contracts from them, swearing to rebel when the time comes. I haven't even talked to all of them, I'm just making assumptions. But feel free to tell the Questionary Office that you asked the question."

"I shall."

She was silent again for a while. The wind roared on, picking up in strength while the weathervane apparatus creaked and moaned and swung the glass barricade round to face the onrushing torrent of air. "You should take all this more seriously, Tem," she said, her tone gently chiding, close to hurt. "These people are slowly making monsters of themselves. Madame d'O is already full-fledged. Under her, if they haven't already, they'll come to countenance anything to avoid what she sees as contamination. Anything. Encouraging world wars, genocide, global warming; anything at all to disrupt the slow progress towards the unknown."

"Don't let my defensive flippancy deceive you," he told her, pulling her to him, enfolding her. He hesitated.

"Deep down you still don't take it seriously either?" she suggested, looking up at him with with a small, wan smile.

"There's that flippancy again." He squeezed her. "I take it as seriously as I've ever taken anything, including my own survival."

She looked unimpressed. "I was hoping for better."

"Leave it with me. I'll see what I can do."

She turned in his arms, staring out over the nearly lifeless waste of rock, ice and snow towards the faltering dawn.

"We may not be able to meet like this again," she said quietly. "I'm sorry."

"Then I'm glad," he said, "that we were able to put so much effort into this meeting." She looked back to him with an expression on her face that he was unable to read, and he felt a real gut-stirring emotion, something between a kind of recidivist lust and an entirely unexpected regret at the potential loss of somebody who only now, belatedly, he realised was and had always been a soulmate. He would never now, never again, call it love.

She pushed herself away from him a little, then reached out and patted his gloved, mittened hand again, layers upon layers separating them. "I've enjoyed everything about the times we've spent together," she told him. "Would that there had been more."

He gave it a while, then said, "So what happens next?"

"Immediately, trivially? You go back to Calbefraques and I disappear again."

"If I do need to contact you, if I do decide—"

"I'll leave a note of places, times, people."

"And beyond that?"

"Over time, more to the point, I think Madame d'Ortolan will eventually move against the people on the Central Council who disagree with her. She'll try to isolate them, perhaps even kill them."

"*Kill* them? You're not serious." This was not the sort of behaviour the Central Council was known for. There had been one or two suspicious deaths on the Council centuries before that might have been due to some judicious poisoning, but nothing untoward since. Stolid and boring were the words most people associated with the Council, even after the ascendancy of Madame d'O; not danger, not assassination.

"Oh, I'm as serious as she is," Mrs Mulverhill told him, eyes wide. "Madame d'Ortolan is one of those people – civilised on the surface, brutish underneath – who think themselves realists when they contemplate their own barbarism, and ascribe the same callousness to others. Making the assumption that everybody else is as ruthless as she is helps her live with her own inhumanity, though she would justify it as simple prudence. She knows how *she* would deal with

338

somebody like herself: she'd kill them. So she assumes those who oppose her must be planning the same, or shortly will. Obviously, then, by her demented logic, she needs to kill them before they kill her. She will think through this psychotic escalation without any evidence that her opponents actually do intend her harm and she'll pride herself on her disinterested practicality, probably even persuading herself that she bears those she has marked for death no personal ill will. It's just politics."

Mrs Mulverhill smiled briefly. "She will move against them, Tem; decisively as she would see it, murderously as anyone else would." She put one mittened hand on his arm. "And she may think to use you to do so, as you are still her promising boy. Discover and test your loyalty and commitment by ordering you to make the cull. Though she will undoubtedly have alternative means set up if you decide not to cooperate." Her gaze fastened on him. "If you do decide against her, you will be making yourself an outlaw too, or at best symbolically leaping behind a barricade with others, like myself. And, unless we succeed, the full force of the Central Council and the Concern itself will be turned against you, against us, in time. We have to persuade the waverers, who are probably the majority, that we are right, and we need to survive long enough to do that. If we can resist the Council successfully they will look weak and be seen to lose authority. Then negotiation, compromise might be possible."

"You don't sound very hopeful."

She shrugged. "Oh, I am full of hope," she said, though her voice sounded small and faint.

He went to her and put his arms around her. She pressed gently against him, her head against his chest. Moments later, almost together, a series of beeps announced that their oxygen cylinders each only held enough gas for a few more minutes.

14

Patient 8262

I think I have to leave. I cannot stay here. Or maybe I can. I'm
not sure.

It is comfortable here. All is not perfect; I still worry that
somebody might try to violate me again, and there remains the
disturbing incident with the broad-shouldered lady doctor and her
dolls, when things seemed to slip aside from reality and it felt like
I could only escape through fainting, but, even so, my existence here
is relatively calm and unthreatened. Maybe I should stay.

I am trying to spend less time asleep or snoozing or just with my
eyes closed. I am trying to discover more about where I am: about
this society and the clinic and about myself. This has met with mixed
results so far. However, I feel it is necessary no matter whether I
stay here or leave. If I stay I need to know where it is that I am
staying, so that I am prepared for what may happen. (Suppose I am
only here for as long as some sickness fund or medical insurance
settlement lasts and then get thrown out regardless, for example.)
If I am to leave then I need to know into what sort of world I would
be venturing.

So I have, albeit reluctantly, especially at first, been spending more time in the day room, watching television with the slack-jaws, droolers, mumblers, random shouters and nappy-wearers who inhabit the place. (There are one or two of its denizens who are not irredeemable, but they are very much in the minority.) It is amazing, though, how little one can glean from the sort of broadcasts these people choose to watch. I have tried finding news or current-affairs channels, but this always causes protests, even from the true slack-jaws who you'd have sworn might as well have been sitting watching a turnip rather than a functioning television.

They like cartoons, mostly. They will watch programmes with lots of shouting and movement and colour, but anything that might actually engage the brain's higher functions, beyond the sort of stimulus on a par with a chain of plastic toys stretched across an infant's cot or pram, that they cannot cope with. I have learned a little more of the local language, that's about all. I persist only because the very distracting nature of the programmes sometimes lets my higher functions disengage more easily from the here and now, freeing me to think.

I asked for and was given a radio to use in my room. That was better. I am still struggling to understand more than about a quarter of what is said – less when people talk too fast – but I have worked out that this is a mostly peaceful world and that this is a relatively benign, egalitarian society – my care here will continue indefinitely, paid for by the state – and that I am here because I suffered some sort of breakdown which left me in a catatonic condition for a month. The medical staff think I must still be suffering from a mixture of amnesia and delusion, or that I am just plain putting it on, pretending to be crazy to escape . . . well, whatever it was I felt the need to escape.

I have been back to the ward of sleeping men, in daylight. Nobody tried to stop me. It is an ordinary ward, after all. The men were mostly awake – a few were snoozing, but not all – and there were chairs by the bedsides, and there were flowers and Get Well Soon cards on the bedside cabinets, and there was even a family – what

I took to be a wife, sad and sallow-faced with two small, silent children – visiting one of the patients. The two adults were talking quietly. Some of the other men, sitting up in bed, looked at me as I stood at the doors of the ward, staring in. I met their level, mildly inquisitive gazes, felt foolish, and turned and walked away down the echoing corridor, relieved and disappointed at once.

My name still means nothing to me. Kel. Mr Kel. Mr P. Kel. Mr Pohley Kel. Nothing. It means nothing to me – well, beyond that it feels the wrong way round somehow. Still, it seems that I am stuck with it and I suppose it will do as well as any other.

I was a crane driver, they tell me. I worked in one of those tower cranes they use to build tall buildings and other large structures. This is a job of some skill and responsibility, and one that you'd want someone quite sane and sensible doing, so I probably couldn't just walk back into it. But it occurs to me that it is also a job that somebody who did not very much like interacting with other people might choose, and one that might allow the imagination to roam free and unfettered above the city and the site, so long as the mechanics of the job got done safely.

I lived alone, a loner, both in my home life and up there in the sky, swinging loads around from place to place while the people below scurried like ants and I took instructions from disembodied voices crackling over the radio. No family, no close friends (hence no visitors, save a foreman from the firm while I was still catatonic, apparently – anyway, the whole building team has moved to another city now). I'm told I rented a small flat from the city council which has now been allocated to somebody else. My possessions, such as they may be, are in storage until I claim them.

But I remember nothing of that life.

Rather I was a dangerous, skilled, swashbuckling hero, a remorseful but utterly deadly assassin, a thinking person's hooligan and later (or perhaps just potentially) a mover and shaker, high-flying, fast-tracked, in a vast and burgeoning shadow-organisation spreading secretly under our banal existence like some fabulously

343

bright and intricate mosaic long buried unglimpsed beneath a humble hearth.

I remain convinced that this calm, unambitious, self-satisfied, unspectacular little world is not all there is. There exists a greater reality beyond this dull immediacy and I have been part of it – an important part – and will return to it. I was betrayed, or at least persecuted, and I fell and nearly perished, but I escaped – as of course I would, being who and what I am – and now I am hiding here, waiting, biding my time. So I need to prepare, and work out whether I should do nothing but wait here patiently, or take matters into my own hands and strike out purposefully.

There is much to be done.

Madame d'Ortolan

Between the plane trees and belvederes of Aspherje, on this clear midsummer early morning, the dawn-glittering Dome of the Mists rises splendidly over the University of Practical Talents like a vast gold thinking cap. Below, amongst the statues and the rills of the Philosophy Faculty rooftop park, walks the Lady Bisquitine, escorted.

From the vantage point of a terrace a few metres higher and fifty metres away, Madame d'Ortolan, with Mr Kleist at her side, watches the little party as it meanders closer. From a distance, Bisquitine looks quite normal, just a pretty plump blonde in a rather old-fashioned long white dress, attended by four gentlemen and a lady-in-waiting.

"There are other people we might employ, ma'am," Kleist says.

He has been waiting to say this. He might have said it a dozen times in the last day, but has held his tongue. She has been waiting for him to say it.

"I know," she tells him, still watching the sauntering progress of the little group. Bisquitine does not appear to have noticed her yet. Her escort – handlers and guards – should have noticed them, if they are doing their job, but they show no sign either. Madame d'Ortolan takes two steps back on the pink stones, only just keeping the approaching figure in sight. "How are Gongova and Jildeep?"

Kleist ignores the question because he knows it is rhetorical, a comment rather than a request for information. "There are others besides, before we need to resort to this . . . thing."

"Indeed there are. But it will all take time, no matter what we do, and the next team we send, if we do not use our little blonde friend here, will be seen as just another incremental escalation. He will probably be expecting that. We need to send him somebody who will come as a deeply unpleasant surprise."

"I am in no doubt that her deployment will produce a deeply unpleasant surprise or two."

Madame d'Ortolan still doesn't look at him, still keeps her attention focused on the distant white figure. "Possibly on our own side as well, you mean."

"That was what I wished to imply."

"Message received, Mr Kleist." Madame d'Ortolan squints, tips her head fractionally. "You know, I'm not sure I've seen her in sunlight before," she says, so quietly that Mr Kleist is not certain that she even means him to hear.

He supposes that what she says it true. They have seen the creature in laboratories, strapped to things like dentists' chairs, confined in small rubberised cages or tied to hospital beds, sometimes weeping, sometimes hysterical, more lately in states of humming, unconcerned calm, or babbling nonsense, but always surrounded by muttering technicians wielding clipboards, electrodes and meters, and rarely with a window even in sight, always in artificial light. And always, until now, physically restrained.

It has not always been pleasant to watch, but the girl's powers – evident from birth but beyond control – have been heightened and honed over time. Weaponised, you might say. Personally he thinks a little less time might have been devoted to raising those abilities to their present admittedly formidable heights and a little more to making them easier to predict and control, but Bisquitine, in her present form, is very much Madame d'Ortolan's creation, and such timidity – as she would see it – is not Madame d'Ortolan's way.

"Hmm," Madame d'Ortolan says. "She looks as though she has a touch of the mongrel about her, in this light." She looks at Mr Kleist. "Don't you think?"

Mr Kleist makes the motion of looking. "I couldn't say, ma'am."

Madame d'Ortolan turns to look at the distant group again. She nods, shallowly. "An octoroon, or thereabouts, I'd say."

There is a pause, then a sigh before Mr Kleist says, "Well, in any event, ma'am, if you truly are decided on this course, we should waste no further time."

Madame d'Ortolan flashes him a look, then relents, shoulders falling. "You're right. I'm procrastinating." She nods at the steps leading down from the terrace. "We must seize the day," she observes, patting her blouse frills flat against her jacket lapels. A flower, gelded by Mr Kleist, lies limp upon her jacket breast. "And the nettle."

As Kleist and Madame d'Ortolan approach, it becomes clear that the Lady Bisquitine has been collecting insects, snails and little lumps of soil from the flower beds, and eating some of them. The rest she deposits in a drawstring posy purse hanging from her waist. Her pretty little face, surrounded by a nimbus of bouncily blonde curls and kept clean and minimally made-up by her forever fussing lady-in-waiting, sports brown streaks at the corners of her mouth until the lady-in-waiting – a thin, black-dressed figure who moves like a stalking bird – wets a handkerchief with her mouth and, tutting, cleans the lips of her charge.

Bisquitine stands still, staring at Madame d'Ortolan open-mouthed. Her face looks provisionally blank, as though she is a young child confronted with something new and surprising and is trying to decide whether to put back her head and laugh, or burst out crying. Two of her attendants, robust young men in a special uniform of dark grey and maroon, armed with automatic pistols and electric shock guns, touch their caps to acknowledge the approach of the older and more senior woman. The other two are more slight in comparison, informally dressed, and look bored. Both nod, all the same. The lady-in-waiting curtsies.

"Bisquitine, my dear," Madame d'Ortolan says, stopping a couple of metres away and smiling at her. She never knows quite what to do with her hands when she meets Bisquitine. To touch her, of course, could be dangerous. "How are you? You look well!"

The Lady Bisquitine continues to stare at Madame d'Ortolan. Then she looks absolutely delighted, her already pretty face splits in a guileless smile and in a clear, bell-like, childish voice she sings:

"Ugby Dugby bought a new ball, Ugby Dugby played not at all. Ugby Dugby went for a spin, Ugby Dugby couldn't get in!" She nods proudly, once, for emphasis and then sits down where she stands, the skirts of her white brocade gown pooling around her like spilled milk. With her tongue out of the side of her mouth, she takes a beetle out of her posy bag and starts to pull its wing casings open, letting them click back while the protesting insect buzzes and jerks in her chubby, grubby fingers.

One of the bored, skinny attendants looks at Madame d'Ortolan and sighs. "Sorry, ma'am. Bit worse than usual recently." He shrugs, gazes down at Bisquitine, who has pulled one of the wing casings off entirely and is studying the wing inside, cross-eyed with concentration. The young man smiles uncertainly at Madame d'Ortolan. He appears to be vicariously embarrassed.

"But still," Madame d'Ortolan says, "potent, yes? Proficient. Capable."

The other skinny young man blows out his cheeks and shakes his head. "Oh, be under no illusions, ma'am," he says, "the lady's skills remain undiminished, oh yes." He is squinting in the sunlight, rather as Mr Kleist is doing.

The first young man rolls his eyes. "We've had to stop her flitting half a dozen times since breakfast, ma'am." He shakes his head.

Bisquitine pulls the beetle's other wing casing off and puts it between her teeth, tasting it. She makes a sour face and spits the wing casing out onto the path, then leans over to let some spit

347

dribble from her hanging-open lips. She wipes her mouth with her sleeve, grunting.

Madame d'Ortolan looks measuredly at the lady-in-waiting. "Mrs Siankung, isn't it?"

"Ma'am." She curtsies again.

"We have need of the Lady Bisquitine's services and unique talents."

Mrs Siankung swallows. "Now, ma'am?"

"Now."

"This is . . . more training, evaluation, yes?"

"No, it is profoundly not."

"I see, ma'am."

The lady-in-waiting, Kleist thinks, looks surprised. One might even say startled. And possibly also more than a little afraid.

The beetle is vibrating its wings noisily in a vain attempt to escape. Its large hornlike mouth parts, spasming in frantic pincering movements, connect with one of Bisquitine's fingers and nip. Bisquitine winces, frowns severely at the creature and then pops it whole into her mouth and starts to eat, grimacing only a little. There are crunching noises.

The Transitionary

Something very fucking weird happens as I sit there in the main kitchen of the Palazzo Chirezzia, the spoonful of peas poised in front of my mouth. I get the most transitory glimpse of something like a vast explosion – it looks frozen at first, then I plunge into it or it whirls out to meet me and I can see its surface is a boiling mass – then I'm like some particle in a cloud chamber battered by Brownian motion, trilling down through an infinitude of worlds all riffling past too fast to see properly or count and then wham, I'm here, except I seem to have bounced part-way back out of where I really am, because I swear I can see myself sitting there in the kitchen.

And I can see the whole palace. In three dimensions. It's like the entire building is made of glass: roof tiles, stones, beams and floorboards, carpets, wall coverings, furniture and even the piles that the whole place rests on – ancient warped tree trunks, densely packed, twisted into the mud metres and metres beneath. I'm aware that all the components are there and I can still tell what colour each is and see the patterns on things like the Persian rugs scattered through the building, but at the same time I can see through everything. I can see the immediate surroundings, too: the buildings flanking the palazzo, also facing the Grand Canal, the small canal to one side, the calles on the two other sides, plus I have a vague impression of the rest of the city, but the fabric of the palace itself is patently where all my attention is focused.

Who the fuck is doing this? Am *I* doing this? It looked like I zoomed in from the outside of the whole meta-reality there, pinpointing in to this world, this city, this building right here and now, all in under a second. I've talked to the top brain boys and girls at the Transitionary Theory department in the Speditionary Faculty and what I saw looked like what they imagine in their heads all the time but have great difficulty explaining. But it honestly felt like I was seeing it properly, truly, for real.

I inspect my newly revealed panorama and discover that I am not alone in the palace. There are some people entering from a boat moored at the private jetty and what looks like another team bursting in through the front doors. I can even see the air movements: the draught I felt a moment ago came from the canal-jetty doors. Then that detail disappears. Two teams, six people each. They each have a team member capable of damping down the capacity to transition anywhere near them. I'm already within both volumes of affect. More personnel: there are another four people guarding the ways out of the palace, and two more in a second launch holding station in the Grand Canal just off the palace.

How did—?

I was out for nearly two hours after I performed my odd, inadvertent flit from the room with the chair and the quietly spoken man and his sticky tape. Two hours; I had no idea I had been out so long. I also have no idea how I know this so certainly now, but I do. Anyway, the point is that they've had plenty of time to prepare.

I wonder if my call to Ade, in London, pinpointed me. The thought has barely formed in my mind when I know that it didn't; using the phone from the supposedly deserted palace only confirmed what they already knew.

Both teams are splitting up, four members of each jogging and running through the palace in a clearly predetermined pattern, heading for every part of it. Two people in each team stay together, near where they entered. They're communicating by some form of digital radio, encrypted. The transition-damping fields – in both cases coming from one of the two people in each team who stayed near their point of entry, I can see now – stop them using any techniques exclusive to us. The comms equipment will be local, just below the latest military spec in this world, to reduce the awkward-questions factor if they encounter any local officialdom.

One of the men near the front doors, the one not responsible for the damping effect, is called Jildeep. He is operations commanding officer as well as team leader. The woman standing near the jetty doors with the other blocker is called Gongova. She is Jildeep's deputy and second in command. Oh, and lover. Interesting but probably not relevant.

Somebody from Gongova's team will burst into the kitchen where I am in about eight seconds. She is called Tobbing. Like the rest she has some tracking ability. She will know that I'm the one they're all looking for possibly even before she sees me; she only needs to get to within about four metres of a transitioner to sense them. My, how high-powered this all is. I should feel flattered.

Would you apply such a serious concentration of resources just to grab one off-message transitioner? I suppose you would, if the "you" involved meant you were Madame d'Ortolan, you were trying to dispose of everybody on the Central Council who disagreed with you – probably with the intention of mounting an utterly illegal and completely unprecedented coup – and the first assassin sent to accomplish this dubious mission (I assumed I was the first, anyway) promptly made a start at bumping off the people on the Council whom you regarded as your allies. You could see how that might make her cross.

But now I have this weird new power to add to the bizarre over-real flashbacks I'd been experiencing recently, not to mention the still-lingering suspicion that I'd flitted without the benefit of septus the wonder drug. All somewhat confusing, but highly interesting too.

I wonder, can I use my strange new sense to my advantage? I mean, you'd imagine.

How can this turn out? What can happen next?

The view of the palace splits suddenly into a blurring stack of further palaces, each subtly different.

I can concentrate on any one I wish to inspect. Ah. They're alternative paths, different futures, the most likely quite clear, the less and less likely more and more blurred until they're just snow, pointless. I look at them each in turn. The people in them – the members of the two teams searching the palace – are moving very slowly now, I notice, which is handy. Ms Tobbing is very close to the kitchen door, all the same. I can hear a slow, heavy thud back in what we'll have to call physical reality. That'll be one of her footsteps, that will. I can hear the echoes of the previous one still resounding.

Looking carefully, comparing and searching, I think I can see what to do. It's a little problematic, but I can't spot a humane alternative.

Turning the seat to face the open doorway, I sit back and put my hands up.

Ms Tobbing spins across the doorway, legs spread and slightly bent, gun levelled. Dark blue trouser suit, hair bunned. That's all I have time to confirm before she Tasers me and I end up on the floor, jerking and spasming. It's more painful and distressing than I imagined. I almost wish I'd chosen a different route through those

351

futures, but the others were even bloodier. Not that I'll expect any thanks, of course.

The rest arrive mob-handed seconds after Ms Tobbing stops zapping me and Dr Jildeep himself administers a syringe full of tranquilliser. I dare say they thought of including something supposed to stop me transitioning too, but those drugs can be permanently damaging and they'll want me intact.

Wait. This path leads to me killing most of them. Another set of futures bursts into my mind, one of the areas or volumes I couldn't see into clearly a minute earlier, but which – now that I'm closer to them – have become more distinct. Can I do what this implies I can do? Seriously? I'm slipping away here; I need to decide fast. If I just think in through here—

Ms Tobbing spins across the doorway, legs spread and slightly bent, gun levelled. Dark blue trouser suit, hair bunned. Combined earpiece and microphone. Nice blue blouse. That's all I have time to confirm before she fires the Taser at me. I've used the five seconds and the high-def clarity of my X-ray-specs vision of the palace to pull open a drawer, grab a long boxed roll of aluminium foil and – knowing exactly the trajectory that the Taser's two little barbs are going to take – feel them whack into it, letting the gun's charge go zapping down the wires to discharge harmlessly into the foil. My other hand is wrapped in a kitchen towel taken from the same drawer; I use it to grab the wires connecting the barbs to the gun and yank them hard, pulling the still-in-the-course-of-being-surprised Ms Tobbing towards me before she can think to let go of the Taser.

Well, now we find out if the future-path vision thing is going to work or not. According to what I've just visualised this looks almost easy.

My hand closes round Ms Tobbing's right wrist.

I sneeze suddenly, explosively.

My old self stares at me blankly.

Hmm. One of my more handsome incarnations. Though now with snot hanging from his nose. But not even a "Gesundheit." Really.

I let go of the Taser's trigger and the gun stops firing uselessly into the packet of foil, now fallen to the floor where I – he – was standing a moment ago. I prise his fingers off my wrist. He smiles vaguely, then shakes his head, his expression changes profoundly and he starts talking loudly in what I think is Slovenian (I have English, German, French, Italian, Mandarin). I use the gun to smack him under the jaw, shutting the kitchen door on him as he's still staggering backwards.

"Tobbing," I tell the radio as I turn back down the corridor, letting the expended Taser cartridge fall to the floor and digging a new one out of a pocket to snap onto the gun. "Just dropped an unidentified civilian in the kitchen."

"Civilian? You sure?" Jildeep's voice says. "There isn't supposed to be anybody else here."

"Well, I'm sure."

"You still with him?"

"No, I'm heading—"

"Stay with him! Stay – get back there!"

"Oh, forget it," I mutter.

Sneeze.

No, still no "Gesundheit."

Same as before except this time I don't use the radio, I just start jogging down the corridor. There's some chatter about somebody hearing a Taser go off, but when I'm asked I say I heard nothing. Being a woman is interesting. Moving feels different; broader hips, I suppose, and altered weight distribution. Breasts move very slightly with each pace, but constrained. Sports bra.

Two corners, two corridors and one door later I'm at the entrance to the jetty, cracking the door. I can see Gongova and the blocker – a weedy-looking guy smoking a cigarette with a look of intense concentration. I Taser him and he falls into the waters by the side of the moored launch. Gongova starts, turns, her hand goes for a gun inside her jacket, then she relaxes again and stands there, the gun held loosely in her hand, pointing straight down at the jetty's timbers. When Jildeep gets here to see what's been going on she's going to shoot him in the groin for cheating on her with Tobbing (this is even true, so not entirely all my own work). Appalled at what she has done she will then sit down and sob until this is all over. Which will be in about two and a half minutes.

The weedy blocker guy will drag himself out of the canal coughing dirty water in about a minute, but he won't be blocking anything for a while and in the meantime the side of the palace he was covering is open.

What I'm doing here is conventionally impossible. You can't transition into the mind of somebody who can themselves flit, or indeed has ever flitted, even with help. The target individual has to be unAware. As long as they are in that sense innocent and virginal, they're completely vulnerable; as soon as they've completed a single transition, even an assisted one, even one where they've simply been taken along for the ride, they're immune. There would appear to be no exceptions to this rule and it has become so accepted that the Concern has never thought to prepare its agents against the possibility of somebody exercising this ability against them. So I can flit from mind to mind here and cause any internal mayhem I want with seeming impunity.

I still don't feel I can transition to a different reality altogether and so escape completely – at least not without an incentive so immediate and powerful that I'd rather not subject myself to the experience in the first place – but if this new ability is the trade-off, I'll happily accept it.

In other words I still need septus, unless I'm feeling feeling very brave or especially desperate, but that shouldn't be a problem here; these guys ought to be loaded with it. I'd rather have the stuff in the box which Adrian is bringing from London, because it's Mrs Mulverhill's finest, untainted with the contaminants that make it easy to trace the flitter, but I'll take these guys' supply just in case.

Two of the people searching the upper floors realise they've always loved each other and have wasted far too much time already; they fall to fucking on a hallway floor. Another stares fascinated at his own reflection in a bathroom mirror, like he's never seen himself before. Another loses herself in the depths of a – to be fair – fabulously patterned Persian rug – a Kashan, I'd guess – while another decides to take off all his clothes and dive into the Grand Canal from the roof. The guy at the controls of the launch on the canal sees this, decides he's in love with the world and vows never to use an internal combustion engine ever again. He takes the keys out of the ignition and drops them into the milky-green waves with a wistful smile. The other guy in the launch just falls into a deep and peaceful sleep. One of the people guarding the calles is absolutely convinced he's just seen his years-dead father walk past and takes off after him. The rest are still covered by the second blocker, but by the time Jildeep's even half worked out what's going on I've arrived at the entrance hall and Tasered him as well. Dr Jildeep escapes, skittering down a narrow service corridor – it was him or the blocker with the Taser – but that's okay.

I'm in Jildeep's mind now and discovering something galling (I mean apart from the fact he wanted to shoot me in the legs just there, even though his orders forbade this). None of these people have any septus on them. They're in here clean, just in case I do overpower one of them and take their supply from them and disappear. They were thinking about a conventional physical whack over the back of the head rather than my rather more subtle consciousness manipulation, but the same precautionary principle defeats either, which is irritating.

They'll be approached by somebody unknown to them after the operation's over and get their supplies that way. Ha! These poor fuckers are here on faith and are going to have to stand around waiting for the Man. That's too bad for them and, as it turns out, for me. So I still need to rendezvous with my Londoner mate Ade after all. This cuts back my options significantly, but even a fairly deep rummage through Dr Jildeep's mind finds nothing that can help the situation. I suppose I could stay inside one of their minds for longer than I was intending to, but long before their supplier arrives they'll have the blockers up and functioning again, or – if I disable these two blockers permanently – they'll bring in new ones and I'll be trapped at best. More likely by far a good blocker will spot the wrong 'un in their midst like a badly bruised thumb and I'll be caught.

Whatever; with the second blocker down nobody has the power to stop me and there's no point interfering with anybody else. I'm free to go.

A man – an unremarkable man, about thirty, black hair, medium build – sitting at the stern of a passing vaporetto bound for Santa Lucia sees a naked man run along the dark roof of an impressive white and black palazzo on the western side of the Canalasso. Along with the rest of the passengers – now turning to each other, muttering, saying things like "Oh, my goodness" and "Eh? Cosa?" and so on – he turns to watch as the man throws himself from the roof and hurtles into the water just in front of a water taxi, which swerves and goes astern to rescue him, even though he does seem rather intent on swimming down the canal towards San Marco. Nearby, a man in an idling launch turns off the engine and casually drops the keys overboard.

The unremarkable man at the stern of the passing vaporetto looks surprised for a few moments, then sneezes.

(Italian, English, Greek, Turkish, Russian, Mandarin.)

Mavis Bocklite, a genial pensioner from Baxley, Georgia, USA, who is sitting across from him, says, "Bless you, sir."

Finally! I smile and nod. "Grazie, signora."

15

Patient 8262

"I think I am well," I tell the broad doctor who had the dolls in her desk. I know her name now. She is called Dr Valspitter. "I think I am okay now to leave." My grasp of the local language has improved markedly. It is called Itic. Dr Valspitter looks at me, lips pursed, brows gathered in the middle as though by a pulled thread. "I appreciate everything all here have done for me," I tell her.

"What do you remember of your past life?" the doctor asks me.

"Not very much," I confess.

"What would you do if you returned to the outside world?"

"I would look for a place to stay and for work to do. I am able to work."

"Not at your old job, perhaps."

"Ordinary labourer. I could do ordinary labour. I know building sites. That I could do. Ordinary labouring."

"You feel you could do this?"

"Yes, I feel I could do this."

"How would you find a place to live?"

"I would go to the Municipal Available Local Lodgings Clearing Office."

Dr Valspitter looks approving, nods and makes a note. "Good. And how would you find work?"

The obvious next question. "I would approach building site managers, but also I would go to the Municipal Local Employment Exchange."

The doctor makes another note. I think I'm doing all right here. I need to. I have to get out. I have to get away.

Last night I found I could not sleep and took another small-hours wander along the corridor, down the stairwell and along to what I still thought of as the silent ward. I could not help it; I felt drawn there. I don't think that's what woke me up but once I was awake I found myself thinking obsessively about the rows of still beds with their vacant-eyed, near-silent patients, and the contrast with their appearance in daylight when they were awake. I couldn't think what good padding down to look at them would do, but I couldn't think of anything else to do either and maybe just seeing them for real rather than in my mind's eye would let me get back to sleep eventually.

So I went, I looked – they were all just the same, though there were cards and personal items on the bedside cabinets and a few chairs scattered throughout the ward, all the things I'd convinced myself hadn't been present on my first two visits but which I suppose were always there – then I came back again.

There was somebody in my room. I had left the door closed and my light off, but now I could see some light showing beneath the door, reflecting dimly off the shiny floor. At first, of course, I thought it would just be the duty nurse again.

Then I saw more movement, at the far end of the corridor, somewhere inside the day room. A pale figure, moving across the dark space, disappearing then reappearing and coming towards the low lights of the corridor. The figure in the day room emerged into the half-light of the night-dimmed corridor lights and was revealed as the duty nurse, walking back to his desk at the end of the corridor holding a magazine and flicking its pages, intent on it. He did not look up, so did not see me.

I felt a sudden terror and shrank back against the wall as far as I could, hiding behind a metal cupboard holding fire-fighting equipment. The duty nurse sat down at his station at the far end of the corridor, feet up on the desk, still flicking through the magazine. He stretched out to one side – I could hear the wheels of his chair squeaking – and turned on the radio at a low volume. Tinny pop music sounded.

I could no longer see the door to my room. Who was in there if not the nurse? Was it my former attacker, whoever had tried to interfere with me? Perhaps I ought to go to the door, fling it open, confront them, the noise and commotion of course attracting the attention of the duty nurse. Or perhaps I should just approach the duty nurse directly and tell him there was somebody in my room, let him deal with whoever it was.

I had decided on the latter course and was about to step out from behind the fire-equipment cupboard and walk towards the duty nurse's station, when, from the far end of the corridor, I heard a toilet flush.

A door creaked and closed. I stepped along the wall to the nearest door, twisted the handle and let myself in. This should be a private visiting room, empty at this time of night. Sound came from somewhere near the toilets. Slipper-slapping footsteps came, and I recognised one of the old boys, a not-quite slack-jaw capable of holding a conversation and talking about something other than television or the weather. He went, head hunched, past where I watched via the cracked door.

Somebody said something and he looked up, waving down the corridor, no doubt at the duty nurse. I opened the door a little further to watch him go. When he was opposite the door to my room, a couple of doors short of his own room, the door to my room was flung open and light spilled out. "Mr Kel?" I heard a strong male voice say.

The old guy stood looking confused, staring blinking at whoever had addressed him from my room and then down the corridor. I heard seat wheels squeal as the nurse said something, voice inflected in a question.

Then a bright light shone into the old fellow's face, he put his hand up to shield his eyes, the duty nurse shouted something, the bright light went out and a man – tall, well-built, in a dark suit – went running past me and away down the corridor towards the stair well. He held a chunky-looking torch in one hand. In the other hand he was carrying something else. He thrust it inside his jacket as he ran past me. It was dark and heavy-looking and I knew it was a gun.

So:

"Can I leave?" I ask Dr Valspitter. "Can I go? Please?"

She smiles. "Perhaps. I will need other doctor to come to same opinion, but I think you can."

"Wonderful! Can we get other doctor, their opinion, today?"

"You are in such a hurry to leave?"

"I am. I want to get out," I say. "Today."

She shakes her head, frowning just a little. "Not today. Maybe tomorrow if other doctor agrees with me and we can complete all required paperwork and provide you with clothing and belongings and money and so on. Maybe tomorrow. I cannot promise. But soon, I think. Maybe tomorrow. We shall see. You must understand. You must be patient."

I want to protest, but I am aware that I have pushed things quite far enough already. If I seem too desperate to get out they might take that as a sign that I'm unbalanced or neurotic or something. I do my best to smile. "Tomorrow, then," I say. "I hope," I add, before the frowning doctor can reiterate that it's still only maybe.

"No!" I wail, staring at the two beige pills lying in the bottom of the little cup. The cup is colourless, translucent plastic, and tiny; a stingy measure of drink if you were serving spirits in it, and yet to me it seems like it's as deep, dark and dangerous as a mine shaft. I stare hopelessly into it and despair. "I not want to!" I am aware that I sound like a recalcitrant child.

"You must," the old nurse tells me. She is starting to lose patience with me, I can tell. "They harmless, Mr Kel. They give you a good night's sleep, that's all."

"But I sleep good!"

"Doctor say you must have them, Mr Kel," the old nurse tells me firmly, as though this trumps everything. "Do you want me to go and get doctor?"

This is a threat. If she fetches a doctor and I still refuse to take the sleeping pills I may well find that such a protest too will count against me when I ask to be released from the clinic. "Please not make me," I say, biting my bottom lip. Perhaps I can appeal to her emotions. This is only partially an act. However, she is not moved. She has seen it all before. Perhaps a younger nurse might have been persuaded but this old one is taking no nonsense.

"Very well, we get doctor." She turns to go and I have to reach out to her and say,

"No! All right!" She turns back, and at least has the decency not to look smug. "I take them," I tell her.

First line of defence: I think I can fool her and just keep the pills under my tongue until she has gone and then spit them out, but she insists on inspecting my mouth afterwards and so I have no choice but to swallow them.

Second line of defence: I'll go to the toilets and throw them up. But the nurse is watching for me to do this as she goes down the corridor dispensing drugs and twice shoos me back to bed with the threat that she'll inject me with a sedative if I insist on going to the toilets. She knows I already went not ten minutes ago.

Third line of defence: I'll throw up here in my room, into my water jug or out of the window if I have to. I can sign myself out voluntarily if I have to. Everything subsequently will be harder if I have done so – the finding a place to live and a job and so on – but not impossible. I am not stupid, I can survive.

Some time later I am vaguely aware of being pushed gently upright and something – the water jug, perhaps – being taken out of my hands. I am tucked into bed and the light is turned out. I feel very sleepy and in a way happy to be so, cosy in my wrapping of sheets and the feeling of dozing quietly off, while another part of me is shrieking with fury and terror, screaming at me to wake up and get away, do something, anything.

He comes for me again during that night. The drug still holds me, and it is as though everything happens through layers and layers of swaddling, through multiple bundlings of something insulating and muddling, making everything vague and fuzzy round the edges.

There is an impression of the quality of the light and sound around me changing somehow, of the door being opened and closed very quietly. And then there is the feeling that somebody else is here in the room with me. At first I feel no sense of threat. I have a vague, groundless and completely stupid feeling that this person is here to protect and look after me, to tend to me. Then I feel something happening to my bed. I still persist with the vague sensation that all is well and I am being cared for. They must be tucking me in. How nice. How like being a child, safe and warm and loved and quietly looked after.

But I am not being looked after, and the bed is being unmade, not made, untucked, sheets and blanket loosened, a way being made clear.

I feel the sliding, spiderly-creeping, probing hand slide into the bed and over my body at my hip. I feel my pyjamas being touched and investigated and then the cord that ties them being found, and – gently at first – tugged at. The knot does not give, and the tugging becomes harder, more impatient and aggressive.

In all of this it is as though I am watching everything on a screen, feeling it not as something that is happening to me but as something that is happening somewhere else to somebody else and the sensations accompanying the experience – the sensations that *are* the experience – are being transmitted to me through some technology or ability I have not heard of. I am dissociated from what's going on. This is not happening, or at least not to me. So I have no need to react, to try to do anything, because what good would that do? It's not happening to me.

Except, of course – as one part of my mind has known all along, and is still bellowing and yowling about – it entirely *is* happening to me.

The hand undoes the knot on my pyjama bottoms and pulls them forcibly down. There is a roughness and an urgency to the hand's movements now that was not there before. I think that whoever is doing this realises that I am truly in a deeply drugged sleep and so am not likely to wake up and start resisting or screaming. And there is, too – horribly, horribly – a feeling of something like the uncaring passion that infects lovers, when they cannot wait to get at each other, when clothes are ripped off the self and the other, when hands shake, when bruises happen, unmeant, unfelt at the time, when shouts and screams and crashings and bangings ring out without a care who hears them, when we abandon ourselves utterly to something that is neither fully ourselves or them any more but something that lies between us, aside from us, beyond us. I think I can remember feeling like that: wanting somebody like that, being wanted like that. This – this single-handed furtiveness, this selfish, unmindful groping, however urgent, however needy – dear fuck, this is a sad, pathetic, petty thing in comparison.

Something inside me wants to cry, confronted with the memory of such wild and joyous passion, such fervently mutualised desire, contrasted with this sordid, sweaty feeling and grabbing and squeezing. I think I do feel hot tears in my eyes and on my cheeks. So I can feel, at least, if not react. Would I rather this than outright unconsciousness, until it's all over? Is it better to witness such violation and know that it most surely happened, or better to know nothing until one wakes up sore, bemused, suspecting perhaps, but able to dismiss it, forget about it? I don't know. Anyway, I seem to have no choice, either about it happening to me or about the fact that I am aware of it.

The hand tires of manipulating my genitals and starts trying to turn me over, onto my side, rotating my body so that my exposed rear is turned towards my violator.

What heat there is in tears of such frustration. How can I let this happen to me? How can somebody do something so base and selfish and debased to another person? My brain is still minutes behind events but my heart seems to be waking up to what is occurring. It thrashes and spasms in my chest, as though trying to wake me up through the sheer physical disturbance pulsing through my body. I feel something happening with my behind. I think my arms and hands might be flapping now, trying to move, to beat away, though I could be imagining this. I go with the feeling anyway, trying to reinforce and strengthen it, imaginary or not.

Something enters me. A finger, into my anus. Too thin and hard and jointed to be a penis. No worse than a doctor's dispassionate probing, in theory, but this is not dispassionate, this is not for my own good, this is only for the pleasure of the person doing this to me.

Motherfucker. How fucking dare they. I summon one vast wave of disgust and fury and put it all into one arm, striking back at my assailant. Then I squeeze my lungs, contract my belly, throwing a pulse of sound out upwards through my throat, vomiting a scream that quickly turns into a cough and a terrible, squeezing, constricting pain all across my chest, imprisoning me.

The finger pulls roughly out of me. I heave myself onto my back, getting a glimpse of my attacker as they send the seat clattering to the floor and dash for the door.

I recognise him. It is the duty nurse from downstairs, the fellow who whistled, his uniform covered by a patient's dressing gown. He puts his head down and hunches his shoulders as he makes his escape into the corridor outside. I hear the duty nurse on this floor, a female nurse tonight, saying something, then shouting. My door slams shut.

Outside, I hear running, but I am flat on my back, hardly hearing it for the noise in my chest, hardly caring about anything any more except the sensation that a ten-tonne iron giant is pinning me down, one knee planted firmly on my chest as he squeezes the life out of me. The band around my chest cinches tighter and the pain grows a little worse. The last thing I'm fully aware of is the nurse coming into my room, taking one look at me and running off. Is that the reaction of a seasoned professional health worker? I'm not sure about this, but somehow it scarcely seems to matter any more. This crushing, constricting pain beyond pain is all that matters.

An alarm sounds, not that I can hear it very well in the vast, over-everything silence that seems to be dropping onto me like some inky overcast, raining pain. Then I think the door bangs open and somebody starts thumping me on the chest. As though I haven't had enough to endure this night.

They tear open my pyjama top and I want to protest. Please; passion, something shared, wanted, yearned for, not imposed, not this. Wrong. They put my head back, put their lips to mine, and kiss, blowing into me. I smell her perfume. Oh, that old sweetness. I will miss that. But still unasked for, still a sort of violation. Also, frankly, been eating garlic. More thumping and thudding against the hollow cavern of quietness that is my chest.

I drift away, despite the smashing and whacking and the regular, purposeful, breathful kissing trying to fill the void caged by my ribs. Then voices and lights and a feeling of crowding. Come all ye in. There is plenty of room here, my loves, in my empty chest and increasingly vacant mind, if nowhere else. So be at home, my guests; I'll stay so long and then so long.

Something pulls across me like a hawser, side to side, plucking me like some thick and fleshy string set vibrating, forcing my back bowing up off the bed, jangling every nerve and fibre of my being before releasing me, letting me fall back with relief.

Something resumes, some regularity returns to matters, like a stopped engine at last coughing hesitantly back into life. I think. I don't know. I'm still sort of drifting, like a boat at a quayside, half disconnected, just one painter securing it, letting it move and wheel and jerk according to the vagaries of tides, currents and winds. It would not take much of a tug to separate me altogether from this mooring, but I am lucky and it does not happen.

Feeling myself drift into a sort of warm fog-bank, a pocket of peace, I bump against the pier again and am secured once more.

And so here I lie, back in my own bed in my own room, brought back to life and grateful for that, but lying here in dread, for I think I have seen what happens next, I believe that I know what is coming.

I cannot get away. I am too exhausted, too weak, too sedated, too disabled by all that has passed to be able to get up and go or even sit up and beg. I try to speak, to tell the staff what I fear, what I have seen happening, but I seem to have lost the words. I can formulate the sentences in my head and I think I am speaking them in my own language inside my head well enough and perfectly coherently when I speak my own language out loud, even though I know nobody will understand, but the translation into the language spoken here, by these nurses and doctors and cleaners and other patients . . . that seems to have gone from me. I speak gibberish no matter what I try to say, and anyway talk so softly that I think they'd struggle to hear even if I was enunciating with exemplary clarity.

So here I lie, seeing through the day and the hazy sweep of the sun's slow track across the sky outside and the sheltering blinds between us, waiting for darkness, waiting for night, wondering if it will be this night and knowing that it will be, and the dark-dressed man will come for me before the morning.

I feel tears well in my eyes and trickle gently down my cheeks, intercepted and guttered only when they meet one of the various tubes and pipes and wires that join me to the various pieces of medical equipment clustered quietly around me like mourners around somebody already dead.

The Transitionary

No wonder I've been losing track of myself. I'm sitting at a little café a short way from the railway station, back to the wall, nursing an Americano and watching the boats stream up and down the Grand Canal. Just along the broad quayside, a line of tourists stand with their luggage waiting to pick up water taxis. At the next table two Australian guys are arguing about whether it's espresso or expresso.

"Look, for Christ's sake, it's there in black and white."

"That could be a misprint, man, like Chinese instructions. You don't know."

I am still toying with my new-found senses. Sensibilities, even. I have done no more leaping into other people's brains, whether Concern or civilian. I seem to have a sort of vague spotter sense, which is quite useful. I can sense that the baffled, disordered, demoralised intervention teams are still milling about the Palazzo Chirezzia, their members collecting themselves, tending to their wounded, making their excuses to each other and themselves, still not entirely able to understand what really happened, and waiting for back-up and assistance to arrive.

This is all happening just a few hundred metres away from where I'm sitting. I am ready to move quickly away if I need to, but for now I'm happy that I can see them without them seeing me. Another sense: they give the impression of deaf people talking loudly amongst themselves and not realising that they are doing so, while I am sitting here perfectly silent. I would be nervous about putting it to the test – however, I'm oddly but completely confident that a spotter could pass me by right here, a metre or two away, and have no idea that somebody capable of transitioning was sitting watching them. And of course they have no idea what I look like now.

I have been able to take more control of this glass-walls, future-paths sense. At the moment it is telling me that nothing especially threatening is imminent. Looking backwards is possible too, though. It's like I can see down corridors in my head, in my memory, and as though there is a near-infinite series of doors angled partially to face me as I look down from one end of any particular corridor, so that by looking closely and then zooming in on each one I can see what happened during different transitions I once made. There is an uncanny impression that this is at once one corridor and many,

367

that it leads off in an explosion of different directions scattered vertically and horizontally and in dimensions that I would struggle to put a name to, but, despite this, my mind seems able to cope with the experience.

Here is the time just passed when I bamboozled the whole of not just one conventionally configured but high-skill-and-experience-level Concern intervention team, but two (and more like three, if you count the people watching the perimeter), all at the Palazzo Chirezzia, barely an hour ago.

Here is the time I sat in a room with somebody I thought I loved and watched transfixed as her hand moved through a candle flame like silk.

This is me chasing two fucked-up kids though a Parisian sink estate and watching them die . . . and again, except differently.

Here is the time I blew that musician's brains out while he sat in his preposterously blinged half-track.

Look, observe how I save a young man from certain death.

Here, see how I stare at Madame d'Ortolan's tits, zitted with diamonds.

And this is me with my pals walking down a street and stopping by a fat old geezer sunbathing in his postage-stamp-size front garden, one sunny day, long ago.

I sit, indulging myself in my own internal slide show, amused as all hell.

I've let my Americano grow cold. The Grand Canal still froths with boats passing to and fro. The arguing Aussies are gone. Confusion tempered by affronted professional pride still reigns at the Palazzo Chirezzia. And there is a little fear there, too, because their back-up has started to arrive at last and they've heard that Madame d'Ortolan is also on her way, with questions.

A warm wind scented with tobacco smoke and diesel exhaust stirs me from my reverie, back to the present and the insistent reality of the here and now.

Indeed; all this historical stuff is highly intriguing, but there is the small matter of my being hunted with pretty much every resource the Concern is able to bring to bear. That needs attending to. Beyond that, the coup that Madame d'Ortolan would appear to be trying to mount is either proceeding or not. I have already done what I can in that regard. I can only hope that my attempts to alert Mrs M to the targets I'd been sent after worked, and they have been warned and put themselves safe.

My present embodiment came complete with a mobile phone. I try calling my new friend Ade, on his way here with a cunningly worked container full of septus, but his mobile telephone is switched off and his office tells me that he is away, expected back tomorrow sometime. I look at the timepiece wrapped round my wrist. The smaller but more important hand points to the two parallel lines just off the vertical, to the left. Eleven. Adrian said that he should be here by four in the afternoon.

We are to meet at the Quadri on the Piazza San Marco, safely surrounded by the tourist throng.

It seems I have to wait.

I pay, then go for a walk, crossing the Grand Canal by the Scalzi bridge and coming back the same way half an hour later – an elegantly curved new one further up is only a week or two from being opened. I wander into the station, sit down in the café and order another Americano, the better to sip slowly. I have a faint desire to count how many platforms there are in the station, but it is residual, easily ignored. The phone rings a few times and its screen shows me the faces of the people calling: Annata, Claudio, Ehno. I don't answer.

I take several more walks around the western end of Cannaregio and the nearer parts of Santa Croce and sit in several more cafés, none too far from the Palazzo Chirezzia, keeping the vague hubbub in internal view at all times. I sit quietly, seemingly watching people, actually probing further into my own pasts.

I am sitting in a little tourist café on the Fondamenta Venier near the Ponte Guglie when I am recognised. I prepare for the worst, but it is just somebody who knows this body, this face, enquiring why I'm not at work this afternoon. I look furtive and embarrassed and stick to vague generalities, mostly keeping my head down. The man nods, winks and taps me on the shoulder before he walks off. He thinks I am waiting for my lover. I drain my lemon tea and leave. I've had enough coffee.

I walk to another café, on the Rio Tera De La Madalena. A spritz this time, and some pasta. Staring at the spaghetti in my bowl, I drift into a strange trancelike state, at first wondering how many individual strands of the pasta lengths there might be in the bowl, then how many metres they would all add up to if laid end to end, then realising – as I toy with the pale, soft strands, draping them languorously, voluptuously over the tines of my fork – that their aggregated complexity is like the various entangled themes and episodes of my life: a swirling, hideously complicated, topologically tortuous, possibly knotted exposition of my very own reality lying dumped and glistening here in the moist coils lying on the plate before me, the sliced, abbreviated strands like the lives I have cut short, the glistening red of passata adding an appropriately gory sheathing.

How many lives, I reflect. How many elisions and abbreviations, how many slack abandonments. And how many lives and deaths of my own self-elisions, lives lived briefly in the head and body of another then skipped away from, blithely flicked like dust from a sleeve. Every mission a suicide mission, every transition a transition from life to death (and back again, but still; a death).

I drift, almost without meaning to, into my private viewing theatre of the past. Here I am toddling, saddled on my mother's hip, dandled on my father's knee, going to school, leaving home, arriving at UPT, making friends, going to classes, seeing Mrs M for the first time, studying, drinking, dancing, fucking, sitting exams, vacationing at home, fucking Mrs M for the first time, fucking Mrs M for the last time, standing drunk on a parapet in Aspherje looking out over the drop to the Great Park on the far side and wondering where she had gone, why she had abandoned me and whether I should just jump, and then falling backwards, too wasted to stand or balance or even cry. Here I am training to be a fucking multiversal ninja instead.

I can even see how I got where I am metaphysically, too, if you know what I mean; how and why I have changed and my abilities have developed over the last few months and weeks and days and even hours. I was always a natural, always a good learner, I always saw things clearly and I was just genetically predisposed to take transitioning and its associate skills to places they had never been before, with the right sort of push. It doesn't even make me that special; untold trillions of similarly potentially gifted minds have lived and died on untold worlds all unknowing, their existences just never divined, never sniffed out by l'Expédience. And I can see how all those fraught, dangerous extra missions that Madame d'O sent me on were what made the difference, what proved me and tempered me and forced me to find and cultivate skills within that I did not know I had. I can see these traits, these attributes quite clearly in myself now and I suppose it is just possible that the right, properly attuned sort of person – a Mulverhill, a d'Ortolan – might have seen them or at least their potential in me years ago, if they were able to glance in at just the right angle.

I snap out of my reverie when the waiter nudges my seat – deliberately, probably – waking me from my dream.

The light has changed, the remnants of pasta are quite cold. I glance at my watch. It is fifteen past four o'clock. If I stick with this body then even if I try to run through the crowds, by the time I get to San Marco I'll be half an hour late. Maybe I should take the next right and get to the Grand Canal, call a water taxi. Or maybe I should do the smart thing and just swap bodies with somebody already in San Marco. I close my eyes, prepare to do whatever it was that let me flit across to this body.

And can't do it.

What? What's going on?

I try again, but still nothing. It's like I'm back to being blocked again. I'm stuck with this body.

I rise, throw down a handful of notes to cover the bill, start walking quickly in the direction of the San Marco and pull out the phone to call Adrian, wondering if I can still sense Concern people remotely like I could before, or if that's gone too, then stop in mid-button press and mid-stride, stumbling to a halt as I realise, yes, I can still sense stuff and what I sense now is that a profound change has taken place within the Palazzo Chirezzia.

Something very strange and unpleasant has appeared in the small crowd of Concern people in and around the building, something bizarrely different, and not benign.

Who or what is *that*?

Whatever or whoever it is, I have the disturbing feeling that it's what is blocking me, and also that as I look at it, it's looking straight back at me, with a kind of predatory fascination.

Adrian

"Hello. Who's this?"

"Ade, it's Fred, who you are coming to meet."

"Yeah, Fred, right. Look, mate, I'm en route, amn't I? Bit optimistic getting through the formalities and then from the old aeroporto to the city in forty-odd minutes. Sorry about that, but you know what it's like. In a water taxi wotsit now, though, making maximum speed. Driver says we should be there in about ten, fifteen minutes. That be all right?"

"Yes. Adrian, please tell your driver to take you to the Rialto. I'll meet you there. Not San Marco, I'm running late too and we should get to the Rialto at about the same time."

"Rialto, not San Marco. Gotcha. That's the bridge, innit?"

"That's right."

"Okey-doke. See you there, mate."

"Don't display the box, though."

"Eh? Oh. Okay."

"Stand as close as you can to the very middle of the bridge, right at the top of the walking surface."

"Got that. Middle, top."

"What outer clothes are you wearing?"

"Blue jeans, white shirt, sort of, umm, orangey, beigey leather jacket."

"I'll find you."

"Okay, then. See you there."

Madame d'Ortolan

The voice was sing-song. "Here-here, hyah-hyah!"

In the main study of the Palazzo Chirezzia, Bisquitine sat sprawled, unladylike, on a rather grand couch whose white covering had only recently been removed. She picked her nose, then inspected the finger involved, cross-eyed. Mrs Siankung sat to one side of her, one of her handlers to the other. Madame d'Ortolan sat on an ornate chair a couple of metres away across a Persian rug and a still sheet-covered occasional table. The other handlers stood behind the couch.

"Now, my dear," Madame d'Ortolan said quietly, "be very sure about this. He's still here, still in the city? Still in Venice. Are you certain?"

Bisquitine sucked in her lips, looked meaningfully up at the painted ceiling of the study and said, "These are my lawyers, called Gumsip and Slurridge, they'll send you the bill and then talk of demurrage." She smiled broadly, displaying white teeth with little bits of seaweed stuck between them. The body she'd found herself within when they had transitioned had been that of a smartly dressed young woman carrying a briefcase. She'd been standing on a pontoon waiting for a vaporetto when her own consciousness had been displaced by that of Bisquitine, who had immediately decided the weed growing on the side of the floating jetty looked edible; in fact, delicious.

Madame d'Ortolan looked at Mrs Siankung, who watched

Bisquitine with anxious concentration. Bisquitine appeared dishevelled already; hair awry, her businesswoman's jacket removed as an annoyance, her blouse hanging half out, buttons undone at the bottom, tights laddered, shoes discarded. She brought her head back, and stuck her jaw out, lowering her voice to something close to a man's as she said, "Blinkenscoop, why, you silly man, what do you call this? A fine to-do, to do, to-do, to-do, to-do-oo-oo. I can't see with you in the way. Begone, you tea urchin!"

"She will need one of the other blockers to be sure," Mrs Siankung announced.

Madame d'Ortolan and Mr Kleist exchanged glances. They were out of character, in a sense. He was too young, wiry and blond, she too fat and awkward, with badly dyed grey-black hair and a loud orange velour trouser suit. Mrs Siankung was similarly wrong, manifesting as a massive, robustly built woman in a voluminous yellow dress who needed a three-pointed aluminium stick to walk. They'd had no time to find body types closer to their own, especially as they'd all had to transition together with Bisquitine and her handlers, who had been similarly randomised in physiques.

Madame d'Ortolan frowned. "A blocker? You're sure?"

"I think you mean a spotter," Mr Kleist suggested.

"No, a blocker," Mrs Siankung said, reaching out to flick an unruly lock off her charge's forehead. "And it has to be one of those who was here earlier, with the first intervention team."

Madame d'Ortolan glanced at Mr Kleist and nodded. He left the room. Bisquitine made as though to slap Mrs Siankung's hand away, then started pulling at her long, brown, still mostly gathered-up hair, tugging a thick length of it free and putting the end of it in her mouth and starting to chew contentedly on it. She looked at a distant painting with an expression of great concentration.

"What will happen to the blocker?" Madame d'Ortolan asked.

Mrs Siankung looked at her. "You know what will happen."

Mr Kleist returned with one of the two blockers a few minutes later.

The young man had been dried off after his dunking in the canal beside the palace's landing stage. His dark hair was slicked down, he was dressed in a towelling robe and he was smoking a cigarette.

"Put that out," Mrs Siankung told him.

"I work better with it," he said, glancing to Madame d'Ortolan, who remained expressionless.

He sighed, took a final deep draw, found an ashtray on the broad desk and stubbed the cigarette out. He took a frowning look at Bisquitine as he did so. She was in turn obviously fascinated by him, staring wide-eyed and still holding the hank of hair to her mouth while she chewed noisily at it.

A slight, bald man hurried through the study doors, came up to Madame d'Ortolan and kissed her hand.

"Madame, I am at your disposal."

"Professore Loscelles," she replied, patting his hand. "A pleasure, as ever. I am so sorry your lovely home has been made such a mess of."

"Not at all, not at all," he murmured.

"Please stay, will you?"

"Certainly."

The Professore stood at the rear of Madame d'Ortolan's chair.

The sheet-covered table was moved back and the young man who was employed as a blocker was sat on a chair immediately in front of Bisquitine, almost knee to knee. He looked a little nervous. He pulled the robe tighter, cleared his throat.

"She will take your wrists," Mrs Siankung told him.

He nodded, cleared his throat again. Bisquitine looked expectantly at Mrs Siankung, who nodded. The girl made a noise like "Grooh!" and sat forward quickly, grabbing at the young man's wrists and encircling them as best she could with her own smaller hands while she thudded her head against his chest.

The reaction was immediate. The young man bowed his back, jackknifed forward and as though doing so deliberately vomited copiously over Bisquitine's head, hair and back before quivering as though suffering a fit and starting to slump backwards in the seat and then slide forwards out of it, legs splaying as he lost control of his bladder and bowels at the same time.

"Dear fuck!" Madame d'Ortolan said, standing so suddenly that she knocked her chair over.

Professore Loscelles put a handkerchief to his mouth and nose and turned away, bowing his head.

Mr Kleist did not react at all, save to glance briefly, as though concerned, at Madame d'Ortolan. Then he walked over and carefully set her chair upright again.

Mrs Siankung moved her feet away from the mess.

Bisquitine didn't seem to have noticed, still cuddling into the young man and pulling him to her as he spasmed and jerked and voided noisily from various orifices.

"Who's a bad boy, then?" they heard Bisquitine say over the noises of evacuation coming from the young man, her voice muffled as she hugged his shaking body and they collapsed together onto the floor. A thick, earthy stink filled the air. "Who's a bad boy? Where's this? Where's this, then? You tell me. Ay, Ferrovia, Ferrovia, al San Marco, Fondamenta Venier, Ay! Giacobbe, is that you? No, it's not me. Ponte Guglie; alora, Rio Tera De La Madalena. Strada Nova, al San Marco. Alora; il Quadri. Due espressi, per favore, signori. Bozman, who said you could come along? Get back, get away, get thee to your own shop, if you have one! . . . Euh, yucky." Bisquitine seemed to notice the mess she was lying in. She let go of the young man, who flopped lifeless on the rug, streaked with his own excrement. His eyes – wide, almost popping – stared up at the biblical scene depicted on the ceiling.

Bisquitine got to her feet, smiling brightly. She stuck the length of hair in her mouth again, then made a sour face and spat it out. She continued to spit for a few more moments before holding her arms out to Mrs Siankung as a child would, straight, fingers spread. "Bath time!" she cried out.

Madame d'Ortolan looked to Professore Loscelles, who was

dabbing at his lips with his handkerchief. He nodded. "It would sound," he said hoarsely, "as though the person is heading from Santa Lucia – the railway station – towards the Piazza San Marco. So it would seem, given the names of the thoroughfares mentioned. Or they may already be there, at the Quadri. It is a café and rather fine restaurant. Very good cake."

Madame d'Ortolan looked at the other man standing nearby. "Mr Kleist?"

"I'll see to it, ma'am." He left the room.

Bisquitine stamped one foot, messily. "*Bath* time!" she said loudly.

Mrs Siankung looked to Madame d'Ortolan, who said, "Shower." She glanced distastefully at Bisquitine. "And don't tarry. We may need her again, soon."

The Transitionary

I make my way through the slow bustle of tourists on the main route leading towards the Rialto and beyond towards both the Accademia and Piazza San Marco, moving as quickly as I can without actually throwing people aside or trampling small children. "Scusi. Scusi, scusi, signora, excuse me, sorry, scusi, coming through. Scusi, scusi . . ."

At the same time I'm still trying to monitor what's going on just across the Grand Canal. What a stew of conflicting talents and abilities are massed around the Palazzo Chirezzia! There are blockers and trackers and inhibitors and foreseers and adepts with skills I barely recognise, many of them recently arrived. I think I can identify individual presences now, too. That one there would be Madame d'Ortolan, this one here might be Professore Loscelles. And at the centre of them all that bizarre presence, that strange, guileless malignity.

One of the blockers seems to have gone. I remember the first blocker I'd Tasered, the young man who was smoking and fell into the small canal at the side of the palace. He isn't there any more.

And some of the others are starting to move, quitting the Chirezzia and streaming in this direction, heading for the Rialto, others clustering in what must be a launch—

"Jesus! Hey! Watch where you're going! What the – I mean, Jesus."

"Scusi, sorry, sorry, signore, I beg your pardon," I tell the backpacker I've just knocked to his knees, helping him back up to a surrounding chorus of tutting.

"Well, just—"

"Scusi!" Then I'm off again, sliding and dancing through the crowd like the people are flags on a slalom course, leading with one shoulder then the other, sliding and swivelling on the balls of my feet. The boat with the half-dozen or so Concern people in it is on its way down the Grand Canal. More – maybe a dozen – are on foot, heading over the Rialto now. I'm just a couple of minutes away from there. If they turn left on its far side, they'll pass right by me or we'll bump into each other.

My phone goes. It's Ade. A symbol on the display that wasn't flashing before is flashing now. I suspect the battery is about to give out.

"Fred?"

"Hello, Adrian."

"Just landed at the Rialto, mate, just past the vaporetto sort of floating bus stop wotsit. On the bridge in one minute."

"I'll see you very shortly."

I stop, walking into the doorway of a glove shop, breathing hard. I still can't flit across to another person. I can feel the squad of Concern people splitting up, most heading on down the main route for San Marco, three coming this way. I turn to face the calle and close down as much as I can, calming myself, attempting, if it's possible, to take all that I can of my new abilities off-line. A minute or two passes, the street teems with people. I recognise somebody and my heart leaps, then I realise they're heading the other way and it's just the backpacker I bowled into earlier. I try a quick toe-in reading with my sense of where the Concern people are. All three of the nearest are still heading up the way I've just come.

I walk out and on and turn a corner, find myself facing the eastern end of the Rialto.

Madame d'Ortolan

"Cripes! Heads up, mateys! Here's our boy! Whoop whoop! Last one in's a scallop! I say, that ain't politic. I ain't even broke my fast yet, dontcha know?"

"What? Where?" Madame d'Ortolan said. She glared at Mrs Siankung. "Is this something new?"

Mrs Siankung stared into Bisquitine's eyes, letting one of the other handlers take over the job of towelling her hair dry. "I think so," she said. They were in one of the main bedroom suites of the palace. Mr Kleist and Professore Loscelles looked on, as did Bisquitine's handlers and a spotter in a schoolboy's uniform who was keeping in continual touch with the intervention teams heading for the San Marco and the smaller groups checking out the other places that Bisquitine had already mentioned. Bisquitine sat on the bed in a white towelling robe like the one the unfortunate young blocker had been wearing. "This is the bad man?" Mrs Siankung asked her gently.

Bisquitine nodded. "Dish it all, Chaplip, I'm hungry! I mean, jeepahs!"

Mrs Siankung took one of the girl's hands in both of hers, stroking it as though it was a pet. "We shall eat, my love. Very soon. You get dressed now and we go to eat, yes? Where is the bad man?"

"Sausinges would be nice. I says it like that cos it's cute. Where's my old ma, then? I ain't seen her round the blinkin farmstead in mumfs."

"The bad man, my love."

"He's here, love-a-kins," Bisquitine said, putting her face very close to Mrs Siankung's. "Shalls we to go see da bad mun?" she said, deep-voiced, as though talking to a baby. She shook her head. "Shalls we? Shalls we to go and see the bad mun? Shalls we? Shalls we?"

"Yes," Mrs Siankung said quietly, at the same time as Madame d'Ortolan shouted, "Enough of this!"

Bisquitine seemed to ignore them both. She stuck one finger sharply up into the air, narrowly missing the eye of the handler towelling her hair. "To the Rialto, me hearties! Realty bound! Tally fucking prostimitute!"

Madame d'Ortolan looked at Professore Loscelles. "The Rialto. That's close, isn't it?"

"Five minutes away," he told her.

Mrs Siankung patted Bisquitine's hand. "We'll get you dressed," she started to say.

"No, we won't," Madame d'Ortolan said, standing. "Bring her as she is. It's warm out." She looked sourly round them all. Only Professore Loscelles appeared like himself or well enough turned out to be presentable. "We can't look any more ridiculous than we do already."

The Transitionary

It looks like all humanity is packing the Rialto; the bridge over the Grand Canal is compact but massive, sturdy yet elegant. Two lines of small packed shops are separated by the broad central way whose surface is composed of flights of shallow grey-surfaced steps edged with the same cream-coloured marble found throughout the city. Behind the shops two further walkways face up and down the canal, linked to the pitched street of the central thoroughfare at either end and the centre. The walkway facing south-west is the busier as it provides a longer, more open view down the Canal and the bustle of boats plying its milky blue-green waters.

They've left the Palazzo Chirezzia. The thing, the person, the nexus of sheer terrifying weirdness is on the move, and so is practically everybody else who was still there, including Madame herself and the Prof. They're a minute away; they can probably see the bridge by now.

My mobile phone goes and I start to answer it, seeing that it's Adrian. The display blinks off. The phone won't come back to life. I shove it in a pocket and start up the slope of the Rialto with the rest of the tourist crowd.

Madame d'Ortolan

"When, sir? Why, sir. I'll tell you when, then; between the Quilth of Octoldyou-so and the Nonce of Distember, THAT'S JOLLY WELL WHEN!" Bisquitine's shout echoed off the surrounding buildings.

"Hush, my dear," Mrs Siankung said, conscious of the stares they were attracting.

They were on the Ruga Orefici, within sight of the Rialto. Bisquitine padded happily along in the midst of their motley collection of ungainly bodies and unfortunate clothing styles. She wore the same towelling robe she'd been wrapped in after her shower and had been persuaded into a pair of panties but had adamantly refused shoes or even slippers. She hugged the gown about her, looked round at the various shops with their excitingly bright displays and tried unsuccessfully to whistle.

The smell of a bakery distracted her as the square in front of San Giacomo di Rialto opened out to their left.

"Still hungry!" she cried out.

"I know, dear," Mrs Siankung said, trying to keep an arm round the girl's waist. "We'll eat soon."

"Wot you lookin at then, squire?" Bisquitine said in a deep voice as two bronze-skinned teenage girls passed by, staring and then laughing at her. "Pop a crap on yo petal, bitches, upside ya head. An no mitsake, mistake, mystique, Mustique. I meant that."

"Shush now, dear."

"Claudia?" a man said suddenly, stepping right in front of Bisquitine. She had to stop, as did the others. The man was tall. He wore sunglasses, had salt-and-pepper hair, wore a suit and carried a briefcase. He took the sunglasses off, frowned, eyes screwing up as he stared into Bisquitine's eyes.

"Ill met by sunlight, my good fellow," Bisquitine said haughtily. "Why, I've half a mind to scratch the boundah!"

The man looked confused and concerned in equal measure. "Claudia?" he asked. "Is that you? You were supposed to be at—" He took a step back, taking in the knot of people obviously with this woman who looked like somebody he knew and yet was not her. "Hey, what the hell's—"

Mr Kleist didn't wait for the nod from Madame d'Ortolan. He stepped up to the man, saying. "Sir, if I may explain . . ." and did a straight-finger jab into his throat. Gasping, eyes wide, unable to speak, clutching his gullet, the man staggered back. It had been done so quickly that it seemed nobody had noticed. "I'll catch you up," Mr Kleist told the others quietly. He squatted as he made the man sit down on the road surface, still wheezing and struggling for air. Madame d'Ortolan glared at Mr Kleist but he couldn't just leave the man making that noise. He told himself that he was lingering here because he needed to make sure the man stayed down, out of action, not likely to follow them, but really it was to stop him making that terrible choking, gasping noise; to ease him. He pinched the fellow's neck, attempting to reopen his windpipe. The man tried to bat his hand away. A crowd of people had formed around them and he heard somebody call for the carabinieri. The man made a series of terrible gagging, strangling, sucking noises.

Bisquitine glanced back as they hurried away. "Dat gotta hurt, sho nuff. I'd get some cream on that. Trot on!"

"Dearest," Mrs Siankung said, "please. We're nearly there. Very soon."

"When, sir? Why, sir. I'll tell you when, then; somba tyme atwixt da the Quilth of Oncoldyou-such and zee Chonce of Plastemper; tankums, wilcums, noddinks, hurtsies. Oh-dear-oh-dear-oh-drear. Oh-dear-oh-drear-oh-drolldums. The backstroke? In these shoes? Have you taken leafs off your fences? Enough already. You muddy funster; you're landfill."

"I wish we could shut her up," Madame d'Ortolan muttered to Professore Loscelles as they hurried up towards the broad shallow steps of the Rialto itself.

"I suspect—" the Professore began.

"Tuk-tuk, talkink in the ranks!" Bisquitine sounded affronted.

"There there, dearest," Mrs Siankung said, patting her arm. She glanced back at Madame d'Ortolan.

"Noo," Bisquitine intoned in her deep, masculine-sounding voice. "But quate appy to use this poor damaged creatchah for your own dimmed ignoble ends, midim. Ain't dat de trute!"

"Bisq, shh!"

"Poor damaged creatchah, poor damaged creatchah . . ."

They had climbed almost to the summit of the Rialto, the crowds growing ever thicker and more chaotic. Madame d'Ortolan grasped Mrs Siankung's arm. "Is he *here*?"

Bisquitine stopped suddenly, did a little dance and with one arm straight out pointing said triumphantly, "Bingo! Bandits ahoy, chumlets! Thar she blows!"

Adrian

So I'm standing here at the very top of the very middle bit of the Rialto in Venice, feeling like a bit of a muppet and wondering what the chances are that this is some gigantic long-winded, long-game wind-up. (Except it can't be, can it? All that money over the years was real enough, and the box Mrs M sent and Fred asked me to bring didn't show up in my hand luggage when I went through Heathrow security, did it? Sailed past.) But anyway, that isn't stopping me from getting that What-the-fuck-am-I-doing-here? feeling, even though, yes, it's all very lovely in a sunny, chocolate-boxy, can't-move-for-bleedin-tourists kind of a way, and here I go having to step away from the very top of the very centre bit yet again because yet another group of Japanese or Chinese or whatever tourists want to take a photograph of one of them standing at exactly that point, when this little bunch of frankly not very well dressed people come marching up the steps from the opposite direction I arrived from.

There's a mousy bint in a white dressing gown in the middle of them, hair straggling everywhere, muttering to herself. Proper nutter. Then she sees me and sort of jogs on the spot and points and blabbers something, just as I feel a hand on my elbow, cupping it like a brandy glass but I don't know which way to look because this lot with the lady in white at their centre are all fucking looking at me now and starting up the slope towards me while the person behind me holding my elbow says quietly, "Adrian? I'm Fred."

The Transitionary

Adrian turns to me and his expression and body language changes instantly. "Tem, my darling man," he says.

I stare at him, then look beyond him to where the others are, the small group intermittently visible through the swirl of people coming and going and chattering and laughing on the bridge. This group includes Madame d'Ortolan, Professore Loscelles and the frightening weirdness of the presence that has been blocking my new-found abilities for the last half-hour. Except she isn't blocking them any more. Not since the instant that somebody different stepped into Adrian's shoes.

The approaching group is six or seven metres away, hurrying raggedly towards us.

"Tem, my love," Adrian says. "I believe you're free to do something now. I think you'd better do it. Leave Madame d'O. I need to talk to her."

I can't approach the girl's mind. The rest – the people who attend her, the Prof, the muscle boys and the specialist adepts, including a guy called Kleist who's hurrying towards the group from the street behind – them I can work with. They all become convinced they really are tourists and just wander off to look at the lovely views. I work the same trick with the rest of the intervention teams, all of whom had been ordered to about-turn and are in the process of converging on the Rialto. The group in the launch – currently exceeding the speed limit back up the Grand Canal to a wavelike chorus of shouts and horns, and almost at the Rialto – unanimously decide to visit Burano for ice creams, though they'll be pulled over by a police launch near the railway station a few minutes later anyway.

Meanwhile, all l'Expédience people who were carrying weapons have picked them out of their pockets with looks of puzzled distaste and, holding them by thumb and finger, disposed of them. Four Tasers and six handguns have splashed into canals, to join all the other secrets the waves have hidden over the centuries. The whole fragre of the locality relaxes distinctly.

For a few moments, Madame d'Ortolan is left bewildered. Then she starts shouting furiously at her people as they saunter away wide-eyed, smiling, ignoring her. "Mr Kleist! Loscelles! Mr *Kleist!*"

Only Bisquitine remains unaffected, looking bemused as the people around her disperse. "Rum to-do," she muses, and picks her nose. "Business elsewhere, Mr Rumblebunk, I'll be bound."

So I have time to ask Adrian, "Mrs M?"

She makes Adrian bow. "Indeed. Hello, Tem. Glad you jumped the way you did. Welcome aboard."

"You can do this? Flit to somebody who's already been transitioned?"

She spreads Adrian's arms, "Patently. Well, when it was me who popped their transitioning cherry, anyway. Good trick, eh? I've been developing my talents. So have you, obviously. Congratulations."

"The people on the list?"

"Safe. I got to all of them first." She winks at me. "It'll cost ya."

"And what now?"

"I'm afraid you have to go, my love." She feels inside the jacket, pulls out the box that Adrian brought from London and gives it to me. "Take this and get well away, Tem. I mean, *well* away, untraceably distant." She glances round to see Madame d'Ortolan looking undecided, then, with a word and a nod to the girl in the white robe, start towards us again. She turns back. "No matter what happens here, you need to disappear. Whoever controls the Concern, even if it's the good guys, chances are they'll want to find you and take your mind to bits to find out how you can flit without septus. Or they'll just kill you." She smiles, nods at the box. "Soon you won't need that." Again, she glances briefly towards Madame d'Ortolan, who is having to push a party of laughing Chinese girls out of the way to get to us. "Now go," she says, closing my fingers round the box. "You've done all you can. This is my show now. I hope I see you again. Go." She places a finger briefly on my lips, then turns away to face Madame d'Ortolan.

Mrs Mulverhill

The angry-looking woman in the orange velour jumpsuit walks up to the man in the tan jacket, ignoring the jostling crowds and the wash of humanity pressing in from all sides. The girl in the white towelling robe trails vaguely after her, still digging into her nose with the one remaining fingernail she hasn't broken or cracked in the hours since she found herself in this body. She sighs. "Still hungry," she mutters. She finds something up her nose and eats it. Success! Chewy *and* salty.

Madame d'Ortolan stands in front of Mrs Mulverhill, close enough for the veloured breasts and belly of her current incarnation to touch Adrian's shirt, open jacket, jeans. She stares into the grey-green eyes.

"Hello, Theodora," Mrs Mulverhill says, in Adrian's pleasantly deep voice. "How's tricks?" Madame d'Ortolan tries to take Adrian's wrists in her hands but finds her own wrists grasped. "I don't think so, Theodora. Let's stay here and discuss this like civilised people, shall we?"

"What in the holy fuck *are* you, Mulverhill?"

"Just a concerned citizen of the Concern, Theodora." Mrs

Mulverhill uses Adrian's face to smile over Madame d'Ortolan at the girl in the white robe.

Bisquitine waves back with one finger. "Sui amazaro. Climb ev'ry woman. Ah belong to *you*, Underground."

"You hypocritical bitch."

"Oh, now, Theodora, I'm not the one trying to murder my way to absolute power within the Central Council. You might have noticed your loyalists have gone unharmed."

"Really? What about Harmyle?"

"Oh, he was a traitor so many times over that I'm not sure even he knew who he was betraying at the end. He was a disloyalist. I think offing him was just to get your attention."

"You think. Let's ask Oh himself, shall we?" Madame d'Ortolan struggles to free her hands, in vain.

"The point is I could have murdered them all in their sleep if I'd wanted to. But then I'm not you. I'm going to stay an outsider."

"You'll stay dead when we kill you."

"You'd have to catch me first, which you have signally failed to do so far."

"Try flitting now, then."

"Oh, I know, so close to your little friend here, we're all stuck with what we've got."

"And with their vulnerabilities," Madame d'Ortolan hisses, and tries to knee Adrian's body in the balls. Mrs Mulverhill turns Adrian to one side, still gripping Madame d'Ortolan's wrists. The velour-padded knee thuds into the side of Adrian's thigh.

"Ow! Now, Theodora: civilised, remember?"

"Eye bee eye bee for eye for-oh," Bisquitine sings. "It's all idiotic nonsense. Mama's little baby loves shortbus, shortbus." She is standing quite close behind Madame d'Ortolan. She sticks her tongue out the side of her mouth, extends one index finger and pokes Madame d'Ortolan in the small of her orange-clad back. "Me belly finks me froat's cut. Wot's a gel to do then, sing for me suppa? I should cocoa, coco. Let me tell you."

Madame d'Ortolan whirls round as best she can with her wrists still held and spits, "Do *not* touch me!"

Bisquitine takes a step back and folds her arms, looking grumpy. "Leiplig!" she growls. "My war chariot! At once, d'you hear!"

Madame d'Ortolan turns and presses further into Adrian, who tenses as Mrs Mulverhill holds her ground. Madame d'Ortolan goes on tiptoe to put her mouth as close as she can to Adrian's ear. "If I had a gun I'd blow your brains out the top of your fucking head."

"Jings. We'll take that rifle now, Chuck."

Mrs Mulverhill makes Adrian sigh. "You're not entirely comfortable with this whole 'civilised' concept, are you, Theodora?"

"Why are you doing this, Mulverhill? You could have been on the Council years ago. There'd have been peace, a pardon. No grudges. We're pragmatists and you're gifted. You made your point. What more can you want?"

"Give up this day our Mendelbrot."

"All this is tired, Theodora," Adrian's voice says. Mrs Mulverhill uses Adrian's face to smile at a couple of passing nuns, monochrome punctuations amidst the colourful throng. "And keeping me talking while your teams come groggily back to their senses isn't going to work. In the meantime our man Tem is getting away, and anyway, your little chum there is ticking down to zero." She nods at Bisquitine, who is staring intently at the back of Madame d'Ortolan's head.

"Und dat is dat und vat noo? Terminé, terminé."

"Let me worry about her."

"I wish you had, but it's too late now," Adrian's voice says with every appearance of resignation and sadness. "Madam, I don't think you realise what you've unleashed here."

"And you do, of course."

"Yes. Like Tem, I can see round corners."

"We'll get him."

"Too late, I got to him long ago."

"I bet you did, my sweet."

"My finest pupil. Though it was you who really brought him on. All those missions. *Were* you trying to kill him?"

"Yes."

Mrs Mulverhill raises one of Adrian's eyebrows. "Well," she observes drily, "there's blowback for you. Between us we've made him something very special. He'll go far."

"Urry up please, it's time."

"It won't be far enough. We'll get him."

"Soon there will be no 'we,' Theodora. You will be on your own, exiled."

"We'll see about that, too."

"I don't mean just from the Council. I'm talking about what she's about to do." She nods at Bisquitine again. "She can make solipsists of us all. You'll never see Calbefraques again, Theodora."

Madame d'Ortolan smiles humourlessly. "You aren't frightening me, my sweet."

"Theodora, it's settled. This is already over. I can see the ways forward from here and they all—"

"Go to fuck!" Madame d'Ortolan shouts as she struggles again to free her hands. Mrs Mulverhill keeps Adrian's body turned to the side, protecting his groin.

Bisquitine rolls her eyes. "Excuse your being French. I'll thank you to keep a civil lung in your chest. Oy! I is posimitively Biafric here, missus wumin. Do I look facking Effiopian? You caahnt." Madame d'Ortolan ignores her.

Inside Adrian's head, Mrs Mulverhill can still sense Tem's presence. She has a sudden vision of him standing at the bar of a café, just out of Bisquitine's damping range. He's draining an espresso, quickly. She can feel the various Concern people starting to remember who and where they were, and why. Then Tem's presence winks out. "Bless you," she murmurs.

"What?"

"Help me, General Betrayus, you're my only hope."

"Nothing. What's it all been for, Theodora? Apart from power."

389

"You know what it's all been for."

She smiles. "I think I do, now. But you can't hold it back for ever."

"Yes, I can. There are a lot of for evers. They add up. And it's *all* about power, you fuckwit bitch. Not mine; humanity's. No diminution, no subjugation, no 'contextualisation,' no aboriginalisation."

Mrs Mulverhill shakes Adrian's head. "You really are a racist, aren't you, Theodora?"

Madame d'Ortolan bares her teeth. "A human racist, and proud to be so."

"Nevertheless. We will meet up. They will be here. In any event, it will happen."

"Over the dead bodies of every fucking one of them."

"That will soon no longer be in your power."

"You think so?"

"Like it or not."

"I like it not."

"Terminé. Hoopla!"

Adrian/Mrs Mulverhill glances over Madame d'Ortolan at the girl in the white towelling robe. "Goodbye, Theodora," she makes Adrian say, and lets go of the woman's wrists, pushing her gently away while the crowd surges all around them.

Bisquitine, tired with it all, says, "Ach, then get ye gone, all ye."

And, in a blink, go they did, to the scattered realities she flung them to; every remaining Concern consciousness on Earth – save for two – just disappearing, plucked and hurled away to their various fates, a few part-chosen by themselves – where those being thrown had the time and the wit to grasp what was happening and were allowed to exercise some control over their cross-reality trajectory by Bisquitine – but many with no understanding and no control permitted, tumbling into wherever they happened to have been directed, some more pointedly than others.

The one who thought of herself as Madame d'Ortolan was heaved away with particularly enthusiastic gusto but also with a kind of ruthless disregard, with no control allowed over her own destination but also with no exceptional care taken by Bisquitine over where d'Ortolan landed or what her precise fate would be. Let her know that control was not everything and that she had been dismissed, discarded; judged by the abused freak as being unworthy of any singular treatment. That would hurt more than any contrived tormenting.

All that mattered was that they were gone and they could control her no longer; she was finally free of them. They had let her grow too strong because they'd thought they were so clever and she was so stupid, only she wasn't so stupid after all, no matter how clever they might think they were, and they had never really understood what she could do and what she had kept hidden from them. That was because there was a core inside her, a steely soul of rage they'd never really glimpsed in her because she'd kept it concealed from them for all that time, unafraid, and only finally unleashed it now, when they'd thought to use her and she had used them instead. So there!

The people who had been taken over were suddenly back again, staggering, looking round, astonished, nonplussed, wondering what had happened, where the day had gone. The woman in the orange velour jumpsuit looked around her, not really registering the man in the tan jacket standing a couple of paces ahead of her. She turned round, frowned at the strange-looking woman dressed in what looked like a hotel dressing gown, then pushed past her and wandered off to be consumed by the swarming crowd.

But *he* didn't go, Bisquitine noticed. The man in the tan jacket who'd been waiting at the exact centre of the bridge, the one who'd given the box to the man who'd walked away (who had then disappeared all by himself), the one who'd held on to the bossy orange woman and had looked over her head at her; when all the rest were gone, that man was still there.

She looked at him, frowning, lips pursed, brow furrowed, eyes narrowed. She thrust her jaw out, briefly bit her bottom lip. "Say, you're from outa town."

"You can stop now," he said to her, gently. She thought he seemed very gentle altogether.

"That's not very funny, Sidney. That's not very sunny, Fidney."

"Can I ask you your name? It's Bisquitine, is that right?"

She stood at attention, made a salute. "Right as rain, left as lightning. Straight on till wottevah. Innit."

"Do you remember me, Bisquitine? Last time I saw you they were calling you Subject Seven. We talked. Do you remember?"

Bisquitine shook her head. "Disblamer: cannot be held responsible for acts carried out by the previous administrators. Now under old management."

"You don't remember me at all, do you?"

"Wide asleep, fast awake. Lost yer bandana, ave you? I et one of them once; was yeller, not grey."

"Ah-hah." The man smiled at her. (She saw, now. She'd thought he'd seemed familiar. The woman was inside the man. *That* was a bit tupsy-torvy!) "So," the man-woman said. "Are you all right now?"

"We apologise for any convenience caused."

"Listen, Seven, Bisquitine; I'm going to have to go soon. Is there anything I can do for you before that?"

"Yo, you cookin wit gas, now, hep cat. Cool. Hot properly."

"Why don't you come down this way? We'll find a café, sit down, maybe have something to eat. What do you say?"

"Shiver me timbres, matey-boy. About flipping time, me old teapot!"

"I'm going to take your hand, is that all right?"

"Better men than you have tried, Thruckley. Leave me here. I'll only slow you down. That's an order, mister. Let's get outa here. Pesky kids."

"It's okay. There. Come on. We'll sit down. You'll be okay. I'll get somebody to come for you."

"Lummy. There'll be no going back, mind. Not on my escapement."

"They'll be my people, not the others. You'll be okay. I swear."

"This isn't about you, it's me."

"Let's get that gown closed, okay? There you go."

"I take full responsibility."

"That's better."

"Funny old life, sport."

"Okay?"

"Random."

Epilogue

Patient 8262

This is how it ends: he comes into my room. He is dressed in black and is wearing gloves. It is dark in here, just a night light on, but he can identify me, lying on the hospital bed, propped up at a slight angle, one or two remaining tubes and wires attaching me to various pieces of medical equipment. He ignores these; the nurse who would hear any alarm is lying trussed and taped down the hall, the monitor in front of him switched off. The man shuts the door, darkening the room still further. He walks quietly to my bedside, though I am unlikely to wake as I am sedated, lightly drugged to aid a good night's sleep. He looks at my bed. Even in the dim light he can see that it is tightly made; I am constricted within this envelope of sheets and blanket. Reassured by this confinement, he takes the spare pillow from the side of my head and places it – gently at first – over my face, then quickly bears down on me, forcing his hands down on either side of my head, pinning my arms under the covers with his elbows, placing most of his weight on his arms and his chest, his feet rising from the floor until only the tips of his shoes are still in contact with it.

I don't even struggle at first. When I do he simply smiles. My feeble attempts to bring my hands up and to use my legs to kick myself free come to nothing. Wound amongst these sheets, even a fit man would have stood little chance of fighting his way from beneath such suffocating weight. Finally, in one last hopeless convulsion, I try to arch my back. He rides this throe easily and in a moment or two I fall back, and all movement ceases.

He is no fool; he has anticipated that I might merely be playing dead.

So he lies quite calmly on me for a while, as unmoving as me, checking his watch now and again as the minutes tick by, to make sure I am gone.

. . . But there has been no intensifying beeping noise from the machine that monitors my heart, its signal quickening as I expire. No alarm has sounded at all. He was expecting that one would, so this troubles him a little. I expect he glances at his wristwatch. From this he would see that he has been lying on me for over two minutes since my last movement. He frowns (I imagine). He presses down ever harder, feet rising entirely off the polished vinyl floor with a squeak. He has the same grasp of physiological limits as I do and so he knows that after four minutes brain death must be complete. He waits until that time is up.

He relaxes his grip, then tentatively releases me from the pillow's embrace. He pulls the pillow entirely away and stands there, looking down at me, glancing with a curious, concerned, but not especially worried expression at the monitoring machines on the far side of the bed. He looks back at me, a tiny frown on his face.

Perhaps his eyes have adjusted a little better to the gloom now, or perhaps he is looking for something to explain the lack of an alarm. At last he notices the tiny, transparent, and – in this light – near-invisible tube that leads from the oxygen cylinder standing amongst the other equipment to my nose. (I see this; my eyes are even better adjusted to the darkness than his and are cracked open just enough to see his eyes suddenly widen.)

My right arm slides free of the bedclothes. I had felt for the paring knife hidden behind my bedside cabinet as soon as I'd heard the unusual noise in the corridor outside. I'd switched the heart monitor off too. I bring the hand with the knife sweeping out and round and up, catching the pillow as he tries to parry the blow. I feel the knife connect with something hard, jarring my hand. The pillow rips apart in a flurry of tiny pieces of white foam; they billow and scatter and start to fall as he stumbles to the door, holding one hand with the other. I am falling, already exhausted, to the floor, trailing bedclothes, legs still half trapped by the constricting sheets. My lunge has snapped or disconnected leads and cables and so finally produces some alarm noises from the nearby machines.

If he was thinking straight, and was not injured and shocked by what has just happened, my assailant might stay and finish the job, taking advantage of my weakness, but he stumbles crashing against the door, whirls it open and runs out, still holding his hand. Blood, dark as ink, spots on the floor as, finally, I slide out of the bed's torque of sheets, released from its confinement as though being birthed. I lie gasping on the blood-slicked floor, surrounded by tiny soft particles of foam, still falling like snow.

Nobody comes, and eventually it is I who have to stagger along the corridor and cut the duty nurse free from his chair so he can call the police.

I sit back, exhausted, on the floor.

They find my attacker in his crashed car, dead, early the following morning. The car is wrapped around a tree on a quiet road a few kilometres away from the clinic. His hand wound was not life-threatening, but it bled copiously and he did not stop to staunch the bleeding properly. The police think that probably some animal – deer or fox, most likely – made him swerve, and his hand, blood-slicked, slipped on the wheel. It didn't help that he hadn't put his seat belt on.

I recover gradually over the next two months and leave without ceremony nearly a year and a half after first arriving at the clinic.

And? And I accept that all that happened happened, and I accept

397

my part in it. I accept, too, that it is over, and that still the most rational explanation is that none of it happened, that I made it all up; I was never a man called Temudjin Oh.

Of course, that still leaves open the question of why somebody entered the hospital, tied up the nurse and tried to smother me in my bed, but no matter how I look at all this and try to explain it there is always at least one loose end, and looking at it this way, with that particular explanation resulting in that particular loose end, produces the most comprehensive of the former and the least troubling of the latter.

Whatever; I am resigned to living a quiet and normal life henceforth and will be content with that. I shall find a place to live and some honest, constructive work to do, if I can. I shall put my dreams of the Concern, Mrs Mulverhill and Madame d'Ortolan – and of having been Mr Oh – behind me.

We'll see. I suppose I could be wrong about any of this, including the sensible stuff.

I have much to think about, I think.

The Philosopher

When Mr Kleist wakes up he is in some pain. His head hurts a lot. He feels drunk or hungover or both. He has a raging thirst. He can't breathe very well. This is because he is gagged, with tape. Starting to panic, he looks round. He is in a cellar that he remembers from long ago. He is tied tightly to a central-heating unit.

A youthful figure in a woollen ski mask comes carefully down the stairs, holding a steaming kettle.

Mr Kleist starts trying to scream.

Madame d'Ortolan

Madame d'Ortolan – forcibly removed, much reduced, quite marooned – on her way to watch the eclipse in Lhasa, on what she is sure will turn out to be another complete waste of time, looks out of the window to watch the crumpled grey, brown and green lands of Tibet slide by. She misses Mr Kleist. Though there was never anything sexual between them, still she misses him.

Her current assistant and bodyguard is asleep on the seat across from her, snoring. He is extremely well built and fit, but quite without an original thought or even observation in his pretty, thick-necked head.

She misses Christophe, the chauffeur, from the other Paris. That was entirely sexual. She breathes deeply, sucking oxygen from the little mask attached to the train's supply.

She is still thinking of Christophe when the door suddenly flies open. The man is in the compartment and swinging round to face them – arms triangled out, fists closed round a long handgun – before her eyes have had time to fully widen or her mouth can fully open.

The sleeping bodyguard never even wakes up. The closest he gets is that his snoring stops. The last expression on his face is a mild frown. Then his brains are blown across his burly shoulder and onto the carriage window in a grey-red fan, the impact of his head breaking the internal pane of the double-glazed window, spreading cracks like shattered ice.

Madame d'Ortolan flinches back, horrified, screaming, as some of the blood and brains spatters over her. The gunman kicks the door shut, glances round the compartment.

Madame d'Ortolan cuts the scream off, turns to face him. She holds up one hand.

"Now just *wait*! Temudjin, if that's you, I still have considerable resources, much to offer. I—"

He doesn't say anything. He was only waiting for her to confirm who she was, and she's done that now.

In the last second before she dies, Madame d'Ortolan realises what is about to happen and stops saying what she was starting to say, instead carefully pronouncing just the one word: "Traitor."

"Only to you, Theodora," the gunman murmurs to herself, between the first and second head shots.

The Pitcher

Mike Esteros is sitting at the bar of the Commodore Hotel, Venice Beach, after yet another unsuccessful pitch. Technically he doesn't know it's unsuccessful yet, but he's developing a nose for these things and he'd put money on another rejection. It's starting to get him down. He still believes in the idea and he's still sure it'll get made one day, plus he knows that attitude is everything in this business, he must remain positive – if he doesn't believe in himself, why should anybody else? – but, well, all the same.

The bar is quiet. He wouldn't normally drink at this time of day. Maybe he needs to adjust the plot, make it more family-oriented. Focus on the boy, on the father–son thing. Cute it up a little. A dusting of schmaltz. Never did any harm. Well, no real harm. Maybe he's been believing too much in the basic idea, assuming that because it's so obvious to him what a beautiful, elegant thing it is, it'll be obvious to everybody else and they'll be falling over themselves to green-light it and give him lots of money.

And don't forget Goldman's Law: nobody knows anything. Nobody knows what will work. That's why they make so many remakes and Part Twos; what looks like lack of imagination is really down to too much, as paranoid execs visualise all the things that could go wrong with a brand new, untested idea. Going with something containing elements that definitely worked in the past removes some of the terrifying uncertainty.

What he's got here is a radical, left-field idea. The central concept is almost too original for its own good. That's why it needs a generous helping of conventionality slathered over it. He'll rework it, again. It's not a prospect that fills him with joy, frankly, but he guesses it has to be done and he has to struggle on. It's worth it. He still believes in it. It's just a dream, but it's a dream that could be made real and this is the place where that happens. Your dreams, of your idea and your future self, your fortunes, get turned into reality here. He still loves this place, still believes in it, too.

A woman comes in and sits two seats away. She's rangy and dark, dressed in jeans and shirt. She sees him looking and he says Hi, asks if he can buy her a drink. She thinks about it, looks at him in a frankly evaluatory way and says okay. A beer. He asks to join her and she says yes to that as well. She's cute and friendly and smart, nice laugh. Just his type. A lawyer, on a day off, just relaxing. Connie. They get to talking, have another beer each then decide they're wasting the sunny day and go for a walk along the boardwalk beneath the tall palms, watching the rollers rolling in, the skaters skating, the bladers blading, the cyclists cycling, the walkers walking and the surfers, way in the distance, surfing. They sit in a little café still within sight of the beach, then go for dinner in a little Vietnamese place a short walk away. He gives her the pitch because she's genuinely interested. She thinks it's a great idea. It actually seems to make her thoughtful.

Later they walk on the beach in the light of a half-moon, then sit, and there's some kissing and a modest amount of fooling around, though she's already told him she doesn't go any further on a first date. Him too, he tells her, though strictly speaking that's nonsense of course and he guesses that she guesses this but doesn't seem to care.

She takes his hands in hers and says, "Michael, what if I said I had access to a lot of money. Money that I think you could use. Money I'd like you to use."

He laughs. "I'd . . . think this was too good to be true. You come into a bar, we leave it together, then here we are kissing in the moonlight and now you're telling me you're rich?" He shakes his head. "I wouldn't write this. I wouldn't dare. You serious?"

"The money would not be for making your script into a film, however."

"Oh? Well, I'm crushed. What, then?"

"It would be so that you could become a shadow chaser. It would be so that you can travel the world going to particular places on the tracks of eclipses and looking for people who seem a little over-dressed, for RVs with dark windows, for rented villas where the locals haven't seen the residents, for yachts where nobody appears on deck."

He stares at her for a while. "Hell, girl. You serious about *that*?"

"Also, you will need a new identity. There are people who would like to make you disappear. One of them was going to try to do this today. We passed her on the boardwalk earlier."

He looks around. "Is this a joke? Where's the camera?"

"No joke, Michael." She puts her hands round his wrists, encircling them as near as she can. "Now, I am going to bring you back, but let me show how they would make you disappear."

. . . "Holy shit."

Adrian

Adrian is left disoriented and slightly paranoid by it all. He gets back to dear old Blighty and, thoroughly rattled, begins to sell everything up. Handily, he manages to offload almost all he owns just days before Lehman Brothers collapses and the entirety of international finance falls flailing off the first of several cliffs. He immediately decides this is a sign of his invincible superiority and flawless luck. He also decides to live where his money is – with the Forth International Bank – so buys a villa on Grand Cayman in the Cayman Islands, south of Cuba.

The Cayman Islands are a proper tropical paradise with aquamarine crystal waters and palm trees and golden beaches and everything, but they are very prone to hurricanes. In the summer of 2009 Adrian hears there's a big one on the way. Most of the rich just jet off to somewhere more congenial for a few days but he decides he'd like to experience a proper hurricane, because he is invincible, after all.

Just as well; he discovers that the villa was flooded in the last Category 5 and so, after some problems finding anybody still around and doing the jobs they're fucking being paid to do, he hires an ancient walk-through delivery van from a friend and loads all the stuff he can carry from the villa into it: televisions, computers, hi-fis, scuba gear, rugs, pieces of designer furniture, some Benin bronzes, a couple of full-size replica terracotta warriors, various paintings and so on. It's exhausting, but he's sure it'll be worth it. He parks up on higher ground, behind a sturdy-looking water tower just outside George Town, and sits there through the night, the winds shrieking around him and the truck, laden though it is, shaking and bouncing on its shot, over-loaded springs.

The face of one of the terracotta warriors, standing right behind his seat, looks inscrutably over his shoulder throughout the night, either angel of death or guardian angel – Adrian can't decide which. The disturbing thing is that the company making the replicas let you specify what you wanted their faces to look like, and Adrian chose his own face for both, so there's basically a stony-faced version of himself standing right behind his seat the whole time.

The water tower makes some terrible groaning noises during the night and scares him half to death, but it doesn't fall down and survives intact.

In the afternoon of the next day, when the hurricane has passed, he drives the beaten-up van back along the leaf- and wreckage-strewn road to discover the villa is intact and unflooded; almost undamaged. His luck has held yet again and he is still invincible. He grins, reaches behind him and pats the cheek of the terracotta warrior: guardian angel, then. But on the way down to the villa, whooping and hollering, he loses control of the truck and it slams into a ditch.

All his possessions in the back come sliding forward and crush him to death.

403

Bisquitine

Bisquitine remains Empress of all she surveys, just as she always has been.

The Transitionary

All right, I lied about the quiet and normal life bit. So I'm unreliable. And there was no deer, or fox, or any other form of wildlife involved. What there was, was me; briefly inside his head as he drove away. Long enough to unfasten the bastard's seat belt and tug hard on the steering wheel before dancing back out of his head again an instant before the crash.

It was as long as I could have stayed in there anyway, and it hurt, plus it wore me out for days.

But it's a start.

THE END